SAVING JASON

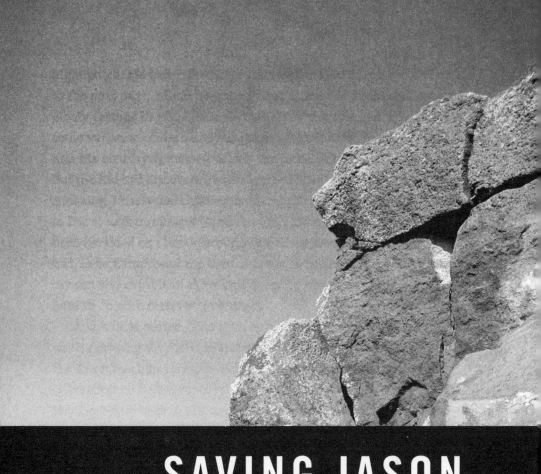

SAVING JASON

MICHAEL SEARS

G. P. PUTNAM'S SONS | NEW YORK

PUTNAM

G. P. PUTNAM'S SONS
Publishers Since 1838
An imprint of Penguin Random House LLC
375 Hudson Street
New York, New York 10014

ISBN 978-0-399-16672-3

Printed in the United States of America
1   3   5   7   9   10   8   6   4   2

Book design by Gretchen Achilles

For Barb

PART I

L ike a flat rock on a still pond, the first bullet skipped twice across the windshield and flew off harmlessly into the night. The second, aimed just slightly lower, broke through, but deflected by the liquid power of angled glass, merely left a long tear in the brim of Mark Barstow's Red Sox cap. In the split second before his view was obscured by the spiderweb of sympathetic fissures radiating all across the glass, Barstow saw two dark figures standing on his front lawn, both in the stance of practiced shooters. He aimed the Range Rover at them and floored it.

Mark Barstow was not accustomed to being shot at; he was a businessman, an experienced financial advisor, a husband and father, and a weekend hunter. Two years in the navy, twenty years earlier, had done nothing to prepare him for this situation. However, he had seen enough action movies to recognize that he was at the wheel of a much more lethal weapon than the two handguns aimed at him. And he had expected something like this. From the moment he and his lawyer had left the prosecutor's office, he had known it was coming.

Bluestone gravel spewed from beneath the rear tires and the big vehicle sped up the driveway. The left front tire hit the raised Belgian-block border at an acute angle, immediately blowing out the nearly bald tire, and slewing the big car hard to the left. The right tire made it over the stone border, but the damaged left wheel acted as an anchor. The car began to pivot.

After an initial panic as the SUV came at them, the two shooters were quick to recover. Both fired multiple shots, shattering both right-side windows. Barstow, his car now sunk into the lawn on the driver's side, threw open the door, rolled out, and came up running. Neither of the assassins trusted automatics—sometimes subject to jamming at inopportune moments—for what they had expected to be "detail" work, requiring no more than a bullet or two, and they quickly emptied their six-chambered .38 revolvers, spurring their quarry into an even greater burst of speed. Barstow ran around the corner of the house and out of sight.

The first call to 911 came almost immediately from a woman two doors down who reported that "kids" were "letting off firecrackers" and "knocking over trash cans." A commotion resulting from either would have been highly unusual in the quiet Great Neck community. Homes were, of necessity, close together, but they tended to be palatial, and a staid quiet was the norm. The second call, three seconds later, from the owner of the house across the street, correctly identified the first sound as gunfire. Nassau County Police Squad Car Number 336, patrolling eight blocks south of Mark Barstow's house, answered the call.

Neither officer had ever fired a weapon while on duty. That was about to change.

Barstow felt one of the last bullets pass behind his head as he ran for the darkness on the far side of the garage. Not noticing the click of the hammer landing on the empty brass shell of a previously fired bullet, he simply ran faster. He slipped through the side door of the garage, locking it behind him. For once, he blessed his wife's insistence that no guns be kept in her house. His locked gun safe, containing a .30-caliber hunting rifle and two over-and-under shotguns—one a twelve-gauge and the other a lighter twenty-gauge bird gun—was stored in a locked closet built into the back wall of the garage. He opened it and removed the twelve-gauge and a box of Winchester Xpert 3-inch #2s—lethal on ducks and geese out to forty or fifty yards and remarkably destructive of human flesh at lesser distances. He loaded the gun and waited.

Except for the hum of the freezer on the far wall near the kitchen door, the house was silent. His wife, Vera, and their daughter, Valeria—still unemployed and living at home, ten months after graduating from the College of Charleston—were, at his insistence, visiting Vera's mother in St. Pete Beach. They had left that morning and wouldn't be back until Sunday night. The outside door rattled as someone tried the locked doorknob.

The two gunmen—realizing that their plan for a straightforward assassination as Barstow pulled into his driveway had now gone wildly off script, veering into the dangerous and unpredictable field of improvisation—made one last attempt at fulfilling their mission. They reloaded and followed Barstow around the side of the garage. The backyard was dark but apparently empty, and the side door of the garage beckoned. Rather than take the point and charge into an unknown situation with the hunted on his home turf, Francesco "Little Frankie" Figundio stood to the side of the door and tried the knob first. Gently. It was locked. He gave it a hard shake and was rewarded with the sound of an explosion. A hole the size of a basketball blew out of the top panel on the door, sending jagged wooden splinters flying in an ever-expanding cone across the side yard.

Little Frankie stuck his hand and firearm through the hole and loosed three quick shots. The empty garage responded like a snare drum, the sharp sounds reverberating and rattling the walls, the bullets ricocheting erratically but ultimately harmless.

Barstow saw the hand with the revolver and watched the short-barreled gun flash three times. Ignoring the whine and ping of the bullets as they careened off metal shelving, concrete floor, and the frame of his daughter's Kawasaki motorcycle, he fired the second barrel of his shotgun at the wall just to the right of the doorway, aiming for chest height. A second hole appeared. A man screamed—a most satisfying sound. Willing to take his victories in small stages, Barstow ran for the kitchen door. He fumbled briefly with the jangle of keys on his chain, cursing in short barks as his panic rose, finally finding the right one and unlocking the door. But before he could squeeze inside, a second hand pointed a gun through the same hole in the door and fired twice.

Framed in the gray light from the kitchen windows, silhouetted against the blackness of the garage, Barstow was an easy target. The only target. Both bullets hit, the first severing his left pinky finger, the second hitting him in the back, breaking his left scapula before sheering upward and exiting, tearing a golf ball–sized hole through his trapezius. He fell forward, dropping the shotgun and spinning as he fell, so that he landed on his back in the middle of the kitchen floor. Without any conscious thought, he began kicking wildly until his foot connected with the swinging door and he forced it closed. The click of the lock as it fell into place was the most reassuring sound he could have imagined. He was bleeding, in great pain, crippled on his left side, deafened by the gunshots in the confined space of the garage, and still outmanned and outgunned. But for the moment he was safe. He found the gun, reloaded, and aimed at the solid, metal-covered, heat-and-flame-retardant door. In the background, he could hear the measured beep of the security system. If he failed to activate the code in another ninety seconds, help would be on the way.

The two gunmen reassessed. The second shotgun blast had plowed lateral stripes across Little Frankie's back, destroying his black leather sports jacket and planting wooden splinters, bits of siding, and half a dozen tiny number-two shot-sized BBs in the shallow furrows. The wound was far from lethal, but it was painful and would require professional medical attention. Frankie stopped screaming and began to curse fluently, switching effortlessly from his native English to the mixed Neapolitan Italian of his paternal grandfather and the Sicilian of his maternal grandfather. They would have been proud.

"Fuck's the matter with you?" the other man asked.

"I'm hit, Gino, you fucking *stunad*. I need a doctor."

Gino would rather have dropped his less-than-useless partner off the bridge at Captree than take him to a doctor, but he was facing a full-out disaster. The odds of attaining success had dropped dramatically. Rather than ambushing an unsuspecting, unarmed victim, they were now pursuing a shotgun-wielding, very dangerous opponent in a fortified position on his own turf. The sound of an approaching siren decided the matter.

"We're outta here. Follow me," Gino said. He turned around once as he ran for the back of the yard. "And shut the fuck up, or I put a bullet in you myself and leave you here."

"Fuck you," Frankie said, but he said it quietly and then stopped talking.

They ran, after a fashion, lurching and limping through the neighboring backyards, tromping through recently turned gardens and tripping over various decorative shrubs and leafless privet hedges. Their car was parked two streets over in the driveway of a darkened house. Though they set off motion sensors in two yards, not one of the three security cameras they passed managed to capture an identifiable photo of them. Minutes later, they jumped in the car and slowly pulled out, avoiding any display of sudden flight. They disappeared into the night.

The two policemen pulled up in front of a dark, silent house. A Range Rover sat half on the lawn, half in the driveway. The vehicle had a flat tire, smashed windows, and bullet holes in the side panels. The only other sign of the recent disturbance was the faint, lingering scent of gunpowder in the damp night air.

The younger of the two called in a 10-34 S2, though it appeared the shooting was over. He added a 10-13, as per SOP. It looked quiet, but backup would be welcome. "We should see if there's anyone hurt," he said to his partner.

"What's ETA?" the older man replied.

"Car Three-Two-Seven in four minutes. The security company sent an alert."

"We wait."

"Someone could bleed out in four minutes."

The older cop thought for a moment. The decision was all his. "All right. I take point." He drew his Glock and started for the front of the large house. He went up the front stoop—a granite structure that would have been more at home in front of a college library—and attempted to see in through the large bay window. Though the curtains were light gauze, the room was too dark. He looked back at his partner and shook his head.

The younger cop was crouched by the abandoned SUV. He motioned for searching around behind the house. His partner shook his head. He preferred waiting. Backup would be there in another minute or two. He held up a hand for caution, but the younger man was already moving.

"Aw, hell," he whispered. He followed around the far side of the house. "Hold up," he hissed as they reached the rear corner.

"There's no one here," the other man replied aloud, giving up altogether on trying to communicate silently. "Whoever was involved here has vacated the premises."

"We don't know that. Now, do as I say. Follow me."

He stayed low and moved slowly, ducking below the windows. A wide, unfenced wooden deck, only a foot and a half off the ground, covered a portion of the yard leading down to a pool, hidden beneath a winter cover. On the far side was a small pool house and a mammoth stone-and-steel construction that seemed to combine a barbecue grill, a sink and countertop, and a built-in pizza oven. On the deck were tables and chairs in various arrangements, with white cushions that gleamed in the half-light of the quarter moon. Sliding glass doors gave entry into the rear of the house. The garage was on the far side. It was all very quiet. Leading with his gun, he stepped up onto the deck, hugging the wall of the house, and peered in through the glass doors. Darkness. Faint shapes. A long dining room. Then a kitchen. Nothing moving. He moved on.

Mark Barstow didn't see him at first. He had been staring into the blackness, his ears still ringing from the shots inside the echoing garage, waiting for that door to open and for the two shooters to make another attempt at him. The last two shots had punched holes through the door, which now looked to him like a pair of unblinking black eyes observing him indifferently as he sweated and bled, barricaded behind the working island in the center of the kitchen. He kept the shotgun aimed at the door. His back was soaked with his blood, but shock was already taking over and he barely felt the wound in his back. The missing finger, however, stung like a thousand wasps all attacking at once. He wrapped the hand in a dish towel and for a moment saw explosions of stars behind his eyelids as he almost passed out. He shook his head. He wanted water. The faucet was only a few feet away. As though entranced, he found that his thoughts were focused solely on reaching that sink. He could wash the blood from his hand and the cold water would help kill the pain. And he could drink. If he could just drink a little cold water, he knew that he would live. Keeping the shotgun aimed at the door, he rose up and took a step toward the counter.

The older cop was already on the far side of the deck when he heard his partner yell, "Freeze!" The word was picked up quite clearly by his chest microphone, as was the next. "Police!" He looked back and saw the younger cop in the approved firing-range stance. He was aiming at the gray glass doors to the kitchen.

It was unlikely that Barstow heard the words. No doubt he heard a sound, but what he saw was a man with a gun stepping into the thin shaft of moonlight that made it down through the stand of tall cypress trees in the backyard. He did not register the uniform; he saw a threat.

"Damn!" His mind returned to crystal clarity. He should have known they would try to flank him—to surprise him again. He whirled and fired once, barely aiming, firing from the hip like some TV hero. He was surprised to see that he had apparently hit his target. The glass exploded outward, the whole sliding door shattering at once, and the tall man—or the shadow of the tall man—fell to the ground.

The policeman felt the blast of the pellets go by and, too late, leapt out of the way of the shards of glass. They ripped through his shirt and sliced the side of his neck, missing the carotid artery by millimeters. The pain was sharp, biting, acidic. He hit the ground and rolled onto his back, too much in agony even to think about returning fire.

The other cop relied on his extensive training. His partner was down, hurt, and vulnerable to further attack. The suspect was still armed and had, despite a warning, fired and hit a police officer. By law and by training, he was allowed—expected—to use whatever force he deemed necessary to defend himself and other police personnel and to subdue the shooter. He fired three times, placing all three bullets in the center of Barstow's chest.

Barstow was dead before he hit the floor.

1

The center lane of the Long Island Expressway was a solid line of steel all the way to the horizon. One large truck after another, all rolling along at ten miles over the speed limit. The right lane was reserved for the undocumented immigrants driving landscapers' rigs, the not-quite-legally blind, and senior tax dodgers in cars the size of small yachts with Florida tags. The far left lane held everyone else. From the guys who just wanted to get where they were going to the truly insane, who drove as though possessed of a death wish. I didn't count the HOV lane, where minivans maintained a steady sixty, while SUVs and the Hampton Jitney did eighty. My shoulders were aching from the strain of keeping every other car on the road at something more than arm's length, and my knuckles were so white they would have glowed in the dark. I have always had a special hatred for the Long Island Expressway.

I was there on a long shot. My job was not—usually—a taxing one. After serving two years of a five-year sentence in federal prison for an accounting mistake that I had let snowball—if they don't get you for the crime, they'll get you for the cover-up—my job prospects back on Wall Street were limited. Most of my old acquaintances wouldn't take my call. But over the next year and a half, I had carved out a niche as a freelance fraud investigator and done quite well. One thing had led to another, and now I worked directly for the CEO of a midsized investment bank, conducting the kind of investigations that the legal and compliance departments found inconvenient. Virgil Becker ran the firm his father had almost destroyed. I had been instrumental in salvaging some of the pieces, and thereafter I collected a ridiculously large annual paycheck for performing what was, in effect, a part-time job. Occasionally, someone or other would object to having their felonious secrets unearthed and I had found myself fighting for my life, or mourning the loss of another. But more often, the greatest danger I faced was the threat of backache and eyestrain from staring at a computer screen for hours on end. Sometimes I just needed to get out of the office and do a bit of field investigating. Which was how I found myself stuck in the center lane on the L.I.E.

Every week, I ran a random search through all of the firm's trades, looking for any pattern that looked unusual. There were always dozens. That's the nature of the business. Then I had to sift through all the anomalies to see if there were any that warranted further investigation. There were surprisingly few. That's also the nature of the business. Most Wall Street crime stays hidden simply because of the massive volume of legitimate trades that happen every day. The program that I had devised wasn't any better than the ones the SEC used—and they had a lot more manpower—but if I waited for them to discover the malefaction, I wasn't doing my job.

The week before, I had come across one of those pesky patterns. One of the firm's brokers had, some months earlier, executed a flurry of trades in penny stocks. Penny stocks are, as one might imagine, stocks that sell for less than a dollar. They are rarely worth even the pennies paid, but every once in a while a stock might pay off with a miraculous new product or discovery. However, it wasn't the kind of business that the firm encouraged—there were too many opportunities for fraud. The dollar amounts were small enough that my program had ignored them until, on a whim, I widened the parameters. The penny stock trades all jumped to the head of the list. There was no obvious evidence of misdealing, but on a slow week I had the time to dig a little deeper. When I continued researching the stocks—all blue-collar types of businesses like plumbers, electricians, and cesspool companies that depended heavily on the use of trucks—I found that twelve of the twelve companies had long-term leases on the same property out on Long Island. That was the kind of coincidence that could go from agita to heart attack. When I looked it up on Google Earth, I saw an immense structure surrounded by a grassy field a few hundred acres in size. It was either a sod farm or pastureland, isolated in the middle of the wilderness of Pine Barrens. It was odd enough to get me out of the office for a closer look.

I began my drop down to the exit ramp a mile in advance of the exit and still almost missed it, thanks to a woman wearing those oversized sunglasses that fit over regular glasses. She sped up when I tried to merge in front of her and slowed down when I dropped back. The trucker behind me finally hit his horn in frustration, which scared the woman into hitting her brakes, and I scooted through. Less than a quarter mile after the exit ramp, I was driving through a landscape of scrub oak and dwarf pine. The edges of the asphalt roadway had crumbled away on both sides so that if another car had come from the other direction, one of us would have had to veer off onto the salt-and-pepper sandy verge.

The break in the wilderness was abrupt. One moment I was surrounded on both sides by an eight- or ten-foot-tall wall of evergreen and gray-brown scrub oak, the next I was passing fence posts as tall as the stunted trees enclosing a grassland resembling a western prairie. I slowed down to examine the territory.

The fence around the property was a grid of thick strands forming four-inch squares supported by tall, thick posts six or eight feet apart. It looked like it would keep out a tank. It also looked solid enough to support half a dozen big men if they wanted to climb over. I thought that it must be for containment rather than security. This idea was bolstered when I saw the inner fence, a single bare wire about four and a half feet off the ground that ran through insulated fixtures on bare wooden posts. An electric fence. It looked harmless from the seat of the rental car, but the wire was heavy enough to carry quite a charge.

Across the field loomed the building I had seen on Google. It was as tall as an airplane hangar, twice as wide, and it had to be the length of two football fields. There were no windows or doors on the side facing me. It was just a long expanse of weathered gray.

I drove along a little farther until I could see the corner of the property and the convergent road, then I pulled off to the side and stopped the car. The sudden silence was disorienting. There was no breath of wind, no birds calling or insects buzzing, no hum of distant traffic or rush of airplanes overhead. I wanted to turn on the radio, to hear some sign that civilization still went on just over the horizon. The sudden ping of the engine as it cooled almost made me jump.

I left the car unlocked and walked along the fence, careful to avoid the bright green poison ivy and the low thistle bushes that shared the roadside with the sparse grass and occasional fern. It was hot.

Around the corner, I came upon the gate—or gates, for there were two, an inner and an outer, forming an enclosed lock the length and double the width of a long semi cab and trailer. The gates were each double-door affairs with electronic locks, counterweighted pulleys, and rolls of razor wire. A sign on each gate announced in both English and Spanish that trespassing was forbidden and that it was too dangerous to even think about coming in. I decided that the restrictions did not pertain to someone who had driven most of the length of the Long Island Expressway to get there, but I wasn't going to attempt entry through those fortifications anyway. There were no signs on the fence, only on the gates, therefore the prohibition ended where the fence began.

I walked back fifty yards or so and began to climb. The metal wires did not sag or buckle. They were made to support weight. Even so, I was sweating by the time I reached the top and swung a leg over. The change in perspective gave me a different view of the field below, and an idea began to form in my mind. I looked for more evidence and found it almost immediately. The remains of multiple fences crisscrossed the gently rolling property. Now almost all rotted away, they had once broken the huge pasture into smaller parcels. Sections where horses could be raised—stallions and mares kept separate until such time that the breeder wanted them together. Enclosures where colts could learn to run with their dams. All this had once been a horse farm. Or ranch. The precise nomenclature escaped me. I was born and raised in Queens.

However, among the now defunct agricultural industries that had once dominated half or more of Long Island was the business of raising horses. American quarter horses. Used for everything from dressage to rodeo. I knew this because of a brief fascination with a girl in middle school who had a less brief, and much more intense, fascination with horses. She and her mother would drive out east every weekend, where they rode hired horses while wearing little leather helmets, black blazers, tall boots, and funny pants. My fascination with her arose because she was almost as good in math as I was, which gave me the impression, ultimately very wrong, that we might have something to talk about. I listened to her rattle on about horses and she listened to me obsess about differential equations. The relationship did not flourish as I had hoped.

There were no longer any horses gamboling about, but the long building now made sense to me. One end of the barn—and I now felt comfortable calling it that—would have held stalls for the horses, as well as storage for feed and equipment. The wider end with the curved roof would have been the indoor riding arena where rider and horse could train together to do the maneuvers required for dressage, or jumping, or even barrel racing or calf herding.

What interest Keegan Cesspool Services—Roto-Rooter's number-one competition on the East End—and the other companies would have in an old horse farm, however, was still a mystery.

I climbed down the inside of the fence. No alarms went off. No armed guards arrived to escort me off the property. No thrashing helicopters hovered overhead. Therefore, I wasn't really trespassing.

The grass under the electric wire was about two feet high. I ran my hand through the top leaves to see if there was any leakage from the fence. I had seen the third rail on the subway arc at times when a train passed by. There was that same electric-train smell of ozone in the air. I didn't want to duck under the wire only to find that there was enough current leaking that I became a quick-fried grounding post. But despite the smell, there was no sharp sting when I touched the grass. I went all the way down to hands and knees to crawl under.

I was about three hundred yards from the barn, most of it through long grass. I was a city boy. Long grass meant man-eating lions, like in that Val Kilmer–Michael Douglas movie, or poisonous snakes, despite the fact that I knew on a purely intellectual basis that there were neither on Long Island. But there were probably ticks, and I could contract Lyme disease or spotted fever, whatever that was. Or at the very least, I might get a spider bite. I cut over toward the packed-earth drive, where the grass was beaten down to a sparse Mohawk fringe. The road led from the gate directly to the barn.

Beyond the barn was a grove of three ancient catalpa trees, each one six or eight feet around. Lazing beneath them in the shade were what I took to be cows—large dark brown lumps. They were far away, resting, and, even to a New Yorker wearing a custom-made suit and Allen Edmonds wingtips, a relatively minor threat. I resolved not to step in any cow pies.

The remaining posts from the old fencing, lined up like pensioned sentinels along the side of the dirt road, were all slightly askew, as though the earth had reshaped itself in undulating waves, or, more likely, something heavy had pushed against them repeatedly. The significance of that escaped me until it was almost too late.

Once on the driveway, I could see the barn much more clearly and from end on. The wall facing me had a single enormous sliding door with the same kind of electronic lock and pulley contraption as the main gate. If that was not enough security, someone had wrapped a thick padlocked chain through the pulley system. If I'd had a hacksaw, I could have gotten through it in not much more than a day or two.

I didn't need a hacksaw. In the middle of the huge door was a smaller door. An *Alice in Wonderland*–sized door with no lock and nothing but a simple lever-handle doorknob. It was too easy. I opened the door and heard the shrill screech of rusty hinges. I paused, waiting to see if I had somehow raised an alarm. Nothing. I walked in and stepped into darkness.

The fact that there were no alarms or hi-tech locks should have been a warning. The owners of the property were either painfully ignorant of modern security techniques or they were arrogantly confident beyond all reason. Or, they knew something that I did not.

I began to explore the dark space. Almost buried under the overwhelming assault from fumes of diesel and other petroleum distillates, there was the faint scent of horse. Certainly not a recent smell, but impossible to ignore. I felt my way to the nearest wall and searched for a light switch. Instead I found a big metal switch box with a long handle on one side. I gripped it and pulled down. There was a loud thunk that sounded more like an axe hitting a stump than anything electric, but it worked. Overhead, banks of fluorescent lights began to buzz and flicker the length of the building, revealing a single open space—the stalls and tack rooms had been gutted and removed—that was now filled with trucks and heavy equipment of every description. Panel trucks, flatbeds, dump trucks, refrigerator trucks, monstrous semis and tow trucks that dwarfed them, septic trucks, a long line of oil delivery trucks, even a half-dozen beverage distributor trucks. The heavy equipment was all earth-moving machinery of one kind or another. There must have been tens of millions of dollars' worth of vehicles there, most in pristine condition.

I walked the length of one row to the far end of the barn where the arena had been. The overhead lights there were dark. The space seemed to hold vague geometric forms and dark amorphous blobs. I searched the wall until I came to another switch box. I pulled the handle. This time, the lights suspended from the high ceiling were all powerful floods. The floor of the arena lit up like an operating room.

It was an operating room. For trucks. Three trucks in the center of the floor were in various stages of being dismantled—or reconstructed—their engines wrapped in thick chains and suspended with block and tackle from steel girders. Parts, some cleaned and labeled, others bathing in tubs of cleaning solvent, were organized neatly around the edges of the space. Along the far wall was a packaging area and loading dock. It was all a factory. But they didn't make things there, they took them apart and sold the pieces. The trucks came in at one end, and if they weren't held for use by D&Y Hauling, McFee Plumbing, L.I. Ice, or one of the other companies on the list, all of whom depended on trucks of various kinds to make their businesses work, they were taken to the far end where they were reduced to their most salable parts, which were then boxed and shipped and sent out through the single small door at the far end. It was possibly—probably—the world's biggest truck chop shop.

I took out my phone and started snapping pictures.

There were too many vehicles to record each one; I would have been there all afternoon. Instead I took samplings and a few long shots for both scale and sheer numbers. Every few minutes I stopped taking photos and emailed them to myself. The moment I realized what this very private piece of property was being used for, I felt an urgency to be on my way back home. The collection of evidence was a necessity, but I did not want ever to have to come back. I had enough to bring to Virgil; he could pass the matter on to the compliance department. My part was done.

I had just turned off the floodlights, casting that end of the barn back into a murky darkness, when I realized what was missing. Guard dogs. I had never seen an auto junkyard without a huge bloodthirsty mastiff or pit bull, or even a short-haired shepherd. By some luck I had arrived on a day when no one was there working, stripping parts or packing them up. But surely they must have had some kind of security. The fencing might have kept out army tanks, but it hadn't stopped me. The urgency to be on my way increased by a factor of ten.

The thunk of the lights going off sounded much louder than turning them on. I made my way to the small door and pushed it open. The hinges sounded their shrill protest again. The sudden changes from light to dark and back again left me blinded as I stepped through the doorway. I was in a hurry, but I stopped and took a second for my eyes to adjust.

The realization that I was not alone came in strobe-light flashes. The first was a sound—a cough. Not exactly a cough, but definitely an exhale. A human could have made the sound, but probably didn't. There was also a smell that hit me just a moment before my eyes focused. It was a wild smell, like what you might get if you crossed a cow with a bear.

My eyes cleared. I was facing a herd of bison. American buffalo. Four very big fellows with horns were standing in a semicircle not twenty feet away. They were blocking my access to the road. My line of retreat. One of them made the coughing sound again. It could have been an expression of anger, or merely impatience. He stamped a hoof on the ground. Anger, I decided. In a group, more to the right and slightly farther away, were eight female bison. Though they were smaller and the horns they wore just a tad less lethal looking, the real clue to their gender was that six of them were swollen and gravid, while the other two hung back, protecting two spindly-legged calves, who watched me with both fascination and fear out of slightly protuberant eyes.

I tried to convince myself that I was in no danger. I was no threat, therefore they had no reason to treat me as anything other than an oddity. An amusement. I would have to pass between two of the bulls to make my escape, but if I showed no hostility they would let me go unmolested. I took a step forward.

The cough this time was considerably louder and its intent and meaning quite clear. I froze. The doorway was just a few steps behind me, but I had read somewhere—probably in *Outside* magazine while waiting at the dentist's office—that bison were among the fastest land creatures, able to run for some distance at forty miles an hour or more. And, they could reach full speed instantly. I turned and ran. I must have hit full speed instantly, too. I was through the door and back inside in a flash, the door hinges screaming.

I let my breath come back slowly. I had been holding it from the moment I saw the bison. My hands were clammy and I smelled like fear. I peered out the door. There had been no movement. The little herd was still there. I watched them for a few minutes and realized that I could easily see them but they could not see me, and so I relaxed. But if I let the door make the slightest sound, they became immediately alert and the bulls took turns coughing in my direction. We were at a standoff. I was stuck until they lost interest—and I would still have the problem of opening the door without making a sound to tip them off—or someone showed up to assist me. Or arrest me. Or worse.

In the waiting game, I had the advantage. The bison were out in the sun on the hardpack in front of the doors. The nice grass and the shade were elsewhere. I had nothing to do but wait. They had to wait and wonder why they weren't waiting somewhere more comfortable. Eventually, the difference began to tell.

The bulls went first. The male of the species always has the shorter attention span. This is why football has halftime. The biggest went first—the one who had first snorted at me and stamped his hoof. He walked a few paces off and began to trot down the field to a bare, sandy spot, where he rolled over, legs in the air, and enjoyed a dust bath. The other three bulls looked like they wished they had thought of it first, and a few minutes later they trotted along after.

There were some huffs and snorts from the cows when the bulls left. They weren't happy about it, but no one went down and tried to shame the boys into coming back. I eased the door open bit by bit, knowing they couldn't see me. If there came a moment where I could escape, I was going to take it.

The calves went next. The two began to stroll back toward the shade. Their mothers, instead of herding them back to the group, followed them. That left six hungry, hot, very pregnant females alone on guard duty outside the barn. A few minutes later, as though by unspoken agreement, they all left at once and headed to the trees.

I inched the door open a bit more and put a leg through.

I almost made it.

OOOOOOOGA! OOOOOOOOGA! A loud horn, the kind you hear on a ship leaving port, sounded twice, sending my heart into my throat and my testicles up into my stomach. I leapt back inside and heard a loud buzzing from an alarm. What the hell had I touched to set that off?

The front gate swung open, red lights flashing, revealing a long flatbed truck that began to come up the road toward the barn. But before I had time to fully panic, or to look for a hiding place, the truck rumbled past the doors and continued down into the field beyond. I heard a muted rumble of hoofbeats and poked my head out. The bison were all following the truck, which slowed after it passed the sandy wallow. The passenger door opened and a lanky man in a denim jacket and ball cap swung out and up onto the truck bed. It was loaded with bales of hay, which he began unloading off the back. The bales hit the ground and broke up into square pallets. The bison began to eat.

That was my chance. The men were busy. The truck and the bison at least three football fields away. With a bit of luck I could get to the fence before they even noticed me. I pushed the door open, dashed through, and began to jog down the road. The door swung shut behind me. The hinges shrieked. I began to run.

I was not a sprinter, never had been, but I was sure that I could cover two hundred yards in thirty seconds. Thirty-two, max. A voice called out and I ignored it. There was no way those farmhands would be able to get the truck turned around and cover the distance to catch me up in time. My fear was the bison.

I did the math. There were too many variables, too many possible rounding errors, but numbers had been my life. If I was going to die, trampled to death by a vestige of the Old Wild West, then I was going out counting.

The truck was a long way down the field from the barn. At least three hundred yards, and more likely four hundred. So I used four hundred because, with the two hundred yards from the barn to the fence, that added up to six hundred yards, or just over one-third of a mile. If the bull started running the moment he saw me—and I knew his eyesight sucked—traveling at a maximum speed of forty-five miles an hour, he would arrive at the electric fence at the same time I did. My heart was threatening to burst out of my chest and I was gasping for air. I still had half the distance to cover.

That was my worst-case scenario—at the full four hundred yards. If the distance was even a bit shorter, I was going to be roadkill any moment. On the other hand, forty-five was a good clip for a healthy bison on the open range. How fast would one of those lazy Long Island bisons move? Over rough, pitted, and rolling terrain? At thirty-five mph, I'd have been able to slow up and jog the last few yards, laughing over my shoulder. The front brain thought this was very funny. The back brain, the place where all the primitive stuff resides, found nothing to laugh about. I ran faster.

The gate was coming up and was, of course, closed. I made a slight turn and ran through the long grass for the fence. That's when I heard the sound of hoofbeats on the roadway. I didn't want to look, but I couldn't help myself. Two of the bulls were already passing the barn, and the truck was finally turned around and was barreling after them. I found that math had abandoned me. I could not do the estimates or calculations. My brain had joined the rest of my nervous system in focusing on one thing only. Keep running.

The electric fence was a dozen strides in front of me. Then ten. Eight. Six. Would the damn animals stop? They must have weighed a ton each. Why would a single strand of wire stop them, regardless of the electric charge? Four. I could feel the pounding of those hooves on the ground behind me. Two. I dove under the wire, sliding through the tall grass, imagining I could hear the crackle of thousands of volts running over my head. I scrambled to my feet, took the last three strides to the outer fence in two hops and a jump. I jammed my toes between the links and climbed as fast as I could.

One of the bulls managed to stop before hitting the fence, skidding to a halt, hooves grinding a pair of parallel trenches in the dirt. The other bull, less experienced or merely more aggressive, hit the wire at full speed. I was already approaching the top of the fence and still climbing, but from the corner of one eye I saw the animal hit. The wire gave way like a rubber band, but there was an immediate crack of discharged electricity and the two-thousand-pound bison flew backward as though fired from a giant slingshot. Every hair on my body stood on end and the mixed odors of ozone and burnt flesh were overwhelming. But I kept climbing.

The bison was down and on the ground, but it was moving. As I threw my leg over the top of the fence and started down the far side, I saw it roll up onto unsteady legs. A long red welt ran down one side of its body. The other bull was already racing up the field. But the guys in the truck hadn't quit.

The truck was tearing down the drive. It would take precious minutes to open the two gates and follow me. I could be in the car and long gone before they would be out. I jumped the last three feet to the ground and turned to run for my rental. I thought I was safe.

Halfway to the car, I looked back over my shoulder. The truck had veered and was now leaping and bucking over the field, headed straight for me. I knew they wouldn't be able to plow through the fence, but that farmhand would be able to climb it and chase after me. I had a good lead, but the truck was eating it up quickly. I had seconds to spare.

Of the few things I did right that day, the most important may have been to leave the car unlocked. I jumped in, started it up, and swung it into a U-turn, bouncing on, off, and back on the pavement, fishtailing slightly in the sand. The truck was coming up inside the fence, but I was on firm, smooth asphalt. In seconds I was pulling away, as they continued to bounce through the field, keeping just clear of the electric fence. The end of the property line—and the corner of the fence—approached. I kept my right foot to the floor and raced away back through the woods toward the lesser hazards of the L.I.E.

The usual westbound slowdown at exit 39 had caused a backup to 41. Creeping along at an average of eight miles an hour gave me time to readjust my adrenaline levels. Fear and aggression became annoyance and exasperation and, finally, acceptance. I could think. I marveled that a spray of relatively small trades had led to me being chased, and nearly exterminated, by a creature almost extinct in the wild. Too bad I couldn't also read the future and see the long list of ills that were to come. That in just a few months my son would be lost in the desert, and that I would face death saving him. And, once again, there would be a death on my conscience.

2

Skeli, the light of my life, the woman of my dreams, and the mother of my unborn child, was sitting across from me in a booth at the Athena Coffee Shop on Amsterdam. She was having a Greek coffee shop version of a salade Niçoise—no potatoes, and red onion and cucumber instead of green beans. Skeli was plucking the curls of onion out and putting them on her bread dish. She was long past the morning-sickness stage of her pregnancy, but food in general had become an issue. Smells and textures had become strange, and things she had once loved had turned toxic. Raw red onion was one of the most virulent of past loves. Mostly she got by on yogurt, lettuce, and a few bites of fish or chicken. And midnight binges of chocolate hazelnut gelato.

"Buffalo?" she said with a teasing grin.

"Bison," I said. I had just finished telling her of my adventures that day.

"I've always pictured them as noble and stoic."

"They're also territorial, protective of their offspring, and really big."

"Why would someone use buffalo instead of guard dogs?"

"Why do I get the feeling you're not taking this seriously? I could have been killed."

"When I told you that I didn't want you to be involved in anything dangerous, I meant no guns or people trying to drown you, and stay away from people who want to beat you up."

"It's not like I seek them out, you know."

"You climbed over the fence, Jason. Weren't there warning signs? Like 'Keep Out' or 'Danger—Guard Buffalo'? You invaded their space."

I was beginning to feel surrounded. "Guard bison."

I waved at the Kid. My son was having dinner in a separate booth across the dining room, accompanied by our good friend Roger. Roger was a retired clown, a practicing alcoholic, and an often rude and uncouth companion whom I had met and befriended years before my troubles with the law began. When I got out of prison, he picked up the friendship as though there had never been a break. I owed him a lot, not least for introducing me to a woman named Wanda Tyler, whom I had nicknamed Skeli. She had been his sometime assistant, when he performed at Park Avenue birthday parties or corporate sales meetings. Jacques Emo and Wanda the Wandaful.

The Kid did not wave back. He blinked. That may have been an important message, but I couldn't be sure. My seven-year-old son, named for both his father and grandfather, had unusual methods of communication. And he refused to be called Jason. The sobriquet was his idea. He occupied a block on the autism continuum, shifting his exact location often enough to keep me and his teachers on constant alert. His mother—Angie, my ex—had never been able to connect with him and it broke her fragile heart. She died protecting him.

It was the autism that defined where we dined. The Athena had demonstrated an acceptance of some of my son's more bizarre eccentricities, such as screaming "Poo" at the top of his lungs when he saw me put mustard on my corned beef, or flying into a screaming tantrum whenever James Taylor's "Fire and Rain" played on the radio, a reaction that, in my opinion, was a tad operatic but thoroughly justified. I had frequently contributed to the waiters' retirement funds with hundred-dollar tips to ensure our subsequent welcomes. So far, it was all working.

Roger was performing an act of supreme generosity by eating dinner with the Kid in order to give Skeli and me a few minutes to enjoy each other's company. Dinner with the Kid could be harrowing to the uninitiated—it could be harrowing to the experienced, too.

"I outran a maddened wild creature to be here with you," I said, giving in to the spirit of her taunts.

"I thought you said you had a quarter-mile head start," she said.

"Not quite."

She laughed. I liked her laugh. It was free and uncomplicated, and I wanted to make her laugh all the time just like that.

"I'm sorry," she said, though not sorry at all. "I'm sure it was scary, but I'm having too good a time picturing you doing the hundred-yard dash and scaling a ten-foot fence in five-hundred-dollar shoes while being chased by a cow."

"Bull," I said. "And it wasn't a bovine, it was—"

"A bison. I know. Isn't a bison a bovine?"

"I have no idea," I said.

"What's the difference?"

"Cows commit murder a lot less frequently than buffalo."

"Ha! Even the world's greatest expert can slip and call a bison a buffalo."

She was having fun, and I was having fun watching her. She could tease me forever as long as she kept up that laugh.

She switched gears on me. "You haven't asked me about my day."

"True. But I thought being chased by a bison trumped the breathless excitement of a physical therapy clinic."

Skeli had been working on her doctorate when we first met. It was the beginning of a second career—or third if you counted the time she spent as Roger's assistant. With backing from me and other moneyed friends, she had opened an office in SoHo, which now took up a lot more of her time than I had expected. That wasn't exactly a problem— I was happy for her success—but I did miss lazy Saturdays and long, relaxed dinners together.

"No, there were no mad bison running around the treatment rooms. We did get another new celeb client today, though." She dropped a name even I recognized. New Yorkers try hard to be unimpressed with fame, but a few signed celebrity photos in the waiting room were good marketing. People would flock to Skeli's office on the slight chance of running into a Broadway legend with sciatica, or an opera diva with a twisted ankle.

"How did she find you?"

"Another referral from Paddy."

Patrick Gallagher was both a Wall Street wizard and a theater producer. He was also one of the friends I had convinced to back Skeli's business.

"Very nice. So business is booming."

"Do I hear a touch of mixed feelings there?"

"Not really. I'm very happy for you."

"And you know it won't always be this way, right? The start-up is the hardest part. Six months from now, the place will almost run itself. I'll have normal hours and we'll have lots more time together."

I laughed in spite of her earnest wish for me to believe. "No, I don't know that. You love being fully engaged. You love helping people. You feel important, and that's a good thing. I don't mind. But in six months, you are going to have a baby to add to the mix and life will get exponentially more complicated. And that's a good thing, too."

We smiled at each other in contemplation of our lives being turned upside down by the arrival of another family member.

"Maybe we should just get a dog," I said.

"Too late, bud. You should have thought of that months ago. What kind of cheese is that?"

I was eating a grilled chicken Caesar salad. When Skeli had started gagging at the smell of coffee or the sight of a rare and bloody steak, I had stopped eating anything that she wouldn't eat—when she was present. If I needed a pastrami fix, or a good burger, I found it on my own time.

"It's Parmesan. Isn't that what you put on a Caesar?"

"That's not Parmesan. It's Asiago. It smells." She gave a half grimace, half smile. "Sorry."

"No problem," I said. "I'll have them wrap it up. Maybe they've got some saltines I could munch on."

She laughed again and my heart soared.

"No. Eat. Eat your dinner. Please. If you send it away, I'll only feel like a crazy pregnant lady and start crying—or screaming. Oh, damn, Jason. I've been sitting on bad news all afternoon and I've got to tell you or I'm going to explode."

Roger and the Kid, with the impeccable timing that good friends and children always seem to have, arrived at our table. "We're heading out," Roger said. "The Kid wants ice cream and I've been sitting long enough. We'll meet you back at your place, okay?"

"'Nilla," my son said.

"That's great, Roger. Thanks. You're sure?"

"I got it," he said.

I held out my hand for the Kid to sniff. He gave a rare smile and held his hand out to me. He did not like to be hugged, kissed, or even touched, usually, but we had discovered this mutually acceptable form of communicating affection. "You take care of Roger, okay? Don't let him eat too much ice cream."

His brow furrowed as he processed this. Roger never ate ice cream. Therefore this gave onto two possibilities: (A) I was losing my mind; or (B) I was making a joke. He weighed these for a moment and responded. "Funny."

They said their good-byes, and Skeli and I watched them trundle off together.

"That's so great," she said. "He's learning to trust Roger."

The Kid did not give his trust easily, but his circle was expanding. It *was* great.

"Ahhh," I sighed in a descending coda. "So tell me your news. You heard from the co-op, right?"

She nodded. "They called. The secretary. What's-her-name? She didn't have to. She said there'll be a letter."

The realtor had warned us. We had been denied by the co-op board.

For the past two months we had been using every spare hour—and there had been few and those hard-won—to hunt for an apartment that would hold our combined family. The Kid and I shared a large one-bedroom with alcove in the Ansonia, a co-op run like a residential hotel. Skeli lived in a rambling wreck on 110th Street in a building that was owned by her ex-husband. She fully expected an eviction notice to arrive within weeks after the birth. Neither apartment would work. The Kid had to have his own room. We needed a three-bedroom.

"Did she say why?"

Skeli didn't exactly answer the question. "She was nice. She voted for us, but it didn't matter."

It wasn't financial. I was being paid close to a million a year and I had an ironclad contract. We had references from Wall Street, Broadway, and even a letter from an FBI agent. The fact that Skeli and I were not married—we had both been married before and shared a distrust of the institution—would not have mattered in twenty-first-century Manhattan, nor would it have if we were multiracial, gay, or members of a Satan-worshipping cult. They didn't know about the Kid's condition, because I had not considered it to be any of their goddamn business, and it would have been illegal for them to consider it anyway. But the one line on the application that asked *Have you ever been convicted of a felony?* had been inescapable. And damning. In some circles, I was famous. Or infamous.

"We could look at condos," she said. "Or check out Queens."

"I grew up in Queens," I said. "I've got nothing against it, but I'm not going back."

"Or farther out on Long Island."

The devil's choice. The Long Island Rail Road or the Long Island Expressway. I would rather be drowned in Asiago cheese.

"Or New Jersey," I said.

She laughed. "Now you're being mean. Cut it out. We'll figure this out."

Real estate in Manhattan. The shared obsession that binds us all. I wondered if people in Hong Kong, or Singapore, or Paris spent as much time as New Yorkers did sharing horror stories of finding, maintaining, losing, or surviving in the quest for the perfect two-bedroom. They probably did, I thought. Paris, for sure.

"Come on," I said. "Let's catch them up. I'll buy you a frozen yogurt." I signaled for the check.

"You sure know how to treat a girl," she said.

3

When Virgil Becker's father ran his investment bank over the cliff, I was called upon to help his son pick up the pieces. Virgil now owed me large. The contract said he had to pay me whether I showed up or not, but I was old-school. I showed up.

"What are you working on?" Virgil asked.

"Penny stock trading. There's a broker out in Stony Brook who's been putting his clients into some microstocks. Compliance cleared it, but I didn't like the way it smelled. I did some looking into it, and now I think it stinks."

"See Aimee when we're done. She can handle it." He tapped a few keys on his computer. "I've got something else I want you to focus on." The computer beeped at him—politely. "She's expecting you."

"Listen, Virgil, this thing with the penny stocks could be toxic."

He wasn't convinced. "How much money is involved?"

Commissions on the trades had run to just over two million dollars. I did some quick math. "Proceeds of around one hundred mil."

He could tell that I wasn't being entirely forthright. "How badly did the account get burned?"

That was the oddest thing about the trades—the clients were making money. "It's complicated."

"What's the hit?"

"Actually, they're up around ten percent. Two years running."

"Well, that's intriguing." His delivery was deadpan.

Penny stocks did not produce steady returns. Each one was like a lottery ticket. And they paid off a lot less frequently.

"I know," I said, "it sounds like I'm chasing moonbeams." I took out my cell phone and opened the file of photos. "But take a look at this before you make any quick decisions." I quickly scanned through the shots I had taken of the trucks, looking for one that might best sell my point. One dark, hurried, often blurred picture after another. Either the flash had not gone off, or when it had, the resulting image showed nothing but starbursts of reflected light. If you squinted and used your imagination, you could see that they were pictures of trucks. They could also have been outtakes from some moody noir movie filmed at night in downtown Detroit. "Never mind," I finished lamely. I vowed to look up how long I had before I could get a cell phone upgrade.

"Hand it over to Aimee." It was an order, but he said it kindly.

"Aye, aye." Aimee Devane was head of compliance for Becker Financial. We did not always play well together. She tended to treat me like the pet cobra—I was convenient for getting rid of rats and mice, but she would have preferred a cat.

"Now do I have your complete attention?" Virgil said it with a smile, but with just a bare hint of impatience.

"I'm with you," I said. "What do you need?"

He checked his watch. "I have just a few minutes to bring you up to speed, then I have another meeting."

"Sorry. The holdup is my fault."

He waved a hand to change the subject. "You've no doubt heard the rumor going around that the firm is in play."

I had not heard it, but then I was not a welcome member of the rumor circuit. Conversations tended to stop midsentence as I approached. My nickname on the trading floor was Darth Vader.

"Who's the buyer?" I asked.

"That's why I need you. Whoever it is, they are being very careful not to reveal themselves. Large blocks of shares trade, but the buyer is always a cloaked account. Offshore, or in the name of a trust or a law firm."

There would be willing sellers out there, too. When the father's

firm was broken up and Virgil took the reins of the remaining brokerage and investment banking businesses, many of the creditors and
investors who had been scammed out of their savings by the father
received shares in the new firm as partial compensation. Now that Virgil had turned the place around and made it a viable business, the stock
price had recovered substantially. Those who had held on through the
whole maelstrom were now being rewarded for their patience, having
been made whole, or almost so, by the rebound. It was found money.

"No one's approached you?" I asked.

"Not exactly. I had a rather clandestine meeting with a lawyer who
claims to represent a consortium of buyers. I said I wasn't interested in
selling, but I'm always willing to listen. I suggested we have our bankers sit in on the next meeting."

"What'd he say?"

"It spooked him. 'No bankers,' he said. 'This is a private matter.' It
was the strangest pitch I've ever heard of. We were having dinner in a
private room at the Waldorf, and he stood up and walked out between
the salad and the entrée."

"How much does the family own?"

Virgil's family made the Borgias look normal. His older brother,
James, known to his friends and enemies as Binks, had become a permanent resident in a rehab facility out in Sedona, Arizona, where it
was easier to keep his heroin habit in check; their sister, Morgan, was
serving time in a minimum-security facility in Rhode Island. The
youngest brother, Wyatt, was an Aspy with limited interests. He lived
with his mother on the family estate in Newport. The mother was a
powerful and protective New England martriarch whose main caloric
intake was high-end vodka.

"Like most of the top employees, I own some shares. Ninety percent of my pay is in stock. A much bigger block sits in a trust. Mother
is the trustee—she set it up after putting up a sizable portion of the
cash I needed to get the firm up and running again. The beneficiaries
of the trust are the four siblings. The trustee votes the shares. There

may be ways around the restrictions that I don't know. All told, however, it comes to less than a third of the outstanding float. Anyone
making a play could end-run all of us, if they had enough capital."

"It would be a lot easier if they had one or more of you on their side."

"If it's family, that makes it . . ." He paused, searching for the
right word.

"Complicated?" I said.

"Venomous," he replied.

4

There was a knock at the door and Virgil called out, "Come in, Jim. You're right on time."

A hint of aftershave preceded the man. Something manly. Old Spice. Bay rum. Kentucky bourbon. Something like that. He looked like he had just come from the gym, his hair still wet from the shower and slicked back like Pat Riley. He had a cocky smile that said, *We both know I'm faster, stronger, smarter, and more aggressive than you ever were or will be, but don't hold it against me.*

I stood up and prepared to leave, but Virgil stopped me. "Don't go. I want you to meet the firm's latest acquisition." He was grinning with barely concealed pride.

The man faced me. If he was at all discomfited by being referred to as an asset, he gave no sign of it. He smiled warmly and extended his hand. I thought that he must not know my history or my current position. Those who did rarely smiled at me, warmly or otherwise.

"This is James Nealis," Virgil said. "He's come on board to oversee all of our investment banking. He'll be focusing on biotech."

"Jim," he said. "Pleased to meet you."

He definitely did not know who I was. We were even. I knew nothing about him. I should have. A hire at that level should have been vetted and I should have been part of the process. The head of all investment banking would be on a par, and if future circumstances warranted, a notch ahead of all other department heads. The position was tantamount to being second or third in the hierarchy. The fact that I had not been consulted grated. On the other hand, maybe my nose was out of joint about having to turn the penny stock kerfuffle over to Aimee Devane. Either way, it wasn't Nealis's fault. I could, at least, be pleasant.

I shook his hand and welcomed him aboard. He was a man of medium height and build, with sharp green eyes. When he stopped smiling, his face became instantly unreadable. He would be a good poker player. Or negotiator.

We all sat down. I gave Virgil a quizzical look to signal that I wanted more information—especially why I hadn't been included in looking at the new hire. Virgil smiled at me instead of answering.

"Jason works directly for me," Virgil explained to Nealis. "He is my last line of defense. When legal and compliance can't fix a problem, Jason often can. The firm would not have survived without him."

He turned to me and continued. "Our people have done well in industrial biotech—white—but we're lagging in the hot areas— agricultural and medical—green and red. I don't expect us to be in position to take on Goldman Sachs anytime soon, but a few small successes will make a big difference here." It was a nice speech from someone not given to making them.

Nealis surprised me. "I know what you do here, Jason. I've heard the talk. It's great work. These times call for strict compliance and it's good for Virgil to have someone he can trust who can work outside the normal channels. It's too easy for a bureaucracy to accept the status quo. You're the man to shake things up."

I thanked him, though I felt like something important had just happened and I had slept through it.

"I'm still getting used to being overhead," I said. On Wall Street, if you are not a producer you are an expense. "It's good to see the firm attracting major talent."

Nealis chuckled politely at my self-deprecating comment and smiled graciously at the compliment. "I'm looking forward to working with you," he said. "My background is *math* also. We geeks need to stick together."

I returned the polite chuckle. I had been a math major up until the point that I realized I was never going to be the next Rasmussen. I graduated a business major. If he knew that much about my background, he had done some deep research. He was more than a few steps ahead of me.

The speeches were over and I had work to do.

5

Aimee Devane had been hired during the bad old days when Virgil's father was running his multibillion-dollar Ponzi scheme that supported his financial empire and a lavish lifestyle. The fact that she had survived the investigation and the ensuing purge said she was a formidable infighter—or that she was squeaky clean. Or both.

Compliance protected the firm, not the employees. Good compliance officers could be a manager's best backup, finding and isolating problems before they became disasters. Bad ones behaved like mad-dog KGB agents. They earned nicknames from the trading desks like Dirty Harry and Popeye Doyle, names that they wore with misbegotten pride. It was a culture that tended to see the world in black-and-white terms and regarded all other employees as criminals, either active or not-yet-active. A sure sign of criminal activity was if a trader was making money—or losing it. I did not see the world that way.

I worked for Virgil and investigated the gray areas. There were plenty. Not every misstep is a crime. And not every trader who makes a mistake deserves to be drawn and quartered. In the end, the game is about taking risks and making money, and traders need to know they have the latitude to take those risks and the confidence that management will back them up.

But the pendulum had swung the other way since the mortgage scams of the pre-crash era. When bubbles burst, they rarely hurt the most egregious offenders. A lot of bad actors had survived unscathed, but the industry as a whole had suffered. Compliance was now the fastest growing department in the firm—and the same applied for all our competitors. Aimee Devane held the reins. If she wanted to shut down a department or branch office, it was gone, with no appeal. I'd been told that she was fair, but all I'd ever seen was tough.

Her department was on the other side of the executive floor at Becker Financial. I walked past the elevator bank and through a double set of doors. Cubicles made a maze of the space with a line of tiny offices against the opposite wall. I threaded my way through until I reached Aimee's secretary, a harried-looking lifer with gray hair tied back in a tight bun and a chain holding her glasses. I announced myself and tried to make myself look patient and in no particular hurry.

Aimee didn't keep me waiting; that wasn't her way. She may have been cold and tough, but she was also much too sensible to put on an act.

"Have a seat, Stafford. What've you got?"

Aimee was also very attractive. That day, she was wearing a pale green suit with an even paler silk blouse. They were a great match for her blazing red hair and hazel eyes. I had heard that she studied muay Thai, commonly called Thai kickboxing, and competed regularly. If the purpose was to help her stay in shape, I would say it was working.

"Penny stocks," I said.

"Every stock trade under ten dollars a share is pulled and reviewed for price to the market, markup, and suitability to the client. Nothing—I repeat, *nothing*—gets by my people."

"'Suitability'?"

"Only sophisticated investors get to play in penny stocks. Even then we watch the action. If the position drops by twenty percent, the broker gets a call from my office."

"Suppose the client was making money? Every time. Every trade. And clearing a ten percent profit regularly over the last two years. Would that raise any flags?"

She cocked her head. "That wouldn't necessarily show a flag in our system."

"But you agree it sounds suspicious."

"Odd, maybe. Suspicious? I don't know."

I nodded. "Worth looking at?"

"This sounds familiar. This wouldn't be the young gun out in C-3, would it?"

C-3 was the branch code for Stony Brook, Long Island. "That's the one."

"Yeah, we looked at him, maybe six months ago. Maybe less. The client is an FA, so no foul. Not our problem."

"FA? Financial advisor?"

"They can trade anything they like. We just execute for them. They take all responsibility for their clients. Becker Financial is only on the hook if they're playing on margin. That's a credit call, not a regulatory issue. My people cleared them."

"It doesn't bother you that all the stocks they trade in are related somehow?"

Her eyes flicked to her computer monitor and back. "You've got five minutes. Convince me."

I told her that I had pulled all the old documents relating to the IPOs—initial public offerings—of the companies involved. There were two different bankers involved, both small firms that had gone belly-up—one during the recent crash, the other back in the tech crash of 2000.

She shook her head dismissively. "They're microstocks, right? How many players are there focusing on that market? Can't be many."

"My five minutes isn't up yet," I said.

She actually smiled. "My office, my clock."

"Rose Holdings," I said. "They all have long-term leases with the same entity."

She gave a half squint. "Who?" Her expression was clear to read. I was stretching.

"Rose Holdings. There is no record of any such company in New York State. Except for the deed on one piece of property."

"You have seconds left," she said.

"Okay, but why would every single one of those companies maintain a fleet of their trucks in the same warehouse? A warehouse that doubles as a chop shop out in Suffolk County." I kept the bison to myself. I thought a mention might hurt my credibility.

"So, it's more than odd. It might even rank as suspicious. But it's nothing to do with us. Call the police, if it's really bugging you."

I wouldn't. I didn't know what I would do, but I really had nothing more than a feeling of vague unease.

She flipped her hands over and raised both eyebrows. I got the message. I had brought her nothing, and she had nothing more to say.

"Thanks anyway," I said.

"Come back anytime," she answered. I didn't think she meant it, though.

needed to swing back and check in with Virgil once more—without Nealis in the room. He was frowning at his computer monitor, but waved me in.

"Did you speak to Devane?" he asked.

"I did. As you said, she's on it."

He nodded distractedly. "I'm worried." We both knew he meant that he was worried about a hostile takeover, not a minor compliance problem. But it was unlike Virgil to allow himself to worry—and even more unlike him to admit to it.

"I'll do what I can," I said, trying to sound confident.

He plastered on a resolute face, which I didn't buy into at all. "I know you will." Then he seemed to realize that, in coming back, I might have my own agenda. "Sorry. You wanted to talk to me. I've been distracted. What is it?"

It didn't pay to be careful with Virgil. He respected directness, not diplomacy. "It's the new hire. What do we know about him?"

He grimaced. "Why? You don't like him?"

I laughed. "As a matter of fact, no, I don't." Top producers, myself included, were rarely known for their social skills. Nealis had made an effort, but I was skeptical. "But that's not relevant. A hire that important? I should have had a chance to do a background check."

Virgil looked at the ceiling at the far end of the room and sighed. "What can I say? You're right? But the firm is growing. A year ago, you and I could have discussed this at leisure. I don't have that luxury anymore. There are too many problems calling for my attention all at once. And one very big one."

"All the more reason to delegate."

"That is a skill that I am still developing. It does not come naturally to me."

"Same here," I said. The transition from trader to manager had been rocky—even before the avalanche.

He acknowledged the similarity with a small nod. "There are sharks and whales, Jason. Nealis is a shark. I'll have to watch him, I know. He's hungry. But he is a very big shark and just what we need here. His production will spin off benefits across every department. He thinks big. Two years from now, I hope I have a team of ten just like him."

I felt a sharp pang of regret for the passing of the small firm, where I had instant access to the CEO, and the knowledge that my contributions were as important as any other's. My role wouldn't shrink in a larger firm—it could be even greater—but the culture would change. We would no longer be a tribe of brothers, following a single trusted leader, but a more powerful empire of competing factions. Politics would have to be factored into every decision—or at least every investigation. All egos bruise, and bigger ones more readily than others.

"I'll be discreet," I said.

"And find out who's giving me migraines, will you?"

"Aye, aye, Captain."

7

While waiting for the elevator, I heard a door open and the sound of two voices. Nealis and another man. A strong Long Island accent. Baldwin or Massapequa, or if not the South Shore, then middle island like Coram or Ronkonkoma. A voice neither usual nor unusual in Wall Street environs, but rare on the executive floor. I stepped back and craned my head to see around the corner. The two men in the waiting area were still talking. They were standing very close, well inside each other's intimate space. I felt a twinge of guilt, as though I were spying on some private moment.

The second man was younger than Nealis with black hair so well-oiled it was phosphorescent, like the wings of a grackle. His face was narrow, all planes, with a prominent nose and chin. He wore a charcoal chalk-stripe suit with a brilliant white silk shirt and a lavender tie. I saw the flash of gold cuff links—polished orbs the size of walnuts.

I ducked back behind the wall a split second before the elevator emitted a loud ping. The doors opened. The moment I stepped in, I hit the button for the lobby.

"Hold the elevator," Nealis called.

My wires are permanently crossed when it comes to buttons that open or close the doors. When the elevator panel uses those arrows that look like Cyrillic parentheses, I am lost. I stabbed and the doors stayed open.

"Hey, thanks," the well-dressed young man said as he entered the car.

I stared up at the floor counter as the numbers flicked by. Some elevator rides are interminable. There was something menacing, or just plain wrong, about him, but I couldn't tell if I was just imagining it.

We reached the lobby and I held back a sigh of relief, but as the doors opened, the voice behind me said, "Excuse me." It sounded more like "Skoos me."

"Yes?"

He examined me closely as though memorizing, rather than recalling, my features. "Yuh Jason Staffud, ahn't yuh?"

"I am." I felt like I had been challenged. I waited for him to announce his name.

"See yuh." He walked out onto John Street and turned the corner.

His casual farewell was much too forced. An act, but a good one. Was it menace that I had sensed? Or fear? But why would he fear me? A chance encounter in an elevator? Not worth examining.

That was a deadly mistake.

8

It was time to find out who was trying to buy Becker, and I knew where to start.

"Richard Hannay's line."

The woman had a voice just like the lady on the *BBC World News* on PBS. I loved that voice. Still, it wasn't the response I had expected when I called that number.

"I'm sorry. Do I have a wrong number? I was looking for Dr. Kimble."

Richard Kimble was one in a list of aliases used by a whizbang computer genius who had helped me out in the past. He was in hiding from various branches of the U.S. government, who collectively believed that he had hacked into high-security systems for the purpose of assisting the Taliban. He had been set up, and a lawyer whom I had recommended was busy trying to demonstrate that fact to Homeland Security, the Justice Department, and the NSA. He was a very good lawyer. I knew, because he was also my lawyer. In the meantime, my genius was maintaining a low profile, living on the far edge of civilized society. And using an app on his notepad to disguise his voice.

"Dr. Kimble is no longer reachable through this number."

"This is Jason Stafford calling. Is there someone else there who could help me?"

"One moment, please. Would you repeat the following phrase for our voice recognition software? 'It is easier to forgive an enemy than to forgive a friend.'"

I did it without stuttering. The man I had known as Richard Kimble—and other aliases—had become a friend, and had forgiven me for risking his life.

The BBC news lady said, "Thank you. We have verification. Would you like to speak with Mr. Hannay?"

The lightbulb went on. The Robert Donat character from Hitchcock's *The 39 Steps.*

"Yes, I would. I would really love to meet with him, if that's possible."

"Is this a secure line?" she asked.

It was a recently purchased prepaid smartphone. "As clean as can be," I said.

"Hang up and stand by for a text." She was gone.

My phone gave a little chirp and I opened the message.

1145A-W4X6

No tricks. No magic decoder needed. Eleven forty-five a.m.—forty minutes later—at West Fourth and Sixth Avenue. The basketball courts in the Village across from the IFC movie theater. I could buy him lunch at the Minetta Tavern.

I rode the express train up two extra stops before getting out, crossing over the platform and taking the second downtown train back to the West Fourth Street station. No one was following me. I hadn't expected to find anyone, but meetings with Richard Kimble, aka Benjamin McKenna, and now aka Richard Hannay, always produced more than a touch of paranoia in me.

At 11:42, I came up the subway stairs and walked along the fence next to the courts. I was early, but Hannay would want it that way. He would already be in the area, watching my back and his. When he thought it was safe, he would approach.

There were two half-court games going on. The downtown game was the more intense. Despite the fact that we were only two weeks into baseball season and the temperature was more like March than mid-April, they were playing shirts versus skins and both teams were sweating.

"You Jason Stafford?" a young voice said.

I turned and saw a hard-faced preadolescent in a black hoodie and black jeans that rode so low on his hips I was surprised he could walk. The laceless sneakers that completed his outfit probably cost as much as my suit.

"Who's asking?" I said.

"You Jason Stafford." It was no longer a question. "Man say you give me twenty bucks if I deliver you a message."

"Bullshit," I said.

"*Saaayy?*" he said in an aggressive whine.

"He said I'd give you ten."

He grinned, unashamed, and proud of his attempt to fleece me. "Don't hurt to try. Looks like you won't miss it, neither."

I grinned back. At least he was an honest pirate. I handed him a ten. "What's the message?"

"He say you can buy him a coffee at Caffe Reggio, if you want."

"Thanks," I said.

"For another ten, I can take you there."

Caffe Reggio was a block away on Macdougal Street. A very short block.

"I'm tempted to take you up on it, just for the entertainment value," I said. "But, no thanks. I'll try and find it on my own."

He shrugged elegantly—a well-practiced gesture—turned, and walked away, his legs bent and slightly spread to keep his pants from sliding any farther south.

I took another look around to see if I could spot Mr. Hannay—or Richard Kimble. The sidewalk held its usual midday cross section of Village denizens. Students and hustlers, housewives and poets, aging gays, and blue-suited businessmen on their way to lunch at Il Mulino or Babbo. If he was one of them, he was well disguised, but then he was always well disguised.

An espresso at Caffe Reggio is not the same thing as the Black Label burger at the Minetta Tavern, but the space was so small and intimate that it guaranteed privacy. It was also another survivor in a city that seems to remake itself every night. A walk through Greenwich Village was always a shock, finding old haunts that had survived, or poignant reminders of places long gone, like the sign for the Village Gate—once one of the great jazz clubs of the world—which still hangs over the CVS pharmacy that took over the space twenty years ago.

I took my double espresso to the table farthest from the counter and sat facing the door. The front page of the *New York Post* looked up at me from a nearby chair. U.S. Attorney Wallace Ashton Blackmore of the Southern District of New York, long rumored to be seeking the nomination for mayor of New York, had made a splash again. "THREE YEARS!" There was a picture of Himself, both fists raised over his head. I flipped to the story inside. Blackmore was "outraged" that too many federal judges were handing out "all-expense-paid vacations" to Wall Street felons, but justice was finally to be done. My friend Matt Tuttle's three-year sentence was today's excuse for sounding off. Skeli and I had been there for the sentencing hearing and had seen Matt's wife collapse as though skewered with a lance.

I closed the paper and flipped it over so I wouldn't have to look at it. The back page was only slightly disheartening. The Yankees were already in last place and the season was only two weeks old. I put the paper on the next table and leaned back in the chair. I waited.

I did not have to wait long. A tall, stooped man with long more-salt-than-pepper hair pulled back into a shoulder-length ponytail came in and went straight to the counter. He was wearing a tweed jacket with leather patches on the elbows and a pair of baggy green corduroys. He looked like a college professor from Central Casting. Maybe the sociology department.

"Cappuccino," he said, "and put it on that man's tab," indicating me with a quick nod. He had a long Sam Elliott mustache that was completely gray.

He came over and pulled the other chair around to my side of the table, so that we were both facing the room. Three black-clad German tourists shared a table out on the street, but, other than the staff of two behind the counter, we were the only people inside.

"I've always liked this place," he said. "It will be a shame when it finally shuts down."

"Is it closing?" I said. It had been there for close to ninety years.

"Well, eventually. Right? This is New York. Nothing lasts forever."

"Hmm. Fraunces Tavern," I said.

"No fair. That place has burned down, blown up, been rebuilt and remodeled, closed and reopened more times than you can count."

"Since 1762. It says so right on the menu."

"Marketing."

It was dark inside the café, and I could barely see the artifice in the man's appearance. He was still in his early thirties, but with the hair dye and artificial stoop, he looked closer to fifty.

"How often do you have to recolor that 'stache?"

"I carry a touch-up kit in my briefcase."

"How's the shoulder?"

Four months earlier, he had been shot while helping me on an investigation. It wasn't a serious wound, but he hadn't been able to go to a hospital because he was very much on the run.

"I had it looked at when I was up in Toronto last month. It's healing."

"You were in Canada?"

"Your lawyer buddy set it up. My wife came up and I got to see the girls for a couple of days." I'd met his family one day in late February. Well, almost met them. The hacker had been waiting for me at the top of the stairs to the subway station at Seventy-second Street. Before I had time to react to seeing him alive and seemingly recovered from our last meeting, he had deftly handed off a Saks shopping bag and merged with the crowd. I waited until I arrived at Virgil's offices before opening the bag. Inside were five packs of one-hundred-dollar bills—fifty thousand dollars—and a note telling me how to make the delivery. The next day—a crowded Wednesday matinee day in midtown—I had a pastrami sandwich at Junior's on Forty-fifth Street. I would rather he had chosen Katz's or the Second Avenue Deli, but Junior's was chaotically busy—excellent cover. An attractive woman in her early thirties with two young girls sat at the next table. At one point, the woman asked me for the ketchup. I passed her the mustard. We all left at the same time. As she went by, she took the Saks bag from the empty chair at my table. Inside were seven packs of hundreds. The extra twenty thousand was entirely my idea. I owed her husband that much and more.

"How are they all holding up?" I asked him.

He forced a smile—it looked painful. "Great. They're tough. Like their mother. Everybody is doing well."

It was too transparent an attempt to self-deceive for me to comment on. "Isn't the FBI or somebody watching them all the time?"

"Twenty-four seven. But the feds weren't going to touch me in Canada without an okay from the government. They followed us around while we went sightseeing for three days, then the girls went back to Buffalo and I disappeared again."

He said it with such a matter-of-fact tone that the story was doubly chilling. I was saved from responding with some idiotic show of sympathy by the arrival of his coffee. He took a sip and dabbed at the long mustache with his napkin.

"Damn. I love cappuccino, but the foam always gets up in my 'stache." He patted it with the napkin again and checked for signs that his gray dye was not coming off. Temporarily satisfied, he took another long slurp. "What have you got for me?"

I'd made an appointment to go and talk with Virgil's mother, but she couldn't see me until the following Tuesday. Then I had waded through public records of recent buys and sells, focusing on larger block trades. I had run out of options. I needed a fresh perspective—and a bit of behind-the-scenes chicanery.

"Find me all the buyers of Becker Financial stock. Not just the front men. From what I've come up with, they're all blind offshore accounts. Law offices or private banks. I need to know who or what is pulling the strings."

"I may need help with something that big."

"Hire whoever you need. Virgil will pay this time. If there is a secretive group trying to buy the bank, he'll need some ammo to fight back."

"How deep should I go?"

"I doubt you'll end up with the names of the real money, but get as close as you can. We've got nothing right now but a bad smell. I'd like to get back to Virgil with something early next week."

"Big job and short timeline. And I imagine he wants me to leave no trace."

"Impossible?"

"No, just expensive. Will he pay in Bitcoins?"

"He'll pay in gold-pressed latinum, as long as he gets results."

"Why, I had no idea you were a Trekkie."

"I'm not. I was a trader. The Ferengi Rules of Acquisition are universal." I paused. "There's something else. Just for me."

"Okay."

"Not a priority, but get me anything you can on a guy named James Nealis. Banker."

"A bad guy?"

"I'm just curious."

"Any chance of my getting shot at again?"

"It's not that kind of case," I said with a barely hidden wince.

"Neither was the first one," he replied, giving me a grin aimed at my discomfort. "Ah, well, the weak in courage is strong in cunning. I will take excessive care this time around. And, listen, thanks for hooking me up with the lawyer. He's given me and my family some hope that we might put all this behind us someday."

I had been paying the lawyer's tab, with the general understanding that it was a loan, repayable if and when this fugitive became a free man again, no longer hunted. I wasn't sure, but I had the feeling that my good friend Larry was low-balling his bills in support of the effort.

"Can I buy you lunch?" I asked.

He shook his head and drank quickly. "I need to keep moving.

Thanks. Another time." He stood up and headed for the door, but stopped as he reached it. "By the way, how much did that hustler gouge out of you?"

"The young guy at the basketball court? He tried for a twenty, but I only gave him a ten." I was a trader and proud of it.

He laughed. "Ballsy guy. I told him to ask for a five."

9

The Kid and I had a tough weekend. Saturday, after his yoga class, we
went for a run in the park. He liked doing wind sprints down Poet's
Walk. I'm no sprinter; I flamed out early. The Kid kept going, burning
up energy that his body would otherwise use to torment him with
sleeplessness, twitches, cramps, and even small seizures.

I took a seat on a bench and listened to a man in his sixties playing
acoustic guitar like John Fahey. A moment later, when the song ended,
I realized that I hadn't seen my son for almost a full minute. An eternity in parent time. I jumped up and looked around madly, but it was
too late. The Kid was gone. The next fifteen minutes shaved a decade
off the years remaining to me and cost me a couple of handfuls of torn-
out hair that I could not afford to lose.

I found him. The Kid was halfway up the face of a giant rock, stuck
to it like a gecko on a beach cottage wall. He was high enough off the
ground that I had to stretch to pluck him off and he didn't like it. He
thrashed and his foot connected with my head, which was not the same
as being deliberately kicked, but it hurt just the same. He had to skip his
usual ice cream treat and we walked home thoroughly disgusted with
each other. I blamed Frederick Law Olmsted for leaving such a dangerous rock lying around where anybody could get into trouble.

Sunday night, I burned the Kid's grilled cheese sandwich. Not
exactly burned. Blackened. I scraped off the charcoal and put the sandwich on his plate—damaged side down—with a dozen microwaved
French fries, four green beans, and a small mound of ketchup. A bal-
anced meal.

The Kid could smell that something was wrong, but I was hoping
that he would smother everything with enough of the red sauce to kill

the taste of everything else—including the burnt bread. It didn't work. He took one bite, began his regimen of ten chews per bite, and started to gag.

My first reaction, and I hated myself for it, was on the order of "Oh, puh-lease, just cut out the big drama." But it was immediately apparent that his gagging, spitting, and heaving was not an act. He was in distress. The fact that the sandwich was not damaging him in any way was a side issue. I stuck my finger in his mouth and began to dig out the sodden mass, holding his cheeks with my other hand to keep him from clamping his sharp teeth down on my finger. I was successful in getting most of the bread and cheese out, but his tongue was still covered with black crumbs and he choked and coughed. I grabbed his water glass and held it to his lips.

"Come on, Kid. Just rinse your mouth. You'll feel better." I almost added "Trust me," which under the circumstances would have been the height of absurdity.

He pushed the water away and the glass flew past my shoulder, emptying its contents down the front of my shirt. The Kid spun away from me and ran for the bathroom. Without thinking, I ran after him. If I had thought, I would have let him go. He wasn't going to hurt himself in there, and he might have been on track to rinse out with mouthwash, which would have been much more effective at killing the taste of burnt carbon. Instead, I jumped up and tried to head him off by circling around the table in the other direction. He saw me coming at him from an unexpected direction and must have assumed that I was chasing him—which, in a way, I was. He began screaming in terror.

I stopped. My body didn't want to, but I let the brain take charge. My body wanted to pick him up and hug him to me until the demons left him. But that never worked, and I had received the bites, scratches, kicks, and punches that came as a result of that approach. I let my arms drop to my sides and squatted down to show a less threatening profile. That didn't work, either. The Kid kept screaming and ran into his room, slamming the door behind him.

"Kid? Son? Are you okay?" I called softly as I edged toward his door.

There was an explosion of banging noises from inside the room. I hoped that he was only kicking something, rather than hitting it with more delicate parts of his body. He was capable of banging his head on something until he bled, and though he had not done it once while living with me, I was always prepared for the worst. At least he was no longer choking and threatening to vomit. The attack passed. The room was quiet.

I heard my phone chirp. It was back on the table. I ignored it.

"Kid? I screwed up your sandwich. I'm sorry. Can I make you another one? I'll do it right this time." I had been scrolling pages on my iPad, reading whatever snippets came up that related to penny stocks. I had not been watching the cast-iron pan. The acrid scent of burnt toast was my first clue that I was destroying the Kid's dinner. I had compounded my error by having been too impatient and pigheaded to make him another. Perfection as a parent was a goal, not a condition, and one that seemed to recede with each new trial the Kid handed me. Rather than earning an A in Single Parenting 101, I was sliding deeper every day into the realization that I would have been better off taking the class pass-fail.

The phone chirped again. I hated that Apple thought I needed a second notification when I did not immediately pick up a text. Did their engineers not consider that there might be something more important in my life than decoding the latest SMS missive from the virtual world? There was probably something in Settings that would allow me to change the notification system, but as there was not a teenager living in my house, I had no chance of finding it.

"Kid. I'm going to open your door. I won't come in unless you tell me it's okay, but I just want to see that you're safe." I waited for a reply. Nothing. But he didn't say no. I opened the door.

He was curled up on his bed, knees practically touching his forehead, rocking slightly and vocalizing in a stream of soft grunts, moans, and vowel sounds that might have been meant as words—as though interpreted by the lead singer in a death metal band. But he was all right. No blood showing. No cuts or red marks. If there was damage to furniture or fittings, I would find it the next day.

"Can I get you anything?" No response. "How about I read to you?" No response. That was a good sign. He wasn't escalating at the sound of my voice. That meant I could keep trying to reach him. "I'm going to come in and sit on your bed with you. Is that okay?" No response. Excellent. I was making progress.

There was no possibility of touching him. A comforting hand on his back would have thrown him into a full-out tantrum. I could offer only my presence. I calmed myself and hoped that the Kid would somehow sense it and be able to feed on it. It may have worked, or it may have been that this latest paroxysm had run its course, but he did grow calmer. The grunting stopped. The violent rocking became a gentle sway. His fingers were beating out his odd, repetitive cadence— stimming. And his vocalizations became a single, soft word. I leaned in to hear him, taking the risk of retaliation for imposing myself into his space. He continued to ignore me. The word became clearer. I heard his whisper.

"Mamma."

There was no word that I could imagine that would have cut as deep. The Kid and I had not spoken of my ex-wife or her death— murder—in months. He dictated what we talked about by ignoring me when I began speaking on a subject that did not interest him. His shadow, a doctoral candidate in psychology at Columbia who worked with my son after school five days a week, had much better luck with getting him to address uncomfortable issues, but I knew—because she had told me so—that on the subject of his mother, he was intractable. But it was unfair in the extreme to lay the blame solely on the Kid for our mutual failure to discuss such a difficult and emotionally complicated issue. My feelings on the subject were a knotted mare's nest of contradictions that I would take almost any journey to avoid examining. There was guilt over the circumstances of her murder, though I had no hand in it directly. Anger, too, but remaining angry at a dead person is one of the shorter paths to depression. But I had not been able to put aside my hurt or resentment, nor my justified fury at her treatment of our son.

"Mamma," he whispered again.

I did not want to have this conversation. Not then. Not ever. I did not want his pain on my conscience. I didn't think I could handle it. It was too much. My mother died when I was no older than my son and I could not remember a single conversation with my father about her. There must have been some, but I did not remember them and that was just the way I wanted it. Angie was not the world's worst mother, but she would have made most people's short list. Leave her and her memory in the past. The Kid had enough other problems, and so did I. Why couldn't we just leave this one alone?

"Mamma."

"Oh, son, your father really doesn't want to do this. I am so sorry. I wish I could. For you. I would do almost anything for you, but I can't do this."

Something in my voice or my words must have reached him because he stopped rocking. His fingers continued to move, but his body was relaxing. He began to uncurl.

"Your whirl," he said.

"What? Sorry, Kid. I didn't get that."

His voice was flat, but he gave equal emphasis to both words. "Your. Whirl."

I was lost. "Your. Whirl," I repeated.

He nodded—so forcefully that I thought he might strain his neck. "Your. Whirl. Mamma."

It made no sense. When I first got out of prison and found my son living in a locked room at his grandmother's house in Louisiana, he spoke only in odd snippets of taglines from radio and television commercials. Was this some throwback? He rarely did it anymore. His normal verbal skills were nowhere near mainstream for a seven-year-old boy, but he had come a very long way.

"Your. Whirl. Mamma." Saying the words aloud didn't help.

"Now!" he yelled, and curled back into a fetal ball.

"No, no, it's okay. I'm trying to understand. Tell me again."

He was fighting for control, his fingers flying. He suddenly threw himself over and leapt out of bed. "Your. Whirl." He marched out into the living room, where he had more room to pace. He strode furiously from his door to the center of the room, then to the front door, then back to where he'd started. He did this circuit three times as I stood in his doorway, watching and waiting for a clue. The parade-ground pacing was one of his tricks for achieving self-discipline, for getting his demons back in their dens. His battle was exhausting him, but he was winning. When he stopped in front of me, he was breathing hard, but focused, no longer frightened.

"Your. Whirl. Mamma."

"Okay," I said. "Show me." Maybe I could get him to draw something for me that would help.

He walked to the telephone—the landline that I occasionally used for sending a fax or to make a call when my cell phone was charging. "Your whirl. Mamma."

Your World. Delivered. The telephone. He wanted to call his Mamma. Impossible. I must have still had it wrong. The Kid knew what *dead* meant. He knew that his mother was dead. That there was no chance of calling her. He was cracking up. I had never read of a behavioral tic like that, but one thing I had learned—autism is always surprising.

"Kid. You can't call your Mamma. She's gone. You know that." I stopped. He was shaking his head in a vehement *NO!* I had it wrong somehow.

"Mamma. Mamma. Mamma." He picked up the handset and held it out to me. "Mamma."

Angie had referred to herself as Mamma, but only in the third person. Her mother was also Mamma. And she was most definitely alive. She called once a week and kept the Kid on the phone for long sessions, entertaining him by reading books or car magazines, hoping for a few words from him before he disconnected. He never said good-bye. He rarely said hello.

"You want to call your grandmother? Have I finally got this figured out?"

He nodded once.

"Okay. We can do that." I took the phone and dialed from memory. Muscle memory. I wouldn't have been able to verbalize the number, but my index finger remembered.

Mamma blamed me for her daughter's death. So did I, for that matter, but her anger was beyond reason. I felt for her and wished peace for and with her. Her daughter had disappointed her in many ways, but blood was all in her world. Angie's brother, Tino, had brokered a kind of détente between us. Mamma had agreed. Refraining from yelling accusations at me was a small price to pay for the opportunity to talk with her only grandson once a week.

"Jason?" she answered. "Is everything all right?"

"Yes, ma'am. But the Kid is having a hard day and wants to talk to you. Is this a good time?"

The Kid was watching me out of the corner of his eye. If it wasn't a good time for her to talk, I was going to have a time explaining it to him.

"But he's all right? He's not hurt?"

"No, ma'am." I had stopped calling her Mamma after Angie was killed. "He's okay." An explanation that he had freaked out over a burnt sandwich and reacted as though I was poisoning him would have left more questions than answers. And he *was* okay. "Just a bit shaky. Can I give him the phone?"

"Let me just turn off my kettle. Yes, give my little one the phone."

I handed it over. The Kid took it and flopped down on the rug, folding himself into a cross-legged sukhasana pose. He could hold it for hours. I backed away to give him some privacy. He didn't really understand the concept yet, but I did.

The offending sandwich was on the table with cold French fries and colder green beans. I took it all into the kitchen and dumped it in the trash. Then got a sponge and cleaned up the spilled water and the black crumbs that littered the table, chairs, and floor. The Kid usually lasted fifteen or twenty minutes on the phone before his inner clock ticked over and he hung up. I found my cell phone and hit the speed dialer for the Athena take-out number. I ordered him his usual and treated myself to a cheeseburger deluxe. They said they were a little backed up, but would be over with the order in twenty minutes. Perfect.

I opened up my message folder. There was a single text. It came from FBI Special Agent Marcus Brady.

It would be a gross and unlikely deception to say that Brady and I were friends. I was sure that if he ever caught me in some blatantly illegal act, he would cart me off to the Metropolitan Correctional Center and feel that he had done a good day's work. But my assistance had served his career. And he had done the same for me. It was a loveless marriage of convenience that often worked out much better for both sides than the buddy-buddy bromances you see in most cop movies.

He wrote: *Barstow & Co. We need to talk.*

Barstow? The name meant nothing to me.

I texted back: *Buzzy. Will call in am.*

I thought I had turned off autocorrect.

Sorry. Busy.

Besides, it was Sunday night. What couldn't wait until morning? My phone chirped again.

Be home 9 am.

10

The next morning the Kid and I were back to what I had learned to think of as normal. All troubles forgiven or forgotten. I could never be sure which system was the operative one in moments like this. The Kid had hung up the phone abruptly when our dinner was delivered, eaten every bite, and gone to bed almost immediately with no hint of a hangover to our drama. I took the reprieve as a gift from the parenting fates and privately vowed never to burn his grilled cheese again.

I dropped the Kid at school, and I made it back to the apartment with plenty of time to shave and shower before Brady's deadline. He surprised me by showing up with two other agents.

"I inserted myself in their case, Jason, because of our past relationship. I told them that if I were here you'd be more willing to cooperate."

Sirens were going off in my head like a three-alarm fire. "Do I say 'Thank you'? I'd like to know where this is going, Agent Brady." I could count on the fingers of one hand the number of times he had called me by my given name. I didn't want to play.

"May I?" The agent who had introduced himself as Brown indicated the couch.

"Sit, please," I said.

"Thank you." Brady and the other agent—I hadn't caught the name—stepped back and gave us a bit of room. I took a seat on my ancient broken-spring armchair. The room expanded again, but I couldn't shake the feeling that they were all poised to grab me if I made a run for the door.

As he lowered himself onto the couch, Brown plucked his suit pants an inch or so higher, so as to maintain the perfect crease. He was both careful and vain. Ex-military, I guessed. I could imagine him making the same gesture in full dress uniform. "Mr. Stafford, you recently made a request to the SEC for information on a certain stock. As it turns out, the U.S. Attorney has also had an interest in that stock. That is the kind of coincidence that makes people in our line of work uncomfortable."

I wanted to throw all three of them out, with an especial kick in the seat of the pants of Special Agent Brady. He had sandbagged me. My lawyer, the wonder-worker Larry, would have cut this guy off before he sat down. That was the smart move. On the other hand, if I called in a lawyer, I would learn nothing about what they knew. I decided to play the game for a bit longer.

"I work for Virgil Becker at Becker Financial. In my line of work, I often find it necessary to request public information from various government agencies."

"Yes, but not very often in these kinds of microstocks."

"'These'? More than one?"

"Right now we are focusing on only one stock. If there are others that happen to overlap, we would see that as more than coincidence, wouldn't you agree? Suspicious, possibly."

Initial public offerings in microstocks don't have to file with the SEC the same way as larger companies. A week earlier, I had requested information on the penny stocks I was concerned about. Only one, I found, had any substantial documentation available. Researching the rest had taken me days.

"I guess it's time for you to open up a bit," I said. "I'm not supposed to guess at which stock we're talking about, right? Maybe you could act it out. How many syllables?"

He favored me with a forbearing smile that held no humor. "What's your interest in McFee Plumbing?"

"That's easy," I said. "Nothing. Recently, I did request public documents relating to the company, but I have lost interest."

"And why is that?"

"Because my boss told me to hand it over to the compliance department. And that's what I did."

"And Ms. Devane is handling the inquiry at this point?"

He knew the name of the head of compliance at Becker. He was telling me that he had already done some homework. Larry would have clamped a hand over my mouth at that point and stopped the proceedings. I wanted to push it just a step further.

"I don't know what the compliance department is doing. They don't answer to me. I work for the CEO only. He wanted me to work on something else—unrelated—and that's what I'm doing now."

"And what would that be?"

"I don't think I can say at this point. I know of no reason to think the cases are related."

"Did you at any time have personal contact with a Mr. Barstow?"

He used the past tense. That was interesting.

"Barstow? I don't think so. Who was he?" I said.

"That's interesting. You use the past tense."

"Only because you did. I don't know the guy."

"You're familiar with a financial advisory firm called Peconic Capital?"

That was the name of the company that traded in the penny stocks.

"Them I've heard of. This guy Barstow? No. What's this about?"

He named two other stock-trading firms that I had never heard of. I admitted as much and turned to Brady.

"Do you want to tell me what's going on?"

Brady had on his poker face. Brown looked over at his partner. None of them liked me asking questions.

"Hey, if it's public information, I'm going to find it, right? Why go all cute on me? I don't know the guy. What else don't I know?"

Brady had to clear his throat to answer. "He's dead. He had agreed to talk to the U.S. Attorney's Office and go before a grand jury. It's securities fraud. In return for immunity on the pump-and-dump, he was going to give up his partners, plus the Jersey bucket shop that was fronting the scam. He also claimed to have something 'really big.' He hinted that it had to do with Virgil Becker and his firm. Then, the night before he was slated to testify, he died in a botched assassination."

That was a troubling circumlocution. How was an assassination both "botched" and successful?

Brown didn't stop Brady from talking, but he was doing his best to send lightning bolts from his eyes. The drive back downtown with the three of them in the car was going to be a tense one.

"Then, all I can say is that I am so glad not to be involved in any investigation of his firm right now." I spoke the truth, if only partial. Someone was dead. *Assassination* was the word Brady had used. This was what Skeli was most afraid of, and she was right. If I had any brains at all, I would stay well clear of it. Aimee could take care of it. She'd probably bite the bullets in half and spit them back. I was sure her steel-plated heart would keep her safe. I stood up, walked to the door, and held it open. "We're done, folks. I am now officially frightened. If that was the point of your visit, you may leave knowing your message was received loud and clear."

No one moved.

"I'm serious," I said. "If you have anything else to discuss, I'll give you the name of my lawyer. Set up an appointment and I'll be there."

"We may be back," Brown said, standing and shaking his suit pants back down over his shoes. "Or we may ask you to come to the U.S. Attorney's Office to tell your story. You wouldn't have a problem with that, would you?"

"I don't have a story." Those sirens were back, screaming in my head.

"Or you could wait and tell it to the grand jury." He made it sound like the Spanish Inquisition.

"Talk to my lawyer."

"That's your right," Brown said.

I could see that he now believed beyond any question that I was somehow deeply involved in something illegal. The picture was painted. He just needed to fit the frame.

They filed out. Brady went last.

"I'll call you," he said.

I wanted to say something cutting, smart, and cynical, but he looked so hangdog and embarrassed, I swallowed the words before they got to my lips.

"Good-bye, Marcus," I said.

I slammed and locked the door. If only it had been that easy.

11

I needed to talk to Larry, my longtime lawyer, but he was in court all morning. I made an appointment for the afternoon and headed downtown for a different form of comfort.

Skeli's office was in the basement of an older building in SoHo. The street level was a storefront, home to a clothing designer whom I had never heard of, which wasn't surprising. Even when I had been married to a model, I had rarely been able to recognize one designer from another.

One floor down, the door opened onto a quiet, comfortable waiting room with indirect lighting. The walls, floors, and furniture were all in shades of gray, from light cloud to dark charcoal. The achromatic look forced one's eyes to focus on the massive flower arrangement that stood on a pedestal next to the reception desk. I smiled. Skeli associated cut flowers with her ex-husband's infidelities; he had brought home flowers whenever he had an attack of conscience. I had been working on rehabilitating her viewpoint, but it was a work in progress. The office manager was my co-conspirator. Kasey was a dark-haired, brown-eyed woman with a permanent case of good spirits. She managed the office, maintained the schedule, and corrected all the mistakes of the billing company. Whatever Skeli was paying her, she was worth double.

"Hey, Kasey. You've outdone yourself. What are these things?" I asked, pointing to a tall, spiked, yellow, bulbous-shaped flower on a long stalk.

She gave me a skeptical look. "I could tell you, but you won't remember for more than a second or two."

It was true. I never did.

I looked around the empty waiting room. "So, is business this slow all the time?"

As one of the three investors in Skeli's upmarket pain therapy clinic, I could have claimed a financial interest in the answer. But I preferred to keep a low profile, appearing solely as Skeli's constant companion. My interest was less for the investment—which none of the three of us would miss—than for her success and happiness.

Kasey gave a half snort, half laugh. "Not likely. Every treatment room is being used right now and we are booked solid right up until nine tonight. Dr. Tyler hates having more than two or three people waiting at a time. She says clients who have to wait use the time to get angry."

"Is she available?"

She checked the monitor. "You're in luck. She's got a break in five minutes. You want to wait in her office?"

I walked around Kasey's desk and entered the inner sanctum. There was a long corridor with closed doors on either side—the treatment rooms—that led, on one side, to a larger room with various weight machines, stationary bikes, and other therapeutic equipment. On the other side were offices and a small employee lounge. The lounge area was empty, so I stopped and made myself a cup of tea before letting myself into Skeli's office.

It was small, but bare enough so that it did not feel cramped. I sat in one of the two swivel chairs facing her desk and waited. She had added a painting to the wall since my last visit, a smiling golden Buddha, seen through multiple layers of gauzy veils and surrounded by shadows that, upon closer inspection, were revealed as representations of birds, fish, and various animals. The facing wall held four framed documents, all attesting to Dr. Wanda Tyler's right and ability to run a physical therapy office. The desk itself was empty except for a black flat-screen computer monitor and a framed photograph.

I turned the picture a bit so that I could see it from where I sat. The shot had been taken on a beach in the British Virgin Islands at the end of last year—just a few months ago. Skeli and I were kneeling next to the Kid, all three of us slightly sunburned and smiling into a late-afternoon sun. The Kid looked relaxed and happy. Content and unafraid. All rare emotions in my son. Skeli was beautiful, of course, but she also looked relaxed. Not exactly blissed-out, but definitely in vacation mode.

I was the odd man out. The long-brimmed ball cap, which identified the wearer as a fan of the Denver Outlaws, hid the bandage on the side of my head and shaded my eyes. I didn't know if anyone else could have seen it, but I saw the residual anxiety there. The fear for myself and those I loved. The guilt over those who had suffered or died.

It had not been a vacation, or at least not solely a vacation. There had been evil, scary men after me, and I had been afraid they would use my loved ones to get to me. It had happened before. My father and his fiancée had escorted Skeli and the Kid to a private island while I dealt with the bad guys. I joined them only when I was sure they would be safe.

The door opened and Skeli came in. "What a treat," she said before leaning down and giving me a long kiss. As kisses go, it was close to a ten.

"How's the newest member of the family treating you?" I asked.

"I'm getting fat."

"You're not getting fat."

"Not yet. I am getting anticipatorily fat."

"There's no such thing. You just made that up."

"Actually, other than the nausea, the bloat, the sweats, and the occasional heartburn in the middle of the night, I feel really great. I think I'm enjoying being pregnant."

Every woman responds differently. Angie, my first wife and the Kid's mother, had fought every change that her body inflicted upon her, taking them all as attacks or, at the least, intrusions. She had spent months red-faced and haggard. Skeli, on the other hand, emanated a secret contentment. And when she smiled, she was smiling for two.

"So why am I honored with your presence in the middle of the morning?"

"How's 'I couldn't bear to be away from you a minute longer'?"

"You have no idea how lovely that sounds. I know you're full of it, but that doesn't alter the effect of the words. But it's a safe bet that there is another reason."

"I do have a downtown meeting later today."

"With the lawyer?"

"A-yup."

"Good luck. How's the little guy?"

"He had a rough night. His father tried to poison him with a burnt grilled cheese sandwich."

"Oh, boy," she said, rolling her eyes for emphasis.

"Right. But we both survived and we had a good morning. Sometimes that's the best I can hope for."

"You know what Camus says about hope?"

"Camus?"

"That the torture for Sisyphus was that he kept *hoping* that one day the frigging stone would not roll back down."

"Mmm?"

"Turn it around. If Sisyphus just comes to love pushing the stone uphill, he will be a happy man."

"I do love my son—it's the autism I hate."

"Maybe you need to learn how to love it, too. You're back to the Pinocchio thing again, that someday your little guy will be a real boy—normal. Don't do that to yourself. Don't do it to him. He's going through a rough patch. You are both doing your best. And if this is what it is—what it will always be—then what are you going to do?"

I was going to go on loving him and doing whatever his doctors thought best for him, no matter what it cost me in money, time, or pain. She gave me another great kiss. It reminded me of Valentine's Day.

Skeli had been forced to cancel our date because of a scheduling snafu at the office. I was home, enjoying a post-Kid bedtime twelve-year-old Irish whiskey and reading The Anti-Romantic Child when there was a knock at the door. It was Skeli. She was dressed in a midthigh-length pink plastic raincoat with a pink bow in her hair.

"Happy Valentine's Day. I brought you a present."

I opened the door and let her make her entrance. I noticed her shoes were a very un-February pair of pink sling-back sandals, not much more than some sequined straps and a medium heel. She vamped in, pirouetted in the middle of the living room, and cooed at me.

"Well, how do you like it?"

Her legs were bare. She was not carrying anything. My brain shrugged off the whiskey mist and focused on the mystery.

"Are you my present?" I said, not even attempting a show of being in control of the situation.

"Aren't you going to unwrap it?" she asked, moving toward me with a catlike glide. She took my hand and placed it on the tag of the zipper. I pulled it down slowly. There was nothing but Skeli underneath. I slid one arm around her.

"Weren't you cold out there?"

"Shhh," she said and took my hand. She led me toward the bedroom.

"And those shoes?"

"I don't know how much longer I'll be able to wear heels," she said. "I did a test this evening."

"And?"

She stopped and turned to me. "Three blue squares. You're going to be a father again."

Joy. Some trepidation. And relief. I knew how badly she wanted this.

"We need to celebrate," I said.

She let the open raincoat slide off her shoulders and drop to the floor. "Aren't you a bit overdressed for this kind of party?"

I pulled my shirt over my head and tossed it on the couch.

"Better," she said, turning and heading for the bedroom again.

I kicked off my shoes and followed.

"What about your shoes?" I asked again, wrestling my pants off.

"We'll pretend these are my spurs."

The kiss ended. "That's a nice smile," she said.

"Thank you. That was just what I needed. Let me repay you by buying lunch."

"I've got clients all day. However, I'll let you buy me a yogurt and we can eat together right here." She leaned over and kissed me again. It was a quick consolation kiss, but still not bad. "Kasey can run out and get. What will you have?"

I gave Kasey some money. Skeli turned off her computer screen, and the two of us luxuriated in companionable silence for a few moments.

She spoke first. "So, what are you and Larry cooking up?"

"I may need his help again. I had the FBI around this morning. They were asking about my interest in penny stocks."

"I thought you dropped that inquiry."

"I did. Now I'm thinking I should have stuck with it."

"I thought you looked a bit stressed when I walked in here."

"I have a nasty feeling that this case is going to circle around on us. Virgil's preoccupied. I've got to cover his back."

She nodded in understanding and the two of us lapsed back into silence.

"You should get a massage," she said eventually.

"Are you offering?"

"Sorry. I don't do massage, but Bric is very good."

"Is Brick a boy or a girl?"

"Bric is a woman. She is a licensed masseuse with ten years' experience and she doesn't do happy endings."

"No. I want no woman but you to touch me."

"Jennifer Lawrence?"

"Nope."

"What's-her-name? Kate."

"Winslet?" I asked.

"No, but I like her. The Kate I don't like," she said.

"What Kate don't you like?"

"The actress. The blonde," she said.

"I don't think her name is Kate," I said.

"No. Not that one."

"I don't know who you are talking about, but if you don't like her, neither do I."

We sat and smiled at each other. Another enjoyable minute passed.

"What are you smiling about?" Skeli asked.

"I'm thinking."

"About what?"

"Jennifer Lawrence."

She threw her head back and laughed. It was a very unladylike laugh. I loved it.

12

Larry, looking sculpted, fit, and exuberant, was soaring twenty feet in the air over a whitecap-flecked Caribbean Sea. His arms were bent, his hands gripping the handle of the kite above, and his torso, wrapped in the harness, curved in an arc. His face was exuding extreme pleasure.

"Barbados?" I asked.

Larry joined me in staring at the framed photo of him kitesurfing. "Jamaica. My girlfriend shamed me into trying it. I was terrified. But after the first ten minutes I was hooked."

He went around his desk and took his place in his ergonomic leather-and-chrome throne. Business was about to be conducted.

"So, you had the FBI in for a late breakfast? Did they steal your silver?"

"I don't have any silver."

"They're not choosy."

"You don't like them," I said, thinking the understatement might detour Larry's favorite lecture topic. I didn't disagree; my own history kept me on the skeptical side of caution when the justice system was the subject. And Larry had the greater experience. He had begun his career working for the FBI before switching to the U.S. Attorney's Office as an Assistant United States Attorney—AUSA—for five years. The abuses he had witnessed firsthand had been the catalyst of his transformation into one of New York's top federal criminal defense attorneys.

"Two out of three are probably okay. The trouble is that the organization is sick. It rewards the one out of three. Paranoids, sociopaths, and crooks. Look who started the thing. All those secret files? You don't think they threw all that stuff out, do you? They're the secret police. They will lie on the stand, plant evidence, and assassinate inconvenient witnesses. And juries love them."

I told him about the conversation. "Brady had the decency to be embarrassed. He brought them there, but he didn't seem very happy about it."

"What do you know about penny stocks?"

"Not a whole hell of a lot." I filled him in on my aborted investigation and its terminus. "I doubt that Aimee Devane will do anything with it. She's very good at what she does, but she defines her role narrowly."

"She's since my time. She worked four years for the U.S. Attorney before going to work on the street. I checked her out with old colleagues. She made her mark there and moved on. They say she was good, but maybe not as good as she thought. Her nickname was 'Am I Divine.'"

"Two years at Goldman. Then Bear Stearns until the crash. Virgil's father brought her in as number two in compliance. Virgil gave her the top slot when he reorganized."

Larry nodded as I spoke. No doubt he already had the information. "She's tough, Jason. Don't underestimate her. If she changes her mind, she will be on the case like a redbone coonhound. Don't be caught standing between her and the bad guy."

"And the FBI?"

"Call me, of course, if they come back. I'll talk to the U.S. Attorney's Office and try to head this off. Meantime, it would be good to continue your investigation. On your own. These guys aren't going to back off and it might be beneficial to have something to trade."

"Virgil won't like it. He wants me full-time on the buyout rumors."

"Sounds like you're going to be busy, then." He stood up. We were done. "Regards to Wanda."

13

It was time to bring Virgil up to speed. I had nothing for him on the takeover, but hearing that the FBI had an interest in the firm's penny stock trades might get his attention. Before I got in to see him, though, I had to outfox the bridge troll. Virgil had a new gatekeeper.

"Jason! What can we do for you?"

James Nealis had been installed in the office next to Virgil. His door was open. Virgil's was closed. Nealis had been hovering between the two when I came off the elevator.

"I'm just here to have a chat with Virgil," I replied.

"He's in the middle of something right now." He said it as though he were the one who had assigned Virgil a specific chore. "Let me have a word with you, if I may. Got a sec?" He was already moving away into his office, his back to me.

I considered not following him, just continuing on my way and knocking on Virgil's door, as per my usual. But maybe I was reading too much into his rudeness. If Nealis had something to tell me, it might be worth my while to hear it. I followed him in and took a seat.

"I'm so glad you stopped by," he began. "I've been trying to get a clear picture of reporting lines, and maybe you can help me."

"I don't know that I can," I said. "I'm not on the flowchart and most of the department heads will only speak to me with express orders from Virgil."

"I was under the impression that you are the chief investigator for legal and compliance. Nothing gets by you."

He was fishing and I couldn't understand why.

"No. I work for Virgil."

"And what does he have you working on now?"

"I think you'll have to ask *him* that question, Mr. Nealis."

"Jim."

"Okay, Jim. You should ask Virgil."

"So, what's your relationship with compliance? Devane? That's her name, isn't it? Are you her secret agent?" he asked with a goofy grin. He was making a joke. Now we were best buds and co-conspirators.

"Devane runs compliance. It's her job to see that the firm operates within all regulatory limits, that all personnel are adequately trained and licensed, and that the firm responds quickly and completely to all our regulators' requests for information."

"And your role?"

"I don't do any of that."

"So how do you interface with Devane?"

I had a friend in B-school who had shown me that an interface is that bit of mesh fabric inside the folds of a well-made tie. We had taken a vow never to use the word as a verb.

"She runs compliance. I don't. I thought you were here to run banking. Moving us up the ladder in IPOs, underwriting, structured finance. Why this interest in my job? Or Devane's, for that matter."

I was careful to make my voice sound as nonconfrontational as possible and to let the words speak for themselves. I wanted him to back off, but I didn't need him resentful. He surprised me. He laughed it off.

"I get carried away. So sorry if I have offended. I came here to make a difference. This firm could be in the top five in a few years and I plan on helping it get there. I could have stayed where I was and been running investment banking at a top-tier firm in a very short time. But I wanted the challenge. I wanted to build something from the ground up. For that, I need to know the players—the big hitters like you, as well as the sergeants who keep the troops focused on the job at hand."

I didn't much like speeches and I had heard that one before. Nealis had offered a couple of variations, like unnecessarily stroking my ego— I had not been a "big hitter" since long before going to prison—but it was the usual new-hire bull. And I would have loved to see the expression on Aimee Devane's face if she ever heard herself described as a "sergeant."

"Jim, I'm so glad we had this chance to open up. Let me know if there's anything I can do to help." I stood up and left without shaking hands. "Don't see me out. I know the way," I called back over my shoulder.

"Hold up," he called before I had a chance to finish making my escape.

I stopped inside the doorway and waited. He came around the desk and produced a small cardboard flyer from his pocket.

"I'm having a small get-together at my place this evening. A chance to meet all the major players in a more relaxed setting." He handed me the card. Drinks at seven.

"Thanks, Jim, but I'm a single parent with responsibilities. Maybe next time."

"Just stop by. I'm sure your babysitter will stay on an extra hour or so. Bring your fiancée."

"Again, thank you. But my fiancée," I almost stuttered. Skeli had twice denied my proposal of marriage, but calling her my girlfriend—or even less comfortable, "lady friend"—seemed to belittle the relationship. I knew that this point was going to become infinitely more important as the birth of our child approached, but I still had no better idea of how to resolve the issue. "My fiancée," I repeated, "works later hours. Let's try to set a date for some time in the future, shall we?"

"I'm in her neighborhood. Just stop by. One drink."

I looked at the card again. The address was in SoHo, just a block and a half from Skeli's clinic. I stopped myself from asking how Nealis knew that. The fact that he knew it was much more important—and told me much more—than the how of it. Why he knew it might have been interesting, but I knew he wasn't going to be straight with me. It was all both intriguing and just a touch scary.

"Okay, then," I said. "We'll see you later."

14

I knocked on Virgil's door. There was no answer. I took out my phone and texted him that I was outside his office and needed to talk. I waited. A moment later he answered.

News?

I wrote him back. **Nothing yet.**

Then?

FYEO.

Come.

I walked in. Virgil was at his desk, looking tired and strung out. He had a phone in one hand and a pen in the other and a yellow legal pad on the desk with a long list of names, some checked, some crossed out, some scribbled over. He was busy.

"I'll make it quick," I said.

"I'm trying to round up support. You don't happen to have a bil or two that I could borrow to fight off a hostile takeover, do you?"

"I'm a little short this week."

"So, what's For My Eyes Only?"

"The FBI. They came to my apartment this morning to ask about penny stocks."

He waved a hand in front of his face. "I told you to pass this over to compliance."

"Aimee's not going to do anything, Virgil."

"If she thinks we're in the clear, I'm okay with that. I have bigger problems."

"There's a grand jury."

"And we'll hear from them through channels. Eventually."

"They told me that one of their witnesses was murdered. Actually, they used the word 'assassination.' It's the kind of word that gets your attention. Like 'tortured' or 'dismembered.' It freaked me a bit."

He smiled. "I seriously doubt that anyone is getting dismembered over penny stock trades."

His phone buzzed. He checked the caller ID. "I've got to take this. Get me something I can use to fight this off. ASAP. I need a miracle. Or an angel with deep pockets."

I wanted to ask him about Nealis and whether he would be attending the cocktail party, but my moment was gone. Virgil was busy trying to persuade another billionaire to take a substantial position in the firm. He sounded relaxed and confident. It was a good act. But billionaires, in my experience, are by nature a skeptical lot. I mouthed "Good luck," and left Virgil to his dwindling list of resources. He was scratching out another name when I closed the door behind me.

I hit the button for the elevator and stood in front of the doors farthest from the executive offices. I didn't want to run into Nealis again. For all I knew, he was totally legit and would help Virgil take the firm into the top tier just as he said, but I didn't like him. It wasn't just that he was remarkably in love with himself, but I had the feeling that beneath his combination of surface charm and arrogance there lay a core of cold ambition and arrogance. And he would gladly sacrifice anyone—even Virgil—to promote his own agenda. But maybe I didn't like him just because I didn't like him.

15

Skeli did not try to beg off on the cocktail party, though she did point out that, as neither of us was drinking alcohol, we weren't going to be the life of the party. She also mentioned that she was tired, her feet hurt, and she was both ravenously hungry and suffering from gas.

We walked the two short blocks to Nealis's building. The SoHo streets were still busy, crowded with shoppers and tourists all speaking in a dozen or more languages, sounding like the survivors of the destruction of Babel. We may have been the only New Yorkers on the street. I filled her in on my meetings with Larry and Virgil and the somewhat bizarre few minutes with Nealis that had ended with the invitation.

"We're in, we're out," I said.

"We're sauerkraut," she said. "Will Virgil be there?"

"I don't know. Why?"

"Because then I will know at least one person who will talk to me about something other than the market."

"Don't worry. I'll talk to you. Most of the people here won't talk to me anyway."

"So tell me again, why are we going?"

"We're here."

There was a line of Town Cars and limos waiting to discharge their cargo of wealthy New Yorkers while a pair of Filipinos in dinner jackets attempted to keep the horde of traders, managers, lawyers, politicians, minor celebrities, bankers, and all their plus-ones moving across the sidewalk and into the lobby of a six-story loft building. I ignored the line and guided Skeli directly to the door. A woman in an ankle-length fur began to make an objection to our cutting the line, but her companion—a senior trader from the structured loan desk—shushed her with a murmur in her ear. Her eyes widened as her mouth closed. Some days being the Darth Vader of Becker Financial wasn't so bad.

"You know, sometimes you are such a jerk," Skeli whispered as we shuffled onto what had once been a freight elevator but was now a mirrored mini-palace that rose with barely a whisper.

"Why? Because I cut in front of those people?"

"You could have charmed them. Instead, you just convinced them that their opinion of you is the right one."

"That presupposes that anything I could do would ever change their ideas about me."

"You miss the point. You can be a nice guy anyway, simply because it feels good. You don't have to be a jerk just to please them."

I opened my mouth to respond and closed it again. There wasn't much I had to say that would have stood up to such emotional logic.

"Think about it," Skeli said.

"I will," I heard myself respond.

The doors opened directly onto an anteroom that would have easily held my whole apartment. Two identically dressed Japanese women—white tights and leotards with pink crinoline tutus—took coats and directed the throng through a set of double doors wide enough to admit grand pianos without fear of scratching the finish. We surrendered Skeli's London Fog and entered the upstream flow.

Nealis stood just inside the doors, greeting everyone by name—a feat that became less impressive when I realized that the woman just behind him held a tablet and wore a Bluetooth device. She was feeding him lines over his shoulder.

"Jason! Great you could come. Thanks so much. Wanda, isn't it? I hope we haven't taken you from your clients. Pain management? I'm right, aren't I? That's your specialty. Great work. There's someone here you must meet." He turned to an attentive young woman who was hovering a few steps away. "Jill, make sure Dr. Tyler is introduced to Doc Pettis." He turned to Skeli and spoke quietly, as though imparting some great secret. "Get him talking about his Chihuly collection. He's a bore, but he'll send you more referrals than you'll be able to handle."

And with that he turned to the couple behind us, and we found ourselves following the perky-eyed Jill through the crowd. There must have been three or four hundred people and yet the space didn't feel overcrowded. The loft took up half a city block.

"Doc Pettis?" I asked Skeli as I struggled to keep pace.

"Spinal guy. One of the best. He did the Olympic high-diver two years ago. You read about him."

I hadn't to my knowledge read about anything like it, but I kept my mouth shut. One learns more from listening than asking questions.

"All his patients go through PT and rehab before he'll cut. He's one of the few surgeons who believes in alternative treatment."

"Ahh," I said.

"Champagne, sir?" A male model in a tuxedo had appeared at my side.

"Pellegrino?" I asked.

"Certainly. Two?"

"Thank you." He moved off through the crowd.

"So, what's a Gilhooly?" I asked Skeli.

"Chihuly. Blown-glass sculpture."

"How do you know this?" I said.

"Because I read."

"I read," I said.

"Something other than the *Journal* and the *Post*."

An unfair description of my reading habits. I also read books on autism. Nevertheless, her point, though phrased for effect rather than accuracy, was well taken. My knowledge of modern art and culture kept safely within boundaries. Though I enjoyed a plethora of musical styles, I tended to listen to work by artists who had first recorded more than twenty years ago. When I read for pleasure, I leaned toward books on baseball. And when I visited art galleries or museums, I gravitated toward the classical realists who painted pictures that looked something like the subject matter. That and the occasional nude.

"I'd guess this artist has never been arrested, right? Otherwise I would have read about it in the *Post*."

Jill stopped us by a small group surrounding a tall, slightly stooped man in his sixties. She introduced Dr. Wanda Tyler to the group and left us. The sparkling water arrived and I handed a glass to Skeli. She flashed me a quick smile and went back to work charming the white-haired doctor. I saw a plate of crab cake appetizers moving through the room and began edging in that direction. No one noticed me leaving.

The crab cakes were good. I wrapped six in a paper napkin before the twenty-something server managed to get away from me. I wandered around looking for someone who might not be terrified to be caught speaking with me. Aimee Devane saw me across the room and gave me the kind of smile that says, *Yes, I see you, but you don't really need to come any closer.* I kept moving.

I saw an ex-mayor of New York, a well-known British actor who had just closed a limited run on Broadway, and an obese New Jersey politician who was pumping every hand he could grab as though unable to stop running for office. I avoided him.

"Whaddaya say, Stafford? How's biz? Whatayagot? What's up?"

Michael "Mickey the Mouse" Moskowitz had been one of my brokers when I first entered the foreign exchange markets. He had wrestled for years with a combined alcohol and cocaine problem, which had finally sidelined his career. Despite having been out of the markets for a decade, he still maintained his connections. The Mouse prided himself on always having the most au courant gossip on Wall Street.

"Hey, Mouse. What brings you out? I thought you only left Long Beach for hurricanes."

"We're in Point Lookout now. But, yeah, I don't get in to Manhattan much these days."

He was older, thinner, and, surprisingly, exuded a touch of good health, as though he might have been eating right and exercising occasionally.

"So what's the draw?" I asked.

"I heard about this party last week and figured I could pick up something juicy. So what are you working on?"

"Gee, what can I share with you that won't interfere with my loyalty to Virgil Becker? Hmm. I've got it. Nothing. Nada. Not a thing."

"Come on, then, ask *me* a question."

"Then you're going to expect me to trade and I've got nothing for you," I said.

"Go ahead. Ask. Maybe I'll give you a freebie."

"Okay. Tell me about our host. He's a big hire and Virgil hasn't let me run a background check on him. What's his story? Can I trust the guy?"

"Come on, we're eating the guy's food. I can't talk about him here. I got *some* standards."

"All right. Here's one for you. Al Mitzner to Daiwoo to run interest rates."

"Nyah. He turned them down a month ago."

"True. They just upped the ante."

"Did they really? No shit. All right, that's good. So I definitely owe you one. Ask me something again. Only, not about Nealis. I can't talk about him." The Mouse actually looked over his shoulder, as though Nealis might be there listening in on our conversation.

"There's a rumor that the firm's in play. What can you tell me? Who's the buyer?"

There was a flash in his eyes that looked like fear. "Don't fuck around, Jason. I said I'm not talking about that."

"I'm talking about a hostile takeover of Becker Financial, Mouse. Not the latest hire. Stay with me."

He waved his hand as though erasing a blackboard. "Really, I can't say much. These people are very hush-hush."

"So you're letting me down twice in a row? That's not like you, Mouse. It would be rough if word of that got around."

He gritted his teeth and smiled, as though something somewhere was hurting really bad but he wasn't going to admit it. "I'll tell you one thing, then we stop talking. Okay? It's a family thing. That's all I'm gonna say. Look at the family."

"*Here* you are," Skeli said, taking my arm in hers and giving me a slight squeeze. "I now know more about the price of blown glass on the art market than I would have thought possible. But I am a certified Friend of Doc Pettis and will be on his referral list. I'm done. When can we go?"

"Let me introduce you to someone," I said, but when I turned around the Mouse was gone. "Sorry, he was just here."

"Who?"

"Just a guy," I said, looking for him in the crowd. But the Mouse had run.

We ditched our empty glasses and I took one last look around for the waitress with the crab cakes. No luck. We wound our way back to the entrance and I slipped one of the Japanese ballet dancers a five for the return of Skeli's raincoat.

I held the coat up for her to put it on—a bit of harmless chivalric sexism that my ex-wife had taught me early in our relationship—and found myself looking through the double doors at the party just as a shift in the crowd revealed two men deep in conversation at the far end of the room. It was much too far to make out what they were discussing, but there was an intensity to the conversation that combined anger and fear. The Mouse was shaking a finger in the face of the hawk-nosed young man I had seen with Jim Nealis outside his office just a few days ago. Despite the admonishing finger, it was the Mouse who looked frightened and the other man who was angry. He did not like whatever he was hearing. If I'd been Mouse, my first concern would be that this guy might get mad enough to just lean over and bite that finger right off.

16

The last time I had been to Chilton, the grand estate across the bay from Newport where Virgil had grown up, I had arrived with revelations that did almost as much damage to the emotional fiber of the family as the collapse of the old man's bogus empire. It had been necessary, but I wasn't sure that I would be welcomed back. Virgil's mother, Livy, had been distant when I called, but she had agreed to see me. That didn't mean she wasn't going to be waiting for me with a twelve-gauge pheasant shooter.

I took I-95 all the way, despite the traffic and the rain. The ferry from Orient Point to New London would have avoided all the worst tie-ups, but would have cost me hours that I didn't have. And the rain would have prevented me from enjoying the view on the ferry ride anyway. I traded stress for time. That rarely pays off, but being home early for the Kid was the greater goal.

The road to the house was unassuming, not much more than a break in the trees with a discreet sign announcing the name of the estate, and another that heralded the security company who watched over the place. I noticed that Livy had changed providers since I was last there—the previous company had been less than reliable.

The gardens needed work. The flower beds around the circular drive were brown and barren. The boxwood needed a haircut. The grass had been recently cut, but whoever they'd hired had skimped on the edging and the weeding. Clumps of crabgrass and dandelions had sprung up in spots. The house, a hotel-sized stone structure designed to resemble some nineteenth-century architect's vision of a Medici castle, needed a face-lift or, at the very least, a power wash. I've always been skeptical—cynical, my ex-wife would have said—about people who need to live in a monument to their own wealth and power, but I felt sad looking at the fading beauty. The place had belonged to Virgil's mother's family and been passed along for many generations. She'd had a bad marriage to a man who had conned the world. He'd taken her as he had his investors. Much of the money was gone, and what was left she had bet on Virgil.

A uniformed maid in her forties welcomed me, told me that I was expected, and led me to a glass conservatory that I had not seen on my last trip. I found Livy sitting in a padded white wicker chair surrounded by tall potted palms. A book with a blue cover was spread on the end table beside her. She was gripping her usual glass of clear liquid, her long, thin fingers wrapped tightly around the glass as though it were the lifeline that still might rescue her from sinking under the unrelenting weight of life.

"Mr. Stafford. How good it is that you have come to visit. Wyatt and I are left too much to ourselves these days. How have you been?"

I played along for a bit, keeping the tone light and conversational. I was in a hurry, but I wasn't going to let her brand me as rude. Rude was beneath her, and therefore could be safely ignored. I needed her.

"And how is Wyatt?" I asked.

"You may ask him yourself. Wyatt!" she called over my shoulder.

I turned and saw that, beyond the grove of palms and a pair of shoulder-high grassy plants in ceramic tubs, was a cleared area that looked out on the harbor. Wyatt had been sitting there all along. In front of him was an easel with paints and the kind of folding field table that artists in English cozy mysteries all seem to have. I stood up and met him by the grasses. He declined to shake hands, but he was more polite and less aggressive than at our first meeting.

"I'm Wyatt," he said. I saw that, despite his recent activity, he did not have so much as a spot of paint on his hands or clothes.

"Yes, we've met," I said. "Jason Stafford. Nice to see you again."

"Mother says some people have trouble remembering names, so it is polite to always announce your own name. I don't have that trouble. Do you?"

"I do pretty well in that regard. I must have gotten it from my father. He was a bartender and remembered everyone."

"Is he dead?"

"No. Retired." Wyatt's directness didn't bother me. Asperger's doesn't often recognize the sensitive nature of some questions. It was a symptom, and once accepted it was invigorating. Anything might pop out next.

"How's your son?"

"Doing well, thank you."

"Has he had any seizures yet?"

Seizures. Another monstrous aspect of autism that the Kid and I had to look forward to.

"None. Not everyone gets them, I'm told."

"No. I did. But he's still very young. Too young to masturbate."

"Uh. Yes." I was doing my best to keep up my end, but the mention of my son and masturbation in the same sentence was a bit of a hurdle.

"They started with absence seizures. Do you know about them?"

Absence seizures were sort of a mega version of tuning out. The Kid tuned out less than he had a year earlier, but there were times when he was simply unreachable.

"Yes, I do. They frighten me."

His eyelids fluttered for a moment. "I need to paint." He turned away abruptly and returned to the easel.

I took a seat facing Livy and found her beaming at her son.

"You have no idea what an effort that was for him," she said with incalculable pride.

"Maybe I do."

She turned to me and let herself search my face for a moment. "Yes, maybe you do. You have surprised me before and now you've done it again. Kindness, I find as I get older, is really quite a rare thing."

"My son is on the spectrum," I said.

She bridled slightly at that, sitting straighter as though challenging me physically. "Wyatt is very high functioning."

I ceded the point. It cost me nothing. "He is indeed."

"How is Virgil these days?"

"You two don't talk?" I was surprised.

"Virgil always tells me that he's 'fine.' He is under considerable pressure, and though he is by far the strongest of my children, I don't entirely believe him."

"He *is* under pressure, but I don't know anyone better able to handle it. He's a rock."

"You'll excuse a mother who objects to hearing her son described as an inanimate object. When he was a child, Virgil was very close with his father. He rebelled, as young people do, but he returned. I think he took his father's unveiling very hard."

This was a version of Virgil that I had never seen. The father had been one of the biggest crooks in history, a cold and distant parent, and he'd cheated on his wife. It was hard for me to think that anyone would have felt any sorrow at his demise—but I wasn't his son.

"Virgil has a problem," I told her. "Someone is orchestrating a hostile takeover. If it works, he'll be out without much to show for all his work saving the place. I'm trying to help him, but I don't have much to go on."

"Impossible. I control the single largest block of shares. I can assure you that I have no intention of selling."

"Or voting with the opposition?"

"I find the suggestion offensive."

"Someone whispered in my ear that the family was behind it."

"Who?"

"Nobody you'd know. But he's usually right."

"Not this time."

"What about Morgan or Binks? Could they have reason to see the firm taken over? Or to see Virgil taken down?"

She wasn't put off by the question, but she took a deep slug of the vodka before answering. "Morgan is capable. She is a very angry woman. But she is in prison and will remain there for another two years—at least. James isn't able to control his own life, much less conspire with others. He is unreliable."

"He's still in the rehab place out west?"

"He is."

James had a vicious heroin habit. Virgil and Livy had pushed, cajoled, and begged prosecutors and judges to let him remain in rehab rather than face the courts. That plan had worked—maybe too well. He was turning into a permanent resident.

"I was thinking that it might be worth questioning him."

"A waste of resources. As I explained, I control the trust. There is no way that any of the children could undermine Virgil without my participation. And, think what you will about my dysfunctional children—all right, *family*—but I would never allow it. They can all squabble as much as they need to, but I will never take sides." She began quietly dismissive but picked up steam as she went along. She finished in a defiant roar. I believed her.

She polished off the last half inch of her drink and placed the empty glass on the end table. "Was there anything else you wanted to discuss?"

"It's been an enlightening visit. I'm left with more questions than answers, but that's my concern, not yours. Thanks for your time. I'll let myself out."

The maid passed me in the main hall, hurrying in the other direction with a fresh sweating glass of clear liquid.

The whole four-hour drive back to New York, I worried over an impossible conundrum. Could the Mouse be wrong for once?

17

You might want to pour yourself a drink," Larry said.

I was in my armchair, staring out at Broadway. Sometimes it was a great place to sit and think. Today it wasn't working. I pushed the mute button on the Bose remote and "One More Saturday Night" ended mid-note. "I'm not drinking these days. Just give it to me."

"You will soon be famous again, if Blackmore gets his way. You, Virgil, and the firm are all targets of his investigation. I offered your wholehearted cooperation as a witness and he, rather reluctantly I think, agreed to a meeting."

"I don't see myself ratting out Virgil."

"Neither do I. But in order to find out what he has, we have to give him a little something. Anything. Just tell him the truth."

"Any other great advice?"

"When you hear me say, 'Don't answer that question,' please don't answer that question."

"That seems rather obvious," I said. I got up and put the kettle on. A cup of tea might help the brain cells to kick in and allow me to find a way through this ordeal.

"One would think, but I am constantly surprised by clients whose only familiarity with the legal system is as a defendant, and yet they firmly believe that their innate ability to talk their way out of trouble is their greatest asset."

"I really don't want to do this."

"Understood. But you overpay me ridiculously to give you the kind of advice that will keep you out of jail. You should follow it, if only for the economics."

"I will do my best." I opened the cabinet and three boxes of herbal tea bags jumped out at me and landed on the counter. My storage method of simply jamming them in up there needed some improvement. I pulled out a few jars of dried leaves to make my own blend and squeezed the three boxes back on the shelf.

"You were a big hit with the FBI. Your file contains both the words 'hostile' and 'noncooperative.' They believe you are hiding something."

"I don't know why they care. This is small stuff, Larry. Compliance doesn't even think what they're doing is illegal."

"It seems your good friend Special Agent Brady sold them on the idea that you are a valuable CI of his."

"I think I resent that. I'm not a snitch. I turn over rocks, and when I find nasty bugs I pass the information on to the appropriate parties."

"Well, when you failed to live up to expectations, they took it personally. You are now on their shit list. Congratulations. My father defended two Black Panthers accused of plotting to blow up a D.C. police station back in the early seventies and he still couldn't get on the FBI's hate list."

"Did he get them off?" The kettle began to sing and I turned it off while I mixed a combination of green tea leaves with a pinch of gingko and some chamomile. The caffeine in the tea would give me the immediate jump start while the flower would take the edge off. The gingko was for long-term benefit. I didn't know whether or not I believed in all that, but I liked the way it tasted.

"Yes, but that's immaterial. They are not a forgiving institution, as a rule."

"Another accolade to put on my mantel. As soon as I get one."

"So are you free tomorrow morning?"

That was a rhetorical question, not meant to be answered. Of course I was free to appear before the Inquisition. "Who's running the meeting?"

"You will be questioned by the great man himself. Wallace Ashton Blackmore, United States Attorney for the Southern District. This is an exceedingly rare occurrence."

The challenge would be to somehow stay out of jail without putting Virgil there in my place. "What time?"

"I'll have a car pick you up at eight-fifteen."

"Make it seven forty-five. We'll drop the Kid at school. He likes Town Cars."

"Who doesn't? See you then."

18

I had nothing to trade except for the fact that I was innocent. Innocence is a greatly devalued asset in the criminal justice business.

I sipped my tea. Still too hot. I punched some numbers into my phone. "I'm trying to get hold of Richard Hannay. Do I have the right number?"

"Please state your name." The voice was as neutral as could be. American. But from anywhere. There was no regional inflection.

"Jason Stafford. We're old acquaintances."

"Please state the nature of your business."

"Just put me through. Or have him call me."

"Sorry. I didn't catch that. Please state the nature of your business."

"Wait a minute. Are you a computer?"

"Ha ha. Do I sound that bad? Sorry. Please state the nature of your business."

"Stop screwing around! Just have him get back to me. ASAP. I can't believe I'm still talking to a computer. Let me ask you something. Do you dream in color? Do you keep file folders of favorite poems? Do you listen to music when you're not answering the phone? Define the nature of the human soul."

"Jason? Are you okay?"

"Nice touch. You sound almost capable of empathy. Almost."

"Listen, let me call you back. This is no longer a good line."

"You don't sound like a computer anymore."

"I'm not. It's a screening program I use."

"Next you'll be promising me a 'free Bahamas vacation' or trying to get me to switch auto insurance. Guess what? I don't own a car."

"Jason. Jason." He tried to interrupt my continuing rant. "I'll call you right back."

The line went dead.

Before I had time to think about what my next move should be, my iPad dinged. I looked around for it. The sound seemed to have come from the other room. I scouted the living room. The couch. My broken-springed armchair. The bookshelf nearest the door. I circled the room again. This time I stopped at the Kid's bedroom door. It was closed. It was usually closed when he was not at home. That way, no one could go in and rearrange his cars on the shelf. Carolina, who provided our once-a-week cleaning service, had a special dispensation, thanks to the Kid's fear of germs, dust, and any other indoor dirt.

I opened the door. My iPad was lying on top of his half-made bed. Another mystery. Life with my son provided so many.

There was a new email message from a Salvatore Albert Lombino, a name that meant nothing to me. I thought about hitting the delete icon, but held off. The timing was too coincidental. I Googled the name. Wikipedia informed me that this was the birth name of Evan Hunter, aka Ed McBain, the man who wrote the screenplay for Hitchcock's *The Birds*. It was Hannay. I opened the message and found a series of numbers, the first beginning with a 1 followed by ten digits. A phone number.

I ran my eyes down the other numbers while I dialed. None made any impression.

"Hey, Jason."

"Do I call you Sal now?"

"No. I'm still using the Hannay persona. Did you look at those numbers I sent?"

"I'm looking now. What am I supposed to see here?"

"I don't know. Anything, I guess." He sounded both tired and defeated.

I looked again.

19 7 23 47
89 31 37 103
223 83 89 311
5 19 41 71
1 3 13 31

"Is this a code? What am I supposed to be looking at? I'm lost."

"Ah. These are all seemingly random names of companies that have recently purchased shares of Becker Financial."

I found my cup of tea and took a sip. It had cooled off just enough.

"Okay," I said. I shifted into my mathematical analytical mode. "Each line is comprised of four numbers. Every number is a prime. No number has more than three digits. Is this true of all of them?"

"Yes to your first and last comments. But I didn't catch that they're all prime numbers."

"Prime numbers sometimes group themselves into little clusters, but that doesn't apply here," I said. "How do you know they're companies?"

"Incorporation documents. We've been able to get into digital files and read a few. Each of these series of numbers is followed by either a 'Co.' or an 'Inc.' or an 'Ltd.' The docs are all filed in island countries in the Caribbean."

"Are there more like this?"

"Maybe, but you'd have to break into the offices and find the physical files. It's not a job for me and my people. But you were right. All the trades were done through law firms and private banks. To get this much, we had to hack into each firm's digital files. These all came from banks. Most of the law firms don't trust electronic files. Those that do have multiple security systems."

"If this is the best we can get, I'm not sure it's worth it."

"Hold up. I have to keep changing phones so I don't set up a pattern. Call me back on this number." He rattled off another number and the phone cut off.

I dialed the new number and he picked up immediately.

"I'm so sorry. Can you repeat your last question?"

"You sound like a computer again."

There followed a shrill beep and an electronic crackle. Then he was back. "Shit! Sorry. I wrote the app for this and I'm afraid it still needs work."

"That's okay, you sound like a normal paranoid again," I said.

"Really. I know I'm acting paranoid, but I also know it's the only thing keeping me safe. It often results in a bad case of cognitive dissonance."

"And a migraine. I was saying that I'm not going to recommend that Virgil sink much more into this until we are confident we can show him results."

"Great things happen when men and mountains meet. Would it help if I sent you more info? Names of some of these law firms or banks?"

I considered for a moment. "I don't think so. It's great that you found some kind of pattern. It shows Virgil that he is right. There is a conspiracy out there to buy up shares of the firm. No doubt about it. But even if I can identify one or two of the names you run by me, it's not going to get us any closer to who is behind it all. I'm going to have to find another angle. And flying to the Turks and Caicos to break into a string of law offices isn't going to do it."

"In the meantime?"

"Can you run these numbers through code-breaking programs? I know that prime numbers have been used in codes often enough."

"I'll need more data points."

"Then spend a few more days on it. See how many more of these you can come up with. We'll talk again early next week."

We made arrangements for me to get another envelope full of cash to him. I was to leave it with the night-shift bartender at the Dublin House up on Seventy-ninth Street. I checked my watch. The Kid and Heather wouldn't be home for another hour—more, if he persuaded her to swing by the dog run in Riverside Park.

"I'll take a walk up there now. Stay safe."

My tea was cold.

19

The night was cool for April, but spring in New York is always unreliable. There have been blizzards, heat waves, floods, and cold snaps during the month. There have also been coyote sightings, a crocodile in Central Park, a tiger in Queens and another in the Bronx, a six-foot boa constrictor that had gotten itself stuck between some rocks, a wild turkey downtown, and reports of a bear up in Riverdale that turned out to be a big black hairy dog. And forget about the rats. Not all of this happened in April, but it was ongoing evidence of the constant incursion of nature upon the city. Most New Yorkers live there—rather than in some more bucolic environ—because they don't want to confront nature on a daily basis. Having to put on a heavy jacket for a five-block walk up Broadway on a spring evening can feel like a major concession to a world that the city fights to keep at bay.

The light was about to change as I reached Seventy-sixth Street and I dashed across to the east side of the street just before the tide of taxis and Town Cars swept past. A horn sounded behind me and I looked back. A slight figure in a dark coat and a long-brimmed hat had tried to make it across behind me, holding back only when the driver of a yellow cab hit the horn rather than the brake and blew by the pedestrian at ten miles over the limit.

I tucked my chin into my coat and walked faster in an attempt to generate the body heat that I was losing through my ears and fingertips. The light at the next intersection was two steps ahead of me, and despite the cold, I decided not to risk making a last-second dash. I stopped and waited. Out of the corner of my eye, I caught a glimpse of the small dark figure across Broadway making an abrupt turn, upsetting for a moment the flow of pedestrian traffic approaching the corner. I didn't stare; I barely looked. But I was on a clandestine mission with three thousand dollars in cash in my pocket. It was not a time for complacence.

Making a feint, I stepped off the curb as though in preparation for a head start the moment the light changed. The figure turned again and began to move to stay slightly ahead of me on the opposite side of Broadway. "Tailing in advance," the hacker would have called it. I stepped back onto the sidewalk and turned to the right, down the side street toward Amsterdam. I moved quickly.

The traffic thinned as I headed up the block, and after passing the back of the comedy club on the corner, I darted across and continued on the north side of the street. I risked a quick look back. My follower had raced across Broadway and was coming up the block behind me. I thought of Hannay's comment on being paranoid and felt a momentary flash of kinship. I sped up.

At the end of the block, there was a bank ATM kiosk and I ducked in and waited for my pursuer to approach. It didn't take long. I had my back against the inner wall, just out of the direct light.

The figure reached the corner and looked around, trying to be casual about it, but failing. Even wrapped in the dark coat, the shape was definitely feminine. And nicely proportioned, I couldn't help but notice. Her hands were jammed in her pockets and her shoulders were high and hunched. She was cold.

She was also unsure of herself and, with her quarry having disappeared, possibly frightened. She looked up and down Amsterdam and her shoulders began to slump. Then the next wave of traffic began to come up the avenue and headlights framed her for an instant and formed an aura around her head. A distinctly red aura. She turned away from the blinding light and I saw her profile. I knew that redhead. It was Aimee Devane.

My first thought was to walk out and immediately confront her with questions and accusations. I quashed the impulse and instead turned my back to her and pretended to use the ATM. I could still see her—though dark and clouded—reflected in the black plastic border above the screen. She finally turned and saw my back in the kiosk. I turned quickly and charged out the door.

"Aimee? What a surprise. I didn't know you lived in my neighborhood." I may have overplayed the moment. She was startled and embarrassed, but she covered well.

"I'm meeting a girlfriend," she said.

"Oh? Where? I'll walk you there. I'm just out for a stroll myself."

We both knew that she had been following me, and we both knew that we both knew. But we stood in the cold, making polite noises at each other and ignoring the obvious. If I had been truly frightened I might have been angry, but what I felt most strongly was curiosity. Why was Aimee Devane following me?

"No, that's okay. It's just a block over."

"Scaletta's? Love that place. Let me walk you. It's a dark block."

"Really, I'll be fine. See you later."

She practically ran across Amsterdam and continued down the side street toward the park—and Scaletta's. I watched until she was out of sight and I was sure she wouldn't be able to circle back and follow me again.

Mike, the bartender at the Dublin House, took the envelope for Richard Hannay and shoved it down behind the cash register. He acted as though receiving secret messages and wads of cash for men with fictitious names and no fixed address was business as usual. Maybe it was. The place had a long history, having first opened in the midst of Prohibition. I debated having a pint before heading home, but decided that my pact with Skeli was more important. And I wasn't going to order a club soda in a dive bar.

A light mist had begun and I turned up my collar and hustled back down Broadway. No one followed me.

20

United States Attorney Wallace Ashton Blackmore was a self-promoting politician with no more respect for the law than any of the miscreants who had ever stood before him. He first made himself famous shortly after the crash by arresting a junior MBS salesman and taking him off the Nomura Securities trading floor in handcuffs. He brought with him four U.S. Marshals and a parade of television news teams. The publicity made Blackmore an instant national celebrity, though six months later the grand jury failed to grant an indictment and all charges against the young man were dropped. The press didn't care. Blackmore was already a hero and a regular talking head on cable.

It cost the guy's family over a million dollars in legal fees and ended his Wall Street career. Collateral damage.

The meeting took place in a conference room that was about ten degrees warmer than necessary. Blackmore's people, led by his top AUSA, John Martin, arrived in shirtsleeves. Larry and I were in suits. No one offered coffee, soft drinks, or water. We were all in place—hot and uncomfortable—for close to fifteen minutes before the great man made his entrance.

What he lacked in charisma and good looks, he made up for with a street fighter's posture and attitude, ready to challenge anyone in the room on any subject. He was shorter than he appeared on television and his comb-over was much more obvious. What came off on the tube as the broad, unwrinkled brow of a great thinker was, in person, a bulging protrusion over a pair of small sunken eyes. If he'd been a parking valet, you would hesitate to hand him your keys.

There were no preliminaries.

"Here's how it's going to work, Mr. Stafford. I'm going to tell you what it is I want from you, and after a bit of pro forma hesitation, you're going to give it to me."

Larry answered. "My client is here voluntarily, Wally. There's no reason for him not to give his complete cooperation."

That wasn't exactly so, but the double negatives were a handy way of obscuring my extreme reluctance to tell Blackmore anything at all.

Blackmore barely acknowledged Larry. "Please tell us why you were interested in a tiny firm called McFee Plumbing."

Larry had prepped me for this one. It was the obvious opening question.

"I do financial investigations for Virgil Becker. The firm pays me, but I answer only to him. When he doesn't have something pressing for me to work on, I look for potential troubles. It keeps me busy."

"And you were 'troubled' by a handful of trades in a stock that's priced somewhere between twenty-three and eighty-seven cents a share?"

"I routinely make requests for documents to various regulatory bodies on a range of issues. McFee was one of many I made that day."

"We'll get to that. Did you discuss McFee Plumbing with Virgil Becker?"

Blackmore didn't waste any time.

"I may have. I don't know whether I mentioned the firm by name. It was one of many."

Blackmore had four men and two women sitting at his end of the table. All six made notes every time I opened my mouth. When they weren't writing, they were staring at me.

"When did you first discuss McFee Plumbing with Virgil Becker?"

Larry held up a hand in the universal *Slow down* gesture. "Mr. Stafford has not said that he remembers speaking with his employer about that specific stock."

"Look, Larry. We're doing this here in my offices as a favor to you, but don't push it, okay? Either your client opens up and tells me what I want to hear, or I will see that he's indicted, and we know where that leads, don't we?"

An indictment would mean my parole would be revoked and I would be back in prison for the remaining sixteen months of my original sentence. There would be a feces-flying court battle over whether my son would live with his grandmother—my ex-wife's mother—in Louisiana or with my father out in Queens. Pop and I would, no doubt, lose that battle, and it was quite likely that I would never see the Kid again.

"Give us a minute, Wally." Larry turned and whispered in my ear, shielding his lips with a raised hand. "He can do that. It's bullshit, I admit, and from what you've told me, I can beat anything they throw at you. In court. Once it's in front of a judge, you're fine, but this *pezzente* doesn't want you to ever get your day in court. He can delay for a year or more and let you sweat it back in Ray Brook the whole time."

Ray Brook was where I had served most of my sentence. It was a medium-security facility in upstate New York. It was cold ten months of the year and hot for the other two and the clientele included both the scared and the scary. I knew where I fit in. I did not want to go back. "What do I do? I'm not lying just to stay out of jail. I've got nothing he wants. I really don't think I know anything."

"Follow my lead."

What choice did I have? "If you save me, you're saving the Kid. Don't forget it."

Larry turned back to face the group at the end of the table. "Full immunity. In writing. Signed by a federal judge."

Blackmore threw up his hands. "You can't expect me to go along with that. Blanket immunity? In return for what? I haven't heard what he's got. How do you expect me to make a deal?"

"Full cooperation. Before we leave this room today, you will know everything that he knows. Guaranteed. But he gets full immunity for anything he tells you here."

"I can't do that, Larry," Blackmore said, shaking his head violently so that the comb-over slipped sideways and threatened to begin flapping.

"And he will repeat it all for a grand jury."

Blackmore should have left the negotiations to one of his crew. He was too greedy, too ambitious, and too in love with himself to see the trap. U.S. Attorneys are appointed by the president. They are administrators. Some, like Blackmore, are also politicians. Rarely are they experienced prosecuting attorneys and they should know enough to delegate negotiations to their staff. But the six men and women with him were all too cowed by his arrogance to speak up. I could see the united front develop cracks and start to crumble.

"I can't get a judge to sign off on that just on my say-so," Blackmore said.

Larry smiled. He had forced Blackmore into telling an obvious lie. Even members of his own team winced at this feeble excuse. One point for the good guys.

"Sure you can, Wally." He looked at his Rolex. "We've got a table reserved for one o'clock at Forlini's. You do what you need to do, and we'll meet back here at, what? Two-thirty? Three?"

Blackmore looked around his group. Finally, one of the women spoke up. "O'Rourke's clerk owes me one."

"Do it." He practically spat when he said it.

Larry stood up. I joined him. We walked out together. Larry had just finagled me a Get Out of Jail Free card and, so far, it had cost me nothing. Whatever happened after lunch, I wasn't going back to prison.

21

I had the sole stuffed with shrimp and crab meat in a white wine sauce. Larry had kale sautéed in olive oil. No carbs. No protein. I didn't question it. If he was on some power diet, it was working. He looked like he was twenty years younger than his age.

"So what happens when we get back there and Blackmore finds out I've got nothing to offer?"

"But you do. He knows some things, but if he really had a case, he'd know you were innocent. And he'd know a lot more than he's saying. He lost the only witness willing to talk to him. Just give him everything you've found and everything you guess. I think you're already miles ahead of him."

I thought it through. Aimee Devane had assured me the firm was in the clear. I couldn't imagine a way in which anything I had to offer would undermine that. The question for me then was going to be whether I could protect Virgil as well.

"Suppose it's not enough? The guy's a pit bull."

"You've got immunity. Worst case, he rants a bit. He'll get over it."

A gray suit with a lawyer inside appeared next to our table. AUSA John Martin.

"Mr. Blackmore wants you two back now. The papers are ready."

"Signed?" Larry asked.

"Judge O'Rourke was feeling magnanimous today, I guess."

"Have you eaten?"

"Uh, no." Martin was grinning.

"Then sit." Larry looked around and a waiter hurried over. "What can we get for our friend that's quick?"

"You want I get him a plate of the linguini alle vongole? The staff lunch. It's all made."

"You eat clams?" Larry asked the young lawyer.

Martin sat. "Blackmore's going to have a cow."

"And you'll blame it on me. Just don't breathe garlic on him when you're making excuses."

The pasta arrived and the Assistant U.S. Attorney ate while Larry told a story about his first mob defense case, where he'd gotten his client off by proving that the feds had manufactured evidence. "The jury had to acquit, but I learned something. They all hated me. I could feel them turn the minute I made that FBI agent look like a bigger crook than my man. The public doesn't want to know what goes on. They want their G-men to be like in the movies. I made him look bad and they didn't like it. Like I say, I won the case, but it wasn't pretty. You two finished? We should head over before your boss gives himself a stroke."

22

Blackmore had ordered a court steno to join us and Larry had a digital recorder delivered. Both sides wanted a clear record of the proceedings. They pushed papers around the conference table for five minutes while everyone ignored me. Finally, Blackmore looked up and spoke to Larry.

"It's time for Mr. Stafford to perform for us. What's he got?"

I had full immunity for anything I admitted to in the interview. I took immediate advantage of it.

"Nineteen months ago, I extorted ten million dollars from a major criminal named Neil Wilkinson in exchange for waiting a few days before I ratted him out. I knew the money was dirty, but I took it anyway. Neil is currently living in Venezuela, where he has been able to fend off all attempts at extradition."

I kept talking even though Blackmore was screaming at me before I had completed the first sentence. If it was on the record, I was clear.

"What the fuck is this, Larry? This is clearly bullshit. Stop the goddamn recording! You! You! Stop recording!"

The steno looked up, surprised to find that the U.S. Attorney was speaking to her. She swallowed a silly smile and stopped typing.

"Larry, your guy can't do this. O'Rourke won't stand for it and neither will I. I'll bury him and have your goddamn license."

"Wally, I had no idea my client was going to talk about anything other than your case." Which was both true and irrelevant, as there was no way that Blackmore would ever be able to prove any kind of collusion. "Can we just calm down and let him tell you what he knows?"

Blackmore settled back in his seat, but he was still pissed. "What is he talking about, anyway? What case is this?"

"Ancient history," Larry said in a soft coo. "Let's stay in the moment."

"When this is over, I'm going after you for the ten mil, Stafford. I may not be able to get you for abetting a fugitive, but I will take every cent you've got left. You get me?"

"Half of it's hidden where you'll never find it," I said. It was parked in a Swiss annuity—anonymous and invisible. "And the rest is in my son's trust fund."

"Then you can tell the little guy he's about to become a pauper."

Larry held up a hand in caution. "Don't rush in there, Wally. Mr. Stafford's son is autistic."

Blackmore, the political animal, understood immediately. If he went after the money that paid for all the extra care and schooling my son needed, the special needs community would never forget. Blackmore wouldn't be able to win an election unless he was running against Bernie Madoff or Phil Spector. Actually, Spector might edge him out in a low turnout.

He was also aware of the fact that the little green light on Larry's recorder was still flashing. Every word he spoke had the power to come back and bite him on his private parts someday.

"Can my client continue?" Larry asked in that same soft tone.

Blackmore nodded at the steno.

I thought of the two million dollars in bearer bonds that I had stolen from a corrupt banker and handed over to a man who had saved my life. There was no point in confessing to that—no one was ever going to come looking for that money.

"There are twelve of these microstocks. They're all remarkably similar. Very low-cap. Minimal documentation. They all trade by appointment only. The companies are all blue-collar-type businesses located out on Long Island."

"We know all that. Let's move it along."

"You wanted to hear everything," Larry said. "Let him tell it."

I continued. "All the IPOs were done by one of two firms. Both small banks. Neither survived the crash. I can't find any connection between them, but both specialized in new issues by start-ups. Mostly old technology, service industry, or buggy-whip manufacturers. One of the firms also did a bunch of tech stocks back in the late nineties. None survived 2000."

"Names?" one of the young lawyers asked.

"Knight Securities and Hawthorne-Doolan. Knight was the bigger firm. They did the tech business."

"Keep going," Blackmore said.

"From what I've been able to find, none of the companies ever made much money for the investors. Zero dividends and they all trade well below the initial offering price. The owners made out all right, but it was the bankers who really cleaned up. They paid themselves huge fees relative to the deal size."

Larry interrupted. "Wouldn't you expect that, though? Even small underwritings have fixed costs."

"Huge fees, Larry. Huge."

"I see."

"The business owners?" Blackmore asked. "What was their cut?"

"Not much cash. But all of them—all of these twelve, at least—got free leases on trucks. Free garage space. Free maintenance. For a one-time fee paid to a company called Rose Holdings, they got to lower their operating costs to peanuts."

Blackmore jumped on the name like a rattler striking. "Who's that? Rose Holdings. We don't have them." He glared angrily at his team. "Why don't we have them? Who are they?"

I pushed on. "I don't know. All I've got is the name and a location. Again, it's out on Long Island. Way out. Manorville. Rose Holdings owns a farm where they raise bison."

"Bison. What do you mean, 'bison'?"

"Buffalo. American buffalo."

"Somebody's raising buffalo on Long Island?" He looked like he thought this might be another indictable offense.

I decided not to share the story of my escape. "There's a big warehouse building. A garage. I'm pretty sure it used to be a place they trained horses. Now it's where they keep trucks—and they run a chop shop there, too, I think."

"You've seen it?"

I nodded. "Once. I'm not going back."

"Why's that?" he said.

"I don't like being gored and trampled on by half-ton quadrupeds."

"You discussed all this with your boss?"

"No. I started to and he cut me off. He wasn't interested."

"He knew about it already," Blackmore said.

"I don't think so," I said. "He asked about the size of the trades and told me to forget about it."

"Why would he do that, do you think?"

"You're asking me to speculate."

"This is not a trial, and I've paid well to hear what you think."

"The broker isn't getting rich off these trades. The clients are doing well. The whole thing doesn't add up to more than a few mil or so. Chump change. And Virgil didn't tell me to bury it. He told me to hand it off to the compliance department. Which I did. Then he put me on something else and that was the end of it."

"But you kept looking into it."

"Yes and no. I did some follow-up, yes, but it wasn't a priority."

"What did Virgil want you to work on?"

I looked at Larry for support, but I didn't get it. "This is kind of a gray area. I don't think it relates to your case." This was where the conversation with the FBI had turned sour.

Blackmore thought he smelled blood. "I decide that, Mr. Stafford. Not you. Ask your lawyer."

I didn't need to. I knew what Larry would say. "Virgil thinks that someone or some group is making a run at the firm. He asked me to look into it."

This news brought on a moment of Blackmore and his team sharing quick looks. They all took notes.

"What did you find?"

I found that I had to clear my throat. We were definitely in the realm of privileged information. "Yes, someone is trying to buy the firm. No, I don't know who. Yet."

"It sounds like my client has a valid point," Larry intervened. "I can't see that this has any bearing on your investigation."

We all sat and thought quietly for a minute.

Blackmore didn't concede, but he did change the subject. "It's called 'parking.' You know the term? My people have traced those trades to another small broker-dealer. This one in northern New Jersey. Not much more than a pump-and-dump boiler room. A dozen brokers in an office park near Montclair. Any of this sound familiar?"

Pump-and-dump was one of the oldest and yet still most prevalent stock fraud scams. The fraudster would set up a minimally capitalized fly-by-night brokerage firm and hire aggressive salesmen to cold-call clients with a hot tip on a relatively illiquid stock. The available flow of the stock must be small enough for the firm to control the pricing. Over days, or weeks, the crooks will tout the stock, driving the price higher and higher. Then, without tipping off the clients, the firm sells its stake in the overhyped stock and lets the whole airy confection collapse. The only way an investor can hope to make anything at all on the stock is to get in early and sell out at the very point that the sales force is pushing it the hardest. Otherwise, it's a loser. Every time. Of course, the safer course is not to get involved in the first place.

"I've examined Becker's books and records. We dealt with a financial advisor. That's the extent of our involvement. The firm has no knowledge of or relationship with any other broker-dealers. Who are these people?"

"I don't believe that," Blackmore said. "The FA has been taking a nice cut out of this business, but the big money is being made by these crooks in New Jersey. There's a kickback somewhere and I'm going to find it."

"Really? I don't think Becker Financial has anything to do with this."

"Have you met with the broker? The financial advisor? What do you know about these people?"

Occasionally, an operation like this would make headlines because they had grown to a size that both the feds and the press found notable, but the vast majority were small-time cons run out of low-rent loft spaces. Much too small-time to be of any interest to a headline-seeking U.S. Attorney.

But if Blackmore could bring down a good-sized firm, one that was being run by the son of one of the more notorious goniffs of recent years, he had a chance of making the front page of all the national newspapers. He had a strong incentive to find a link between these small-time crooks and Becker Financial. And to Virgil Becker in particular.

"No," I said. "I've never met any of these people."

"You never met"—he checked his notes—"Mark Barstow? Larry Grella? Daniel Parks?" He continued to rattle off a list of names, to which I just shook my head. I knew none of them.

"All right. Let's just talk about the broker. Joseph Scott. What's his relation to your boss?"

"None, as far as I know. Virgil's not the kind of boss who has the front-line producers up for a drink and a slap on the back. I doubt that he's met half of the salespeople who work for him. He's got sales managers and branch managers for that."

"So why would Virgil protect this guy?" Blackmore asked.

"He wouldn't. You're looking at it wrong way 'round. Why would he risk the firm for some nobody out in Lake Grove or Stony Brook or wherever? Even if the guy was a top producer, it's not worth his while to get involved. It makes no sense."

"I want you to meet with this guy Scott. You'll wear a wire."

I had heard stories about people who had been trapped that way. They lived a life of constant fear and suspicion until the feds used them up and spit them out.

"Not a chance," I said.

"That's not in the agreement, Wally," Larry said.

"Screw the agreement." He turned to the steno. "Not another fucking word. Not one more word. Understood?" Back to us. "And I am not 'Wally,' Larry. I am now Mr. Blackmore, and I want what I paid for."

"I'm not wearing a wire," I said.

"Shut up!" Blackmore yelled at me.

"Quiet, Jason," Larry said. "We're out of here." He stood up and I hopped to my feet, too. He picked up the recorder off the table. "We've cooperated, Mr. Blackmore. I'm sorry my client didn't make your case for you, but he's done nothing wrong. If he uncovers any wrongdoing, I am sure that he will report it to the proper authorities, just as any good citizen would do. Good-bye."

"Wait! You walk now and I'll tear that agreement to pieces, no matter what O'Rourke says. Read the fine print. If you're holding back or I can prove you're guilty of anything you haven't talked about, you will go to prison. And not just for the balance of your sentence, wiseass. I will put you away for so long, nobody, but nobody, will remember your name. I want Virgil Becker and you are going to help me get him."

Larry held up the recorder. The green light was still blinking. "If you have any more questions for my client, please submit them in writing."

Neither of us said a word until we were in the elevator.

"I trust you've got that five mil tucked away someplace safe," Larry said.

"It's not over, is it?"

"No. Blackmore is a vindictive little man. We should both watch our backs. I hope you don't have any more surprises hidden away, Jason. We won today, but only because we had a winning hand. Next time, he'll be sure to have stacked the deck."

"What's his next move?"

"Hell if I know."

23

After dinner I spent a few hours poring over the meager information I had. Strings of numbers, whether prime or not, and an admonition about "family" weren't worth much. I had misplaced my tablet—again—and though I strongly suspected that it might have found its way into my son's bedroom—again—I wasn't going to risk waking him. I took my laptop, cell phone, and a cup of tea and plunked down in my chair.

Richard Hannay picked up on the first ring. "I set up a website for us."

"Why do we need a website?"

"To exchange messages and talk in private. It's a fortress. It would take a small army of hackers a week to get in. By that time, we'll have been warned and moved on."

"Interesting. Can we use it to talk?"

"And video. We can even conference through it if you want to include people you know are secure. I set up a similar arrangement for communicating with my wife and the girls."

"Sounds great. When did you come up with this?"

"This morning. Think in the morning. Take a look."

He directed me to a page that advertised a purveyor of off-sized machine screws, nuts, and bolts. Blazoned across the bottom of the screen was a red banner declaring SITE UNDER CONSTRUCTION—COME BACK LATER.

"Don't hit the log-in button, it's an alarm. Go to the top right and click on the logo of the little fat man."

He walked me through the sign-in procedure—which required not one, but three log-in pages, each with a long password and a CAPTCHA box. "To deter the bots." The whole process took minutes—an eternity in computer time.

"At the prompt, I want you to start talking. It doesn't matter what you say. Read the newspaper or give the Pledge of Allegiance. It's just to give an imprint for the voice recognition software. Then hit the video button so the system can do facial recognition. It's not perfect—I could scam it—but it's good enough."

"Good enough" was computer-speak for "top-of-the-line."

"You created a facial recognition program? From scratch?"

"I borrowed it from a Disney app. It works better than anything I could have written."

"Talking to you, I often get the feeling that I am standing on a promontory, looking at a future that I do not understand."

"Ain't that always the way. Keep talking. I'll stop you when the program is ready."

I recited the words to "Friend of the Devil," stopping when I got to the line "I'll spend my life in jail."

"That's fine," Hannay said. "You're done."

A new window opened and I was looking at Hannay on the screen. It was like Skype, but with two bar-graph monitors along the border that registered both facial and vocal recognition. They flickered up around the ninety-five percent mark.

"Very cute," I said. "And no one can eavesdrop?"

"They'd have to be better than I am. Or have a lot more resources. NSA or Homeland Security could do it, if they knew where to look."

"So, what do you have for me? Anything new?"

"Two more companies with similar number combinations. Nothing more."

"Then hold up on it. I need to find another angle." I thought for a moment. "Did you ever get a chance to check that name I gave you? James Nealis."

"You said it wasn't a priority."

An idea came to me. "Did I? See what you can do. But I do have another name I would like you to research for me first. Scott, first name Joseph. He works for Becker out on Long Island."

"Want to take a guess on how many Joseph Scotts there are in the greater New York area?"

"He's young. Early thirties, tops. At least mid-twenties. He's a broker, he's licensed."

"That helps. When do you need this?"

"How's tomorrow morning?"

"Hah! You're looking for real depth."

"Anything. I want to have something to hold over this guy when I talk to him. Then give me Nealis."

"Check in with me around nine."

I stayed there in the chair, running one search after another, jumping from James Nealis to number series to Joseph Scott and back again. Hours later, all I had accomplished was to run down the battery on the laptop. I plugged it in to recharge and closed my eyes.

24

A small hand plucked at my shirt.

"Breakfast."

The Kid was up and must have been standing next to me for the last few minutes. Sunlight had replaced the reflected light from down on Broadway. It was morning.

"Breakfast. Right." What day was it? The Kid had put on a pair of blue jeans and a bright yellow sweatshirt that was a recent favorite and a major change in his likes and dislikes—the year before, he would *never* wear yellow. In fact, yellow was now his number-one favorite color in almost all things. Red was now banished. The outfit made him look like a miniature suburban dad ready for the weekend chores, but he had done it himself and that was what mattered. Bright Colors = Thursday. The Kid and I kept a calendar on the door in his room and he started every day by placing a big black *X* on the day just finished. He never forgot.

Breakfast was also in transition. Skeli had somehow persuaded him to try yogurt and it had been an immediate hit, throwing his whole weekly schedule into chaos. Scrambled eggs—no spots—once eaten on Monday, Wednesday, and Friday were now only to be served on Tuesday and Thursday. Cereal was no longer allowed, it being "for babies." Syrup, and either pancakes or French toast, was for the weekend. Once I made the proper adjustments, I found that my life was greatly improved by this. I never had to struggle to keep the syrup off his clothes before school, and preparing lemon yogurt meant nothing more than tearing off the foil cap and giving the Kid a spoon. Exactly the kind of food preparation at which I excelled.

"I'm on the case, my boy. Go sit down and I'll get your juice and vitamin."

I jumped up too quickly and my screaming back reminded me that sleeping in an ancient broken-spring armchair was a dumb thing to do at any age. I began putting his meal together, feeling both rushed and chagrined. Two eggs—both spotless—whisked to a golden froth and poured over a single pat of melted butter.

"You want cheese today?"

He smiled.

Neither of us smiled often enough. I smiled back.

I grated a sprinkling of cheddar cheese over the eggs while they cooked—another of the new culinary extravagances the Kid allowed—and in minutes had redeemed myself as father of the year.

"Here you go." I put the plate in front of him and returned seconds later with a glass of water, a thimble-sized serving of no-pulp orange juice, his vitamin, and his morning meds. "I'm going to take a quick shower. You eat up and maybe we'll have time to play a game or read a bit before we leave."

I cheated and stayed in the shower a full minute longer than necessary, letting the hot water soothe the muscles in my lower back. The Kid took a yoga class every Saturday morning; maybe I should consider it. Maybe I would start it over the summer. Or next fall. Later, at any rate.

While I shaved, I planned out the day. First order of business was to send Heather a text. The Kid had a doctor's appointment that afternoon. Next, I needed to get to the bank for some cash to pay Carolina, the housekeeper. Then I had to rescue Virgil and the firm. Maybe when I was done, I could end war, fix climate change, and save the planet from an alien invasion.

It was time to confront the broker—Scott. Joseph Scott. I would call his branch manager and insist that Scott come into Manhattan for a sit-down. He wouldn't be on his own turf. He'd be easier to trip up. If I needed to bring in Virgil or Aimee as heavy artillery, they'd be an elevator ride away. And I would be at least two steps ahead of Blackmore.

Showered, shaved, and dressed for battle with the forces of evil in a blue custom suit from Saint Laurie, white shirt, and solid red tie, I was back to the Kid in ten minutes.

I found him with the missing iPad propped up in front of him. The eggs were untouched and congealed into a dull lump. His juice was exactly as I had left it, the vitamin beside it. He had taken his medicine. Small miracles keep me sane.

A cartoon was playing on the small screen. Disney. Mickey and Goofy. A female version of Goofy in a polka-dot dress was terrorizing Mickey. I didn't see much humor in it, but I accept that I was not the target audience. The Kid, however, wasn't laughing, either. He was rapt, barely blinking often enough to keep his eyeballs moistened, with his mouth slightly agape. But he was not reacting to any of the antics. I felt like the machine had just stolen my child's brain and replaced it with straw.

The female Goofy was supposed to be Goofy's grandmother. I realized that if I had figured that out, I was already much too involved in the show. It had me. Another few minutes and I would be as slack-jawed and zombie-eyed as my son. I pulled my eyes away and took a deep breath.

Only then did I put together the chain of events that must have preceded this moment. In the few minutes that I was out of the room, my son had retrieved my iPad, searched for and found this cartoon featuring his favorite Disney character, Goofy, and had made it play. He had done this without being able to read, as far I knew. Could he have accessed the cartoon without reading or writing? Or had he been hoarding his skills until he found some use for them other than keeping his teacher happy—a goal that would not have motivated him in the slightest?

"Hey, Kid. Eat your breakfast." When faced with the inexplicable, retreat to your last known point of reference.

He ignored me. Of course.

I wanted to tell someone. Skeli. My father. Roger. His uncle Tino. But what would I say? I had no idea what had happened. The Kid was watching a cartoon on my iPad. And???

"Come on, son. It's a school day. Finish up." I had to address, at least, the cartoon. We did not own a television—upon a doctor's recommendation. "You can watch the cartoon later." I reached across and put my hand between his staring eyes and the small screen. For a moment he did not react, then he calmly took hold of my hand and gently moved it to the side.

The timer beneath the image showed only another minute and thirty-two seconds. The smart move was to wait. Intervention might prove costly. The Kid could easily explode if I tried to remove the iPad. Rather than watch, and make myself crazy in the process, I retreated to the kitchen and washed up the bowl and pan. I deliberately took my time.

When I came back to the table, the vitamin and juice were gone and the Kid was eating eggs with his left hand—sans fork—and swiping at the screen with his right index finger.

"How did you learn how to do that?" I asked.

He gave me the scowl that meant he thought I was acting "stupid." Maybe so.

"Okay, I'm stupid. But teach me. I want to learn how you did that." I reached over and hit the button at the bottom of the screen. The image disappeared and the home screen appeared. It was covered with apps, most of which I routinely ignored. "Go ahead. Let me watch how you do it."

He sighed. Obviously, I was too stupid for words. He swiped the screen and the second page of apps came up. He pointed to an icon of a frowning face. He touched it and opened a new screen showing images of cartoon characters. He scrolled through. Found Goofy and touched it. A page came up listing Goofy cartoons and other images and their address on the Web. I noticed that many of them were highlighted. He had visited here often. I watched him scroll through to the next page, where he stopped and chose. He poked and another Goofy cartoon began. I let my breath out. I was stunned. The app was some variation of the same image recognition that Hannay had built into his security system—possibly the same one he had "borrowed." But the Kid had discovered it and learned how to use it all on his own. Amazing. I knew that children on the spectrum were using computers to learn, to communicate, and to play. I knew that the iPad had once been heralded as a breakthrough device for the ASD community and had, in fact, improved the lives of many. What I didn't know was that my son was capable of showing interest in any technology that didn't have to do with cars. I was stunned.

And a little scared. Thoughts of what else he might come across while perusing the Internet stopped me dead. I needed to either lock the damn machine in a safe and hope the Kid wasn't also an intuitive safecracker or find some way to childproof the thing. I vowed to get Heather's help with it, just as soon as I cleaned up the other few thousand issues demanding my immediate attention.

The Kid held a last morsel of scrambled egg in his hand through the next four minutes. I watched with him. Goofy encountered various annoyances while on vacation, some of disaster quality, but none life-threatening. The Kid laughed this time. I did not. Well, I chuckled once.

Eventually, the end credits began to roll and the last of the eggs disappeared. I grabbed the iPad and closed it. The Kid did not object. He was in a good mood. I had anticipated a meltdown.

"Brush your teeth, pal, and we'll go."

He jumped up and ran to the bathroom. If that was what ten minutes of Goofy in the morning led to, I was prepared to rethink the whole ban on watching television. What do doctors know anyway?

The Kid was back, Velcro-lace shoes in hand, in much too short a period of time.

"Did you brush?" I said. "Two minutes?"

He nodded quickly. Much too quickly.

"You have nice teeth. You need to keep them that way."

He threw his shoes. One went across the living room and hit the wall. The other flew at me, but without much conviction. If he had thrown it harder, I would have believed it was on purpose. As it was, it barely reached me and ended up sliding under the table.

"Sorry. Sorry. Sorry." While he did not sound in any way sorry, he did jump up and retrieve both shoes. He plunked himself down on the floor and pulled them on.

"Teeth," I said when he was done.

He stomped into the bathroom, where he began to sob loudly. I followed him in and put toothpaste on his brush and handed it to him. He glared at me.

"If you do a good job brushing your teeth, we can watch two more Goofy cartoons tonight after dinner."

He thought about it. Making deals was usually a self-defeating exercise with him. His memory did not work in such a way that I could demand performance after the reward. And he would promise anything, say anything, agree to anything, to fill an immediate need. He had no control. But this time, with the promise of reward for a chore that was a basic requirement anyway, he gave it serious consideration. He nodded once and began to brush.

I noticed that his hair was looking a bit shaggy in the back. Time for another haircut. Each one was torture. For me, for the stylist, but mostly for the Kid. The day had just started and I was exhausted.

25

Roger called as I was starting the dishwasher—my last act of house-keeping before taking the Kid to school.

"I've only got a minute," I said. "I'm on my way out the door."

"You're famous all over again."

"What's up?"

"You made the paper. Front page."

I understood. "The *Post* or the *News*?" Roger never read anything but the tabloids. The differences between them might not have been apparent to the tourist or casual visitor to town, but they were obvious to every New Yorker. If you made the front page of the *Daily News*, you had a chance, though slight, of being treated fairly in the story.

"The *Post*."

"Great. What's it say?"

"There's a not-so-nice picture of you. You got your usual scowl. You look like somebody's idea of a hit man or something."

"What's the headline?" I waved the Kid out into the hall and locked the door behind us.

"One word. 'RAT' with three question marks."

"Rat? What the hell does that mean?"

"You want me to read you the article?"

"No. I'll get a copy downstairs." I was already moving down the hall to the elevator. "Just give me the gist."

There was no answer. The Ansonia had originally been designed to house musicians. The halls were big enough to move grand pianos, and the walls thick enough to dampen the sounds of neighbors prac-ticing scales at all hours. There were spots in the building where cell service dropped out completely.

"Roger? Roger? You still there?"

A sharp crackle answered me. I stepped into the elevator and hit the button for the first floor. "Stay with me," I said into the dead phone. I repeated it twice more, giving my faith in technology over to a more primitive reliance upon the power of threes.

The elevator doors opened, and being careful not to step on any of the black tiles, I ran across the lobby, the Kid hopscotching behind. We did not walk on black tiles. Kid's rules.

"Can you hear me, Roger?"

"Yeah. Did you get all that?"

"Yeah. No. No. Just tell me, why are they calling me a rat?"

"It says you're going to testify before a grand jury."

"That's bullshit!"

"Don't shoot the messenger."

"Sorry. But it's still bullshit. I've got to go. Thanks for the warning."

Raoul, the day doorman, held the door open with one hand while waving the newspaper at me with the other. "Front page of the *Post*, Mr. Staffud!" He was impressed and excited, and no doubt thought that I should be as well. Other tenants of the building had made the front page from time to time, but Raoul had always treated my notoriety as something even greater than their celebrity. I was not the has-been villain of a four-year-old fraud that no one cared about anymore; I was evil enough for the *Post*.

I handed him a five. "Get us a cab, Raoul. We're in a hurry today."

"Sure thing." He ran to the corner and stuck his hand in the air.

My phone rang again.

26

Good morning, Jason." It was Larry, sounding calm and relaxed. I felt neither. I wanted to strangle him, because he wasn't as frantic as I was. "I don't know if you've seen the *Post* yet today . . ."

"What the hell is this? We had a confidential meeting with that son of a bitch. I never agreed to testify. This is crap. Who talked to the press?"

"It's just noise, Jason. Relax. You have your immunity, and if you come up with something for Blackmore, we'll talk before turning anything over. He's just applying pressure."

"Blackmore? The goddamn U.S. Attorney did this?"

Raoul came huffing back up the block, a yellow cab following slowly.

"Based on my years of experience facing off against the worm? Yes, I would say he's the one who did this."

"Fuck him."

"*There's* an unappetizing thought."

"Don't make jokes. I want to kill the guy." Unfortunately, this came out of my mouth just as I was settling into the backseat of the taxi next to the Kid. I saw in the rearview mirror the cabbie's eyes widen. "It's a figure of speech," I told him. I gave him the address of the Kid's school and sat back.

My phone beeped at me. Another incoming call. I checked. Marcus Brady.

"I've got Brady calling me now."

"You should take it," Larry said. "Call me later. We can still make this work."

"How the hell are we going to fix this, Larry? Everyone at Becker will cut me dead after this."

"I'll call Virgil. He'll listen to me."

"Well, that'll be nice. I'll have *one* person on my side."

"Talk to Brady and call me later. I want to know his take on this."

One of the last strongholds of privacy in New York City—the backseat of a yellow cab—had succumbed to the siren song of the Internet sometime during the previous administration. The same Napoleonic mayor who wanted to control how much salt and sugar I consumed apparently thought it important that I view ads for Blue Man Group every time I rode in a taxi south of Fourteenth Street. Why hadn't New Yorkers risen up in revolt against this assault? Sadly, because most of them secretly liked it, I thought. The damn thing started nattering at me moments after I closed the door.

Unless the taxi was an unusual vehicle in some way, the Kid usually just sat back and watched whatever inanity was being broadcast from the screen facing us. Not today. He had wrapped his arms around his shoulders and was squeezing hard. His face had the teeth-bared grimace he made when he was angry.

"Later," I said to Larry, and switched lines. "Brady? Hold on just a sec. I've got to talk to my son." I held the phone to my chest to mute it. "Hey, Kid. I see you're upset. Can I help you? Is it because I'm a little upset, too?"

He gritted his teeth and growled.

"Okay, okay. I'm more than a little upset. I agree. Out of control? Maybe, but I'm okay now. Can we talk about it?"

He spoke through the gritted teeth so that his voice came out sounding like someone possessed by demons. "You said a bad thing."

I reviewed my conversations with Roger and Larry. I had said a great many bad things.

"You're right. And I'm sorry. I shouldn't use those words. I will try very hard not to say them again. I'm having a hard time. You understand that, don't you? When someone has a hard time, they don't always act the best."

"It's bad to kill." His voice sounded a bit more normal.

The cabbie looked back at me again in the mirror.

"Well, I didn't mean it," I said, trying to be quiet enough to exclude the driver.

"Kill. K-I-L-L. Kill."

Wonderful. Two years of school and my son was just learning to spell. And his first word was *kill*.

"Really, Kid. I don't want to kill anyone."

He pointed to the *Post* in my hand. "Rat. R-A-T."

And his second word was *rat*. I needed to have a word with his teacher. "Very good. I need to talk on the phone now."

"'Kay."

He wasn't okay, he was still upset. He just wasn't in extreme crisis mode. But it was a window—a small one—and I needed one right then.

"I'm going to talk to Mr. Brady. Remember him?"

"The FBI man," he said. He had lost the growl, but none of the volume. The cabbie's eyebrows shot up again.

"Well, he needs to tell me something, so give me just a minute. Okay?"

He mimed biting down on something; he had once bitten Special Agent Brady. It had been justifiable self-defense. "'Kay," he said.

I punched up the volume on the television.

"You can watch until we get to school," I said. He was already mesmerized.

27

B rady? You still there?"

"I'm here. You saw the paper?"

I had it in my lap, but I hadn't opened it to look at the story. Roger was right. The picture was not flattering. I looked a little like one of the bad guys in an old Charles Bronson movie, but I couldn't remember which one.

"I have it here."

"I want you to know I had nothing to do with that. Blackmore is in charge and I'm out. He thinks I'm contaminated because of our history."

"Look, Marcus, you've been straight with me in the past and I'm sorry for your troubles, but today I just don't have any more room on my plate. Know what I mean?"

"I'm not looking for sympathy, goddamn it. I'm calling to warn you."

"A little late. You think? My life just got flushed down the drain. I figure the circle of people who will still speak to me just dropped into the single digits. I don't know if I could round up enough to man the infield."

"I told Blackmore that he just put a bull's-eye on your back. Someone went after Barstow. Two shooters. They screwed up and Barstow fought back, wounding one of them. They took off when the cops arrived. Barstow was wounded and confused. He fired at the cops and put one in the hospital. The other one took him out."

"Why didn't you tell me all this the other night?"

"Because the conversation ended abruptly when you kicked us out."

"Did they ever find the two shooters?"

"One. He washed up on Fire Island."

"How'd they know it was him?"

"Shotgun wound in the upper back. Blood matched to the scene. But that wasn't what killed him."

"No?"

"No. Someone put a twenty-two-sized hole in the back of his head before dumping him in the bay. He went out with the tide. By the way, you might not want to eat any local-caught blue crabs for a while."

"Who was he?"

"Small-time punk named Figundio. A nobody. Suffolk County cops are 'making all appropriate efforts,' which you can take to mean they've got more pressing concerns."

"Was he mobbed up?"

"None of our people knew him. But that could just mean he was too far down the roster for us to notice."

"All right, I'm scared. But as long as I stay clear of Blackmore, no one has any reason to come after me."

"That's not a strategy. Blackmore will just keep squeezing. He has something else cooking, I know it. This is just a feint."

"A powerful feint," I said. "What does he follow it up with? A nuclear strike?"

"Like I told you. I'm no longer on the inside track on this. But he and his people looked like a wolf pack following a strong scent of wounded prey. There's more coming."

"What's your idea? How do I fight this thing?"

"You can't. Come in. Let me get you and your son into WITSEC. I can make it happen with one call. Then you can work with Blackmore or not. You're untouchable."

"I go into any kind of witness protection program and that's admitting I'm a rat. I can't do that. I don't have a lot of friends, I admit, but that makes the ones I *do* have that much more valuable."

"Not one of them would want you dead."

The cab was edging up the queue in front of the school. I started fumbling for my wallet. "I've got to go, Brady. Thanks for your concern. And I need to watch my back. But I still have a job to do. And I think that once all the facts are out there, no one will have any reason to shut me up."

"Then they'll take revenge."

"There's no profit in revenge. A guy back at Ray Brook told me that."

I swiped my credit card, added the biggest precomputed tip on the screen, and jumped out. The Kid was still watching the television. "Brady? We'll talk later." I tucked the phone in my pocket and looked back into the cab. I found myself staring back at my own face. It was an old photo. An earnest young black woman in a cutout in the lower corner of the screen was relating some of the high—and low—points of my life. The word RAT scrolled across the bottom banner.

"Damn it," I said. I covered the screen with the newspaper. The Kid turned and scowled up at me. "Sorry. Time to go to school, bud. Come on."

His teacher was waiting for us out front. I tucked the *Post* under my arm so as not to draw attention to it. I doubted that she had seen it, but some of the parents might have. Ms. Wegant didn't smile at me, but then she never did. The Kid and I performed our hand-sniffing ritual and he surprised me by skipping into the building.

Despite Brady's warnings, I felt relieved. The school would keep the Kid safe. For today, at any rate. One step at a time.

28

On the way down the hill to Broadway, I called the main number at Becker and asked to be put through to the branch manager out in Stony Brook. He was an old warhorse named Yazinski. I'd met him, but never had any dealings before.

He answered with the branch code. A true company man. "Becker. C-3."

"Mr. Yazinski?"

"Speaking." There was a deep whiskey-gravel in his voice.

"This is Jason Stafford. I work for Virgil—"

He cut me off. "I know who you are."

"Good. I need to speak with one of your people. Today. In my office."

"I see you made the paper this morning."

I ignored him. His tone was polite, even slightly amused, but I didn't have the time or the inclination. "Joseph Scott. I checked. If he takes the Ronkonkoma line, he can be in my office by ten-thirty."

"What do you want with Joey?"

"You'll be informed if there is anything relevant."

"Because if this is about those penny stock trades, he's been cleared by compliance. They've been all over it."

"Just have him report to me. I'm in conference room B just off the trading floor."

"Does Nealis know about this?"

I was getting tired of his resistance. I had the bigger club. "Nealis is banking. I work for Virgil. So do you. You'd better go talk to Scott, otherwise he'll miss his train."

29

Virgil deserved to see me in person when I made my attempt to explain the *Post* headline. I didn't call; I took the subway and made it downtown in ten minutes. A light mist was in the air on John Street when I came up the stairs. I hustled across the street and into the familiar building.

I swiped my security card at the stile and walked through. The rolling bar moved an inch and stopped, landing a lateral punch just below the belt, but not low enough to do any damage.

Still smarting, I stepped back and swiped it a second time before pushing. Nothing. It still didn't work.

I held up the card to the guard in hopes that he would buzz me through, but instead he waved me over.

"Good morning, Mr. Stafford. May I see your card, sir?"

"What's up, Jerold?"

Without answering, he ran the card through an electronic reader and kept his attention on the monitor in front of him. When he spoke, he avoided eye contact. "I'm very sorry, Mr. Stafford, but I have to confiscate your card."

"Why?"

"That's what the system tells me." He swung the monitor around so that I could see the message. I didn't bother reading it.

I held back a sigh of annoyance. "Who do I talk to? Is this a security snafu?"

He swung the monitor back and read the message again. "Compliance, sir."

"What the hell? Jerold, why would compliance have anything to do with building security? What's going on?" And what had I done to piss off Aimee Devane?

He had still not allowed himself to look directly at me. Now his face shut down entirely. "I can give you the number, sir."

"Keep it," I said with a petulant sneer, which I instantly regretted. Jerold hadn't done this to me, he was just the unfortunate bearer of bad news. "I have it," I said with an effort at keeping my tone neutral. "I'll be back when I get this straightened out."

Smokers had been banned from standing directly outside the front doors of the building, but the aroma from around the corner was thick in the damp April air. I felt ridiculous dialing Virgil to whine about what was no more than a misunderstanding or, at the worst, a turf battle. I dialed the private line.

The call went directly to a recorded message. "The mail box of the party you are trying to reach is full. Please try again later."

A buzz of anxiety began to nag at the back of my brain. There was an unpleasant pattern beginning to form. This was way beyond having ticked off Aimee Devane.

The mist in the air began to coalesce into an insistent but light rain. I huddled against the side of the building and ran through my options. None were attractive. I manned up and rang the chief of compliance.

"Mr. Stafford?" Aimee answered. "I've just had a call from the manager of C-3. What do you think you're doing?"

"Why were you following me the other night?"

"You were told not to pursue that investigation. Are you that incapable of following a simple directive?"

"Is that why you've had me locked out of the building? Don't turn this into some squabble over territory. I need to talk to this guy Scott. In case you haven't noticed, I'm getting seriously squeezed by the feds, and getting to the bottom of this penny stock bullshit is the only way I see of straightening things out."

"No longer your concern. As of forty-five minutes ago, you no longer work for Becker Financial."

"What? Why? Because of the damn newspaper story? It's nonsense. Yes, I spoke to Blackmore, but I said nothing that would implicate the firm or any senior exec. I just put in a call to Virgil to explain all that, but his private line went straight to voicemail. Trust me, when I get through to him, he'll understand."

"Oh." She sounded almost sympathetic. "You are not up to date, are you? I had your card confiscated on orders from Nealis, not Virgil."

"Nealis? He can't fire me. I don't work for him."

"As a matter of fact, he can. And you do. Or did. He's running Becker ever since Virgil was arrested this morning. A little less than an hour ago. And the first thing Mr. Nealis did was to get on the squawk box and announce that you were fired. I heard the trading floor cheering from two floors up."

Virgil had been arrested. Blackmore's one-two. The *Post* article, as provocative as could be, was still only a feint. It blocked me from being able to help Virgil. Any move I made on his behalf would be seen as suspect by his friends, family, and anyone in the business.

"Aimee, I need someone to believe me. I didn't do this. There is no way that I gave up Virgil to that prick Blackmore."

"I've dealt with Blackmore before. I believe you. It doesn't change anything, though."

"How do I help Virgil if I'm locked out? You've got to let me talk to the broker. This guy Scott. He's the key. There's more going on than you know."

"That's not an encouraging start, Stafford. I never thought of you as much of a team player, but now you're straight-out telling me that you've been holding out on me. And, you expect me to help you. I've dealt with a lot of traders over the years, but that's a level of chutzpah I haven't seen before."

"This is not about me. I can dig Virgil out of this—I know it—but

I can't do it alone. Talk to me. I'll give you everything I've got. We can do this together."

"Trust you? Based on what evidence? I never understood Virgil's faith in you. You are the epitome of loose cannons. You are also a liar, a cheat, and a crook. I've spent my career forcing guys like you out of the business. Why should I give you one iota of trust?"

"Very simple," I said. "I get results."

She took a long moment to digest that. I let her have the time before I continued.

"If Nealis is permanent, how long does he let you stay around? Help me get Virgil back and he will never forget it. Write your own ticket. He'll stamp it."

"Stop. I don't need that. I'll help Virgil because it's the right thing to do. I still don't trust you, but I don't see anybody else riding to his rescue."

"Then meet with me. Now. Come down and we'll get a coffee around the corner someplace. I'll give you everything I know, suspect, or imagine. Please."

She didn't answer for almost five seconds. The longest five seconds I had experienced since asking June Schuyler to the senior prom. (June said no. Actually, what she said was "I don't think so.")

"Give me ten minutes."

30

The building across the street had a recessed doorway, where I waited out of the steadily increasing rain. I would be able to see Aimee as she came out the doors, but I couldn't see much of the street. That was a mistake.

My cell phone chirped with a text message. Hannay.

Call STAT.

I didn't have time. Aimee would be down in one minute and I wouldn't be able to stall her while I contacted Hannay and got his latest report.

Later. Haf hour.

I looked up. Aimee was standing across the street under a black-and-white *New Yorker* umbrella and looking up and down for me. The rain was now a torrent and the sidewalk had emptied. She was the only person in sight. I called out and dashed across to meet her.

"Where to?" I said, raising my voice over the roar of the deluge.

"Come on," she said. "No one will be in the Iron Horse at this hour. We can get a coffee at the bar."

The umbrella was on the small side for two, but she let me keep my head covered. My back was getting soaked. We turned the corner and headed for the middle of the block, hugging the building and rushing from one awning to the next.

A black Lincoln pulled to the curb just ahead of us. An unremarkable sight in lower Manhattan. We kept walking. All four doors opened at the same time and four young men in sweatshirts and ball caps got out. I saw them but took no notice. Then they were standing on the pavement blocking our way. I stopped. Aimee looked up and then at me.

"Are you Jason Stafford?" one of them said in a deep voice. He towered over me.

"*Who?* My name is Howard Johnson," I answered quickly.

"That's him," said a short, pinch-faced man holding up a copy of the *Post.*

A minivan pulled up to the curb in back of the Lincoln and the side door slid open. Two more men jumped out.

"Get in," the man with the newspaper said. "Hurry up, we're all getting wet out here."

"What about her?" the first man asked. He was wearing a black Syracuse sweatshirt with orange lettering. He had the kind of forehead you rarely see outside of the Museum of Natural History. If he had gone to Syracuse, it must have been for rugby.

Another one of the group spoke at the same time I responded. "Let her go." For the briefest moment, I had hope that I could keep her out of what was to come. He had a mousy ponytail sticking out from underneath his cap.

"Screw that, she saw us," the first man said.

The man with the paper was obviously in charge. He made his decision. "Bring her."

Aimee moved first. I don't believe I had ever seen anyone move as fast, outside of a Jason Bourne movie. She swiveled on one foot, thrusting a raised elbow up behind her. It connected with the face of one of the young thugs and he went down like a dropped sandbag. Her off foot came up and, with a kick that Mia Hamm would have envied, landed in the groin of the guy with the newspaper. Two down. She stabbed at another man's face with the open umbrella. He backed up quickly.

The other three men had been as frozen in surprise as I was. We all moved at once. Two of them grabbed Aimee from behind, inadvertently getting in each other's way. I leapt into the fray, snatching at the ponytail with one hand while swinging a roundhouse punch that never connected. The Syracuse man, who seemed to have the mass of a small planet, stepped up and tapped me on the temple with a leather-covered sap. I sank to my knees. I wasn't knocked out, but I was no longer even a bit player in the fracas.

Aimee landed on the pavement in front of me with two men on top of her. She was wriggling madly, but they each had an arm and were lying across her legs.

"Kill the bitch," the newspaper guy yelled in a gasping rasp.

"No," I mumbled while trying to get my arms and legs to obey any of the simple basic commands I was sending their way.

"I got this," the man with the sap said. He leaned over and tapped her. She stopped wriggling.

They scooped us up and tossed us in the back of the minivan. Someone laid me across the bench seat and sat on my back while another wrapped my hands and ankles with duct tape. When he was done, he slapped another piece over my eyes. I fought the urge, but my brain decided that it was time for a reboot. I went away for a while.

31

Aimee was staring down at me. She was alive. So was I.

"How're you doing?" she asked.

"My head hurts."

"Welcome to my world."

"Where are we?" I said.

"No idea. I was starting to think you weren't going to wake up."

I rolled up to a sitting position. The room started spinning and my headache got a lot worse.

"Please don't vomit," she said.

We were in a room. The walls and ceiling were covered in sheet metal. The floor was linoleum. Aimee was sitting on a folding chair. On the floor beside her was a battery-powered camp lantern that seemed to be already halfway through its cycle, the light adequate to see our surroundings—and each other—but not enough to read by.

"I'm not going to throw up," I said, though there was more hope than faith in the statement.

"Glad to hear it."

I held my watch up to the lantern. "Is that right? I've been out for hours."

"I don't know. What time is it? They took my phone."

"It's after three." I checked my pocket. "Mine, too." Heather and the Kid would be at the neurologist's for the Kid's monthly checkup.

"So who are those guys?" she said.

"Give me a minute."

There was only one chair and she was sitting in it. I crawled over and sat with my back propped up against the wall. The room returned to a more stable condition. It was then that I noticed the balled-up wad of duct tape in the corner.

"They left us untied?"

"No," she said, shaking her head in both negation and amusement. "I took your tape off after I got rid of mine. I was worried about your circulation. Your hands were turning blue."

I looked at them in the dim light. They both appeared to be fine. "Thank you." I felt my brow and around my eyes. Still tacky, but no other residual issues. "How'd you get untied?"

Instead of answering, she stood up and clasped her hands behind her back. Then, slowly sitting, she folded her body back through her arms and brought her wrists up to her mouth. She mouthed biting.

"I'm impressed."

"Lots of yoga," she said.

"I was also impressed by your moves when they surrounded us. That's not yoga."

"No. Muay Thai. Twelve years. But I'm not so proud of myself. It didn't work, and it could have gotten us killed."

I had a feeling that getting killed was still a strong possibility, but I kept it to myself. "Still. One against six."

"I reacted. If I'd been smart, I would have just turned and ran. My training got in the way. Are you going to tell me who those guys are?"

The claustrophobia that had first descended upon me during my two years' stay as a guest of the federal government began to kick in. The walls were closer. Every time I blinked, the room got darker and smaller.

"Just give me a goddamn minute," I said, though it came out in a low growl that spoke more than the words.

"I liked you better unconscious."

There wasn't much to say to that. I pushed upright, using the wall for support, and forced myself to look at our surroundings. The walls were no longer advancing. They were behaving just like walls—only covered in metal.

"Have you noticed? Our voices echo, but there's no outside noise. It's like a recording studio in here."

"You don't cover the walls of a recording studio in metal sheets."

"No. And usually the door has a knob." I had worked my way around to the far end of the room, where there was a door in the middle of the wall. Where a knob would have been, there was just a hole. I bent over and looked in. Or out. It didn't matter, there was nothing to see. No light. Nothing.

An idea began to take shape. "Hey," I said. "Look under that chair. Is there a plug? Or a drain of some kind?"

She stood up and moved the chair. Mounted in the floor was something that looked very much like a shower drain.

"How'd you know?"

"I think I've figured it out." The words L.I. ICE and a logo of a giant ice cube bracketed by two smiling penguins came to mind. "This isn't a room. We're in the back of an ice delivery truck. And I'm willing to bet I know where it's parked."

She looked around the space. "An ice truck? All right, I'll buy that. But how do you know where it's parked?"

"Are you wearing heels?"

She looked at me as though I had spoken in Farsi, but she turned her leg so that the lantern light fell more directly on her shoe. She was wearing black pumps with a solid, sensible two-inch heel.

"Damn," I said.

"What?"

"Sorry. I need a six-inch spike. If this is an ice truck, the door release is through that hole. You run a screwdriver or an ice pick through there and it opens the door from the outside."

"And me without my ice pick," she said.

"Or even a hatpin."

"You're about three generations too late for that, I'm afraid."

I tried pushing the door. It was as unyielding as the wall around it.

"Don't you carry a pen?" she asked.

I laughed. "A pen? I'm not as old as I look." I walked the perimeter, banging my forearm against the wall at random points, hoping for a hollow response. All I got were sharp echoes.

Aimee waited until I got back to my starting point by the door. "So when are you going to tell me who these guys are and what they want with us?"

I tried the door one more time.

"They left us a light," I said.

"And two water bottles." She pointed to the far corner where two twenty-ounce bottles of Dasani rested against the wall. "Which means they're coming back. But I don't know whether that's good news or bad. What do you think?"

"Why were you following me?" I said.

"You don't believe in coincidence, do you?"

"Not since about second grade."

"Who the hell are those guys?" She was close to yelling.

I turned to her reluctantly. I still had a ton of questions, but it was time to share with her the few answers I had stumbled upon. "This may take a while."

I told her about the microstocks, the one-hundred-year leases on the trucks and the garage, the chop shop, and even the bison. I told her everything. Well, not everything. At least not right away. I put off the part about the financial advisor getting killed until I couldn't avoid it any longer. I'd like to think that I was protecting her from the worst news, but I knew better. I was having trouble facing it myself.

32

There's too much of it that I just don't buy into, Stafford. Why kill the FA when there's nothing for the feds to hang on Becker?"

"Parking," I said. "That's conspiracy. RICO. Right?"

"Let me list the problems. First, who murders over a reporting violation? That's nuts. Next. Intent. It's not parking if the financial advisor believed that his clients were taking legitimate risk. You'd have to prove that there was a prearranged timing and price where the clients were 'guaranteed' a profit. *And*, you'd have to prove that our broker knew about the arrangement before it would impact the firm."

"They killed a man. He was set to testify and they murdered him."

"You don't know that. We know he was killed. You have no idea why, though. Maybe his wife hired the hit man. Or the daughter did. What you have is an ugly coincidence. That's all."

"Blackmore believes he's on to something. He must have more information that he's not showing."

"I told you when you first came to me with this, I looked into it. There is no case."

"So why is Virgil in jail?"

"Because Blackmore is a grandstanding politician, not a prosecutor. Virgil will be out on bail by tomorrow morning. He might already be out. Blackmore doesn't need to actually convict him of anything. He's already got what he wanted. His name in lights as being tough on Wall Street crime."

"And next year he can run for mayor on that," I said.

"Eventually, Virgil's lawyer will get the case thrown out and he can go back and pick up the pieces of whatever's left."

"There won't be much. If he hasn't lost the firm already, he will have in six months. The press will make sure he never comes back."

"And what happens to us?" I said.

She shrugged. "We're back to my original question. Who are these guys? And what have they got against you?"

I picked up the water bottles and handed her one. "If they wanted to kill us, they'd have done it already. They gave us water and light. You have to think they want us alive, if not comfortable."

"I think you're whistling past the cemetery. We've been abducted, Stafford. Kidnapped."

There wasn't much to say.

We turned out the light before the battery went dead. Sitting in the dark kept my claustrophobia in check. It also meant we didn't have to stare at the despair in each other's faces.

Aimee stayed on the chair and I laid down, blocking the door. If our captors returned, I'd be the first to know. Time passed. Hours, but we disagreed as to how many. It would have been simple enough to turn the lantern back on, but we both felt it was better to preserve what few resources we had. The dark seemed less oppressive knowing that we could dispel it at any time with the flick of a switch.

My head still hurt and I felt drowsy. Concussion or depression? Either way, the brain was shutting down, refusing to examine my predicament because there were no happy endings. No lucky breaks. When the door opened behind me, we were going to be killed.

Only, when the door opened, I rolled out and down a flight of steps, banging into two or three sets of legs on the way down. Three male voices were all yelling at me and at one another. I rolled down the last step and up onto my feet. I ran.

I ran right into the arms of a fourth man. It was the big man with the sap. He took me by one arm and began to reach into his pocket.

"Oh, no," I yelled. "I'm sorry. It was an accident." I dropped to my knees. "Please don't hit me again."

"Get up." He helped by pulling straight up on the arm in his grip. I got up.

"Get him in here," someone said, and I found myself propelled on windmilling feet up the steps and back inside the truck. My few seconds of freedom had cost me a severe pain in my shoulder, but I had learned that my deduction had been correct. The lights were dim in the huge garage—the big banks of fluorescents had not been turned on—but I had seen enough anyway. And we were being held captive in an L.I. Ice truck with the two stupidly grinning penguins on the side. The faint smell of long-gone horse closed the deal.

The inside of the truck felt uncomfortably crowded. My claustrophobia began to creep back, with the walls developing a liquid look as though they had morphed from solid planes to mere surfaces through which I could fall, and like Alice, fall forever. I sank down and sat on the floor. It helped a little.

Aimee had not moved from the chair. The lantern had been tossed in a corner. The light coming in through the door was all we had. It wasn't much, but I could see the four men, who now stood over us. There was the little nasty guy who had identified me from the *Post*; his big friend from the Stone Age with the big *S* on his chest; a slightly older man—mid-thirties, I guessed—with flat, expressionless eyes, wearing a suit and tie and sporting the kind of pompadour you might see in a road company revival of *Grease*; and the impeccably dressed, good-looking man whom I had first seen with Jim Nealis—and last saw arguing with the Mouse.

What is she doing here?" The little man was no longer in charge. The speaker was the guy I'd seen with Nealis. His accent made it come out "doon he-ah" and the way he said "she" made it sound like a slur.

"She was with him," the weasel said in an aggrieved whine. "What were we supposed to do?"

The young boss turned to the man with the pompadour and rolled his eyes. They were surrounded by screwups.

He turned to Aimee. "What were you doing with him?"

"How are you, Mr. Scott? Jason, I want you to meet Joseph Scott of the C-3 branch. I think you were looking for him earlier today."

"I asked you something. What were you doing with him?"

She looked up at him with half-closed eyes. It was a languid and satiated look. "None of your business. It's personal."

"Get out. You expect me to believe you were on your way to a nooner with this old guy? Not a chance."

If there was any chance that Aimee could pull this off, we might just get out alive.

"What do you know about it? Your idea of a hot affair is a tube of KY warming gel and your laptop." She turned to me. "He's been warned about watching porn at his workstation."

Stone Age man thought this to be very funny. So did the little weasel. Scott smiled, but he wasn't amused. The other guy could have been a monument to Stoicism.

"No more BS, lady. You two are working together. What's he been telling you?"

"Usually he just tells me he likes to do me from behind, but I like being on top—so we compromise. And, like I said, it's really none of your business. Can I go home now?"

"I assume you two have met before," I said.

"Shut up, Stafford. I'll get to you."

"I told you we looked at his trades," Aimee said to me. "He was clean."

"How can he be clean?" I asked. "I told you what this place is. There's got to be forty or fifty trucks hidden here."

That got a reaction, but not the one I expected. Scott laughed. "'Hidden'? What's hidden? It's a garage." Then it hit him. "And how the hell do you know what's outside?" He turned on the three musclemen to see who had screwed up. They looked as surprised as he was.

"And the chop shop," I said.

They looked even more bewildered.

"I saw it all a week ago."

The weasel spoke. "That was you? You was the asshole who got chased over the fence?"

The hard-eyed man looked at him. *"What's this?"*

"Last week. Like he said. We were out here feeding the herd when out of nowhere some idiot in a suit goes running off across the field and got the animals all stirred up. That's when that young bull got the fence burn."

Scott broke in. "What the hell were you doing out here?"

"Investigating penny stock trading. I found this place by searching documents. I saw the chop shop."

"Chop shop? What chop shop? It's a garage. They park trucks here. When the trucks break down, they fix them."

"I don't know how it fits in, but it's part of your scam."

"What scam? Don't you get it? There is no scam!" He was screaming. "And you!" He poked a finger in the weasel's face. "You had to drag her into this? What am I supposed to do with her? This is kidnapping. Unlawful imprisonment. Those are federal charges, numbnuts."

"You told us—"

"I told you I had to talk to this rat. I didn't tell you to assault the goddamn chief of compliance. Did I tell you to do that? Gino, did I tell you to do that?"

The stoic looked at him with the smallest sneer. "Maybe we should be having this conversation somewhere else?" He made it a question, but it sounded like an admonishment.

It was finally dawning on me that, while I still firmly believed these four fools were involved in some dangerous conspiracy, it had little to do with penny stock trading or stolen trucks. In a flash, I understood everything and nothing.

I felt sick. I wanted to laugh maniacally at the cast of four stooges, but the reality was that I'd been caught looking the wrong way—playing Blackmore's game rather than taking care of business. I was the stooge. I had let Virgil hang. And now, looking at the man who Scott had just called Gino, I knew that I might pay for that mistake with my life. Killing me was the only way to cover their tracks. They'd have to kill Aimee, too. Another noncombatant. Another innocent. Another mistake on my part and another death due to my incompetence and arrogance.

In my cowardice, I hoped that they would kill me first so I wouldn't have to watch her die.

Scott heard Gino's words, but chose to ignore them. "I've got a couple more questions for you, old man. And take it to heart, you will tell me what you know, or I will have Gino gut you like a fish. Then I will sit here watching you hold your intestines in your hands while you bleed out."

I believed him. He wasn't funny at all anymore. But he was making threats. That meant he was scared, and that fact terrified me. He was afraid of what I knew and who I might have told. If I'd had any inkling of what that secret might be, I could have used that power to take charge and possibly save both our lives. But I had wasted my efforts on a chimera and I was clueless. Clueless, and soon to die because of it.

Aimee shifted her position in the chair, pulling her long legs back underneath her. She could read our future as well as I, and she was about to make a move to forestall it. But the risk was too great. I was flat on my ass and would never be able to get up in time to be of any use. And while no one was yet waving guns around, I would not have been at all surprised if either Gino or Scott was strapped. Even a knife would have immeasurably tipped the odds in that enclosed space.

"Let her walk away and I'll talk," I said.

"Did you think we were negotiating?!" Scott screamed in my face. "We're not *trading*. This is how it works: I ask questions and you answer them. Simple enough? Now, what did you tell the goddamn feds?"

The most direct method of prolonging our lives was to just keep talking. "They wanted to know about the penny stocks. McFee Plumbing. The whole pump-and-dump scheme."

He started screaming again. "I don't care about that small-time crap. Or those idiots in Jersey." He turned to Gino. "Fahchristsake, you do a favor and you never hear the end of it, you know what I mean?" And, more reasonably, to me again: "Don't give me that, okay? I want to know what you told them about me."

"I don't know. What should I have told them? They had your name." I was dancing as fast as I could, but I couldn't keep up. If we weren't talking about penny stocks, I was lost. I had no idea what to say.

"They had *my* name?" He spoke to Gino again. "Fucking Barstow again. The guy didn't know how to just keep his mouth shut. The only thing that guy was good for was drinking my cousin's scotch." He turned back to me. "So what else did that *finocchio* tell the feds?"

"How do I know? I wasn't there. What? You think I'm their little buddy? They don't *tell* me things. They *ask* me things."

Gino pulled a long, thin-bladed gravity knife from an inside pocket. With a well-practiced flick of his wrist, he opened it.

"Wait!" I yelled. "They told me he had something big. Something that involved Virgil. That's all I know. I swear."

"Something big?" Gino had taken over. He was waving the knife in front of my eyes as though he might decide to stab me there first. "Something big? Like what, asshole?" He jabbed a feint at my left eye and I jerked my head away. "Talk to me!"

Scott backed away nervously. He had just lost control of the situation and that scared him. It scared me, too.

Aimee made her move. She exploded off the chair, her legs like powerful springs shooting her up and forward. Her right arm was straight out and aimed for the throat of the throwback in the Syracuse shirt. If she had connected, she would have crushed his larynx and shifted the odds more in our favor. I was still more liability than asset, but it didn't matter. The weasel stepped in.

He had been suckered by her once and was not going to let it happen again. He reacted on the instant, grabbing her wrist and pulling, cutting off her attack and tipping her weight. He ducked and let her own momentum send her flying over his shoulder. She landed with a crash.

But she wasn't done. Her hands hit the floor first, breaking her fall, giving her the chance to leap back to her feet, ready for a second attack.

The big man was ready for her this time. He had been slow to respond, but once moving, he was a blur. He stepped inside her punch and hooked her ankles with a sweep of his leg. She went down hard. She did not spring back up. She moaned and stayed down.

Gino had moved quickly, too, and he now stood over Aimee with the knife. "Enough with the floor show," he said. "Let me finish this bullshit right now."

"No," Scott said. "There's been too many mistakes made."

Gino spoke in a grating hiss, his anger barely checked. "This guy knows nothing. Look at him. Right now he'll tell you anything just to go on living another few minutes. But it's bullshit. He doesn't have any idea what your cousin is working on, Joey. You want to talk about mistakes? You. You're the mistake. There was no need to grab him. You panicked and screwed up."

Scott surprised me by responding with a cool head. He didn't react to Gino's tone or his words. He spoke calmly. "You were right, Gino. This conversation should take place somewhere else." He turned and walked to the door. "All of you. Come with me."

The weasel and the big caveman went out on his heels. But before Gino followed, he took a minute to stare into my face. He flicked the knife closed and took a short-barreled gun from behind his back. He put the barrel to my temple and spoke quietly. "I promise you this. I'll make it quick."

34

The door was thrown shut and the truck was again enclosed in darkness. I realized that I had been holding my breath for an impossible length of time and I gasped in air like a drowning man.

"You okay?" It was Aimee.

"Wh-wh-what? Yes. I'm okay," I said.

"He didn't cut you, did he?"

How could she sound so strong? She had been moaning moments before. Seemingly in pain and only semiconscious.

"No. No. I'm okay."

"I thought he was going to cut your eye out. So I created a diversion."

She had taken a beating and risked her life. A thank-you would have been inadequate. "I owe you."

"Who's this 'cousin'?" she said.

"No clue."

"Neither do I."

I heard her moving and then felt a hand on my ankle.

"Is that you?" she said.

"I would certainly hope so," I said.

We both found this insanely funny and a chuckle built into a burst of full-throated laughter. When we passed hysteria on the laugh chart, Aimee began to hiccup. I wiped away tears composed of three parts fear and one part relief that we were both still alive.

"What next?" I said.

"I think we've got at most two hours, and most likely at least one before they make their—*hic!*—move. Damn! How do you—*hic!*—get rid of hiccups?"

"Something about drinking water while standing on your head. I think."

"Well, that's not happening."

"Or a big scare."

There was a pause followed by more peals of laughter. She stopped first and began to take long, controlled breaths.

"Oh, that's good. I think that did it. I'm better."

"Then tell me why we've got an hour."

"Or more. Scott isn't the boss—we just saw that, right? This cousin is really in charge. Or at least, Scott's not the sole boss. But he's not going to be the one to dirty his hands putting us down, either. *Hic!* Oh, damn! He's got plenty of muscle to handle those kinds of chores."

"Agreed. Hold your breath and count to one hundred."

"I'm fine. Really. That was the last one. So Scott needs an alibi. He needs to go to someplace where he'll be recognized and surrounded by people who will vouch for him. Believably."

"I can see it."

"*Hic!* Damn! On the other hand, they can't leave us here for too much longer."

"Because as long as we're alive, we're a risk."

"A big risk. Though we seem to be well contained for now."

"Well, we're going to change that," I said.

35

We were ready for them when they returned. And they were almost ready for us.

The door was wrenched open so hard it slammed back against the outside of the truck and a blinding white light stabbed into the darkness, seeking us. But we had each taken up position on opposing sides of the doorway. When the light hit me, I lunged forward and stopped abruptly, drawing the first one up the steps to grab me. It was the caveman. Of course.

Aimee hit him behind the ear with the lantern battery and he went down to his knees. He wasn't coming up again right away. The weasel was behind him, holding a big spotlight. He swung it around to highlight Aimee, and I saw a Taser in his other hand. She saw it, too, and rushed straight into him. He fired and there was an immediate crackle as he pumped fifty thousand volts into her stomach. She went down and began to jerk like a landed fish. Gino was coming up the steps behind the weasel, gun at the ready. If I let him get all the way up, we were finished. And if there were more thugs behind him, my best course of action would be to lie down and play dead.

I grew up in my father's bar. A friendly local gin mill in College Point, Queens. Most of the regulars knew one another and maintained a camaraderie that tended to smooth rather than ruffle feathers. But every once in a long while, someone would need to be ejected. Pop's technique was to come out from behind the bar via the kitchen so he'd be behind the bellicose drinker. He'd grab the poor slob by the back of the belt with one hand and the back of the neck with the other and propel him out onto the street. Once he got him outside, he'd give one last push, then come back in and lock the door. If they insisted upon making a fuss, he would then call the local precinct and let the cops handle the drunk. He told me, "You put your hands on another man and anything can happen." The keys to success were surprise and speed, not strength or agility. "Once you get the guy moving, don't stop until you're in the clear."

The weasel hunched his shoulders as soon as he felt my hand on his neck. It was a natural reaction, but it did nothing to release my grip. And it helped to get him slightly off balance. I grabbed his belt and lifted. He came up onto his toes and swung the spotlight wildly, trying to get at me. He held on to the Taser, and as I ran him to the door and tossed him down onto Gino, the wires popped out of Aimee's stomach and followed the weasel. He and Gino tumbled down the few steps, landing with the weasel on top. The spotlight smashed, which actually made it easier to see, rather than the opposite, as the twilight of the few wall lights made dimly lit pools surrounded by areas of near total darkness.

I turned and lifted Aimee to her feet. There was no time to see whether she was capable of action. I simply grabbed her arm and pulled her. She staggered past me and dropped through the doorway. I heard a man's scream followed by a gunshot.

There was no choice. The only exit, the only possible escape, was out that door. I ran for it.

A huge hand grabbed at me, managing to snag the back of my suit as I went by. The Cro-Magnon was back in action, if in a limited way. I leapt out the door and the jacket ripped up the back and I fell, spinning as I did, leaving half of my suit in the man's grasp.

I landed on a squirming mass of struggling arms and legs. Aimee was on top, but if Gino had been able to extricate himself from underneath the weasel, he would have been able to take her apart. She wasn't fighting so much as thrashing. She was still half dazed.

I rolled to my feet and kicked at where I thought Gino's head was. I clipped the weasel instead and he screamed again. The gun was on the ground in front of me and I kicked at it, sending it skidding out of the light.

When I turned back, Aimee was up and running. By instinct or accident, she was heading deeper into the lines of parked trucks. She wasn't moving fast and she reeled like a kitten in a windstorm, but she was moving. I followed.

A Taser delivers a high-voltage, low-amperage charge. It works best from a distance of four or five feet because the two points need to be far enough apart to allow the current to arc. Aimee had been right on top of the weasel when he shot her. She'd been stunned, but she was recovering quickly. She ducked between two big semi cabs and out of the light.

There was a roar like an enraged bear behind me. I looked back over my shoulder. The big guy had charged down the stairs and was coming on fast. The weasel was up and moving my way. Gino was on his feet, bent over, searching for the gun. I dodged between the next two trucks and kept running.

The lack of overhead light helped us and hindered them. It wouldn't be long before one of them—my bet was on Gino—would figure this out and head for the electric panel. Once those big strips of fluorescents were turned on, we'd be easy to trap. We had a narrow window to squeeze through.

I looked around wildly, trying to orient myself. They would expect us to head for the main doors—the largest and most obvious exit. If we headed the other way, we would have to cross the whole open expanse of the area that I had thought was the chop shop. But there was a small door there beyond the work tables. I tried to weigh odds, but there were too many unknowns.

A voice hissed at me. "Down here." Aimee's head was poking out from under a long flatbed truck. I threw myself on the ground and rolled under with her. She ducked back into the darkness and I stayed with her.

"I hope you know what comes next," she whispered.

"Shh." Large lumbering legs passed just feet from where we hid. The caveman. He kept going down the line of trucks, only bothering to look underneath when there was a light nearby. He sped through the truly dark splotches. I risked peeking my head out and watched him make the turn at the end of the row. "Come on. We go."

I took her hand so that we wouldn't be separated. We dodged among the trucks, avoiding all of the brightest puddles of light. The big man and the weasel were calling out to each other as they searched the area behind us, reporting to Gino as they cleared a section. They were approaching the main door. We were at the other end of the garage. The old riding rink was in front of us and only a few rays of reflected light ran this deep into the building. I could see the hulks of partially rebuilt trucks in the center of the space, but only as massive shadows of black upon black.

"You holding up?" I asked.

"I'm good," she said.

"Stay close. Not much farther."

Though the space was mostly open, there was plenty of clutter stacked on the dirt floor. We had to edge forward, sliding one foot ahead of the other, but we were making it. More than halfway to the far wall, I caught sight of a flash of light on glass. There were four small panes of glass in the upper half of the door. It was straight in front of us, only another twenty feet or so to go.

That's when the lights came on. One of the gang had finally reached the electrical panel and thrown the switch. But it wasn't the main panel that controlled the long strips of fluorescents, nor the meager low-watt wall lights. The big glaring floods over our head all came on at once. We were standing, lit as clearly as in an operating room, in the middle of an expanse with nowhere to hide. Like cockroaches caught in the middle of the kitchen floor when the light comes on, we did exactly what they do. We scurried for the nearest bit of cover.

A massive engine block hung by chains from an overhead winch and we dashed behind it. A gunshot sounded and a bullet ricocheted off the side. The huge piece of machinery rang like a wounded bell.

Gino had found his gun.

I looked over my shoulder. The door was less than ten feet away. If we stayed where we were, Gino could just walk up and shoot us. We had to take the chance.

"Ready?" I said.

Aimee looked back.

"Suppose it's locked?"

I laughed. "Then we're really screwed."

She didn't find that nearly as funny as I did.

It should have worked. A handgun is notoriously inaccurate beyond ten feet. Even professionals who practice shooting often tend to spray bullets during the heat of a firefight, depending upon noise, ricochets, and quantity of ammunition rather than a well-placed solo shot. It was because of this that police departments had moved away from the five- or six-shot revolver to the larger magazine semiautomatics like the Glock. I had learned all this by watching an old *Law & Order* rerun many years earlier.

I moved first, dashing out in an arc, away from Aimee and what I thought was the safer course of a straight run for the door. I hoped to draw fire away from her. I hit the door shoulder-first, surprised at the lack of resistance. I fell through the opening, rolled up onto my feet, and turned to look for Aimee. She was right behind me, one foot still inside, when another shot sounded. Her face contorted, but she kept on coming.

"Go!" she yelled.

The night was both starless and moonless. The field was almost as dark as the inside of the ice truck. But my eyes adjusted quickly. I couldn't see much, but I knew which way to go. I took her hand again and we ran.

36

We dashed across the road and into the field. At that moment, the choice between taking our chances on being ignored by a herd of bison or dying at the hands of those three stooges was a layup.

"Just keep moving," I said. I would tell her about the local wildlife when we had more leisure.

The ground was rough, rutted and cracked, and surprisingly dry for that early in the season. The grass was uneven, cropped by the herd to a few inches in places, tall and already tasseled in others. Aimee was tiring, I could feel it. I needed a good-sized patch of long grass. We would be invisible on such a night.

A floodlight came on over the door to the building, but we were well outside its reach. It wouldn't help our pursuers at all, reducing their night vision rather than revealing their prey, but the dim light that far out in the field was just enough to navigate by.

The grass rose almost to my waist. That was the spot. I ran another two steps and dropped, pulling Aimee down with me. We lay facing back the way we'd come and parted the grass directly in front of us.

"Not a sound," I whispered. "We'll wait here and see what they do."

The floodlight placed our pursuers on a stage. Gino came out the door first, then turned to call to the others. They stepped out through the doorway a minute later. The three men conferred. Then they walked to the edge of the pool of light, taking turns looking in various directions, as though they were afraid to step off into the darkness. The big man was holding a blood-soaked rag to the back of his head. I hoped he was in a lot of pain.

Aimee shook me and held a finger over her mouth in the universally recognized signal for silence. I had been chuckling softly and hadn't even noticed until she told me to stop. She was breathing heavily, almost panting, but doing her best to stifle any sound.

"Are you all right?" I whispered.

She shook her head.

"What?" I asked.

"I think I'm in shock," she said.

I could barely hear her. I leaned in closer.

"In shock?" I said, seeking clarity. Shock from what?

"I'm shot." She reached around and touched her back. "And I'm bleeding." She showed me her hand. In the dim, grainy light, the blood on her fingers looked black—but it looked like blood.

My plan collapsed. I had thought that if we could make the fence and get to the road, we'd be able to walk to the highway in less than an hour. The L.I.E. was patrolled enough that a cop would find us in minutes once we got there. And as the road to the highway was straight as the path of a bullet and bordered by dense woods, we would have plenty of warning if a vehicle came after us, and plenty of places to hide along the route. Now I needed to get Aimee to help immediately. I needed a vehicle and a way of exiting the gate. Chances of coming upon either in short order looked to be impossible. If she didn't die of shock, she would simply fade away with loss of blood. Without help, she would deteriorate quickly.

I checked on Gino. He and the others were still gathered under the light. He had pulled out a cell phone and was engaged in what I guessed was an intense and unpleasant conversation. Reporting to the front office on his failure to murder us.

They were blocking our other avenue of escape. Riskier, but faster, and more direct. The building was filled with vehicles, some big enough to breach the gate if I could get enough momentum going on that dirt drive. There were at least two or three big Mack trucks that would turn those gates into kindling and scrap metal. I didn't know much about driving a Mack truck, but I thought once I got it rolling, matters would pretty much take care of themselves.

"What are you thinking?" Aimee whispered.

"I think I heard something." We were both still and silent. There it was again.

The sound was a deep cough. Real terror returned. Less than ten feet from us, a bull bison rolled up onto its feet and coughed a third time. I looked at Aimee to warn her and saw that she had already taken in the new threat. Her eyes were wide and losing focus. Terror and loss of blood had turned her face pasty white.

"I meant to tell you," I whispered.

I reviewed what I knew about American bison. There were a few that lived at the Bronx Zoo. The Kid found them fascinating. I had read the guidebook to him a half-dozen times. Unfortunately, there had been no succinct advice on how to survive an encounter in the middle of the night while on the animal's home turf. I did know that the bulls kept away from the herd except during mating times. The cows were all either about to calve or were already being followed by little ones. So it probably wasn't mating season. A relief, as I did not want to find that I was between a bull buffalo and the object of his affection.

We could be surrounded by resting buffalo or steps away from the only one for a quarter mile. They didn't sleep much, I remembered, so if the beast had just awoken there was little hope of its nodding out again anytime soon.

Somewhere behind us, another twenty yards or so into the dark, there was the electric fence. If we could get past it, the way I had the first time I had been caught out there, we would be safe. Safe from this horned battering ram on four legs. It began grazing. It looked peaceful, almost docile, but I had seen the transformation once before.

I gestured *Follow me* and rose to a low squat. Aimee tried the same and staggered and fell. This time, she whimpered when she went down. Shock was wearing off and soon she would be feeling the pain. I had to get her to move.

The bull coughed again. I risked a look in its direction. It had stopped grazing and was watching us. Trying to determine whether we were a threat or not. Bison had few predators in the wild—wolves and bears mostly—but humans made the list. I reached down and helped Aimee to her feet. I moved very slowly. The beast blinked but otherwise did not move.

"Can you walk?" I said, speaking as quietly as I could.

"Yes," she said without much conviction.

Looking back toward the light was disconcerting. Gino and the two thugs were easy to see. The bison was now framed in light, a dark silhouette. Yet when I turned and looked ahead toward the fence—and the electrified wire—I could only see for a few feet. I felt that they must be able to see us since we could see them so clearly. But they couldn't. My senses told me one thing, but the brain knew better.

"I'm going to carry you," I said. I stood in front of her and draped her arms over my shoulders. I bent and took her weight on my back, then rose and lifted her off the ground. I didn't yet have a plan, but escape seemed to be our best chance to survive.

I stumbled through the grass. Aimee wasn't heavy, but she wasn't able to help me, either. I could not imagine how I was going to get her over the fence, traverse the forest, and do it all in time to save her life. So I stopped thinking about it and just kept moving. Her feet dragged behind me. I stopped and hitched her higher and she gasped in sudden pain.

"Hang in there," I said. "Not much farther." I had no idea how far it was to safety, but I would not admit it to her or to myself.

A large dark shadow passed a few yards ahead of me. It took me long seconds to realize that it was another bison. Another solitary bull. It was peacefully grazing and ignored us. I paused to let it go by.

But the animal stopped suddenly and raised its head, sniffing the air. A breath of wind had carried our scent to it. I froze. The beast swung its head around—it was spooked. It lowered its head toward me and began a series of short hops, meant to frighten me into retreat. It frightened me, but there wasn't much I could do about retreating with Aimee on my back. I stepped sideways, and it huffed loudly and continued its dance. The sound of its distress and aggression had become impossibly loud in the otherwise silent field.

I risked a look back over my shoulder. Gino was arguing with one of the men and pointing in our general direction. The situation was easy enough to read. I was afraid to move, but more afraid to stand still. I had no choice; I had to keep moving. I headed for the fence again, slowly and steadily. No sudden movements. No threatening actions.

The blond-wood posts, eight or ten feet tall, began to appear, like ghostly signposts, ahead and slightly to my right. I had been walking in a tangent, approaching the fence, but not by the most direct route. I made the adjustment.

A moment later, I pulled up and stopped. There was another bison curled on the ground directly in front of me. Another few steps and I would have stepped on it. I looked back. The agitated male wasn't following, but he hadn't given up. He was watching and occasionally stamping or coughing a warning. But around him, two other shapes appeared. I had carried Aimee right through the group of bachelor males. Five of them were all around us. The reason for Gino's reluctance to follow us out into the dark field was now apparent. We were surrounded by painful death. Stealth and subtlety weren't going to help us. I hitched Aimee higher again and moved quickly around the sleeping bull, taking long strides.

The fence was suddenly much closer and I stopped again. Somewhere in front of me was a single thick strand of electrified wire, with enough of a charge to stun a bull bison. Enough to kill a stumbling human and the woman on his back. I closed my eyes and counted to ten. When I reopened them, my night vision was stronger. I inched along. My peripheral vision caught the faint glint first. We were there.

"I'm going to put you down and pull you underneath the fence. Just stay low and you'll be fine."

She murmured something. I couldn't understand her words, but I didn't need to. She was conscious and capable of following instructions.

I eased her to the ground, not daring to look back, then I slipped under the wire and reached back for her hands. Though I tried to be gentle, the pressure on her wound must have been dreadful. She gasped once, but held back any further sound as I pulled her across the intervening space. And then I had her. We were both between the tall outer fence and the electrified wire. I stopped and took stock of our situation. And came near to despair.

We were safe from attack by bison, but we were no closer to escape. Aimee couldn't climb the outer fence, and I couldn't carry her over. She was still bleeding and it was too dark for me to determine how serious her wound might be. I looked back. The three men had disappeared. They weren't in the field. I wasn't reassured. I knew they hadn't given up.

"We're going to be okay now," I said. Maybe she believed me, though to my ears I did not sound at all convincing. "Stay here. I've got to reconnoiter."

I rose up and, running in a bent crouch, made my way along the fence, looking for any break, any possible spot where we could get through without having to climb over. It was futile. The fencing was in excellent shape.

The bison didn't like my movements. They couldn't easily see me; I was nothing but a dark shadow flitting along on the far side of the wire. But they could smell both me and the scent of fresh blood in the damp air. They all began to stamp and huff. They sounded like a cross between a chorus of bullfrogs and Roger in the morning. From across the fields, the herd of females and calves picked up the agitation of the young bulls and began to reply with plaintive lowing. Then there was the sound of the alpha male, somewhere in the same direction, roaring. It wasn't anything like a lion's roar really, but it communicated all the same information. The boss was there and in charge.

37

From the garage came the sound of the little door screeching open. The bison all turned their heads to look.

The three men walked out into the light. Even from that distance, I could see that they were all holding handguns. Somewhere in the building, there must have been a cache. Gino probably knew what he was doing with a gun and the weasel looked at least minimally competent. But the Missing Link stuck a long-barreled silver revolver down the front of his pants. I hoped that he would trip and put a hole through his privates.

They walked toward the field and split up. Gino and the weasel came straight on, but moved very slowly. Cautiously. I could tell by their body language that they were already frightened. The big guy jogged far around to the left before coming down toward me—flanking me. He was surprisingly fast for his size.

From the driveway came the sound of a gunshot. I looked and found enough spilled light from the barn to see Gino, weapon in hand, firing into the air. He shot three times and began walking through the grass toward the young male bison. He had, no doubt, deduced that their commotion was the result of our presence. And he was coming to finish us.

If the gunfire was meant to frighten off the bison, it didn't work. Maybe it was merely meant to distract them from the approach of the other shooter. But the bison were so domesticated that they did not register the sound as dangerous. Instead they continued to focus on me. They ran, stamping and grunting, along the electric-fence line, both angered and fearful. I threw up my hands and shouted hoarsely and they scattered like a flock of pigeons, only to immediately form into a compact group and return. They were still ignoring Gino, who had advanced to less than a football field away. He was close enough to be in silhouette; I could see his outline clearly, but not his features. Soon—another minute or two—and he might see me, the distant light reflecting off of my face or white shirt. I panicked. With no plan other than retreat, I turned and ran back toward where I had left Aimee.

I realized immediately that Gino was driving me, herding me. The shooter coming down from the other side would complete a pincer and they would have us both.

Gino fired again. This time, however, he was close enough to the animals that they reacted. With the unison of a flock of starlings, they turned and ran. They didn't go far—twenty yards or so—before wheeling and looking back. The weasel came forward, and for a moment stood facing off against the herd. Neither side was willing to make another move until they had fully assessed all the dangers.

Gino still couldn't see me, but the big man was now coming up along the fence, deep in darkness. His eyes would have adjusted and he would see me any second. He pulled the weapon out from his pants.

I bolted. He saw me and chased after. We ran parallel along the fence. I didn't know whether he could see it or not, but we were both dangerously close to zapping ourselves into eternity.

He fired. It made a lot of noise. I wasn't a great target, but if he was simply trying to scare me so much that my legs turned to Jell-O, it came close to instant success. I staggered, fell, picked myself up, and ran for the outer fence. I leapt up and hit the fence two feet off the ground, grabbing hold with my fingers and pulling myself higher.

Another shot rang out and this time I heard the bullet whistle by, close enough that I believed that I could smell it. And then I heard the roar of the bull again. Much closer. I risked a look over my shoulder and saw, once more only in silhouette, a bison. A behemoth of a bison. Like some truant from the last ice age, snorting, roaring, and stamping the ground. He had arrived to defend his herd.

The three shooters saw it, too. Gino and the weasel turned and ran, but the guy who had just been chasing me was penned between the bull and the fence. It was only thirty yards away. A heartbeat or two once it began to move. Courage or stupidity? He faced it, aimed carefully, and began to fire, smoothly and regularly, giving himself time to pull the weapon back from the recoil and take aim again. Four more shots. Then he calmly opened the cylinder and began taking bullets out of his pocket and carefully inserting them.

The bull wasn't polite about it. It didn't wait for the man to fully reload. With a long hop, it began its charge.

I don't know if any of the bullets hit their target, but if they did, they didn't slow the bull down. It covered the intervening ground in seconds. When the younger bulls had chased me the week before, the ground had seemed to thunder and reverberate, but this attack was so quick, over thick grass, that it was almost silent. The man looked up from the gun and his calm evaporated. When the animal was only yards away, he turned to the side and ran.

He ran the wrong way.

He hit the electric fence belly-first. The lightning bolt that arced from the fence sounded like the demise of Gog and Magog. It boomed, hissed, and sizzled. The combined scents of burnt flesh and ozone filled the air. The man remained upright, jerking in horrifying spasms for what seemed like minutes but must only have been for a second or two. The gun dropped from his hand and he fell, slumped over the sagging wire.

The fence was designed to stun a buffalo, which was then supposed to immediately recoil. It was not made for prolonged contact. One of the big lights over the barn burst, flinging a fireworks of sparks over the yard. Back inside the building, the circuit breaker overloaded, tripping off not only the fence but the main electric as well. The other light over the barn door went dark, the fence released the dead man, and he finally sank to the ground.

38

All the buffalo, the big bull included, moved far back from the fence. They recognized the crackle and sparks and respected them—and the smell of scorched flesh had them spooked. The bull kept his distance and made sure the more curious of the younger males kept theirs, too. One in particular retreated far down the field.

I jumped from the fence and ran to where I had left Aimee. Without the distant glow from the barn light, the night was pitch-dark again and it took me a few minutes to find her. I bumped into the dead electric fence more than once in the process, scaring myself witless each time.

Aimee was in trouble. Her breathing had become shallow, her pulse was faint, and her skin was cold. Shock was well under way. I had to get her to a hospital. There were plenty of vehicles in the barn and only two men left. The odds were atrocious, but there was no alternative. Somehow, I needed to outwit or overpower them or she would die.

The bison had all lost interest and moved off a good distance, swallowed by the night again. The big bull was lowing and roaring—he may have been hit by a bullet—but he was on his feet and moving. His adversary was never going to move again.

I pulled Aimee under the fence and once more hitched her up onto my back. I started back across the field. She felt heavier.

"Leave me," she moaned close to my ear.

I could not leave her. The ghost of another woman was there with her. And if I could save this woman, then maybe the ghost would finally let me be.

"We're leaving here together," I whispered to her. "Just do me a favor and keep breathing."

She moaned again.

The long building was a black wall against the black sky, an illusory goal, but the shadow loomed larger as I approached it. I was heading in the right direction at least.

I carried her across the rutted dirt drive. We were almost at the barn when the light came back on, an alarm like an old-time firehouse bell went off, and the wall-sized rolling steel door began to rise with a rumbling clatter.

Aimee whimpered in my ear at the sudden noise and explosion of light. But she was still alive. I took her to the side of the barn and laid her down in the shadows.

"I need to find us a way out of here. I'll be back for you. No matter what."

She didn't reply. In the dim light, I could see her face again. She was beyond pain. She needed a hospital and soon.

A big diesel engine ground into life, and a moment later twin high beams preceded a Mack tractor truck out of the door and into the yard. The lights swept over the field and caught the group of young male buffalo grazing peacefully again. They looked up disinterestedly and went back to their midnight snacking. Nothing else moved.

A second truck started up. The lights came on. I saw what they were doing. They would have a fleet of large trucks, lights covering the field. Then they could each take a truck and hunt us down—if we were still out there. As it was, a stray flash of light as a truck made the turn could easily frame us on the wall and it would be over. I needed to move.

The second truck—another big tractor cab—pulled out and lined up parallel to the first, their lights covering a swath forty yards wide over the field.

The driver of the first truck jumped down from the cab and strode back into the building, leaving the truck running, lights on. It was Gino. He carried the gun by his side. I pressed my back up against the wall and waited for him to pass inside. He didn't see me.

I was frozen with indecision. The risk of trying to take one of the trucks while one of those two was there and keeping watch was too great. Doing it with Aimee slung over my shoulder was impossible. But the risk of staying put was almost as great. I huddled there while a third truck rolled out and lit up the field. Then it was the weasel's turn to bring out another truck. The two men continued to alternate until six trucks were lined up, all idling loudly, high beams slicing the darkness into narrow strips of gray bordering swaths of brilliant white. Nothing more happened for at least another ten minutes. The two men sat in the bookend trucks, scanning the field for any sign of us— or the caveman, though by then they must have realized that it was his demise that had caused the electrical blackout. The lights from the line of trucks revealed highlights from the ground between them and the fence, but little detail. If we had still been hiding out there, we could have stayed low and been invisible.

Gino must have realized that the plan wasn't working. He jumped down from the cab of the truck and jogged to the other end of the line. He and the weasel conferred for a few minutes, with gestures that indicated their plans. Gino returned to the Mack, gunned the engine, and slipped it into gear. The two trucks—the big Mack with Gino on board and a honey wagon with the logo YOU DUMP IT, WE PUMP IT spelled out in brown—pulled out onto the grass, plowing it down as they ground slowly toward the fence. About halfway there, they turned, allowing the lights to sweep like large, and deadly, spotlights. But there was nothing to see but grass and the tall fence. They continued.

Eventually, on one of those turns, the lights would pass over us hiding against the wall and we'd be discovered. The odds were strongly against us no matter what I did, but they were never going to get any better.

"Aimee? Come on. We're going to get out of here now." I tried to get her arms over my shoulders again, but she was limp. There was nothing for it but to lift her in my arms and carry her clutched to my chest. She would not weigh any less that way, but she would be marginally easier to hoist and keep in position. I squatted beside her, tucked my hands underneath her, and with an explosive jerk, I rose up. Her head flopped back and her arms and legs dangled. She had been reduced to an awkward burden. I held her to my chest and scurried toward the nearest truck.

It was another big semi cab. I didn't know how to drive one, but I didn't have much choice. Aimee was already beginning to slip out of my grasp. I staggered to the opposite door, propped her on the running board, and climbed up. The engine was idling and the cab unlocked. I swung the door wide, jumped down, and lifted Aimee into the passenger seat. I sat her up and strapped her in.

"We're almost there," I said. "How are you holding up?"

She didn't answer. She might not have heard me. Pain and loss of blood were ganging up on her senses. Her body and brain were sealing off all nonessential systems. There wasn't much time.

Lights swept over me as one of the two big trucks out in the field made a turn for another pass. I froze, hoping that I had not been seen. Immediately, I realized that there was no point. If I'd been spotted, I needed to escape soonest, and if by some fluke they hadn't seen me, it was still time to break out. I slammed the door behind me, climbed over Aimee, and half fell into the driver's seat.

There was a big red button labeled BRAKE. I pushed it. Nothing happened. I pushed it hard and it sank. The truck rolled a few inches. There was a clutch and a tall gearshift. How hard could it be? I held down the clutch, revved the engine slightly, shoved the shifter into the spot where first gear was on every manual transmission I had ever seen, and let out the clutch. The truck began to move—in reverse. I was headed directly for the barn, going fifteen miles an hour—backward.

I pulled the truck out of gear, and shifted into where third ought to be. The engine growled at me and the transmission bucked unhappily. But it didn't stall. I pressed down on the gas, spun the wheel, and headed for the main gate.

"No comments on my driving, okay?" Maybe she could hear me.

The bright high beams swung by again, washing the cabin with blue-white light. They were on to me. I shifted up two gears and the truck bucked again before accelerating like a muscle car. With no load or trailer, the 400 horsepower and 1,300 pounds feet of torque on the average big diesel goes straight to acceleration. I had to race through the gears to keep up with the roaring engine. The gates were a hundred yards ahead and approaching quickly. The tall side mirror showed both trucks bouncing across the field after me. They had already been moving when I started and were traveling faster, so they appeared to be closing in. I triangulated our relative positions. The septic tanker had a slight chance of beating me to the gates—I had to assume that it had been stored empty. I raced up the gears and kept the pedal to the floor. The engine howled every time I pushed my foot down on the clutch. It was going to be close.

The Mack cab bounced onto the drive behind me, but now my head start was beginning to pay off. I looked again and saw that I was even pulling away.

The tanker was coming in at an angle on my left. It hit a deep rut just before the driveway and bounced hard and high. For a split second, the weasel let up. It wasn't much, but it was enough. I kept the accelerator floored and squeezed through in front of him. The double gates were right there.

"Hold on. This is the tricky part," I said. Aimee didn't answer.

I hit the first gate while still shifting and the wheel was almost wrenched out of my hand. I let go of the shift and held on to the wheel. Planks, two-by-fours, hardware, and whipping strands of barbed wire flew in all directions. But I was gone before it all registered. The outer gate was sturdier, but that just meant it was louder when it cracked and exploded as I came through.

I pulled the wheel hard to the left and bounced onto the asphalt. The truck felt like it was ready to roll over, but it surprised me. It held the road and barreled on. The next turn was coming up fast. A left would take me out toward the highway and the hope of finding help and a hospital. Straight would lead me deeper into the desolation of the Pine Barrens. If they caught me there, I would have no chance. But if I could get to the highway, I could soon have every highway patrolman in Suffolk County out to stop me. And that would be enough to turn the tables. I turned left.

The truck gave that same vertiginous pull as if it wanted to fall over on its side. I let the truck take the turn wider, thumping off the pavement on the far side and plowing briefly through the underbrush. Short pine trees and scrub oaks snapped at the window on the passenger side, while others sank beneath the tall chrome grille.

The first of my pursuers took the turn. Gino in the Mack. Like the vehicle I was driving, it had no trailer. It was all about horsepower and torque. But he was the better driver. He seemed to have some idea of what the hell he was doing. I did not. He downshifted into the turn and took it slower, but much steadier, keeping it under control. I was merely hanging on, hoping that my lack of knowledge wasn't going to get me killed.

I aimed for the road and the truck responded, bouncing back onto the tarmac again. I tasted blood and found that I had just bitten my tongue. But I was ahead of the other two trucks, and while they were in pursuit and, I was sure, intent on killing me, they were following me to where I wanted them to go.

The transmission seemed to have an as yet inexhaustible number of gears. I was in sixth and the engine was howling for another change. I pulled the stick back and the gears ground and the truck bucked. I shoved it into neutral and tried again, double-clutching this time. Much smoother. I was barreling along at seventy through the dark woods. A faint glow up ahead signaled civilization and safety.

That's when the truck behind me struck. Gino came racing up and hit the rear end of the tractor. It was barely a tap, but the effect was terrifying. The truck began to yaw and I felt as if all control had disappeared. I remembered hitting black ice in upstate New York when I was first learning to drive in college. I steered into the skid and let up on the accelerator. The wheels grabbed and I pulled the truck back into line just before it rolled off into the woods again.

I knew what he had done. An asymmetrical push from behind doesn't need to be forceful to be effective when a vehicle is traveling at fifty miles an hour or more. A gentle nudge can be deadly. I needed to keep directly in front of the truck behind me, so that if he tried it again, I would be able to take the blow solidly in the center. I moved the truck onto the crown of the road and tried not to think about what would happen if some poor citizen wanted to come down from the other direction.

There were now two sets of headlights behind me; the honey wagon had finally achieved some momentum and was coming up strong. The woods whipped by. I risked another quick look at Aimee, but no miracle had happened. Her head was hanging to one side, her eyes staring at the dashboard. I thought I should feel something, but my adrenaline kept me from going there. I would pay for it later.

The highway was just ahead. I hit the brakes and double-clutched down two gears. The Mack raced up behind me on the left and gave another nudge. The tanker was just over my right shoulder. I felt the truck begin to slide and I downshifted again. The wheels grabbed, but there wasn't time—or room—to make the turn onto the on-ramp. The tanker's lights filled the right-side mirror. I wasn't so much driving as being driven.

The Mack was coming up again for another push and I swerved to the right, just before passing under the L.I.E. The tanker truck veered away. The weasel overcompensated. He must have panicked. He didn't have time to register what he'd done. The truck hit the concrete overpass at close to seventy miles an hour and the lights in my mirror went out. The sound of the crash was magnified in the short tunnel, but I wasn't around long enough to absorb it. I felt no shock, no horror, just relief that I was now being pursued by only one crazy killer rather than two. I immediately flipped back to the task at hand.

The next on-ramp was also a right turn and I was on top of it.

There was no time to downshift again. I mashed the brakes, pulled the wheel over, and hoped that the tires would continue to hold the road. They did. Barely.

The curve was tight, sloped for sedans and station wagons moving at thirty or forty, not for a giant diesel cab tearing through at fifty. I leaned into the turn, as though my puny one hundred and eighty pounds might make a difference. Somehow the truck held the road and I was on the L.I.E. and running back up through the gears.

There was no traffic, though there was a steady stream heading the other way. They would be of no help to me. A green sign flashed by announcing the exits for Riverhead. No! I was traveling east, not west. Farther from the city and what I thought of as safety. Was there a hospital in Riverhead? I didn't know. It didn't matter. There would be other cars up ahead. Someone on the road would have a cell phone and be only too happy to report two semis playing bumper cars on the highway in the middle of the night.

Gino had somehow made the turn back at the on-ramp and was still behind me. I kept to the left-hand lane. The trees along the edge of the road were taller and more substantial than they'd been closer to the farm. If I ran off the road into them, I doubted that I would survive. But the wide grassy dip that bordered the oncoming lanes looked like it might slow the truck rather than mangle it.

I hit the horn and turned on the brights as I came up on a black BMW 3-series coasting along all alone in the passing lane. He pulled over, but not before tapping his brakes twice just to demonstrate his displeasure. I didn't bother to hit mine, I just kept on coming until he moved to the side.

The Mack was riding right down the dotted white line, blocking both lanes. He also hit his horn and brights. The BMW had nowhere to hide. His only escape was to outrun us. He stepped on it and went from seventy to over a hundred and left the two of us barreling along alone. But a mile down the road, just before the crest of the next rise, the brake lights on the Beemer went on and the car drove off onto the verge. We whipped by him, and as our headlights swept over him, the driver gave us a two-handed, middle-finger salute.

I looked over at Aimee and our eyes met for just a moment. She had nothing left and it showed. She was giving up. I needed to end this soon and get her help or it would be too late.

I watched the speedometer creep up into the low eighties, and just as I crossed the slight peak, I swung over so that I was straddling the white line as well. The swift glint of light reflected off glass caught my eye as we raced past a thick copse of vine-laden fir trees. Finally. Hiding behind the wood was a Suffolk County police cruiser clocking speeders as they came over the top. Two commercial trucks, thirty miles over the limit, riding the white line. The cop must have thought he had won the lottery. His flashing lights came on before he even hit the road.

One of us wanted to be stopped by a policeman. I was surprised to discover that Gino didn't much care. I took my foot off the accelerator and immediately slowed by ten miles an hour. The Mack was on top of me, immediately coming up on my left side. But this time he wasn't content to simply run me off the road.

The window next to me exploded and the windshield began to spiderweb around a hole the size of my thumb. I registered the sound of the gunshot long after the evidence of its passing. There was a second crack followed by the whine of a ricochet off the back of the cab. He had failed at getting rid of me earlier; he was going to finish it now. I sped up.

Behind us, the police cruiser had his siren blasting, but he was hanging back fifty yards or so. He must have seen or heard the gun. If I could just stay alive for another quarter of an hour, there were sure to be other police reinforcements gathering ahead.

Gino must have figured out the same thing at about that time, because there were three more shots in quick succession. I thought at first they must have been wild and desperate as none came close to the cab. Then I realized that he was firing at the tires. An experienced trucker would have no trouble handling a blowout, even at the speed we were moving, but I was no trucker. I was learning as I went along. A slow panic began to build in my chest. The odds of our making it through the next fifteen minutes had just swung to a good bit less than even money. A trader isn't supposed to take those long shots.

A white pickup truck appeared in my headlights. Some hardworking laborer was hugging the right-hand lane and moving at exactly one mile an hour under the limit. Coming home from a bar, I guessed. I swerved around him and he flashed his brights at me in protest. No doubt, my rudeness was quickly forgotten as the other semi flew by, followed a moment later by the cop car, siren screaming. If the drinker was a religious man, he would have been saying a few prayers of thanks at that moment.

Another police cruiser was waiting for us a half mile up the road. He pulled out from the grassy median, lights flashing, and pulled into the center of the highway. I had an instant in which to decide whether it was okay to hit him, attempt to get around, or stand on the brakes, risking another series of shots from behind.

I stood on the brakes.

The truck began to fishtail. I wasn't going to have to worry about getting shot. No one could have hit that target, especially from the helm of a speeding semi. The wheel felt like there was nothing attached to it. I tried steering into the skid, but the truck immediately began to yaw in the other direction. Aimee flopped forward, the seat belt keeping her semierect. That was when the Mack clipped my right rear tire.

There was a pop, followed immediately by a second. It sounded harmless enough. But the yawing immediately increased. I reached over and pulled up on the red brake handle. The truck began to hop and buck like a wild horse, throwing me sideways, where I landed on top of Aimee. I had strapped her in, but neglected my own seat belt. The truck leaned to the right and I tumbled down onto the floor at her feet, cracking both my nose and the back of my head in quick succession. I may have blacked out, but if I did, it was only for a split second. The horror hadn't let up, but at least I didn't have to watch it happen.

Being crammed into that space saved my life. The truck ran off the highway on the right, toward the tree line. But before it hit, the truck lurched and rolled onto its side, plowing a wide swath through new grass, budding wildflowers, and saplings before coming to a rest twenty feet off the road.

My feet were above me. The ground was somewhere behind me, just beyond the passenger door. Aimee, hanging from her seat belt, loomed down over me, her head twisted at a sharp angle from her shoulders. Her neck was broken. I could not imagine why mine wasn't.

I checked my fingers and toes for feeling, just to be sure. I hurt everywhere, but I could scrunch my toes and wiggle my fingers. The fact that I was extremely uncomfortable—all my weight was on the back of my neck—and unable to move were my greatest concerns. That was good. If I was complaining, I was alive.

More sirens and flashing lights. Police. Rescue units. I lay there and waited. Aimee's dead eyes stared down at me, but I couldn't look back.

PART II

FOUR MONTHS LATER

The black birds had gone quiet again. Devils. Eyes that could see movement from miles away. The coyote depended upon scent, and while he could smell carrion at a great distance, the damn crows always had the advantage.

Coyote waited. He was hungry, but he could wait. He was good at waiting. The crows began to screech again. They were smart. They talked together, sharing greetings, warnings, and information about food, predators, weather. Coyote had learned to watch the crows for first signs of danger. Today they were talking about food, but they had not feasted yet. Something had them unsettled. Coyote crept to the top of the ridge far above the arroyo.

Men had been there—truck smells, a crushed cigarette—but were gone. Nothing since. The smell was strong. Coyote almost turned and ran. Only the sick and desperate went near humans, usually to their deep regret. But mixed with the man smell was the smell of decay. Coyote waited and sifted the other scents on the wind.

The crows rose up in a fluttering black cloud, squawking shrilly in anger and frustration. But not fear. Coyote moved to the lip of the dry riverbed and looked over the edge. Twenty feet below lay a naked man, spread-eagle on the bare ground. His arms and legs were staked down with loops of bent metal. A pool of dried blood had soaked into the sand around him. His face and body were red and blistered from the sun. He had lain there for more than a day. Deep wounds and bruises covered his torso. His manhood had been cut away and stuffed into his mouth. He should have been dead, but he was not.

The man's head moved. That was what had set the crows aflight. His body was already beginning to rot, yet he was still alive. But not for much longer. Coyote would wait. He was good at waiting.

39

Aimee's dead eyes were still staring down at me. I awoke with that image two or three times a week. There was no point in trying to get back to sleep. Aimee would be there waiting for me. I rolled out of bed, hit the bathroom, and pulled on jeans and a T-shirt. I had calls to make.

Just before sunrise was best. New Yorkers rise early—even pregnant physical therapists—and in order to catch Skeli before her workday started, I called soon after four, Tucson time. There were stars at that hour. And planets. Venus, Mars, and Jupiter were all up and easily identifiable, and the star guide app I used informed me that Neptune was at its most prominent point of the year. I also learned, after much frustration, that I would need a telescope to see it.

Skeli and I met each morning in the online chat room designed by Mr. Hannay, who now went by the name of Manny Balestrero. The security for our meeting place was, according to Manny, "some of my finest work." It needed to be. There had been a second attempt on my life even before the emergency room sent me home that night. Hospital security had detained a young man in a dark windbreaker who had been asking "what room" I had been assigned. When the Suffolk County Police took a look, they immediately arrested him for criminal trespass and possession of a handgun without a proper permit. Special Agent Brady got the wheels rolling, and by noon the next day, the Kid and I were in WITSEC and on our way to the Grand Canyon State.

The Kid and I were in the program until Wallace Ashton Blackmore closed his investigation or brought me back to testify. Depending on the results of a future court proceeding, we might one day return to our old lives, or live out our days hiding in the Great American Desert.

Blackmore was the gatekeeper and his prime motivation was media attention. He had garnered plenty of that by arresting Virgil—though he was released the next morning without being charged—and he would earn much more when he put the final pieces of a racketeering case together. But if some other case came up that would result in national attention, he might easily chase off in another direction.

Gino was going to do serious time. The only question was where he was going to do it. Ballistics had matched the bullets from the Barstow crime scene and the single bullet in Aimee's back to the gun he had with him when his truck went into the trees. Nassau County wanted him for the Barstow shootout and Suffolk County wanted to indict him for Aimee's murder. But Blackmore wanted to try him in federal court as part of the racketeering case he was trying to build. So the delay worked for the U.S. Attorney as well as for the defendant. The Suffolk County DA knew it was a layup for his team, but was content to wait and spend the rest of the summer on the beach at Davis Park. The only losers were the Kid and me. Stuck in limbo—hiding out in the desert. Waiting to find out whether I was to risk my life and testify or abandon any hope of ever returning to our past life. Every delay was both a relief and a stake in my heart.

The problem for all the prosecutors involved—county and federal—was what to do with Joseph Scott. Everyone knew he was involved—no one doubted my story—but the evidence to convict wasn't there—yet. The boiler-room pump-and-dump operation in New Jersey had been rolled up, but Scott's connection was tenuous. Worst case, he'd get a slap on the wrist for the securities parking. The most serious charges—ordering the hits and the kidnapping—were going to be a hard sell because none of the thugs were talking. I could place him at the scene, but nothing more substantial.

Blackmore wasn't giving up. He was one of the most underhanded, self-promoting U.S. Attorneys Larry had ever seen—and that included some truly infamous ones—but he was tenacious and a true believer that behind every coincidence there lurked a conspiracy. He held the threat of my testimony over Scott's head as though it were a weapon of mass destruction. I didn't know whether Scott or his lawyer believed I was a real threat or not, but I wasn't willing to bet my life on it.

"What news, my love?" Skeli greeted me. Manny had set up the program so we could see each other as well as hear. She looked like heaven.

"I miss you."

"That's news?"

"Nothing changes here. What do you hear?"

"Not a lot," she said. "Your father is now down twelve pounds and very proud of himself. They stopped by the office late yesterday." My father and his new wife had recently returned from a six-month around-the-world honeymoon cruise. Pops had put on twenty pounds. Estrella hadn't gained an ounce. I had not spoken to either of them since the wedding. "What else? Nothing, really. I've got a checkup appointment this Friday and your daughter has been very active. If this is any sign of things to come, she's going to be a soccer player. What's up? How's the Kid?"

"Kid is unchanged. He doesn't hate it here, he just hates that it's not there, if you know what I mean. I suppose we are identical in that regard. I handle it better, that's all." And we both missed Heather. Most days, we were each other's only company—except for the two live-in bodyguards. "I talked to Larry." I spoke to Larry almost as often as I did to Skeli. "Nothing new. Blackmore drags his heels. The case goes nowhere. Same old, same old." I hated to hear myself sound so discouraged—and discouraging. "Let me see. There's a new bodyguard coming today." Virgil was paying for the guards. Occasionally, one or the other would rotate out.

"Who's leaving?"

"The good one."

"Josh?"

Josh was ex-army, having served a full twenty years. He had a wife and two kids in Baltimore and had never taken to Tucson. He hated the heat, the food, the sports teams, and the fact that, as a six-foot-five, two-hundred-and-eighty-pound black man, he stood out in a town that was almost one-half white and one-half Latino. There were more Native Americans around than brothers. He and the Kid got along well, and we would miss him.

He would be leaving me with Hal. Hal was a sad man. A loner. Unmarried and, at forty-four, he was reaching the effective end of his current career, with no plan for the future. He was alert and, I assumed, competent at his job, but he had a black hole where his personality should have been. He had been with us for a month, and I could not remember a single sentence of conversation with him that revealed any emotion, sense of humor, likes or dislikes, thoughts, dreams, hopes or regrets. The man was a cipher.

"Josh wants to take some time at home for a bit. Who knows, he might be back." That last bit stood as my attempt to look more on the bright side. I gave up trying and just let myself feast on looking at Skeli. "You look lovely. Did you have your hair done?"

She was just out of the shower and still had a white fluffy towel wrapped around her head. "Hah! I'm thinking of cutting it all off. Just until she's done breast-feeding. Dawn tells me that babies get distracted by hair and don't feed well, so they suck in a lot of air and get colicky later." She had met Dawn in a parenting class. Dawn was also a first-time mother, and fifteen years younger than Skeli, but she had read every book on the subject. So, while she had an encyclopedic cache of information, much of it was contradictory, outdated, or so speculative and unscientific as to be downright dangerous.

"I think that's only with girl babies," I said. "You put a breast in a man's mouth—at any age—and he will not get distracted, I can pretty much guarantee."

"This is a girl baby, sport. And I don't want you thinking about women's breasts."

"Just yours. I haven't been able to touch you for four months."

"One hundred sixteen days," she said. "Hey, I just got a text." She picked up her cell phone. "Virgil. He says, 'Nine-thirty.' He means you, right? What should I tell him?"

Virgil and I had burner cell phones that we very rarely used to speak to each other. We never called anyone else and, as both phones were purchased with cash, neither could be traced back to us.

"Just say 'Okay' and then delete the whole conversation."

"Will do." She looked deep into my eyes—or where it looked like my eyes were. It was more than a little strange. The cameras were inches above our images so that our eyes never really met. It worked a little better if we sat farther back from the computer, but that tended to allow in too much background and cut the sense of intimacy. No matter what, it was a poor substitute for a hug. "I love you," she said. "Come on home soon. And safe."

"I love you, too. Have a great day."

"Give my love to the Kid, too."

"Always."

She closed out first. The screen went fuzzy with vibrating diagonal stripes the way old tube televisions sometimes acted, or the way messages from outer space always began in black-and-white sci-fi movies.

I checked the time. Too early for Larry. Virgil's call wasn't for another hour and a half. I put on a kettle for tea, filled the coffee machine and set the timer, and went out front to watch the nighttime sky show come to an end.

Twilight begins about an hour and a half before sunrise. In New York, that sentence would have no relevance. It never had for me. During a brief period in my early twenties, that time was bookmarked by the bars all closing at four and the delis and bodegas opening at six. The streets were quiet, except for the late-cruising Town Cars and the first wave of yellow cabs haunting the hotels and hoping for an early fare out to the airport. Commercial garbage trucks and bread trucks made their respective pickups and deliveries at the same restaurants and cafés, which would not open for hours to come.

In the desert, twilight belongs to the birds. The bigger owls were finishing their nighttime forays, and the smaller ones were just coming out to do their hunting. Next came the doves—the mourning and white-winged. A family of quail crossed through the alley behind the house, the mother peeping *Keep up. Keep up. Keep up* to her scurrying chicks.

The kettle whistled and I went back into the kitchen and made a cup of Earl Grey, and toasted a single piece of rye bread on the griddle. I ate it plain—no butter or jam. My sense of taste had somehow diminished. Not an entirely unsurprising event, considering the assaults that my palate had been forced to endure. I understood that spicy food helps you sweat, and that's a way of keeping cool in a hot environment. But everyone in Tucson had air-conditioning. It was impossible to avoid it, even if you were the type who enjoyed seeing the thermometer cross over into the hundred-degree-or-greater zone on a daily basis. So why were there jalapeños on everything from appetizer to dessert?

The most egregious attack had been an accident and entirely my own fault. If I'd been paying attention, it could all have been avoided.

I steered clear of making personal contacts, believing that three grown men living together in a house with a single, very weird child was enough of an oddity without having to draw further attention to myself by refusing to discuss anything about my past—or my son's—with neighbors, storekeepers, or service industry employees. But I had made one exception—taking the Kid to the local library and letting the adult-section librarian help him research car books.

Ms. Claire Wood was my age, a widow for the last eight years, with a son just starting on Wall Street, and not much else to tie her to southern Arizona but the fact that she loved it there. All this she told me in the first five minutes after the Kid got settled in the reading room. She was obviously lonely, quietly attractive, and had made immediate note of my naked ring finger. I let my guard down—more because I felt a bit sorry for her than because I had any real plan—and accepted her invitation to attend an art opening—"Just some wine and cheese and a few of the local artists"—later that week.

I showed up in jeans and a white button-down shirt, as square and unremarkable as I could make myself, and already regretting venturing out. Someone—probably the artists themselves—had sprung for better than the expected wine and there was a table of interesting-looking appetizers, too. I was wearing my computer glasses, both as an accessory to my disguise as the world's most boring man, and because, if I was going to be looking at artwork, I could always fiddle with the glasses when I needed to avoid making a comment. The glasses, though, tended to distort images at a distance, around the periphery of my vision, and items very close up. They were only good for staring at a computer monitor for long periods, which was when I normally used them.

After making my way around the room, I noticed that the artists much preferred painting at sunset than at any other time of day—possibly due to the declining temperature, or possibly due to the approach of cocktail hour. One woman artist had broken with the rest and had included native fauna in her compositions. She concentrated on rabid-looking coyotes, curled rattlesnakes poised to strike, giant tarantulas, and evilly grinning Gila monsters. Even her sole sunset featured a pair of savage javelinas, tusks glinting red in the dying light. The javelinas we had seen at the Desert Museum looked more like smallish feral pigs. Harmless, but not quite Disneyesque. Peccaries. Who could fear an animal called a peccary? But this artist's peccaries looked like the man-eating kind. More Marvel Comics than *Lion King*.

Though I was tempted by the chilled bottles of Mumm Napa sparkling Brut Rose and Jordan Russian River Chardonnay, I stuck with the seltzer from Costco. I played with my glasses, sipped my ersatz cocktail, and successfully circled the room without having to engage in conversation with any of the other guests.

Our host, the widowed librarian, was no longer *quietly* attractive. She had gone all out with a loose caftan that did nothing for either her shape or her complexion. About a hundred tiny bracelets jingled on her forearms and her oversized hoop earrings brushed her shoulders. I imagined that the look she was going for was "artsy," but the wild assortment of colors and shapes in the fabric of her garment upstaged every painting on the walls.

She waved at me from across the room and I feigned nearsightedness and adjusted my glasses. Then I retreated back to the relative safety of the food table, where I failed to engage an elderly man in conversation about baseball and the fortunes of the Diamondbacks while looking over the fare. I avoided the sushi. One of my prime survival strategies is to never eat raw fish more than twenty miles from an ocean.

I noticed that the older man was wearing a hearing aid, which he must have turned off—a defense not unlike my glasses. He saw me looking at him and asked, "Were you talking to me just now?"

"I was," I said. "I was talking about baseball."

"What?"

"Baseball." I did not raise my voice—that would have been futile. I overenunciated so that he could read my lips.

"Stupid game," he said, and turned away.

I took a minuscule bite of a fried pepper. The melted cheese squeezed out, burning both my tongue and the palm of my hand. I needed something cool and soothing. Out of the corner of my eye—I was still wearing the stupid glasses, mind you—I saw a bowl of guacamole. I scooped up a golfball-sized glob using a round rice cracker—idly wondering as I did why there were no chips—and put it in my mouth. It wasn't guacamole. It was wasabi.

My sinuses felt like they had been blasted with a chemical freeze. My eyes teared and my nose ran. It gushed. I couldn't get enough air into my lungs to cough effectively. I took a glass of chardonnay and swallowed all of it in one gulp. I poured another and downed that. It didn't help, but it did draw concerned looks from the art lovers nearby. The third or fourth glass began to have some effect and I was able to make my way out of there soon after. We had since been frequenting a different library.

40

The shower in the guest room shrieked its high-pitched, tortured scream. Too much water pressure being forced through inadequate mid-twentieth-century pipes and fittings. The house needed to be renovated or bulldozed. I could make a good argument for either. Josh was up and beginning his day. The coffee machine clicked on. I took my laptop and a second cup of tea and went back out to the veranda.

The dome of the sky was already turning blue, but the valley was still deep purple. The foothills up behind the house twinkled with a few lights. Early risers in the moneyed class? More likely their household staff getting up to clean the drowned lizards out of the pool.

I opened up the website again and logged in. Larry had left an alert. I clicked on his icon, and a moment later we were virtually face-to-face.

"You look good," he greeted me. "Well rested."

"I can't adjust to the time difference, so I go to bed soon after the Kid. What's the news?"

"Gino's lawyers got him another postponement. Doctors' orders."

Gino was still shuttling back and forth between surgery and rehab for the injuries he got when his truck plowed into the woods. Even without the reports from his medical team, Suffolk County Court would have given him the delay. The wheels of justice turn slower in August than at any other time of the year—except for Christmas week.

"What about Scott?"

"Still on admin leave. The SEC wants his license pulled, but Blackmore has them holding off."

If I had taken the time to look at the bigger picture, rather than getting caught up in the penny stock minutiae, I might have learned something about the young Mr. Scott. Manny had tried to warn me minutes before the abduction—he had found it all quite easily—but even if the message had come through in time, I don't know what I would have done with it. Special Agent Brady filled in some of the holes that Manny had not explored.

Joseph Scott was the fifth son and eighth child, born of the third wife of Frank Scotto, once an active member of the most powerful New England crime family and now a long-retired businessman living in a nursing home in Boca Raton. After his second stint in prison, Frank and his two brothers had broken ties with their Providence associates and moved to the north shore of Long Island, where Frank remained on the FBI's most-investigated-to-no-effect list. Scotto avoided contact with all members of New York's Five Families, though Brady guessed that he was paying tribute to at least one of the Mafia leaders. The three brothers dabbled in various businesses: home-heating-oil delivery; real estate development; hard-money lending; payday loans; restaurant laundry supply; truck and heavy equipment leasing; a beer and soda distributor; commercial carpet sales and installation; cardboard packaging manufacture; and, through their sons, sons-in-law, and a stepson from Frank's second marriage, a chain of cut-rate eyeglass stores; a manufacturer of CPAP machines to treat sleep apnea; a bank; and a structured settlement firm. Dabbling paid well. As Frank had outlived his three wives, avoiding the economic debacle of divorce, he had amassed, according to his FBI watchers, a pile of dough that topped two hundred million. The brothers had not fared quite as well, but each one had left an estate of over ten million dollars. At times, some of their employees had been caught gaming the system in one way or another, and some had served time for it. But nothing had ever stuck to Frank or the brothers, no matter how hard the feds tried. They had maintained files on the family for years, expecting all along that they would someday uncover evidence of extortion, loan-sharking, identity theft, unlicensed gambling, import and distribution of controlled substances, arson- or murder-for-hire, corruption of public officials, truck hijacking, or any of the other traditional organized crime staples. Nada. Not even tax evasion. Eventually, the feds had to grudgingly admit that the family had gone legit.

Young Joseph, his surname cropped at birth at his mother's insistence and with his father's blessing, briefly attended Chaminade High School, but graduated—a year late—from Hargrave Military Academy. The more regimented environment had provided him with enough self-discipline to make it through St. John's and he graduated with a BS in business. Before getting his broker's license and coming to work at Becker Financial, Joe had been a dabbler, fashioning himself after his father, it seemed. But Joe didn't have the knack, or maybe he was in too much of a hurry. Or too busy being young and reckless. At one point, he ran a chain of laundromats and was known for paying his bar bills with sacks of quarters. One by one, the stores closed. He avoided personal bankruptcy with a bailout from the family. His big brother, Frank Jr., had a brokerage account with the C-3 branch at Becker Financial and made a call. Joseph Scott became a banker.

"Why hasn't the little shit been indicted?" I asked. "Can't Blackmore show conspiracy or something?"

"Criminal conspiracy doesn't get Blackmore what he wants. He wants a RICO charge. Racketeering. The penalties are much greater and they include asset forfeiture. If he gets an indictment under RICO, then he can include everything in one trial. RICO is like the Death Star for a federal prosecutor. Scott alone isn't worth the trouble. But if Blackmore can use him to bring down Virgil and his firm, he can land a multibillion-dollar gold mine.

"He has to prove that there is an ongoing enterprise and he needs to make all the links for the grand jury. Blackmore thinks that Virgil's firm qualifies, but it's a long shot. He'd have to back into it by proving that Virgil either abetted the crime or looked the other way. But you tell me he directed you to hand it off to Devane. Compliance.

That's exactly what he's supposed to do. Beating up on Virgil isn't going to work."

"Virgil's still locked out of his own firm." And there was little that I could do about it until my own pressures lightened up. "I'm going to be talking to him in another fifteen minutes."

"Wish him luck from me," Larry said.

41

How are you, Jason? Is there anything you need?"

Despite the offer, Virgil sounded like he was on the ropes. More than a little stressed. Aimee's death still troubled him, and the ongoing investigation was a constant drain on his energy. He was no quitter and would go down fighting, but I didn't want him to go down at all. He had been publicly arrested, but never arraigned, leaving him in a limbo created by Blackmore—neither accused nor acquitted, but still under suspicion. Fearing customer backlash, the board had asked him to stay out of the office until the matter was settled. Forcing Virgil to do nothing qualified as cruel and unusual punishment.

"What's the news from home?" I asked, vying with my nature to be chipper. "And talk about anything other than the Yankees. I think their hitters melt in the heat. Maybe they'll do better in September."

Virgil was not a baseball fan, and having grown up in both New York and New England, his loyalties would have been forever split between rivals. He put up with my banter, but didn't engage.

"The news here is not good. The board met in a special session yesterday. I was not invited. That was galling enough, but the letter they sent me today is worse."

"But they can't do that, can they? Take a vote without the chairman present. Isn't that a violation of something or other?"

"My vote wouldn't have stopped this."

"Tell me."

"The board has always been split between those who support my efforts and those who dislike my presence on principle. They were screwed by my father, appointed by the court, and would be happy to see me leave."

"You've told me."

"I know. Excuse me. I'm meandering. At any rate, two members of the board tried to push through a vote to kick me out and replace me with Nealis. The rest of the board balked. Nealis, to his credit, headed things off. He told them he wouldn't accept unless he knew he had the support of a majority of the shareholders."

"I'm surprised. He doesn't owe you any loyalty. You two don't have a history."

"No, it was a nice gesture. But the board took him up on it. They've drafted a resolution and called for a shareholder vote to be conducted at the annual meeting."

"Okay. That's not until late September. We've got a month and a half to prepare."

"And, they've moved up the meeting to the end of August. We have three weeks."

Virgil and family did not control enough shares to dominate the vote, but they wouldn't need a lot of other supporters to win. The question was how many shares were now being held by whoever had been attempting the hostile takeover and how those shares would be voted. In three weeks, Virgil might lose everything.

42

The Kid didn't like the new guy. He didn't give him much of a chance. Willie arrived in the late morning. Josh was gone by noon. He and the Kid sniffed hands when they said good-bye. Willie drove him to the airport and the Kid locked himself in his room. Two days later, things hadn't improved. The Kid came out for meals, ignored all conversation, ate quickly, and returned to his room. I tried to wait him out. Meanwhile, he had the iPad and his cars.

Willie made the effort, but the Kid just wasn't having any of it. Willie warmly greeted the Kid whenever he showed himself, asked politely if he needed anything, and always made some upbeat comment. Admittedly, he was no Mister Rogers. Willie had a forgettable face, with the kind of blond hair that might also be described as brown or red, but which was so thin and limp that it didn't matter what you called it. One ear was noticeably higher on his head than the other, but as he wore a weather-beaten Padres cap at all times, indoor and out, the ear hardly qualified as a distinguishing trait. Otherwise, he was an alert, sharp-eyed, athletic, and somewhat grim man in his late thirties—a bodyguard.

But Willie also cooked, which greatly improved the quality of life at our hacienda. I still fixed the Kid's food—he wouldn't have it any other way. But Willie made a real dinner for Hal and me every night. He did the shopping and insisted on doing the cleaning up. I offered my help—I could load a dishwasher as well as the next man, I thought—but Willie refused. Hal heard that and didn't bother to offer. By the third night's meal—featuring thick spears of asparagus wrapped in prosciutto, an arugula salad with Gorgonzola and pine nuts, grilled zucchini smothered in olive oil, and a roasted rosemary chicken with a skin so crispy it crackled—Willie had made himself an invaluable member of the team.

"Kid? It's your dad." Of course it was. Who else would be bothering him?

It was morning on the fourth day since Willie's arrival, and I had determined it was time to break the logjam.

"Kid? We need to talk. I'm coming in, okay?"

My son had barely spoken to me in days. In general, he spoke much less than before we went into hiding, when I had disrupted his life in almost every conceivable way. But the past few days had been extreme and I felt that I had to remind my son who was in charge—a choice that is almost always the wrong one.

He didn't answer.

"Okay. If it is not okay with you for me to come in, now is the time to say so." At home we had used two knocks separated by ten seconds for both of us. The Kid had the privacy he craved, and on the nights when Skeli slept over, I had some assurance that we would not be surprised during our more intimate moments.

The Kid still didn't answer.

"Right. Here I come."

The Kid was in bed, covers pulled up to his chest, two pillows propped up behind his head. He was watching something on his new iPad. He was using my earbuds. I had refused to get him earbuds because I believed that they could be harmful to young ears. Allowing him to use them would also have meant that I couldn't eavesdrop on what he was doing. So, he was using mine. The pair with the built-in microphone that had gone missing two weeks ago, and I was sure had dropped into the recycling bin when I was putting twine on the newspaper pile.

I had to give him credit. He did not tear them off, or try to hide them. He showed no signs of feeling guilt or even mild embarrassment. He kept watching.

I sat down on the bed next to him. It was another Goofy cartoon.

There was a period during my fourth grade when I had discovered and gobbled up a series of books by a man named Walter Brooks about a bunch of talking farm animals. The fit passed in a few months, but I realized much later in life that the themes of fairness, honesty, and decency, combined with intelligence, compassion, and more than a touch of shrewdness, had all stayed with me. The books had arrived at exactly the moment in my life when I could appreciate their depth. I suspected that the Disney writers weren't on a par with Mr. Brooks, but maybe, in that moment, Goofy was giving my son just what he needed. I let him finish watching, then I gently unplugged the earbuds and put my hand over the screen.

"No more right now. We've got to talk."

"You talk."

"Yes, you're right. When I say that *we* have to talk, it usually means that I'm going to talk and you're supposed to listen. That's called a lecture. Or sometimes a talking-to, as in 'I'm going to give that child a good talking-to.'"

"Not good. Bad."

"No, it's not good. But like a lot of things, it's not so bad, either. It's necessary. You can think of it like eating vegetables."

The Kid rarely responded to metaphor. The concept confused him.

"You may not like it, but it's good for you. And you won't see the positive results right away, but someday you'll appreciate it."

He began tapping out his peculiar rhythm with his fingertips. Stimming. There were times when it was annoying, but it was harmless. It looked weird, and I hated to imagine that strangers would think my son was weird—though I had to admit that sometimes he was just that. But it helped him keep his planets in orbit and his galaxies from crashing into one another.

"I know you are sad that Josh went home. I miss him, too." Josh didn't cook, but there was a stability to him, a feeling that he was fully grounded, a calm that none of the other bodyguards who had billeted with us had shown.

"Stupid."

This always meant that I was missing the point. It may also have meant that he thought I was stupid, but I elected not to see it that way.

"All right, then. You tell me."

The fingers kept flying.

"Are you upset that Josh gets to go home and you don't?"

"STUPID."

Ahhhh. His vehemence betrayed him. Of course that was part of it. It was always part of everything. He wanted to be back where he felt comfortable. Where the doorman knew his name. Where the parking attendant in the garage let him walk around, looking at the cars. Where the lady who cut his hair was used to his terror of the scissors and had devised various harmless, yet effective, stratagems for him— from always having on hand a big picture book of cars for him to look at while she worked to giving him car stickers as a reward for good behavior. He missed the Athena, the subway, the dog run in Riverside Park, and even his school. I was sure that he missed Skeli, my father, and Roger. Damn. So did I.

But he was still telling me that there was something else. Maybe it had not started with Josh's leaving. Maybe it was the arrival of Willie.

"Is it Willie? Is he the problem?"

The Kid pinched his ears and pulled them as if trying to get them into alignment. I laughed. He looked at me in surprise; he hadn't been trying to be funny.

"Are you telling me you don't like the guy because he has funny ears?"

The Kid scrunched up his face.

"No. Okay. Please. I don't understand. What's wrong with Willie?"

"He's bad."

43

It took another day, but I finally persuaded the Kid to come out for a quick early-morning trip to the zoo at Reid Park. The park was close enough that we could have walked there, but we would have risked dying from heat prostration on the return trip. The forecast was for one hundred and two by midafternoon.

But we planned on leaving right after breakfast, driving there in the Lexus LX. I made up water bottles while the Kid cleaned up and got dressed. Willie and Hal both wore light windbreakers, so I knew they were armed. No sane human wears a jacket of any kind in Tucson in late August.

The deep rumble of an automobile came to a stop out front and a moment later there was a knock at the door.

"Somebody get that," I called out, wondering who it could possibly be. The sales guy from DirecTV? I thought we had permanently discouraged him. The gas man? Hadn't we just seen him the previous week? Wrong time of year for Girl Scout cookies.

Hal stuck his head around the corner.

"I think you should get out here, sir."

Two U.S. Marshals had come to visit. Their news wouldn't be good.

The living room wasn't a small room, but the presence of two more tall, broad-shouldered, and grim-faced men made it feel that way. I was a touch over six feet and the shortest man in the room. I was wearing my habitual frown, but for once I had a good reason.

They wanted me to move. Not to return to New York, but to scurry to another hideout—someplace more remote and therefore safer, so they said. The story came out in drips of coveted information, as though they expected me to obey their directive simply because they said so. They were scaring me.

"I'm not trying to scare you. I'm telling you how it is. You might not want to hear it, but we believe you're in danger. It makes sense to move. As soon as possible." The marshal who was speaking had introduced himself as Marshal Reyes. He wore black, silver-toed cowboy boots with his suit. The other man, Deputy Marshal Geary, wore khakis, a loose polo shirt, and boat shoes. He had to be the only man in Arizona wearing boat shoes. It didn't matter. Except for the clothes and hair color, all marshals looked alike to me. Call it an ex-con's predilection.

The mutilated body of a murdered man had been found in the desert. He had gone missing from the program. The service was reviewing all of their clients' cases, looking for connections or possible leaks.

I craned my neck back and looked down the hall. The door to the Kid's room was still closed. I had been trying to get him to come out all week and now I dreaded his overhearing any of the conversation.

"How did the killers find him?" I asked. "I was told you fellas had a perfect record."

"That's true. We have never lost a client who followed the rules. That tells you that our guy wasn't following the rules."

There's really only one rule while in the WITSEC program: Do not contact any former friends or associates. All the other rules are variations on the theme.

I wasn't very good at following the rule. The secure chat room that Manny had set up was violation number one. Skeli and Larry also had access. Virgil and I had the bat phone. Skeli sometimes read me messages from Roger, so he was aware that we were in touch. None of them knew exactly where I was, or any other way to contact me, but according to the letter—and the spirit—of THE RULE, I was in daily violation.

The bodyguards knew about the chat room. The marshals did not.

"I don't want to move. I don't want to move my son. He doesn't do well with change. He's having a hard enough time as it is."

It certainly wasn't my love of Tucson. I had absolutely nothing against the town, except for the heat, the food, and the sports teams, but it wasn't home and never would be.

Hal, with one month's seniority over Willie and hence the spokesperson, leaned in and cleared his throat. He had been clearing his throat before speaking ever since he arrived in Tucson. It must have been either the dust or the pollen, because it certainly wasn't the humidity. "If the marshals recommend a move, we are contractually bound to go along with it, Mr. Slater."

Slater was my WITSEC name. John Slater, known as Jack. I had asked for John Slaughter—the local version of Myles Standish or Daniel Boone—but the marshals vetoed it. They intimated that I wasn't taking the process seriously. That wasn't it at all; I was simply too terrified, confused, and concerned for my son in order to make any intelligent decisions.

Hal continued. "And if you don't take their advice, we are required to cancel your contract." Hal was always polite, but he was a big guy and he rarely smiled. That lent an air of restrained anger to everything he said. He wasn't angry, but he was serious. As serious as a loaded weapon.

They would pack up and go. They were both there twenty-four seven, on duty even while sleeping. I accepted their presence as a cold necessity. I felt safer with them around. I just didn't like the necessity.

"So, you lost one of your clients." I waited for Reyes's response.

"Essentially, he left the program."

The distinction mattered much more to him and his superiors than it did to the rest of the world. The guy was dead either way.

"Being beaten, stabbed, tortured, and left for dead out in the desert is not how I want to end my days, but I don't see the connection."

Reyes and Geary gave each other that *We know much more than we're telling, but maybe we have to say a little something more* look. Every time you got two or more cops in a setting, you were guaranteed to see it at least once. "The client was very high profile."

"Yes, but you're not moving every man, woman, and child in the program, are you? What does this 'high profile' guy have to do with me?"

Hal looked out the window as though he had suddenly lost interest in the conversation. I realized that he knew the answer. Willie tried to catch his eye, but Hal was focused on a big Spartan Air Force cargo plane coming in to Davis-Monthan. The air force mothballs them there and they're about as common in Tucson as cactus wrens.

I waited. Eventually someone would fill the silence.

Deputy Marshal Geary surprised me. He broke first.

"According to your file, Mr. Slater, you had previous contact with the snitch."

Everybody in the program is a snitch. That's what they call us and why they'll never understand that, no matter what they do for us, it is always going to be "they" or "them" and "us." Never "we."

"Thank you," I said. "Hal? You have anything you want to add to that?"

He shifted his gaze back to me. "I had a message about it first thing this morning. HQ isn't sure if there's any correlation. They're getting back to me." The security firm that Hal and Willie worked for did their own research.

"They make any recommendations?"

"Maintain, pending further developments."

I did not have a large circle of friends or acquaintances who might be somewhere in the program. In fact, I could think of only one possibility. He wasn't a friend. He was instrumental in my ex-wife's murder. He didn't order it, but he could have stopped it.

"This wasn't a certain South American banker, was it? I thought someone told me he was in a cheese shop in Florida."

When witnesses are also federal prisoners, they're protected from a potentially murderous and revengeful general population by being housed in special facilities throughout the BOP—Federal Bureau of

Prisons. These secluded wings where the "rats" are kept are known as "cheese shops." It's not just the inmates who call them that. Every employee of the justice system uses the same nomenclature.

"His family pulled strings and cut him a deal. He was relocated to Sacramento with a new identity."

Castillo was his name. Tulio Botero Castillo. We had met while I was chasing down some missing money for Virgil. Castillo came from a prominent banking family in Colombia. I had engineered the ploy that forced him to choose between testifying or getting killed in prison. He wasn't a nice man—though he had impeccable manners— and he would have felt no remorse if it had been me who was found half eaten by coyotes and other scavengers, but I felt another notch carve itself into my battered psyche. Someday I would have to come to terms with all of the ghosts from my past.

"California? What was he doing in Arizona?"

"He drove to Phoenix two weeks ago, after checking in with his handlers for his biweekly. He checked into the Valley Ho in Scottsdale, but checked out three days later. Then he went off the grid."

That was what I called an unsatisfactory response. It had great detail, but no pertinent information.

"What happened? How'd you lose him?"

The two marshals shared another quick look. "We have reason to believe that he was using the Internet to contact members of his family."

That sent an electric charge through my brain. It zapped a few million nerve cells, and I was sure my body jerked. None of the men in the room reacted, but they must have caught my distress.

"There are ways to cloak that," I said.

Deputy Geary spoke. "And I'm sure there are ways to get around the cloaking. The thing is, he didn't follow the rules."

"By choosing to remain here, you will, in effect, be removing your-self from WITSEC. You understand that, don't you?" Hal was a by-the-rules kind of guy. I didn't like him or dislike him. Personality was not what he was good at—or there for. If you were stuck sitting next to him on a long bus ride, you'd want to have a good book to read. But when he weighed in on something, he was direct. There was no bull-shit with Hal.

I didn't want to move. The Kid didn't want to move—unless it meant going back to his school, Heather, the Greek coffee shop across Amsterdam, and all the other markers of his old home in New York. But if I stayed, I was not just risking my life, I was risking his as well. There really was no other way to decide it.

"Ah, screw it," I said. "Where're we going?"

"We were thinking Las Vegas," Marshal Reyes said.

"You've got to be shitting me. Las Vegas?"

"New Mexico."

"No," I said.

"It's a college town," Geary said in what I thought was supposed to be a cheery contribution.

"I've been there," I said. "I bought gas there once."

"What'd you think?" Geary said.

"They kept a clean restroom."

"It's quiet," Reyes said. "It's a little more rural than Tucson."

If that was meant to sound reassuring, it failed the test. Did I have a choice? No.

"How far is it from Il Mulino?"

They looked at each other. "I don't know," Reyes said. "What's Il Mulino?"

"An Italian restaurant in Manhattan. I miss it sometimes."

Reyes smiled. "Don't worry. I'm sure they've heard of pizza in New Mexico."

"I will attempt to keep an open mind," I said. "New identities?"

Geary handed me a thick envelope. "John Sauerman. We kept your initials."

"When do we leave?"

"As soon as you're packed."

"Let me go break the news to my son."

walked through the dining room toward the back of the house. The hall was the darkest—and coolest—point in the house. With all the doors closed, the AC vent overhead blasted the small space. It could be over one hundred on the front stoop and eighty in the kitchen, but the hall would feel like a meat locker. Only a bit of reflected sunlight made it into the hall, and the overhead light got a workout, night and day. We had already been through a box of bulbs in the few months living there.

I hit the switch, more out of habit than necessity, and was not terribly surprised to find that, once again, the bulb was shot. I ignored it and continued down the hall. My foot brushed something on the floor, and before I could stop myself I had sent a line of five Matchbox cars flying. Standard response was muffled anger and the delivery of a monologue to my unresponsive son on the hazards of leaving his toys in the middle of a thoroughfare. But I found that I didn't have the heart for it. I scooped up the cars and filled my pockets.

"Kid!" I called to the closed door. I knocked, counted to ten, and knocked again. "Kid, I'm coming in."

I tried the knob. The door was locked. That was forbidden. When I discovered that his bedroom could be locked from the inside, I attempted to replace the whole assembly. I removed the knobs and all the metal bits inside and brought them to a locksmith, who informed me that I would have to change the door. The door, I learned when I then went to a window and door purveyor, was a custom size and delivery of a new one ordered on the spot might be early October, with luck, and would cost as much as two months' rent. I put the pieces back—thrilled with myself that the mechanism still worked—and sat my son down for another one-sided talk. He reluctantly agreed that his safety was of primary importance, and that it therefore made sense to Never Lock the Door. Now he had locked it again.

Frustration—and parental anger—had blinded me. There was a thru-line and I had missed the connection. The Kid had been lining up his cars—an activity that straddled the border between play and compulsion—in the hallway. From the hall it was possible to hear even a muted conversation in the living room, and none of us had been trying to be quiet. Therefore, the Kid had heard us. He had then run into his room, upset enough to abandon his cars, and locked the door.

Those were all conjectures, but the evidence, cause and effect, and two years of history with my son led me to those conclusions.

I reviewed the conversation we had been having in the living room. The description of the body had been detailed. At least two assailants, and possibly as many as four, had beaten and tortured the man for hours before crucifying him in the sand. Then the local fauna had gone to work. Explicit references to body parts and bite marks had been mentioned. All this while I had stupidly assumed the Kid was in his room and well out of earshot.

So, the Kid had obviously heard the horror of what had been done to Castillo and then run into his room and barricaded himself against a similar fate. That was my working hypothesis. It fit all the known facts. It just happened to be wrong.

A thump sounded on the other side of the door. I put my ear to it. A minute later, there was another thump. The mats. A suggestion of Heather's, passed through Skeli when she heard that the Kid was not transitioning well. I had hung a big wrestling mat on his wall and placed another on the floor below it. The Kid loved the arrangement. He rolled, jumped, fell, and threw himself against the padded wall and floor until he staggered with exhaustion. It had terrified me at first, but I quickly learned that it was less harmful than letting him bump into furniture or leap off the landing on the basement stairs, and it usually led to a long nap, which was my reward.

"Kid, you need to unlock the door. I'm here to help you."

Thump.

Thump.

Maybe I could get one of the marshals to shoot the lock.

Thump.

"Kid!"

Thump.

I took out my wallet and scrounged through it for my library card. It was thinner than a credit card, flexible, yet sturdy. It slipped between door and jamb and I swept it down to the catch. There were two more thumps while I jiggled the fittings, bending the card and forcing it harder against resistance. I felt the card snap in half.

"Willie! Give me a hand. The Kid's locked himself in."

Willie, in addition to his culinary skills, we had quickly learned, was, of the four males living in the house, the one most handy with tools. I didn't bother calling a marshal because I associated them with locking things up rather than breaking in.

Willie arrived in a moment with a long, thin screwdriver. He forced it under the jamb next to the knob and jimmied the door. We winced in unison at the sound of splitting wood.

"Sorry."

"No, don't think about it. Just do it."

He did. The door swung open.

"Thanks."

"No problem."

"Kid? Kid? It's me. Your dad. I was worried about you, guy. I'm coming in. I'm not mad about the door. I understand. You're scared and I don't blame you." I repeated those words as I walked in and looked around his room. He had heard us and had gone into hiding.

I looked under the bed, though it was the most unlikely spot. Nine out of ten kids would have hid under the bed, but not my guy. Too dirty. Dusty. Not a chance. But I looked anyway because I'm an NT (neurotypical) and what the hell do we know. I checked the closet, the bathroom, the shower, the laundry hamper, and under the drawing table. He wasn't anywhere. I began to feel the first stirrings of panic.

"Willie, get in here. You look. He's not here."

Willie repeated my steps. I felt like screaming at him "He's NOT under the goddamn bed, you idiot!" but I held it back.

Willie found the Kid's escape hatch. In the back of the closet, a panel of loose drywall had been shifted aside. Through the gap we could see into the closet of the adjoining bedroom. The twin-bed guest room the bodyguards shared.

I couldn't help but give a silent "Attaboy!" for my son's ingenuity. He had created a blind with the locked door, making me and Willie waste valuable time while he escaped into the other bedroom. It was a ploy. It required multipart strategy, an understanding of my patterns and responses, and a good bit of chutzpah. Nicely done. I was *less* concerned rather than more. It meant that he was somehow in control.

"Check your bedroom," I said. "I'll look in mine." The odds of the Kid having hidden in the shared bathroom were down around zero. A single errant pubic hair or smear of toothpaste left in the sink would have had him sobbing with anxiety.

It took me seconds to search my room. I had a few suits in the closet and some shirts on hangers, a bed with no head- or footboard, and two large plastic baskets—one held clean underwear and socks, the other held dirty. I lived simply when in hiding. The windows were all shut, the blinds down and closed. The room was cool and in twilight. I felt a wave of exhaustion and wanted to sink onto the bed and put a pillow over my head. Could I just have one hour, a half hour, an uninterrupted ten minutes where I did not have to cope? Where I could just relax and let all cares go? Obviously not.

"Not over here," Willie called.

"Check the bathroom," I called back. If I was down to pinning my hopes on his having hidden in the bathroom, I was getting desperate.

He was not in the bathroom. I called Hal and the marshals. I assigned roles and we began to search in earnest. The house was small. In less than two minutes, we had an answer. He was not inside.

"The kitchen door," Hal called.

We ran to join him. He was already heading outside. "It was unlocked," he yelled over his shoulder.

The only time the rear door was unlocked was when one of the adults was going through it. Otherwise we all used the front door—which we kept locked as well. My head—and heart—were circling back through the panic mode, leaving the amused relief to fend for itself for the moment.

Some previous occupant of the house had installed a vinyl-coated chain-link fence surrounding the backyard—most likely to be used as a dog run, judging by the burnt yellow splotches in the sparse lawn—with a lockable gate leading to the garage and driveway. I had installed a trampoline with netted sides for the Kid to let off steam. Otherwise the yard was bare, not a tree or a shrub, nowhere to hide. The Kid was not there. The gate was locked.

"He must have climbed out," Hal yelled. He vaulted the five-foot-high fence—an impressive feat. I didn't wait to see if the two marshals could duplicate it.

"Follow me," I said to Willie, and ran back through the house to the front door. The door was open. The Kid had sandbagged me twice.

We burst out the door and across the parched and dusty front yard. Hal and the marshals had beaten us to the curb. They stood there in indecision, their heads whipping to and fro, their eyes squinting against the midday glare, looking for any sign of the Kid.

"Just spread out and run," I yelled. "He's fast, but he won't last."

Hal gave orders. I waited. The neighborhood was a quiet suburban street with too many green lawns and deciduous trees that sucked up precious water like sponges. The families were all working-class of either Anglo or Mexican heritage. Two-car families, but one of the vehicles was most likely a pickup. Many of the wives worked. At noon on a school day, it was as deserted as a ghost town. All it needed was some rolling tumbleweeds and a mangy coyote to resemble a film shoot for a southwestern apocalypse. Nevertheless, five grown men running through the streets, obviously hunting or chasing someone or -thing, would soon be noticed. One of my neighbors, a good citizen, would be calling the police sometime soon.

Willie had the presence of mind to hop into the Lexus and search via car. I stood by the marshal's car and waited.

They had arrived in a 1970 Plymouth Barracuda, the product, no doubt, of a civil forfeiture, our legal system's middle finger to the Fourth Amendment. The Cuda had the big 440-cubic-inch engine with the Six Pak exhaust. When the marshals first pulled up, it had sounded like a cross between an army tank and one of those cigarette boats. Though 1970 wasn't a great year for American muscle cars, as emission standards became more stringent and safety standards added weight, a seven-liter engine made up for a lot of deficiencies. The car had been repainted at some point, in a nonstock electric-blue metal flake, destroying the value for any serious collector, but the Kid wouldn't have cared.

What sight would have driven all fear from my son's mind and left him in slack-jawed amazement? Only a small dog or a big-engine car. I opened the passenger door and slid in next to him. He was in the driver's seat, hands on the wheel, too short to see over the dash, but not caring—his eyes were focused on the instruments, his mind adrift in some private fantasy. He was humming a single note. It was his happy hum, not the pre-meltdown one. Not the one that led to tantrums or trances. No, this was the hum that he sometimes made when communing with a furry animal—a dog or a sheep. He was as much at peace as this world ever allowed him.

"Hey, guy," I said.

He hummed.

"We're going to have to move again. Today. Can you stay here while I go pack?"

He kept humming.

"Well, okay. I'll get Willie or Hal to sit with you until we're ready to go. You'll be okay."

The humming stuttered and I thought I might have gone a step too far. He blinked rapidly.

"Okay. I'll ask Hal."

The humming continued.

I got out of the car and dialed Willie. "C'mon back," I said into the phone. "See if you can get the others. The Kid's here. He's okay."

"I see the marshals," he said. "You better call Hal, otherwise he'll just keep hunting. He's like a coonhound."

I called Hal. He took longer to answer and longer to convince that both the Kid and I were all right. While we were talking, he came in sight around the corner.

"Come sit with him while I get started packing."

We loaded the back of the Lexus. The wrestling mats and our bedding took up a lot of the space.

"The Kid can ride with the two of you," I said to the marshals. "It'll be a treat for him. He'll behave. He'll probably hum until he gets tired and then he'll sleep. Call my cell if you need anything. We'll be right behind you."

"You're the snitch, not your son. You should ride with us, too."

"That puts one adult in the backseat of a Barracuda with the Kid. Which one of you two is going to sit there for the next seven hours, because I can goddamn guarantee you that it's not going to be me."

The two of them did their mind-reading look again. I gave them a few seconds while they silently debated.

"I wouldn't be at all surprised to have local police stopping by sometime soon to find out why men with guns on their hips were running all over the neighborhood not too long ago." I flashed them the smile that Skeli calls my Wall Street Asshole Grin.

"Fine," Marshal Reyes finally answered. "But you and your buddies stay right behind us. You drop back more than a football field and you're riding the rest of the way in the backseat with your son."

"We can do that," I said. I moved the Kid's car seat to the back of the Barracuda, gave him the Matchbox cars from my pocket, and told him I'd see him for lunch. "We'll find you a place with really good grilled cheese."

We were packed and gone in another six minutes. Hal left the house keys under the mat.

45

Travel out west is not so different from what it was two hundred years ago. You steer toward the horizon and stop when you need to sleep. The choices for a map-obsessed Easterner were remarkably few and dictated by geographic obstacles—mountain ranges, bottomless gorges, or rivers that were either flooded or dry, never in-between—or the sheer vastness of empty space. Drive three hours from New York City and you can see ocean beaches, mountains, rivers, forests, and deepwater lakes. Three hours from Tucson we had yet to see anything but cacti. A car passing in the other direction was an event.

"Did you notice anything about that little escape hatch in the closet?" Willie asked. He was driving. Hal was playing with his phone.

"Like what?" There was a shimmer like sunlight on water on the road up ahead. It had been there, at about the same distance from us, for a half hour. At what point does a mirage cross over into hallucination?

"He took that section of the wall apart. It would have taken him quite a while to cut through that old drywall and clean up the mess so we wouldn't find it. He didn't do all that in the few minutes he was in his room after breakfast."

The Kid was so frightened—of something, of someone, or of everything—that he had felt it necessary to create that back door. And, to keep it a secret, even from me. That thought gave me a shock of conflicting emotions—none of them happy ones. On the other hand, he had carried it off successfully, created it, used it, and evaded five grown men until he had been distracted by a vintage Barracuda.

"How long do you think it took him?"

"I wouldn't guess."

"We're coming up to Deming. We should stop and eat," Hal said.

I pulled my eyes away from the contemplation of a mesa—or butte, I did not know how to tell one from the other—that vaguely resembled the front of a locomotive, if you squinted enough. Getting out of the Tucson area had been the priority. Lunch had been forgotten. The Kid would be hungry. "I'll call them," I offered.

Cell phone service had been spotty out where the nearest tower was well over the horizon, but the signal was strong as we approached the town.

"Your son's been asleep for the past two hours," Deputy Marshal Geary said. "Are you sure you want to wake him?"

"He does that after a panic attack. He'll wake up as soon as you start to slow down—and he'll need to eat." He would be ravenous. The attacks, whether seizures or bursts of running or other activity, left him exhausted and calorie depleted. He might even eat a green vegetable.

"Does he have any food preferences? Special diets?"

"Any place that'll make him a grilled cheese and French fries will be just fine," I said.

Hal looked up from his smartphone. "There's a Denny's."

I spoke into the phone. "Hal found a Denny's."

"He's joking, right?"

"I don't think so."

"We'll find something better. Just stay right behind us."

I relayed the order to Willie, who nodded and kept driving.

"Denny's not high-class enough for you?" Hal said with just enough of an edge to his voice that I couldn't tell whether he was truly offended or attempting a joke.

"Do they make a good green sauce at Denny's?" I responded.

"Denny's feeds America," he said.

"I think we can all agree on that."

––––––––

Willie followed the Cuda off the highway and we began threading our way through the main street of Deming, New Mexico.

"So who was this Castillo that got axed? How do you know him?" Hal asked.

Willie looked at him in surprise. I was surprised, too. Hal was the first bodyguard to ask any question that might pertain to my past. And this was the first time he had done it. As far as they were concerned, I was John Slater—now Sauerman—who had sprung into existence in May of that year and I needed constant protection. End of story.

I tried answering with the bare minimum. "He was a banker who got involved with the wrong people. A drug cartel from Honduras. He chose to testify rather than go to prison." I elected not to go into the details of how I had helped put Castillo in the position where he was forced to make that choice.

"Sinaloas? Don't they run everything down there?" Willie asked. The taboo had been broken. My past was now fair game.

"From what I understand, it's more like a free-for-all these days. Maras versus Zetas versus Zacapas versus Sinaloas. The DEA took out some major players, thanks to Castillo, but it seems that just makes room for some other bunch of crazies to take their place."

"So which group would have come after the banker, do you think?" Hal said, his eyes concentrating on his phone.

Every bit of information that I knew about the heroin smugglers came from Special Agent Marcus Brady. It had been shared with me on a confidential basis, and I did not want to give it away in casual conversation. "Why the interest?"

"I'd like to know who I'm protecting you from."

"Or what we might be in for," Willie added.

That made sense and helped to alleviate my quandary. "Fair enough. The people he helped put away were from different groups all over Central America. But the main group called themselves Mijos. They're an offshoot from the Honduran MS-13 branch. With Castillo's information the United States and Honduras were able to crack down on them. Hard. If there are any of them left, they've been reabsorbed back into the Mara."

"That's a nasty crowd," Willie said. "They get kids—young kids, preteen—and train them to be *sicarios*. They feed them on cocaine and hate. By the time they get turned out, they'd kill their own mothers on orders."

I did not want to think about teenage hit men on my trail. Luckily, just then the Cuda pulled to the curb in front of a washed-out-looking café that advertised both SOUTHWESTERN AND AMERICAN CUISINE and Hal said, "Lunch." We pulled in next to the marshals and I saw the Kid peeking over the edge of the rear passenger window, looking for me. I gave him a wave. He looked worried and still half asleep.

Willie got out and went over to talk to the marshals. He and Reyes went inside the café to see that it was safe—and, I hoped, to check that the chef could put together a good grilled cheese. The rest of us waited in the cars.

"That was a bit of a surprise," I said.

"What's that?" Hal asked.

"You've been here more than a month and never asked any of those kinds of questions."

He stared straight ahead. "I'm just being cautious."

"And your partner?"

"It's the first time we worked together. I think he enjoys fraternizing more than necessary, but that's not a bad thing in our business."

I regretted saying anything. I'd been looking for words to calm my uneasiness and I'd gotten them. Only to discover that I needed more.

"I'm going to check on my son," I said, reaching for the door handle.

Hal held up a hand. "Don't exit the vehicle until Willie gives the all clear. Please," he added a beat later. That barely qualified as a request.

There's not much point to having bodyguards if you don't pay any attention to their advice. I didn't like taking orders—just on general principles—but I stayed in the car. I watched the Kid. He wasn't in distress; his worry was his natural "at rest" state. He sometimes lost the look when he felt safe in his own space, but I hadn't seen him without it since we came west.

Willie stuck his head out the door and, with a big grin, waved us in.

46

The house in New Mexico was not in Las Vegas proper, it was a few miles out of town, up a long serpentine valley that cut through the foothills, and just north of a place called Devil's Gulch. As the marshal had said, it was distinctly more rural than Tucson. And a long way from Seventy-third Street.

It was a bigger house, with four bedrooms and three baths on two floors, and a professional kitchen—which made Willie happy, and by extension, Hal and me, too. The Kid and I shared the upper floor and a balcony that ran the full length of the front of the building. My room had a sliding glass door that opened onto the balcony overlooking a barn and corral. I showed the Kid that if he was ever so afraid that he needed to find me, he could come down the hall, or go out the window onto the porch and come into my room by our "secret passage." We tried it out together a couple of times so he'd know how to do it. I made it a game, but he wasn't fooled. It was serious preparation.

The balcony was the only spot in the house that had any kind of a view. My room faced west, but the hill behind the house blocked everything but the tops of the Bear and Barillas Mountains. The front of the house looked out onto a rust-brown valley that felt more like a border than a vista. If the house had been higher on the ridge, we might have been able to see the town down below and the beginning of the Great Plains, which seemed to begin just the other side of Route 25. If you dropped a tennis ball down our driveway, it might have rolled east all the way to the Mississippi, ending up somewhere near Memphis. In back of the house stood the small corral and a lean-to, where the property owner had warehoused his small herd of cattle.

The long drought had done in his entrepreneurial dreams. The house—and the outbuilding—had been empty for over a year.

Willie took charge of making the house livable, overseeing two short Latinas from town who worked harder and faster than any team of eight men, cleaning every surface and disposing of the desiccated dead mice we found in the traps that had been left behind. Willie said the presence of the mice was a good sign. It meant that no snakes had taken up residence.

Hal, the Kid, and I took a drive farther up into the foothills. To an Easterner, the flora and the land looked sparse and sere. Dwarf-sized pinyon trees, too water-starved to grow much over four or five feet tall, shared the landscape with sagebrush and a spiky plant that I didn't recognize. To a grown-up city kid like me, it looked like an alien planet. The nearest house was down in the hollow on the far side of the next hill. I thought it strange that, rather than build on a site with a view, this homeowner, like the man who owned the house we were renting, had chosen to place his home in the shadow of these bleak mounds. I said so to Hal.

"Water," he said. "There's little enough of it up here. You don't want to have to drill an extra hundred feet or more, just so you can see a whole lot of nothing."

It was an alien planet.

The road petered out halfway up a canyon. Beyond that point was nothing but wilderness. Well to the west, blue mountains colored the horizon. Santa Fe was over in that direction—beyond one and a half million acres of mountain forest. I was as out of my comfort zone as I was ever likely to be in my lifetime.

"Let's go back to the house," I said.

The Kid looked at me. He'd picked up on it, too.

"Tell you what, son. We stay here long enough, we'll open a New York–style kosher deli. Steam our own corned beef and pastrami. We'll introduce these folks to latkes and tzimmes. Too much? Maybe you're right. Okay, then we'll open a bakery and get rich selling black-and-white cookies and semolina bread. Just think, these people have been living their whole lives without fresh-baked seeded rye. We're going to show 'em what they've been missing."

I was losing my mind. I wanted my life back.

47

Parenting an autistic child is like hitting a baseball. The best you can hope for is one in three, and that's if you are truly stellar. One in four keeps you in the game. Sometimes you're just going to be trying to draw a walk. You will strike out more often than you would like. And every once in a while, you're going to get beaned.

But you can't ever take your eye off the ball.

I had begun homeschooling the Kid over the summer. I wasn't a natural. The Kid did not miss his friends—he had none. The other students had been tolerated, nothing more. But he did miss routine and those who helped him to maintain it. I was a poor substitute for the combined powers of Heather, Ms. Wegant, her assistant, and even Mrs. Alysha Carter, the lady dragon who guarded the gates at the school. For my part, teaching was much more difficult than trading had ever been.

"The . . . house . . . is . . . red."

"Excellent," I said.

The Kid had such a strong memory that he could often "fake" reading. I had to create new books for him every day, otherwise he would simply repeat, as though by rote, the information from the previous time we had covered that lesson. Regular reading books were only good once, or twice at most. He could effortlessly do the same trick with any book on cars. Getting him to actually sound out words or to remember their meaning beyond the subject of cars was the challenge. He had come a long way in the past few months, but each new word was a hard-won victory.

I started every reading session with flash cards. Each one had a picture—a prompt—and a word. I made them myself with three-by-five cards and cutouts from magazines. If I thought he had memorized a picture—and so was able to cheat on the word—I would drop it out and replace the picture later in the day.

Neither of us was a particularly patient human being. I had to bring enough for both of us.

"Next page."

I also made books with pictures and simple sentences. He memorized the books even faster than the cards. The more complex the context, the easier it came to him. I thought this was a good thing. It meant that he was smart. But was he smart enough to fool me? Easily.

"The . . . cat . . . runs."

"Try again. What's that letter?"

"J."

"Right. What does 'J' sound like?"

"Jason." He put his teeth together and blew out, showing me how to make a 'J.'

"Excellent. So is there a 'J' sound in 'runs'?"

His eyes drifted away. He did not like to be corrected or to have me demonstrate his mistakes. I didn't know any better.

"What letter is this?" I pointed.

"T . . . U . . . V." He emphasized the right answer. He knew the alphabet in three- or four-letter groups. He could only find a letter by finding the group.

"Good. And what's next?"

He looked away.

"Come on. Stay focused," I said.

He put the back of his hand to his mouth and began making fart noises.

"Does Heather let you make those noises? Does Ms. Wegant? I don't think they do."

The noises stopped. The Kid picked up his pencil and took a bite off the end. He did not just nibble on his pencil. He bit off a chunk of it and crunched it into a million soggy splinters.

"You *may not* do that! Not allowed."

His mouth opened and a soup of drool and gnashed pencil ran down his chin and onto his shirt.

I grabbed a paper napkin and wiped crud out of his mouth.

"What is your problem?" I was yelling, which meant that I had already lost control of the situation. The frontal lobe was trying to maintain and regain, while the darker, more primitive parts of my brain were recommending more violent courses of action. "Stop this! Pay attention and do your work."

He flopped facedown on the table, almost, but not quite, banging his forehead into it.

"Read this, damn it! What did the cat do?" I was screeching. It was wrong and I knew it.

The Kid reared up and screeched right back. "The cat jumps," he blurted out. He picked up the book I had lovingly made and turned the page.

"Awesome. Well done." I was exhausted.

"Ooooooh. The big dog is fat." He laughed. It sounded like a cat with a hair ball.

He had made a joke. The caption read THE BIG DOG IS *FAST*. But the picture I had chosen showed a running Saint Bernard, shot from an angle that made him look like he was sporting a good-sized beer belly. Or brandy belly.

"Very good, son." He knew the word *fast*. The great thing was that he understood the difference well enough to make a joke out of it—no matter how lame.

The front door opened and Willie came in bearing two bags of groceries. We'd been four days at the house and had already drifted into a regular schedule. Willie made a run into town every morning before the heat became unbearable. The Kid and I worked together. Hal stood watch and played with the apps on his cell phone.

"How's everybody?" Willie said. "I found a restaurant if you want to venture out some night. The El Fidel. The lady at the gas station says it's as good as anything in Santa Fe." He rattled on as he put away the supplies.

The Kid shut down in Willie's presence. He put the book down and his eyes went blank. It was as though a switch was thrown and he went into stasis. I wasn't going to get him to concentrate until Willie put the food away and left us in peace.

"You need a break?"

The Kid didn't answer, but his eyes flicked in my direction.

"Take five minutes. Yes," I answered before he even got the question out. "You can watch Goofy. One cartoon. Just one. Then we go back to work."

He scowled. I knew he was going to try for two and that I was going to let him. He knew it, too. He didn't see the point in my making an annoying and useless insistence upon only one and it ticked him off. He was right, but I wasn't going to admit it to him.

I needed a break.

"I'm going to get some air."

He looked up with a questioning look.

"Some *outside* air," I said.

He opened the iPad and was gone.

Dust devils were racing down the valley and there was a brown haze over the eastern horizon. It was going to be a scorcher. Mid-nineties. Every day had been a scorcher. It had not rained so much as a drop the whole week we had been there. The waitress at Daylight Donuts, where we'd had breakfast our first day, told us that August was their "rainiest" month.

"It gets downright dry come the fall."

I saw the flash of reflected sunlight off Hal's mirrored sunglasses across the yard. He had set up a blind on the hill where he could sit and watch the road below. He could see the whole valley from there. It should have been comforting to have him on watch, but instead it was a reminder of why we were there.

I realized that he was talking on his cell phone. Reception was better up there than around the house.

The two bodyguards had set up motion sensors along the road—there was little enough traffic—but the coyotes and a herd of javelinas kept setting them off. The pigs weren't going to leave—they saw us as interlopers on their territory—so Hal shut the system down and we relied on more primitive surveillance.

There's no such thing as quiet in New York City. Even in the Ansonia, with its thick walls and renovated double-paned-glass windows, there was always a background hum, punctuated with occasional sirens, car horns, or the clash of metal upon metal when some fool ran the light at Seventy-second Street. The valley was quiet. Even the wind was quiet.

"That town was once—" a man spoke behind me.

"Whoa!" I yelled. I turned around. It was Willie. "Shit fire, you scared the piss out of me." My heart was threatening to beat its way out through my eyeballs. "Why the hell are you creeping up on me?"

"*Hmpf.* Sorry."

"No, I'm sorry." I pulled myself together and tried on a laugh just to see if I could do it. "I must have been miles away. I did not hear you coming." The laugh hadn't gone over with the level of cool required, so in desperation I just kept talking. "You were saying something about the town? What about it?"

"Las Vegas—this one, not the other one—was once one of the most lawless, wide-open places in the West. Doc Holliday lived here with his lady. Wyatt Earp, too, for a while. He was the town dentist. Holliday, that is, not Earp."

"Oh? I knew a man once who had a bit of a fixation on those folks." Virgil's father had named all four of his children after the Earp brothers.

"This old guy bagging groceries down at the Lowe's told me all this. Jesse James. Billy the Kid. Somebody called Dirty Dave." He laughed. "They were all through here at one time or another."

"Jesse James?" I was no expert on the Old Wild West, but I thought the James Gang did their business more in the Midwest.

"That's what he said."

I looked back to the house. "How's Jason the Kid?"

"He went up to his room."

"I better get him back to work." My heart wasn't in it.

"He doesn't like me." Willie stated it as a fact. There was no emotion in his voice. He might just as well have been going on about Doc Holliday.

"He trusts very few people, which is a very logical reaction to his experience. Most people have no idea what his world is like. They approach him with a set of expectations that only confuses him." In other words, cut the guy some slack. A lesson that I had to relearn every day. I had just failed another of our lives' little tests.

"Time to spell Hal," he said. He sauntered across the road and climbed the hill.

I walked back to the house.

48

The Kid stayed up in his room and I let him. A break from schoolwork—and from each other—seemed a good idea. I didn't check on him until lunchtime. Much later on, we deduced that he had most likely been gone for close to an hour by the time I knocked on his door.

"Hey, Kid. Time for lunch. We'll go for a ride after. Come on down."

I waited the prescribed ten seconds and knocked again.

"Hey, son. I'm coming in."

The room was empty. I checked his closet. The bathroom. The room was hot, despite the air-conditioning—hotter than the rest of the house. The window was open. The "secret passage."

I looked out onto the balcony. There was no sign of him. I checked my room. The bathroom. There was nowhere to hide. He was gone.

I had thrown together sandwiches for lunch and Hal was halfway across the yard, delivering one of them to Willie, still on duty up the hill. I called to him.

"Hey! Hal. Help me. The Kid's not here."

That brought him running. Willie couldn't hear me, but he saw that something important was happening. He jogged down the hill to the house.

Hal took charge. "Let's not panic, okay? We've been down this road before. First, we search the house. Look in every cabinet, every closet. Check for false walls. We start down here. Keep up the patter. Let him hear us talking to each other. And stay in sight of each other. That way he won't slip by us like he did last time."

We worked the downstairs for five minutes. Five wasted minutes, in my opinion. I had been on the main floor all morning. If the Kid had come back downstairs, I was sure I would have seen him.

Upstairs took no longer and produced no clues. I stopped looking and took an inventory of the Kid's meager possessions. I could find nothing missing. His books and clothes were all there. His car box held sixty or seventy cars—a new Matchbox car being the only birthday present guaranteed to elicit a positive response—and I would have challenged anyone other than the Kid to know if there were any missing.

I went back out onto the balcony. Nothing moved anywhere on the far side of the valley. Beyond the corral the hill rose up steeply.

Willie came out and joined me.

"Anything?" he said.

"No."

He examined the railing. "Here's where he went over."

I looked and saw nothing unusual.

"He shinnied down the leader. You can see the scrape marks." Dust clung to every exterior surface—and many internal ones, as well. Once the marks were pointed out to me, they were obvious.

The rain gutters and leaders on the house were made of thin aluminum and were fifty or sixty years old. I would not have trusted them to hold up a squirrel, much less my son.

"Oh my god," I said. "He really did this, didn't he? What the hell was he thinking?"

He wasn't thinking. He was running. His father had yelled at him over some stupid reading lesson.

"We need to call the police," I said.

"Hey, let's not jump ahead. There's a lot at stake. I don't think the marshals would want you to have that kind of attention right now."

"Screw that. My son is out there." I swept my arm to show the desolation around us. It looked like the far side of the moon to me.

"Wait. Let's see if we can find him first. That's all I'm saying," Willie said.

I didn't so much agree to the delay as I just went along with a calm individual who was willing to make decisions. I was a wreck. I felt like I understood heart attacks for the first time in my life. We grabbed Hal on the way and the three of us went outside to explore.

The bottom of the aluminum leader was pulled away from the wall. Hal pointed out where the Kid landed. It looked like nothing but scattered dust.

"Someone needs to stay here in case he comes back," Hal said.

"I don't think I can do that," I said. "I'll finish going nuts."

"Willie?"

He nodded. "Stay in touch. Take water."

A few minutes later, Hal and I started up the back slope. Somehow I had expected him to be bent over looking for signs, like some Indian tracker from an old Western movie. He didn't. He stayed upright, as tall as he could. His eyes were constantly sweeping across the terrain. I tried to emulate him. It was hard work. My feet had to find their own way over rough ground. We were both wearing hiking shoes. Mine were suede and ankle-high. Hal's were thick leather and laced halfway up his shins.

"Watch for snakes," he said.

"Great."

"It's too hot for them to be out and about. Just don't kick over any rocks without looking first."

There were thousands of places all around us where a small seven-year-old child could hide. It was hopeless. The trees were short and sparse, not much more than shrubs, but as we moved higher, the trees became taller and our horizon shrank.

"Stop and drink," Hal said.

"We've got to keep going." We had only been searching for half an hour.

"Drink. Otherwise you're going to keel over from heatstroke and I'll have two emergencies to deal with instead of one."

I had a half liter of water with me. The first sip seemed to evaporate in my mouth. I was surprised a moment later to realize that I had polished off half the bottle in one long gulp. And I was still thirsty. Was the Kid carrying water?

Hal took off his glasses and wiped his face. Without the mirrors hiding his eyes, he looked much more human. And he looked worried.

"We're kidding ourselves," I said.

"Yeah."

"He could be hiding five feet away and we'd never see him," I said.

"Yeah."

"So what do we do? I can't go back and just hope he gets hungry and comes home."

He took out his cell phone and looked at it. "Nothing. No bars."

"Who do you want to call?"

"Willie. It's time to bring in help. I want him to start making calls."

"Let's head back. Call him on the way," I said.

49

"What the hell, Willie? What do you mean you didn't call?"

It took us another half hour to get back to the house. A half hour of nightmarish imaginings of what was happening to the Kid. A full hour wasted. Hal had finally gotten a signal and had told Willie to bring in the local police.

"I spoke to the marshals. They said to wait 'til they got here. They'll be able to control the situation."

"This isn't about turf, you idiot! I'm calling the sheriff's department."

"No, no. Reyes has a chopper bringing him in. Just wait another half hour and they'll be able to search the whole county, if need be."

Hal looked as astonished as I was at Willie's failure to act. "We're a hundred miles from Albuquerque. By the time they get in the air and get here, it's going to be another hour or more."

"But they'll be able to fly over and find him in no time. What's the sheriff going to do? Besides, if you bring in the locals yourself, you risk having your cover blown."

Blowing my cover was a different problem. It wasn't less important, it was less immediate. One thing at a time. First thing was to get the Kid as much help as I possibly could.

I told Siri to dial the county sheriff. Five minutes later, we could hear a siren coming up the road.

50

The deputy contacted the sheriff, who, upon hearing that it was an autistic child who was missing, called the state police. They turned it over to the state SAR—search and rescue—coordinator, who said he would be on-site in two hours. I fumed.

By the time the marshals arrived in a five-seater Bell helicopter, I was fighting recurring waves of panic. The pilot set the bird down in the corral and Hal and I went out to meet them.

Deputy Marshal Geary jumped out, crouching and running, with one hand holding on to his Diamondbacks' hat. He joined us at the rail fence.

"I really wish you had waited before calling in the locals. This is going to be a circus in a little while."

The response from the police felt like it was happening on a geologic timeline. I wanted to scream at someone, but couldn't even find someone high enough up the chain of command to make it worthwhile.

"Maybe you're right," I said. "But the more people looking, the better. What do we do now?"

"You come with us. If we see your boy, we look for someplace to set down and you get him. Simple."

I hated traveling in helicopters.

Hal said, "Do you have room for me?"

Geary shook his head. "You hold the fort. We'll keep you posted."

I climbed over the fence and followed him to the helicopter. Marshal Reyes gave me a squint-eyed nod as a greeting. The pilot handed me a helmet with a built-in mic and showed me how to turn it on.

"Keep it turned off unless you've got something important to say. No chatter. But if you see something, don't hesitate or waste time being polite. Jump right in."

I nodded and strapped myself in.

The pilot took us up, and in minutes we were moving up and over the hill that Hal and I had covered earlier. The two marshals and I watched the ground. The pilot took occasional glances down, but focused mainly on flying the machine. We crossed over another line of hills into the next valley. The trees were taller there and wider—fuller. They cloaked the ground. I realized that there was a lot of terrain that I was missing. A small child, or even a large man, could have hidden from us down there. If the Kid was lost and wanted to be found, we had a chance. If, on the other hand, he was angry or frightened, he could evade us by simply standing still.

We rose again and passed over the dry bed of a small stream, an ancient gray house in a clearing, and a rough dirt road that ran to it.

"We should check the house," Reyes said. "He'll be looking for shelter."

He was applying logic to my son's behavior. I had my doubts.

"I'll radio base and have the sheriff send out a four-wheel drive," Geary said.

I flicked the switch for my mic. "He's not there," I said.

Reyes looked at me. "Why not?"

Because the house looked both unsafe and dirty and probably had spiders or scorpions. The Kid would rather roast in the sun than take the shade in a structure like that. "Trust me. He wouldn't go there."

Reyes thought about it for all of two seconds. "Have them check it out anyway."

So much for trusting a father to know his son.

The pilot crisscrossed over the land, keeping the helicopter moving slowly westward. I felt the onset of motion sickness. Whenever I looked up, the horizon seemed to be swooping and spinning. If I looked down, I just felt sick.

We crossed another dried-up riverbed. It was about twenty feet across and looked to have once been two or three feet deep. But it was now covered in young pinyon trees. The river had been dry for years.

On the far side was a large clearing where bare rock broke through the surface. The helicopter rose unsteadily as we passed over. My stomach did some more acrobatics.

"Thermals," the pilot said as he corrected. "I'm going to have to stay up higher."

If we stayed up higher, we weren't going to be able to see anything on the ground at all. The helicopter search was pointless. We were wasting more time.

I flicked the switch again. "I want to go back."

Reyes snapped at me. "What? We've just started looking."

"We can't see a damn thing. The Kid could be anywhere down there and we'd never know."

A herd of javelinas, spooked by the noise of the helicopter, broke from the cover of a copse of taller trees and stampeded along a game trail. The lead animal veered off the trail into another stand of pinyons and the others followed. They disappeared as though they'd never been.

"You see that?" I said. "That's what I'm talking about."

"Yeah, but if your son hears us go over, he's not going to hide, is he? He's going to come out and wave and be happy we found him. Am I right?"

"No," I said in reflex. My son was not that simple. "Maybe. But he doesn't think like that. This is a waste of time. You guys do it, if you want, but take me back to the house."

Reyes didn't like it. "When we need to go for fuel, we'll drop you on the way." He turned away, dealing with me by ignoring me.

We rode around for another hour. The view didn't change. The trees got taller and there were fewer patches of sagebrush. There were more rocky escarpments breaking through the crust of the ground, and when I looked back over my shoulder, I could see that we had risen above the foothills by a thousand feet or more.

"He never made it this far," I said. "He's not fast enough. And the constant climb would have exhausted him. We need to turn back."

"We could refuel now," the pilot said.

Reyes looked like he had just downed a twelve-ounce glass of humility and it wasn't sitting well.

"Drop him back at the house." He turned and looked at me. I thought he was about to blast me to assert his control over me, my life, my son, the search, the universe, but he stopped himself. "Jesus Keeriste. You're mighty green, you know that?"

I refused to vomit in the confines of a small helicopter cockpit. I took long cleansing breaths and told myself that I would be back on the ground soon.

51

I felt better as soon as we started back. The pilot flew in a long curve away from the mountains, no longer searching with the nauseating crisscross pattern, and avoiding the more obvious places where thermals might catch us and toss the helicopter up in the air like a child's balloon. In a few minutes, we were passing over the edge of Las Vegas and the foot of the road that led up to the house. A deputy sheriff stood beside his car, blocking the road. He watched us soar overhead with a thoroughly dissatisfied look on his face.

The house was surrounded by pickup trucks, some with horse trailers attached. We flew over and the pilot began to set us down in the corral. A man in civilian clothes tried waving us off, but scooted out of the way when he saw that we were coming in anyway.

"Who's that crazy son of a bitch?" Geary said. No one bothered to answer.

The moment the skids hit the ground, I popped the latch, jumped to the ground, and ran for the fence. Terra firma never felt so good.

"What the hell is going on here?" Reyes was right behind me, yelling over the noise of the engine and the still-moving rotors.

The civilian yelled right back. "You got to get that thing outta here. We've got to unload our horses."

"Who are all these people?" Reyes said. He yelled back at the pilot. "Shut her down."

"We're the SAR volunteers. Who are you?"

"I'm the guy in charge."

"I don't think so," the man said.

Another civilian-attired man approached across the yard, flanked by two state policemen in black uniforms. The man in the center was grinning; the staties were not.

"Hello, gentlemen," the man said. "Which one of you is the parent?"

"That's me," I said. I almost introduced myself as Jason Stafford. "John Sauerman."

I guessed the man to be in his early fifties. His hair had been brown, now going to gray, cut short in an efficient buzz. Though he held himself far too relaxed to be ex-police or -military, he exuded the air of command. He was wearing a checked short-sleeved shirt, well-worn jeans, and hiking boots. I liked him immediately. He was going to find my son.

"Roy Robertson," he said, extending a hand. "I head up S and R for the state. Who's this gentleman?"

Reyes flashed his badge. "U.S. Marshal Reyes. We'll be running this operation."

"Did I misunderstand? Is this a hostage situation? I thought we were looking for a missing child."

"I'm going to want all communication with the press to go through me. You must understand that our presence here reflects the sensitivity of the situation. Mr. Sauerman is under our protection. Therefore, as senior marshal, I will direct the search. You and your people will take orders from me or my associate, Deputy Marshal Geary."

"Are you in pursuit of a fugitive, Marshal?"

Reyes grimaced. "We're looking for a seven-year-old boy," he said, enjoying giving the guy a dose of scorn.

"Then you are invited to participate in my search. If you would like to work with our press liaison, I will arrange that. Is that helicopter yours?"

"Yes, but . . ."

"Then please have your pilot take it somewhere else. Anywhere else. My people need a place to keep their spare mounts."

"This is federal, Mr. Robertson. You'll take your orders from me. That helicopter may be our most valuable asset in finding the child."

Robertson looked at me. "I'm sorry about this, Mr. Sauerman. Just give me one more minute to sort this out." He took out his phone and speed-dialed a number. "Hey, Cindy. It's me. Is she in?" He waited a few seconds until a second voice came on. "Thanks for taking my call, ma'am. We've been called out on a missing child over in San Miguel County and there are U.S. Marshals present. We are having a conversation about jurisdiction. Would you be willing to speak with them?" He listened for a moment and then handed the phone to Reyes. "The governor would like a word, Marshal Reyes."

Reyes took the phone as though he thought it might bite him on the ear. He listened for a few seconds, then said, "I understand." He disconnected and handed it back. "You're still going to need me, and my chopper."

"Marshal, you ask anyone here, I'm an easy man to work with. But they'll also tell you that I lack patience. It's one of my greatest failings. And I do not like to repeat myself. Now, will you please get that machine out of here?"

Reyes wheeled around and stomped back to the helicopter. Robertson took my arm and guided me toward the house. "Mr. Sauerman, please tell me anything and everything you can about your son. I understand that he has ASD. How severe are his limitations? Is he verbal?"

I started talking.

52

One last question. I realize that you may be limited in how much you can tell me—or want to tell me—but the presence of U.S. Marshals here raises some concerns. We have worked with the feds many times before and we respect each others' drives and abilities. But I need you to give me your trust and be as open with me as you possibly can."

"I'll do my best." We were sitting across from each other at the dining room table, a rough-hewn, thick-plank affair that had been painted with a clear plastic finish to a depth of about a quarter of an inch. We each had a cup of steaming black coffee. Robertson had ordered everyone else outside.

"You see, Mr. Sauerman, I can't put my people at risk. They are volunteers. They will brave rough terrain, heatstroke, snakebite, and even being stalked by mountain lions, but if there is any reason they might be harmed by a member of the human species, I cannot put them out there."

I did trust him. I couldn't say why exactly. Maybe it was his solid self-confidence, or maybe it was simply relief that a calm and capable man was taking charge of the search for my son. Or it may have been desperation.

"I believe that my autistic son has gone 'walkabout.' Children with ASD do that."

"I know that," he said. "We call it elopement."

"Or wandering. No one knows exactly why they do it."

"We are operating under the assumption that this is what we are dealing with here."

"Or he may be pissed off at me. I gave him a hard time this morning."

He smiled. "I've got four boys."

I continued. "As to your question, I know of no reason why or how my son and I would be in danger here. We came to this place to avoid that kind of danger. I have to believe that we have been successful."

He stared at me so long that I felt an urge to confess even more. I wanted to tell him about Aimee's death, my wife's murder, the drug cartel that might still be after me more than a year after I had helped send some of them to prison—including the now-dead banker. I wanted to explain that, although I had made a mistake and spent time in prison, I was not that man anymore. I didn't say any of that.

"Find my son, Mr. Robertson. Please."

53

A topographic map covered the table. Robertson and I had been joined by three of his team leaders.

"We'll start with a search through the various buildings here on the property. Mitch, I want you to start on that immediately. Then check on other houses on this road. Look into everything. Barns, woodsheds, even dog houses. Often, autistic children will head for shelter. He could be hiding here on the property, for all we know. Mr. Sauerman, would your son have any specific phobias in that regard?"

"Dirt. Anything dirty, moldy, or covered in spiderwebs will creep him out. If it even looks like that, he'll stay away."

"So we can leave out the dog houses," Mitch said.

"Actually, he likes dogs. All animals, really. He has no fear of mammals."

"Is he a runner?" the other man said.

"He's a sprinter. He can duck and weave, and he can move quickly when he's scared, but he can't do distance. He has no control that way, he just gives it his all until he drops."

"That's good info, but I want to know if he has a history of elopement. Has he done this before?"

I remembered a chase through our old neighborhood when two FBI agents surprised us. The Kid had moved like lightning. "Yes and no. He runs when he's scared, but he doesn't just wander off and disappear. This is a brand-new symptom." New symptoms of his autism seemed to arrive on a seasonal cycle. I was never prepared. The episode in Central Park and his brief disappearance in Tucson began to take on a different hue. "The best I can say is that he's never done anything exactly like this before. Not this extreme or for this long."

"Betty, you have the local knowledge. Talk to your people. I want to know about abandoned houses or outbuildings. Also caves. I very much doubt he's made it up into the Sangre de Cristos yet, but we'll want the information at hand."

"We passed over an old house in the helicopter," I said.

Betty nodded. "About five miles west? The Haines place." She tapped the map.

"It's exactly the kind of structure he would avoid," I said.

"Gotcha," she said.

"I've got to ask. We didn't see much when we were up in that helicopter, but isn't there some way we can use it? It seems you could cover a lot of ground in a short period of time."

Robertson smiled indulgently. "My people are looking for sign. Dropped items. A scuff mark from a sneaker in a dry wash. A gum wrapper. A dried-up puddle where he stopped to take a piss. Even a loose thread. You don't see any of that from the air. We'll put people on horseback to get to a search location, but once there, it's all about eyes on the ground."

"What about technology? Those thermal whatevers?"

"Thermal imaging?" He shook his head. "The average human at rest in a neutral environment shows an image of about ninety-eight and a quarter degrees Fahrenheit. Would you like to take a guess at the ground temperature up in those hills right now?"

"Weather said it was going up to ninety-four today."

"Weather temp is taken at between four and six feet off the ground. Ground is going to be an easy ten degrees warmer."

"So a person wouldn't even show."

"A grown man or a group might show up as faint shadows, and if they were moving, you might be able to pick them out with military-grade equipment. But a small child? Nothing. Hiding or standing still? Not a blip."

"What about dogs, then? He's not afraid of them, and I've got plenty of his things to get a scent."

"Similar problem. It's the heat, Mr. Sauerman. Scent is carried on oils. Perspiration. Amounts so finite we can't even test for most of them. But a dog can smell them. The problem out here is that once the sun goes to work on those oils, the odor rises off the ground and gets dispersed. On a still day, the dogs just get confused, because the scent seems to be everywhere. If there's even a breath of wind, they won't find anything at all."

There was a hot breeze coming up off the plains.

"How familiar is your boy with the area?" Betty asked. "Would he know how to get to Storrie Lake, for instance?"

"We've only been here a few days. I wouldn't know how to get there."

"People with ASD often head for water," Robertson said. He pointed to the map. "What about these creeks?"

"They're both out of probability range," Betty told him. "And they'll be very low this time of year."

"Where do you get all this?" I asked. They were a lot more educated on folks with autism than the average law enforcement professional.

"SAR is about two things, Mr. Sauerman. Statistics and eyes on the ground. Lost-person behavior is the statistics. There's an international database covering rural, wilderness, and urban settings for people in various age groups, or with specific disabilities. It's updated regularly and as comprehensive as they can make it. One thing I can tell you is that recovery of autistic children has a very high probability of success within the first twenty-four hours. We plan on finding your son."

54

"Y ou mentioned mountain lions before," I said. I hadn't wanted to say it, but I had been thinking it so much that it just popped out.

It was later in the afternoon and the Kid had not yet been found. Robertson wanted me to stay at the house with him. I was more valuable as an information resource than as a searcher. The teams reported in over the radios regularly, which helped me to control my soul-destroying anxiety. It sounded like things were progressing. If I had been out in the field, I would have been defeated by the immensity of the problem.

"Not likely. Big cats don't come down unless they're driven down. This time of year, there's plenty to eat up in the mountains. It's cooler. There's water. I wouldn't worry about that problem."

"What would you worry about?"

"We think we're going to find him," he said. "Safe."

"I've heard coyotes at night."

"No doubt. But have you seen one? Our western coyotes are small. They might take a small pet, but even a small seven-year-old is big compared to them. They'll protect a den, but they don't usually attack. They run or hide."

Searches of the house and barn had turned up nothing more than another two shoe marks in the dust near the corral. The house over the hill, where an older retired couple agreed to keep an eye out for any seven-year-old children—lost or not—revealed no sign of him. The teams were now focusing on a small but hourly expanding circle of probability. Robertson and Betty had broken up the map into search cones, beginning at the IPP (Initial Planning Point)—the house—and fanning out across the hills. They had assigned probabilities to those cones based on geography. Some areas were too steep or, for some other reason, less accessible to a small traveler. One group had gone off in three pickup trucks to investigate the lake area and surrounding waters.

Hal was nervous with all of the strangers coming in and out of the house and roaming around the property. He stayed near me. Willie made a big pot of chili before heading out with one of the search teams. Robertson didn't question why I had two armed men living in the house with me, and I made no effort to explain.

My iPad chirped. Incoming email. A beer ad with an outdated coupon for discounts on Rolling Rock longnecks. That was Manny's way of letting me know that there was someone in our chat room who wanted to talk. It was after nine in New York, so I guessed that it was Skeli.

"I'll be in my room for a little while. Sing out if there's any word."

Robertson was busy examining the map again and didn't look up. "Will do."

Skeli looked tired. I couldn't imagine what I looked like.

"You're still at the office," I said. Her diploma and licenses covered the wall behind her.

"The last client just left. Benny's straightening up the equipment and then we're walking out." Benny was one of the therapy technicians. He was a big, gentle blonde from Iowa who had come to New York to seek his fortune on Broadway, but had enough foresight to pick up a marketable skill along the way.

"You okay?"

"Yes, we're doing fine." She looked down at her belly and back to me. She smiled. "Missing you."

"And I, you."

"You don't sound good."

"You're right. I'm stressed. The Kid went missing today."

"Oh my god. Is he back? Is he okay?"

"No. The state search-and-rescue people have been looking for him all afternoon." I filled her in on the little that I knew. "This is all a mess. We should never have come out here."

"You didn't have a choice."

"There's always a choice. I pulled him out of the only world that he understood—that he felt even remotely comfortable in—and brought him out to this very weird place. This would not have happened if we were still in New York."

"You don't know that. And he would not be better off if you were dead. And *that's* what might have happened if you were still in New York."

"I could have found a way."

"Well, find it now. That's got to be your goal. The only way you can help him right now is by making plans for the future. So do it."

"Anybody ever tell you you're one tough broad?"

"I know they're going to find him, Jason. So do you. He's hiding right now. But when he gets thirsty enough, or hungry enough, or forgets whatever it was that spooked him, he'll show up. Meanwhile, you have dozens of trained people out there doing what they do best. You said so yourself."

I had. She was right.

"As long as that asshole lawyer, what's-his-name, Blackmore, keeps you in purgatory, he wins and you lose. There must be some way you can turn this thing around. You're the smartest man I know." She looked away. Someone had just come into the room. "Give me one minute, Benny, and I'll be ready to go." She looked back at me—at the screen. "Is there any way that I can help? Pass messages to Virgil? Or talk to your FBI buddy?"

"Thanks. I don't know whether there really is a way out of this mess, but I'm the only one who's going to look for it. Do you pray?"

"Not since I was about the same age as the Kid," she said.

"I never got the habit. Times like these, though, I understand its appeal."

55

"Mr. Sauerman?"

Neither the voice, nor the words, registered. I heard them, but I did not understand how they might apply to me.

Skeli made a good point. I was in hiding because someone was afraid of something that I supposedly knew. Some vital piece of information that would disrupt their plan, and possibly send one or more people to prison. The fact that I had no idea as to what that might be was irrelevant. They believed and were afraid, and had, therefore, sent someone to kill me. If they were afraid, I had the power. I just needed to find the key to use it.

"Mr. Sauerman?"

The Kid was going to be found. That mantra was for my own fear. If I let myself think anything else, that would be all I could think about. Fear for him would drive out every other thought. I had let my fear rob me of my home, my family, and even of my own identity. I did not want to ever face a man with a gun again. Nor could I bear the death of another innocent, sacrificed in lieu of my own sorry ass. But I could still fight back with what I had left. My brain.

"Mr. Sauerman. Sir!"

My head snapped up. It was one of the state cops at my bedroom door—they all looked identical in their black uniforms—and I had the immediate realization that he had been trying to get my attention for some time. But who the hell was Sauerman?

"Yes? What's up?" I asked. Of course. *I* was supposed to be Sauerman. Sauerman was a frightened man on the run. Well, I was a frightened man, too, but I was no longer running.

"IC wants you downstairs."

Incident coordinator. Robertson.

"Thank you."

Robertson and two of the team leaders were at the table. The woman, Betty, had a bowl of the chili, which she was attacking with ferocity.

"You need to hear all this. There've been some developments. They found sign. Some yellow threads on the edge of a patch of bougainvillea. It looks like the boy hid there at one point. Our people could have walked right past him."

"But he's gone again."

"Yes, but this tells us where we need to concentrate. I can bring in teams from more remote areas and get everyone in this area here." He pointed to the map and a purple-outlined cone that covered a few hundred acres.

"What says he hasn't already walked out of the area?"

"This border? Very steep and all rock. It would be like trying to climb up the side of a thirty-foot-tall frying pan on your hands and knees. There's plenty of places for a small child to hide all along the base, but climb over it? No. Not during the day."

Sunset was not far off. I guess he saw that thought on my face.

"We'll post people on that ridge all night if we have to. We're close, Mr. Sauerman. This is very good news."

"You're right. Thank you."

"But night is coming. We'll continue, but usually we try to attract people at night. Fires, big lights, horns. Anything to give someone who is lost a beacon of some kind. Autistic children don't usually respond."

"You're right. Big noise scares him. Hurts, actually. He might find light interesting, but not a fire or floodlight. Christmas tree lights, maybe. Sparkling, twinkling. Or colored lights."

Robertson looked at Betty. "Can we find something like that?"

"I'll make some calls," she said.

"Lastly, sir, we have a developing press problem. We can't ignore them. We set up a dummy command post down at the high school gym. I'm going to drive down there in a little while and talk to the reporters. I don't know your issues or why the marshals are interested, but a moment in front of the cameras might help us. People see a grieving parent on the local news and maybe remember seeing the boy walking along a road, or hiding in an outhouse."

"Let me think about it."

"That's fine. But I want you to know. They're not going to stay down there and be well behaved for very long. I'm surprised they're not up here already. By tomorrow morning they'll be right outside the door with trucks blocking the road and folks poking cameras in the window. They'll dig until they get every last bit of information available. It's going to be very hard to keep secrets, if you know what I mean."

"I understand."

He wanted me to say more, but I wasn't ready. I still wanted the Kid found in the next minute—or five.

"Now that we know the general area, wouldn't I be more valuable up there?" I asked. "He might come to me."

Robertson looked pained. "You're not trained. Sorry. If we put you out there, we have a greater likelihood of doubling our problem rather than resolving it."

"I want to go."

"Sir, I am not sending an untrained man out at night into that kind of terrain. And as it is an official SAR site, I can have you detained, if need be."

"If you don't find him tonight, then I'm going out there in the morning."

"We're going to find your son. I still believe he is close by and relatively safe."

"I'll talk to the press in the morning. When we're finished, I'm going out there."

"I don't make trades, Mr. Sauerman. I find lost people."

"I *do* make trades, Mr. Robertson, and I'm going to help you find him. Send one of your volunteers with me. If he hears my voice, he may come. I should be up there now."

56

Robertson knocked twice and put his head in the door.

"I've arranged for a press conference tomorrow morning at seven. Up here. They've all promised to hold back until then."

My laptop was open on the bed next to me, but I was having a hard time concentrating.

"And I go looking for him right after," I said.

"And I'll be going with you. Try and get some sleep." He spoke in a quiet, kind voice.

"Thanks."

Sleep wasn't on my agenda. Daybreak was seven hours away.

I had to expect that my picture would be all over the world the next morning. The story of an autistic child lost in the high mountain desert would be the number-one human interest story of the day. The distraught father speaking to the media for the first time would be irresistible.

I would be recognized. Outed on national news. How long would it take for the press to realize that John Sauerman, resident of Las Vegas, New Mexico, was actually Jason Stafford, the ex-felon who had graced the front page of New York's other favorite tabloid?

Better they hear it directly from me. The torrent was coming; it made sense to meet it head-on.

There was another knock at the door.

"Come in."

It was Hal. "You okay? I'll be in the next room."

"I'm fine. Thanks. Willie?"

"Still out with the team. They've put up a forward camp at the LKP. He'll sleep there."

LKP. Last known place. Twelve hours in and we had all adopted the jargon.

"See you in the morning. I'll probably be up for a while."

"You want company?"

"Thanks. No."

"Good night, then."

I tried lying down and closing my eyes. As soon as I let my mind relax, the images of horror swept in, screaming for attention. My son, cold, terrified, dehydrated, in pain, stalked by animals that flew, walked, or slithered.

I got up and went out onto the balcony. It was the night of a new moon. The stars looked close enough to touch. I took a chair, put my feet up on the railing, and tried to think of anything but my son.

People who grow up in cities learn about constellations from books. I'd been to the planetarium in Manhattan exactly three times in my life. The only constellation I could identify with any degree of confidence was the Big Dipper. There were times when I couldn't find it. A friend in college had explained that it was upside down and, therefore, looked different to me. I believed him because he had no reason to lie, and if he was playing a prank, it would have been the only one he ever attempted. Sometimes I could find it, sometimes not.

But at least the Big Dipper looked like a cup at the end of a long curved handle. A dipper. Other constellations looked nothing like their names. Man's desperate attempt to create order out of chaos. *Impose* order. And it *was* an imposition. Wasn't the display—which must resemble what the ancients saw every night—magnificent without having to be chopped into recognizable pieces? Did early navigators determine that a particular grouping resembled the Babylonian god of war? Wasn't it more likely that some shaman called it that as part of some religious quackery designed to keep the peasants in fear of their universe?

The universe is filled with mysteries enough. Why does man create mysteries where none exist? It merely highlights their ignorance. I had never been a student of astrology and was resigned to the idea that I never would become one.

Mathematics was filled with such supposed mysteries that, upon deeper investigation, were revealed to be mere coincidence or wordplay. Some, like Russell's paradox, or Euler's Königsberg bridges puzzle, were instrumental in opening up other fields. Others, like the seventeen camels, the rope around the Earth, or Ulam's Rose, revealed less about the workings of the universe than they did about the limits of mathematics as a form of communication.

Ulam's Rose. I sat up. Ulam's Spiral. I ran back into the bedroom and grabbed my laptop.

It took me less than a minute to find Manny's messages. They went back for a few months. Of course, he wasn't Manny then. Who had he been masquerading as back in April? The writer. Evan Hunter. I Googled him quickly and found the answer. Salvatore Albert Lombino.

I did a search for messages from Lombino. The one I wanted was the very first. The buyers of the shares of Becker Financial. The coded names of the buyers. Lists of numbers. Prime numbers.

Ulam's Spiral has drawn more than one young mathematician into its spiderweb of meaningless confluence. If in some distant future or alternate universe, the mystery of the spiral is solved, it will have more to do with our understanding of the workings of our subconscious than any new mathematical theorem. Chaos exists. Some events are truly random. The fact that we see patterns speaks to how we perceive reality—how the brain works—rather than to any intrinsic grand design.

Ulam was a twentieth-century mathematician who, during a sleep-inducing lecture at a conference he attended, began doodling a spiral shape composed of numbers in order, highlighting all the prime numbers:

17	16	15	14	**13**	
18	**5**	4	**3**	12	
19	6	**1**	**2**	**11**	
20	**7**	8	9	10	
21	22	**23**	24	25	26

He noticed that prime numbers tended to align on diagonals as the spiral increased in size. Then he saw that there were longitudinal and latitudinal lines. Later, when he was able to see computer-generated results, the lines became even more apparent. Eventually, a spiral was created that used numbers of several digits. When the resulting picture was reduced in size to an image that could be seen all at once, in its entirety, by the human eye, it looked like a rose. Ulam's Rose. The scientific mind looks for cause and effect. If lines exist, there must be an algorithm that can predict them. But in the case of Ulam's Rose, there is none. It's like seeing shapes in clouds.

During my junior year at Cornell, a cruel teaching assistant had assigned the problem to our class on a Thursday. My study group spent a long sleepless weekend modeling the spiral and running test after test for repeatable patterns. When we dragged our defeated selves back into class on Tuesday, the laughing grad ass told us, "You are all so arrogant as to think that every problem can be solved. You must develop humility to be great mathematicians." I hated the jerk.

I set up an algorithm, plugged it into Excel, and sat back and watched as the spiral grew. I limited it to two figures to save time. I doubted that I would need more to see the patterns I needed. I asked the program to highlight all prime numbers and they all turned **bold**. Lines appeared. I switched back to Manny's email and compared.

1 3 13 31
19 7 23 47
5 19 41 71

The numbers matched. I checked a full page just to be sure. I was right. The numerical names of all the blind accounts that had been purchasing shares in Virgil's firm had all been taken from the meaningless patterns that exist in Ulam's Rose.

And that told me two more things. The man who was behind the takeover of the firm—the great mastermind—was a mathematician. Or had at least studied enough math to be aware of the Rose. And he had the same sense of humor as that asshole of a graduate student. Add to that the more obvious points—that he must know securities laws and how to evade them—and the picture became clearer. I knew someone who fit that image.

Second, I had a connection—tenuous, and easily coincidental— between the penny stock trades and the takeover. Rose Holdings. Rose Holdings was the name of the real estate company that owned the bison ranch/truck garage.

Blackmore would sneer. Special Agent Brady would think I had been out in the sun too long. But that fragile bit of information was just what Manny would need to find more evidence of the connections.

It was a small thing, and I was desperate, but I felt the power shift in my direction. I sent a message to Manny and another to Virgil. Neither would be up at that late hour, but it didn't matter. The next morning was soon enough.

I went back out onto the balcony and leaned against the railing. The Big Dipper was right-side up. There was a flicker of light in the corner of my eye and I looked up. There was another. Directly overhead, shooting stars were blossoming from a stellar cornucopia. Flickers became long flashes that started as a comet and ended with a wink. There were hundreds. They came faster and faster.

My neck ached. I realized that I had been watching for almost an hour. The star show slowed, then stopped. I waited, but there were no more. It was over.

I felt cold and lonely again, just the way the Kid would feel.

Somewhere up in the hills a coyote barked. A *"Yip. Yip. Yip."* More playful than angry. A second coyote answered. Then they howled to each other. Others joined in. There had been silence during the meteor shower, but now the coyotes were letting loose. It was both scary and majestic. I couldn't tell how many voices—possibly a handful, maybe more.

And I thought of the Kid out there alone, cold, and frightened, listening to this chorus, and a cold chill ran up my back. I did not fall asleep for hours.

57

I didn't see the sun come up. My balcony faced west. But I felt the heat rise even before the sun was fully up. It was going to be another hot day.

My laptop was still open. I checked for messages. Nothing from Virgil and just a short single sentence from Manny. *I'm on it.*

The smells of coffee and bacon frying were already wafting up the stairs. I cleaned up and dressed carefully for a day in the desert. Sturdy hiking shoes; light, loose-fitting pants; a long-sleeved shirt; and my Yankees cap. I slathered sunscreen on any body part that had the slightest chance of being touched by sunlight.

Hal was at the table, eating breakfast with three of the volunteers. Robertson had temporarily moved his maps and was looking at satellite images on his laptop. Other members of the team drifted in and out while I ate. No one talked much.

I watched over Robertson's shoulder as he sectioned off areas to be searched. He was using a series of red lines of varying width to mark the borders. One section had a line considerably wider than any of the others.

"What's there?" I asked.

He looked up. "Where?"

"The thick red line."

"This is the rock outcrop I mentioned. A wall. Ten meters tall and one hundred eight meters long. On the far side it slopes off gently, mostly bare rock. Not much cover."

"We flew over it yesterday. We caught a thermal off it that threw us up a dozen feet or so."

He chuckled. "And then dropped you right back, I bet. It's a good sight marker. When you're out there staring at the ground for hours on end, it's necessary to be able to look up every once in a while and immediately get your bearings. I set up search patterns with these kinds of natural markers. I could give everyone GPS coordinates, but technology tends to develop quirks in extreme environments. The most efficient tools my people take into the field are their eyes and their brains. You ready for your fifteen minutes of fame? Those reporters will be up here soon."

I had already experienced more than my share of fame—or infamy. "What would happen if we left now and skipped the big show?"

"Well, I'd lose credibility with that crowd, and I can't afford that. They've got people who listen to state police radio all day, and when they hear my name, they hit the road. Lost hikers, hunters, children, you name it. It's all good copy. Sometimes they can even help. The only way I can keep them in-line is to play fair. Otherwise, they'd be up the trail with their high heels, blow-dried hair, cameras, and microphones, getting in our way or getting lost on their own. We promised them a worried father. We have to give it to them."

"Then let's get it over with."

"Amen." He checked his watch. "They should start arriving in another fifteen minutes."

"Sounds like they're early," Hal said.

Then I heard it, too. Vehicles coming up the gravel road.

"Showtime," I said.

58

It wasn't the press.

A state police cruiser came into the yard, lights flashing, followed by two black Ford Explorers. They all pulled to a stop and the doors flew open. Marshals Reyes and Geary stepped down from the backseat of the first SUV.

"Mr. Sauerman, we need to talk," Reyes said.

Robertson put up a hand. "You can have your talk, but not right now. There are about two dozen reporters due to come up that road any minute to talk to Mr. Sauerman. It won't take long."

"I'm afraid our news preempts any such action."

The yard now seemed full of police. Six more deputy marshals and two state police were out of the vehicles and standing behind Reyes. Geary was still wearing the boat shoes. All the other deputy marshals had cowboy boots, though only Reyes had the silver toe-caps. Maybe it was a tribal method of denoting rank.

"What's going on, Lieutenant?" Robertson asked.

One of the staties answered. "It's their ball, Roy. I've requested a tactical team to back them up. You need to hear what they've got to say."

"Let's talk inside. I don't want the press to show up in the middle of this," I said.

Ten big men crammed into the combined living room/dining room. I sat on the couch and felt a sharp edge poke me in the back. I reached behind the pillow and found the Kid's iPad.

"Let's get on with it, boys. I want to get out and find my son today."

"I understand," Marshal Reyes said. "But this is important."

He laid it out quickly. The DEA had received some disturbing information from Mexican authorities. An unidentified person had made a series of telephone calls from Las Vegas, New Mexico, to a landline phone in Mexico City early in the week. That phone was on a list of numbers used by members of the Mara. There was no record of the conversation, but there were subsequent calls from Mexico to a cell phone in the States. DEA tracked it to a house in the Tucson suburbs. When they went in to investigate, they found an abandoned home—there were still plenty of those to be found all over the Southwest. The DEA talked to neighbors. Four young Latinos had been living there alone—squatting. They had pirated electricity and cable from a nearby house and mostly stayed indoors ordering pizza, Chinese, and burritos. They went out sporadically, driving a white double-cab Toyota pickup.

"Okay, I see why you're nervous. But I've barely been in Las Vegas. The odds of someone recognizing me on one of the three times I've been to town are negligible. It's coincidence. That's all."

"I'm not done," Reyes said. "There was evidence that the basement of the house had been used to hold at least one prisoner. DEA called FBI who called in an evidence response team. Within twenty-four hours, the ERT matched blood and fecal matter to our client. The dead guy found out in the desert. They contacted us and here we are."

"So these Maras are the ones who got to Castillo?" I understood the marshals' concern for my welfare, but there was something else they hadn't yet said.

"The evidence is solid."

"And where are they now? The Maras?"

"We have to accept the possibility that they have taken your son."

I was as stunned as anyone in the room. In the silence, we all heard the sound of more vehicles coming up the road.

Robertson recovered first. "Marshal, I have to tell you, we have evidence that the boy was in these hills as of late yesterday. We've narrowed our search down to one valley. I believe we're going to find him within the next few hours."

"You're not seeing the whole picture. That's why I'm now in charge."

I lost it. It sounded like he was fighting over turf again. "Are you out of your mind? That is the most tenuous bull-pukey nonsense I can imagine. Based on a phone call? You don't even know if it was just some poor landscaper trying to get a message to his mother."

Reyes leaned in close, his face inches from mine. "Are you willing to bet lives on that? Because that's what you'll be doing. These *sicarios* get their kicks from pain and death. They like to leave their victims to bleed out rather than put them down quickly. They take machetes and start by hacking off hands or feet, then arms and legs. Do you have that picture in your head? Good."

I didn't back away. "I'm afraid. I never said I wasn't. But it was fear and running away from fear that got me and my son into this mess. I'm done with it. So, I decide from now on. And I have decided that I'm going into those hills and bring my son home."

"I can't let you do that."

Cars and television vans began rolling into the front yard, sending up clouds of brown dust.

Robertson said, "That's the press arriving, Marshal." He spoke calmly and reasonably, wringing some of the heat out of the argument. "We're leaving just as soon as we talk to these folks."

"These Maras are well armed. If they come up here, it'll be a bloodbath," Reyes said. "Your people won't stand a chance against them."

"Marshal," I interrupted. "If I am no longer in witness protection, then you have no say in what I do or don't do. So, I respectfully want to take myself out of WITSEC. It's been a mistake. I won't let it happen again."

The reporters were out in the early-morning sun, piling out of cars and trucks, cameramen behind. The clamor was muted, but wouldn't be for long.

Reyes had lost and he knew it, but he had to try one last time. "Mr. Sauerman, I must insist that you rethink your position."

"The name is Stafford, okay? Jason Stafford, of New York, New

York. Hal? I know I just voided your contract, but I wouldn't mind having someone to lean on when I talk to the press."

"I'm with you," Hal said.

"Allow me to do the introductions," Roy Robertson said.

"All right, but get it right. The name is Jason Stafford."

59

Hal stood to my left, slightly in front. Robertson was on my right with the state lieutenant to his side. The deputy marshals flanked us on both sides. I may have quit the program, but they weren't quite ready to walk away. Reyes and Geary, however, remained in the house.

"I'm going to save you all some research time. My name is Jason Stafford. I'm from New York. Until a few minutes ago, I was protected by the WITSEC program as a potential witness in federal court."

They were all screaming questions long before I finished speaking. I ignored them all and continued.

"Yesterday morning, my seven-year-old son went missing. We believe that he's up in the hills. I'm going looking for him as soon as we are finished here. You'll understand if I leave suddenly. I'd like to get started."

I began to pick out particular voices and their questions in the melee. I answered as best I could.

"No, I will not comment on a federal investigation. I'm here to talk about finding my son."

"Yes, it's true. My son has ASD. He is verbal and intelligent, but his likes and dislikes, fears and strengths, are all varying and unpredictable."

"No, I don't believe he has been taken by any person or persons. There does seem to be a rumor to that effect going around."

"I believe he's gone walkabout. It happens to forty percent of kids on the spectrum. He is probably disoriented, lost, hungry, and thirsty, and I'd like to go find him as soon as possible."

"Yes, I believe he is alive, but I think that is a dumbass question. I will believe that until I see good reason to change my mind."

"Ask Mr. Robertson, he's the expert."

Robertson took over and the crowd quieted down. They knew him and proffered him a modicum of respect. He answered their questions tersely, but gave them a few good lines of copy, too.

"Mr. Stafford! Mr. Stafford!"

The woman didn't need to yell, everyone else had calmed down.

"Yes, ma'am."

"How does it feel to have your child lost in the high desert? What are you feeling right now?"

"Impatience. I'm very worried for my son and want to get started."

"You don't appear to be distraught. Are you always so controlled?"

She had already written her story.

"Yes, I am." I turned to Robertson. "Can we go now?"

At the back of the crowd a deputy sheriff who had been sitting in his car at the head of the driveway put on the lights and siren and peeled out onto the road. Heads whipped around to watch him leave. The rest of us stood in various stages of amazement or confusion.

A second sheriff's car came hurtling down the road from up in the hills. Lights, no siren. Two reporters turned and ran for their cars. The rest of them looked like they thought it might be a good idea.

The state police lieutenant strode over to his car and conferred with his driver. A moment later he burst into action, running around the car and jumping into the shotgun seat. The car fishtailed twice leaving the driveway.

The reporters all turned and ran for their vehicles.

The marshals were standing around like bachelors at a bridal shower. They knew they'd rather be somewhere else, but weren't sure where.

Reyes burst out the front door. "Mount up. I want no radio chatter."

Robertson stepped in front of him. "You mind telling us what's going on?"

"I just got it from the FBI. Those four Maras? They stopped for gas just up the road from Ribera. A deputy saw the truck and radioed it in.

They're now holed up in the store. There's a tactical team coming up from Albuquerque, and CIRG has a SWAT team on standby."

"I suppose they were on their way here?" I said.

"That's a working hypothesis," Reyes said.

"And now they're not."

"You're cocky, Stafford, and I don't like that. In my business, over-confidence is the number-one killer. If those punks were on their way here, it was because someone gave you up, and that someone is still out there."

I didn't have an answer. He waited to see if his words had made any mark. They had, but I didn't give him the satisfaction.

I let his words in and examined them for the first time. There were plenty of weak links in the chain of events—too many alternative explanations for a series of coincidences to be considered evidence of a possible attack on me or the Kid. But if by some remote possibility, the few facts did add up to a real threat, the consequences would be ghastly.

The call from Las Vegas to Mexico City was key. If someone had recognized me and made such a call, who was it? The odds of it being a random stranger were impossible to calculate. At any rate, much too low to consider. That left only the people who knew where I was—the marshals and bodyguards, Skeli, and Larry. The last two were out of the running. Much as I hated to admit it, the marshals also had to be excluded. They had too much to lose. That left Hal and Willie.

An image came to mind of Hal sitting on the hillside in his make-shift blind, watching the road below, and talking on his cell phone. Another arose, this one of Hal questioning me about my past history with the Mijos and Castillo on the drive from Tucson.

Willie had been there, too, and with his frequent trips to town, he had ample opportunity to make the call in question. And the Kid didn't like him, had never trusted him. The Kid was afraid of almost everyone outside of a very small group. But my mind kept coming back to our conversation soon after Willie first arrived. "He's bad."

60

Robertson was on the phone, checking on his order for a pair of ATVs to get us all up to the LKP camp—I would have been useless on horseback. They would be arriving momentarily. Hal filled backpacks with bottled water. He looked different to me already. His solitary, stoic nature now seemed mendacious and sinister. I plunked myself down on the couch and tried to look like I wasn't going mad with a psychic mix of paranoia and impatience. I landed on the Kid's iPad. Again.

The computer survived the experience. So did I. I held it in my hands and felt the Kid's presence. Emotion threatened to overwhelm me, and I forced myself back into front brain mode. I was going to find my son, and to do that I needed a clear head.

I turned on the iPad and put in the Kid's password—8, 1, 1, the number of our apartment at the Ansonia. His magic image-finder app was open and running. It hit me. It was too simple. Anyone could have taken my picture, run it through this app or one like it and found my true identity. I wasn't exactly a celebrity, but my face had been in the news more than a few times, most recently thanks to Blackmore's machinations. How that unknown person had known who to call to sic the Maras on me was a separate mystery, but I thought I had the first clue. Leaving the witness protection program was the wisest thing I had done. Nowhere was safe. Hiding didn't work. If I had to live the rest of my life with a constant bodyguard, that was a better existence than cowering here at the end of the road. It all fit and made sense to me. The Kid and I were going home—just as soon as I found him. It took only another minute to find that all of my deductions were wrong.

I swiped the page to see what pictures my son had last researched.

Cars. The marshals' Cuda. A swaybacked, bone-thin dog from Deming. An ancient Chevy pickup he had photographed on the street in Las Vegas. A blurred long shot of the valley that, after some manipulation, revealed four indistinct shapes that could have been javelinas. There was only one picture of a person. Only one. Willie. The Kid had caught Willie at the kitchen counter the previous morning, looking directly into the webcam. The picture must have been taken moments after I went out for some "outside air." It was a good shot. It looked just like him. I touched the search button and waited.

The app flashed rapidly, one image appearing instantly as the previous near miss was rejected. Sometimes the mistakes were ludicrous—women or old men—sometimes even humorous—a sleepy-eyed cartoon mule. The program began to slow. Fewer pictures appeared, but they were much closer to the original than any of the previous possibilities.

"Ready to roll?" Robertson said.

I looked up. He and Hal were standing by the door.

"Give me one minute. I just came up with something," I said.

Robertson looked surprised. "Okay."

"I'm loading the off-roads," Hal said, walking out with three bulging backpacks.

The app continued to work. From the rejects, I could see why the program was being forced to work so hard. Willie had an unremarkable face. He looked like a thousand other men. There were too many faces that were almost a fit. Willie was the noncelebrity. The face that would disappear in any crowd.

Then the screen stopped flashing and resolved into four quadrants. Each held a headshot of a face that could easily have been Willie. One man had a mustache, small and groomed, no bigger than a toothbrush, but it practically jumped off the screen. Another face was half covered with a thick black beard, but I could see why the app had chosen it. The shape of the eyes, the nose, and the forehead were an excellent match. They could all have been the same person.

I kept staring. The fourth face looked the least like Willie. The nose longer, the cheeks less angular. But the eyes were very much like Willie's. And then I saw why the computer had chosen that image.

"Would you ask Hal to come back in here?" I said. "I want him to see this." I clicked on the one face that was, without a shadow of a doubt, Willie's.

They were both back in less than a minute.

"Take a look," I said. "You know this guy?"

Hal took the iPad. "What is this?"

"This is the Kid's iPad. That's what he was playing with yesterday. Just before he took off."

"Well, they all *look* like Willie. But this guy *is* Willie. He's had some work done since this picture was taken—the nose for sure—but there's no doubt. It's him. Look at the ears. There can't be more than one set of ears like that in this world."

"Click on that face. See what you get."

He touched the screen. "Oh shit."

61

Willie was a dead man.

EX-DEA MAN KILLED IN METH LAB FIRE

Huntingburg, Indiana—Justice finally caught up with the killer Walter Lee Collins this week. The ex–DEA agent and convicted murderer, currently under federal indictment in the Southern District of Florida for soliciting and accepting bribes, drug trafficking, money laundering, and a host of other related charges, was killed in an explosive fire that erupted during an eight-hour siege by U.S. Marshals, federal agents of the DEA, and Indiana state troopers of a farm in this rural section of southwest Indiana. According to ISP 1st Sgt. Adam Wheeler, "The farm was being used as a meth factory. We don't yet know what initiated the explosion, but there were large containers of volatile chemicals on the premises." Identification is pending on the bodies of two other individuals, assumed to be co-conspirators, found in the ashes of what had once been a hog-raising housing system on the property.

Collins was a ten-year decorated veteran of the federal agency and a member of an elite task force that operated in Southern Florida. The team was restructured in 2008, and two senior members were allowed to resign after allegations of abusive and possibly illegal practices, though no charges were ever filed against either agent. After reassignment, Collins's performance evaluations slipped dramatically, triggering an internal investigation that eventually revealed a pattern of criminal activities going back three years. Local authorities in Florida believe that Collins was tipped off to the investigation and was able to flee prior to arrest. Today's events end a two-year nationwide search . . .

"Your son could read this?" Hal said.

"No. But he knows enough to get the gist." He knew the word *kill*.

"How old is this article?"

"Three years. Our Willie has managed to fly under the radar for quite a while."

"We have to get the marshals back here."

"I have to get up into that backcountry and save my son."

"And I need to protect my people," Robertson said.

"Then let's move," I said. "No radio. He might be listening in. Cell phones only."

62

From the air, the foothills had appeared desolate and unmarked, but coming up on the ATVs, we followed well-used trails through a forest of short trees. I understood much better the problems of tracking someone through this wilderness. Off the trail, the ground was rough, rocky, and as dry as moondust. Tracks might show up in the sand or be filled in by the merest puff of wind. Outcroppings of rock might be a single large stone, or the tip of an underground mountain.

Two miles up a series of dusty trails was the LKP camp. It would have taken us an hour to hike up to it. The ATVs got us from the canyon where the road petered out and up to the camp in ten minutes.

They had set up self-supporting tents in a semicircle. A rope was stretched between two trees, and six horses were tied to it. They looked miserable. Facing the tents was a canopy about ten feet a side. Hanging from it, like a decoration at a Brooklyn block party, were strings of multicolored Christmas tree lights. Underneath it—the only shade in sight—was a long folding table and camp chairs. Betty sat there with a handheld radio, a cell phone, and a map. All the tools she needed.

"I've called all of my teams," she said as we approached. "Your man is out along this area here." She pointed at the map.

Robertson and I huddled over it. The lines of elevation through that section were close together, indicating a steep series of inclines.

"They don't get much signal over there, unless they're up on a rise."

"Can you show me where you found the yellow threads?" I asked.

She dug in a backpack and retrieved a large plastic ziplock freezer bag. "Here they are. The patch of stickers where we found it is just down that trail—maybe ten meters."

They were the same color as his shirt. "We'll start there," I said.

"Hold up," Robertson said. "I don't want to bump into this nutter stumbling down the swash of some gully over here."

"I'll be with you every step," Hal said.

Robertson smiled at him. "That goes without saying. But I want to avoid trouble. We're here to get the child. Let the marshals come back and take on the bad guy. It's their job."

"I think we now know who called in those Mexican shooters," Hal said. "If I get a chance to take him out, I will do it."

"Well, let's hope you don't," I said. "Who takes point?"

"I do," said Robertson. "You two stay close. Betty, if you hear shots, call all your people in and get them back down to the house. I don't want any of our volunteers taking a stray bullet."

"Clear," she said.

Robertson led the way. I followed a few steps back, with Hal not far behind me. We strode quickly at first. That section of the trail had been covered extensively already.

"Let your eyes relax. You're not looking for something specific. You're trying to find an anomaly. Broken twigs, bits of color that don't belong, marks on the ground. We stop and look at anything."

A quarter of an hour later, I was already feeling the effects of dehydration. Sweat evaporated faster than it ran, so it was hard to explain why my lips felt like they were cracking and my brain was working at half speed. How had the Kid survived twenty hours of this? There was something about that question that began working on me. How had he survived? Answer that, and I had a good chance of finding him.

We stopped for a drink of water and a quick planning session.

"I want to cover this section from this cliff to the arroyo over here," Robertson said, pointing them out on the map. "Once we get over this next rise, you'll be able to see the cliff. It's a big rock face due south of us."

"It's the biggest chunk of rock out here," I said.

"We'll hike down to the arroyo. It runs roughly parallel. We can then do diagonal sweeps between the two, working our way up toward the end of the valley. Questions?"

"The cliff faces north. The base will be in at least partial shade all day." I was trying to think like a lost child. My lost child.

"Good point, Mr. Stafford."

Crossing the top of the next rise, we were hit by the full heat of the morning sun. I pulled my cap lower, but it was like looking into a furnace. Color disappeared. My eyes were so dry it hurt to blink.

"How's everybody?" Robertson said. "It gets hotter, if you can believe it. I started doing cave rescues years ago, because climbing down into dark, rattlesnake-infested holes in the ground beat walking around in a hundred-and-twenty-degree desert heat."

He was talking to keep us alert. It was too easy in that heat to let the mind drift and concentration slip. It worked. I shook off the lethargy and focused on the Kid.

We came to the arroyo. The sides had once been steep, but too many dry seasons had caused them to collapse. Vegetation had spread across the wide, dry creek bed. We stuck to the trail.

"Javelinas probably cut this. There's deer and elk farther up in the mountains, but they don't get down this way much. Nothing for them. But if you see a family of those pigs coming through, don't hesitate. Jump off the path or they'll run you right over. They're aggressive sons-a-bitches and they've got tusks. They'll hurt ya."

"There are a lot of them here, too. We've been seeing small herds of them every day since we arrived," I said.

"Could be the same group. They move around a lot. You probably saw them most in the morning and late afternoon. Watch your step. There's a rattler under that tree."

The little pine was about six feet off the trail and only about knee-high. It was almost bare of needles and looked more dead than alive. The snake was curled around the base, hugging the sparse shade, and so well camouflaged I had to stare hard to make out the triangle-shaped head against the mottled, dusty brown soil. It was smaller than I expected—only three feet long or so.

"Keep moving and he won't mind you. Most people get snakebit because of curiosity. That or stupidity."

I was not curious. Neither was Hal. We both stayed on the far side of the trail as we moved past it.

The Kid would have been curious, I thought. Not stupid, but not knowing any better. That cold hollow returned to the pit of my stomach. I refused to answer the question of what I would do if we didn't find him.

63

We swept back and forth across that section of the valley four times. We saw no more snakes, but, according to Roy Robertson, that was due to our failure to see them rather than there being only one rattlesnake in the whole valley. We took a break in the shade of the cliff each time we reached it. We drank water—"rehydrated" was how Robertson put it—and let a film of sweat appear. Then, stepping back out into the sunlight, the sweat instantly evaporated, and for a minute it felt as cool as springtime.

"Coyote," he said, pointing at the ground.

I saw what looked like dog tracks in the sand. There seemed to be a lot of them.

"We may be near a den," Robertson continued. "Keep an eye out."

"I thought you said they weren't dangerous."

"All wild animals are dangerous. What I said was they rarely attack. But they will defend a den."

"It looks like there were a lot of them here," I said.

He smiled. "Does it? Or it could be just a few moving around—agitated over something."

I looked up. The cliff looked like a single rock, the face smooth and weathered. Two-thirds of the way up—some twenty feet over our heads—the rock was split laterally in a long gash, creating a recess that in spots was two feet tall but dwindled down to nothing.

The crevasse was well-shaded from the sun. I imagined the rock would still be cool in there. If I'd been a child looking for cover, that's where I would have headed.

"Could the Kid have climbed up there?" I asked.

Hal looked up and ran his hands over the smooth rock. "I've done some rock climbing and I know I couldn't do it."

Robertson stood back and eyed the whole wall. "We should check. I don't see how the boy could have managed it, but I don't like not looking into every possibility."

The cliff was a lot taller than any of the rocks in Central Park, but no steeper or smoother. I didn't know how the Kid could have done it, or where he'd get the confidence to try, but in my mind I could easily picture him creeping up the face of a mountain. Coming down was a different story entirely.

"If he's up there, he has no idea of how to get down," I said. "He'd be like a cat in a tree."

"I don't believe it," Hal said.

"Hey, Kid!" I called out. "It's your dad. It's Jason. Come on out. I want to take you home. Your real home, okay?" I didn't expect an answer, so I wasn't disappointed when I failed to get one. "How do we get up there?" I asked. "Anybody got a ladder?"

"No, but we can rappel down," Robertson said. "We'll hike around the base and come up the back side. According to the map, the land flattens out up there. I've rope and some equipment in my pack."

"Now?" Hal asked. We had only covered about half of the valley.

"I don't think he's there, because I don't see how he could get up there," Robertson said. "But it's out of the sun and safe from everything that walks, runs, or slithers down here. If I could climb up there, that's where I'd want to be. Let's go. We can come back and finish our sweep later in the day."

The lines on the map appeared in my mind. "Head up to the east. It looks steeper, but it's not. The west-side approach goes through much rougher country."

Robertson checked his map and a moment later agreed. "He's right."

For the next half hour, we made our way up a steep incline at the upper end of the valley. All three of us were reeling with exhaustion by the time we got to the top of the rise, but looking back we could see that the top of the rock was now slightly beneath us. We rested for a minute while Robertson scanned the valley with his binoculars.

"There's a group of searchers a bit to the west. I can't tell if your man Willie is one of them or not."

There seemed to be a lot of vegetation for a desert. A lone man could have hidden nearby and easily followed us without being seen. "He could be anywhere," I said. "We can't worry about him. Let's just stay alert and find the Kid. The sooner we're out of these hills, the better."

"Agreed," Hal said, but he didn't stop looking.

It took us only minutes to hike back down to the top of the cliff.

"Hey, Kid. Can you hear me?" Still no answer.

The rock was solid up top with no place to dig in anchors. We dropped our backpacks and executed a quick reconnaissance of the cliff.

"Can you two take my weight?" Robertson asked.

"I'll go," I said. "He doesn't know you. And besides, if anyone is going to fall, I'd rather it was me."

Robertson ignored every maniacal word I said. "Can you take my weight?"

"Yes." I would.

"I've done this kind of thing a hundred times or more. Follow my instructions and we'll do just fine."

Hal and I each took the end of a line and wrapped it around our waists. Robertson hooked both ropes to his harness and made sure they ran free and stopped when he squeezed the clamp.

"Just lean back and let the harness do the work. I'll take him to the bottom and you two can hike around to join us. Questions?"

"Suppose we're not in the right place? Suppose you have to move."

"Then I'll find a spot to take the weight off and you two can take turns sidestepping."

We stood ten feet apart and about six feet from the edge. Robertson controlled the lines. He walked backward, paused at the lip, and then continued down out of our view. He wasn't heavy, but I was relieved when I felt a sudden slack in the line.

"I'm here, but too far to the west to see much. We're all going to walk slowly back to the east, one step at a time. Stafford, you first. Then me. Then Hal. Got it? No time for rehearsals. Let's do it. Waltz tempo. One, two, three."

On one, I stepped to my left and waited. A moment later, Hal completed the pattern.

"Good. Maybe three or four more like that and I'll be there. I've got to lean out to clear an overhang, so be prepared to take my weight again. Ready? Three steps this time."

We crossed another five feet and waited. Even if we all screwed up enormously, the remaining fall was only twenty feet. A fall would be damaging but not fatal. The greater danger was either Hal or me losing our balance and getting pulled over the edge.

"This is a good position. I'm going to stand on the crack here. Stay braced in case I slip. Got it?"

We both yelled an acknowledgment. The tension on the line disappeared. I found that I was holding my breath as though every cent I ever had, every love I'd ever known, and every atom of my being was on the line and the roulette wheel was spinning, the ball already jumping in the opposite direction.

"Mr. Stafford?"

My heart stopped.

"Your son is here. He's okay."

Life went on as before. The universal clock ticked away another second, but I had aged a lifetime.

"Thanks, Roy. What can I do? How do I help?"

"You two just hang loose for a minute. He's having a drink of water."

The rather impractical desire to jump over the edge and somehow fly down to comfort my son was almost overwhelming. The instinct for self-preservation—I would have broken my neck, I was sure—took over and prevented me.

"How does he look?"

"Not too bad. A little sunburn. Your dermatologist won't like it. Dehydrated, for sure, but his eyes are clear. He doesn't seem to be afraid of me."

"That's great," I said, because I couldn't think of anything else.

"Or the bats."

"Holy hell, no."

"They're clean. Not too many. Maybe a handful. They don't act rabid, but you'll probably want to get him to see a doctor soon anyhow."

A New York doctor. "Marvelous." I wanted to rush to the rim to try and get a look at my son, but in the process I would have given Robertson enough slack to break his neck. "Just get him out of there and down."

"I'm working on it."

He spoke softly to the Kid—too soft for me to make out any words. Whatever he said must have been magical, because he called up again a minute later. "Can you take both our weights? I've got a harness on him, but he can't rappel. You'll have to lower us."

Hal yelled back. "We don't have enough slack. I've got maybe ten feet I can give you—maybe another four to six feet if I walk to the edge, but that doesn't do it. You'll still be too far off the ground."

"That will have to do."

The Kid growled loud enough for us to hear.

"You okay, son?" I said. "That man is my friend. He's there to help you."

"We're all right. He's got a handful of toy cars up here. I guess he was afraid we might leave them. Give me a minute. Well, well. There's two empty water bottles up here. Your son's a pretty smart guy."

I hadn't even thought to count the water bottles back at the house to see if any were missing. Smarter than his dad.

"Let us know when you're ready," I said.

It wasn't an approved mountaineering technique. The tension came on the lines in a sudden jerk, enough that it would have pulled me off my feet if I wasn't prepared for it. Hal and I watched each other, trying to match the other's work as we slowly paid out the line.

"Keep talking to us, Roy. We can't see a thing."

"We're okay. Keep a-coming."

The line ran around my back and off to my left, so that as I eased with one hand, I could brake with the other. The tag end was coming closer.

"We should get closer," I said.

Hal nodded.

"Just a foot at a time."

We took the first step. The weight threatened to pull us off balance.

"Easy," Robertson called out.

"Easy for you to say," Hal grumbled.

"We're going to do it again," I yelled.

We took two more steps. That took us within a foot of the edge of the cliff. As the angle of the rope steepened, the weight increased substantially. The strain was starting to tell. By craning my neck I could see the Kid dangling below, strapped to Robertson, his arms wrapped around the man's neck.

What I couldn't see was how much farther they had to go to reach the ground. I had another three feet of line.

"Give us a read. How much to go?"

"Six feet? Seven?"

"We don't have that much line left."

"Give me what you've got. We'll be fine."

A twisted ankle miles from the camp during the midday heat could be a huge problem. A broken leg might be a death sentence.

Hal and I let out the last few feet of line. It was psychology, not physics, but the load felt twice as heavy as it had a moment before.

"That's it," I cried.

"Okay. Give me just a second."

Hal and I had all of our attention focused on the two bodies dangling below us. We had forgotten about Willie.

I was looking straight down, trying to guess the remaining distance to the ground, when I felt Hal's line go slack and the full weight of Roy and my son almost pulled me off the cliff. Hal was falling, his body limp and spinning as though he had been pushed. I dropped the rope and tried to save myself.

Robertson hit the ground and rolled easily, the Kid on top of him. They were down and safe. Hal's arms hit first. He collapsed into a lump and didn't move. I teetered over the drop, windmilling my arms in an attempt to fly backward just an inch or two to where my balance would return. It was no use, I was falling.

A hand gripped my shirt and plucked me back to safety. My knees were rubber, my mind overwhelmed with relief. I didn't question my good fortune, I exulted in it. Until I hit the ground and saw Willie standing over me.

He held a big semiautomatic handgun pointed at my face. The bore looked like a tunnel to hell.

"Get up. Slowly."

64

I rolled up onto hands and knees, feeling like I had been saved from a possible lingering death, only to face a quick and certain one.

"Don't shoot. I won't try anything." It was no lie. I had nothing left.

"On your feet."

"Stafford? Stafford?" Robertson called out. "Where are you?"

"Look out!" I yelled.

Willie smacked me across the back of the head with the pistol, not hard enough to stun, but it shut me up. To seal the deal, he fired the gun twice, barely aiming, down at the bottom of the cliff.

"No!" I screamed, leaping up at him.

He easily swatted me away. "Get moving. That way." He pointed with the pistol back up the trail to the hills above us. I started walking. He grabbed my pack and slung it over his shoulder.

I staggered forward, realizing only when I was up and walking that I was bleeding. Trickles of blood ran down from the back of my head, soaking into my shirt. I smelled of blood and fear. I was a predator attractor. Soon, I would be transformed into a vulture attractor.

"You didn't have to shoot them," I said.

"I didn't. I aimed to miss."

"So, you just shot *at* them."

"I don't kill innocent people," he said.

"I read about you. You're a convicted murderer."

"You read about that? Then you also know I'm dead. One statement is as true as another." He waved the gun to get me moving again. "It was line-of-duty. But the DEA was under pressure and they needed a fall guy. They offered me up as sacrifice."

"You're not going to kill me?"

"No. I'm holding you for delivery. That's what the client wanted."

"So, what is your deal?"

"You alive. In exchange for a suitcase full of hundred-dollar bills."

"I can get you a better deal."

"Too late. If I don't show up with you, they come after me. It makes the decision process very streamlined."

"I can get you a new identity. Make you a millionaire. Set you up anywhere in the world."

"Right now, I'm being hunted by the FBI, DEA, and the marshals. That's enough, don't you think?"

"You may be disappointed, you know. Your friends are going to be late. That's if they show at all. You'd be better off making a deal with me right now."

"Is that right? What happened? Their plane get redirected? Turbulence over Cincinnati? Don't bullshit me, please, Mr. Stafford. It's been tried. I'm not a good candidate."

He knew my name, therefore he knew my history. Discovering it was no more difficult—easier even—than finding out his background.

"If you know me, you know I can deliver what I promise."

"Can we drop this? Keep moving."

"They were recognized. Practically every law enforcement agent in the state is down by Ribera right now. They're holed up in a gas station. I just hope they've got brains enough to surrender, because they're not getting away."

"Who are you talking about?"

"The Maras. The four kids from Tucson. The *sicarios*."

Willie laughed. It wasn't a nice sound. "Dude, the Maras don't even know your name. I tried, don't get me wrong. I spoke to some people—made a few calls. If any of that Mijos crowd are still alive, they've got other concerns. I tried to make a deal, but there were no takers down south. Sorry if that disappoints."

"So who, then?"

"Who do you think?"

"Someone from the East Coast, maybe?"

"Snap."

"Give me a name." I knew the name, I just wanted the confirmation.

"Ho ho. Keep walking."

"One million dollars. Where do you want it?"

"In my hand. No? Sorry. No deal." He pushed me hard. I stumbled but stayed on my feet. "Come on. Up the hill."

"So if you're not going to shoot me, why shouldn't I run?"

"I didn't say I wouldn't shoot you. I said I wouldn't kill you. I don't think these people would mind if you arrived with an extra hole or two."

The hill fell away before me and I could see where we were headed. The abandoned farmhouse with the sagging roof, sunbaked walls, and slanting porch. I had my bearings. We had been traveling in a north-westerly direction—away from the morning sun—and had come just over a mile. That put the LKP base camp three miles to the east and a touch north. If I could get away, and stayed on the game trails, I could cover it in half an hour or less. The big question would be water. Willie had my pack. I'd need to get it away from him, or at least get into it.

The aliens had taken all the bicycles.

What? What was the matter with me?

I felt dizzy. Light-headed, and at the same time headachy. Heat prostration. Loss of blood. The combination would kill me long before I got to the camp.

"I need water," I said. My voice croaked. "If I don't get water, I won't make it another ten steps."

Willie must have felt it, too.

"Don't do anything we would both regret." He stripped off the backpack and removed two bottles of water. There would be four more and then we would be done. Our tongues would turn to shoe leather. Our eyes would shrivel in their sockets, but by that time we wouldn't care. We'd be comatose.

I tried to take a sip of the water but gulped half of it down before I was able to stop myself.

"Thank you," I said. My fantasy of a minute earlier had fled. I was beaten, humiliated. Grateful to my captor for a simple sip of water. How quickly Stockholm syndrome sets in.

"Move," he said, pointing down the hill toward the house.

A distant drumming played on my eardrums. For a moment, I was sure I had imagined it. Then I heard the regular beat of a helicopter and my hopes returned—and were immediately dashed. The helicopter was there to take me away, not to rescue me.

"They're coming. We've got to get out in the clearing, so hustle, old man."

Willie was no more than ten years my junior. The heat was getting to me again. The insult stung.

"Screw you. See if you can keep up." I started running down the trail.

Willie laughed at me and let me get a ten-yard head start before coming after me. I poured it on. The helicopter was coming closer. I looked wildly around for taller trees, more cover, and broke from the trail. The ground was rough, I tripped, but kept my legs churning and managed to stay upright and moving.

"Get back here!" Willie yelled. I ignored him and he was forced to follow.

I could see the helicopter swooping over the small valley in short arcs. They couldn't see us. I knew because I had been up there just the day before.

The machine flew right over me. I wanted to scream and cower, but I kept moving. The chances of escaping the helicopter were better if I stayed still and hidden, but I couldn't with Willie coming behind me. Another narrow game trail appeared before me. I stepped onto it and ran for all I was worth. I could hear Willie closing in on me.

He fired.

Terror releases adrenaline.

Special Agent Marcus Brady had once lectured me on the ineffec-
tiveness of handguns. It is next to impossible to hit a man-sized target
at twenty paces while running over broken ground. I believed him.
Nevertheless, when the gun boomed behind me, my adrenaline levels
soared.

Despite the noise generated by the helicopter, the pilot or one of his
passengers must have heard the sound of the big semiautomatic
because the machine tilted suddenly and flew straight for us. I ran,
trusting the canopy of pinyon trees to keep me at least partially hidden
as I pounded down the path.

The helicopter passed directly over me—and kept going. But as it
went, it flushed a family of javelinas, who burst out from the shelter of
a dense thicket of sagebrush and onto the trail. They were coming
straight at me, barking like terriers with head colds.

Without hesitation, I dove headfirst into the surrounding shrubbery.
At least a dozen of the creatures rushed by me. I looked back. Willie was
frozen in the middle of the narrow trail. The wild pigs hit him at knee
height. He staggered and, too late, tried to run out of the way. He was hit
again and again, in less than a second, until he fell awkwardly—awfully—
to his side and emitted a sharp scream of pain. The animals kept running
and disappeared a moment later, leaving dust and a groaning man.

I stepped back onto the trail, alert for the pigs' return or the presence of any stragglers. Willie was on the ground. I checked his hands.
They were empty. The gun had fallen only a few feet from him, but it
was no threat. Willie's right leg was bent at the knee—the wrong way.
He wouldn't be moving on his own any time soon.

The helicopter returned, moving slowly this time, hunting for us. I
stayed low and off the trail. Someone must have seen Willie lying in the
open because the machine lifted up and flew down toward the clearing
in front of the house, where it came down in a tornado of brown dust.

I picked up the gun. It was heavy.

"Just tell me who sent you and I'll let you live," I said.

Willie looked me in the eye and saw right through me. "Bullshit. You're no killer."

He was right, and I had no backup line. I threw the gun into the brush.

"I'll find you, Stafford. You won't even see it coming."

I rolled him onto his side and he screamed from the sudden pain.

"Thaaat's nice," I said. I took three bottles of water out of the backpack and gave him one. "It's going to take some time for them to hike up here and find you. I'll be long gone." I rummaged some more and took the binoculars, sunscreen, and two power bars. He wouldn't need them and I might.

"I should have just killed you and brought them your nuts in a plastic bag," he said, his voice cracking from the pain.

"Why do they want me alive?" I said.

He laughed. "I think they've got a few questions for you before they kill you."

They wanted to know what I had already told Blackmore. They would torture me to find out and then kill me themselves. Willie wasn't an assassin—he was just a traitor for hire.

"You should get that leg looked at, sport. It's not going to mend well." I stood up, kicked him once in the leg just because I could, and ran up the trail.

65

I stopped running when I reached the ridgeline. The helicopter sat in the center of the bowl of the valley, rotors spinning slowly. Three figures were spread across the bare front yard of the old house. They were being cautious, moving slowly up toward where they had heard the last shot. I dug out the binoculars and focused on each one.

They were all young—early to mid-twenties—dressed in sweat-shirts and jeans. I did not recognize any one of them, but they could have been part of the crew who had taken Aimee and me. If they weren't, they were stamped from the same mold. They were already sweating copiously. They were nervous. They didn't belong and they knew it.

All three were armed with long weapons—two rifles and a shot-gun. How would the dynamic change now that I was no longer in custody? Would they try to take me alive, or had this become a simple manhunt? I didn't want to be around to find out. I dropped the binoculars. I was well within range of one of those rifles. If they saw the glint of sunlight reflected off a lens, I would make an easy target. I got down on hands and knees and crawled over the top of the hill. I didn't get up again until I was well out of sight.

Once on the far side of the hill, I took my bearings. The cliff wall was an easy marker. If I kept that rock to my right at an ever-increasing angle, I would eventually run into the wide arroyo. I pictured the map in my mind. There was a long ravine a mile in front of me. I would need to keep more to my left to pass around it. I'd never be able to climb down into it and back out again. It was too steep and too narrow.

I took a sip of water and set out. Three miles. Minutes in a helicop-ter. Twenty-three minutes on the lap track at the Y. Twice around the reservoir. I'd done one lap in under ten once. I'd been a good bit younger.

Three miles—not quite a 5K—in midday sun in the desert. The rarified dry air at more than seven thousand feet making each breath an effort. Three miles pursued by killers with weapons that could kill at a thousand yards.

A single shot rang out. I froze. The sound echoed softly and when it faded it left a silence more intense than before. The single shot had not been for me.

Willie had become a dangerous liability for them. If I got away, Willie would be a wanted man. A wanted man with the need for hospital care. And probably willing to trade a name for leniency. Dangerous. He had to be eliminated.

I picked up the pace.

Crossing the searing heat of a shadeless rock outcrop, I had the thought that the men behind weren't trackers. They were just meathead toughs from Long Island. They were dealing with the same heat, thin air, and lack of familiarity with the land as I was. My odds improved.

The band on my cap was becoming a tourniquet around my head, squeezing and interfering with blood flow. I needed to take it off. If I took it off, I knew that I would feel better instantly. My shirt, too. I staggered to a stop and tried to remember how to manipulate buttons.

Damn. Water. I needed to drink more water. Skeli told me that all the time. Keep the damn hat and shirt on and take another sip. And keep moving.

I heard the helicopter. They were searching the last valley. I was long gone from there. They would spend valuable time learning the inefficiencies of tracking from the helicopter.

Keep moving. Drink water. The wound on the back of my head was bleeding again. Rivulets were running down my back. Skeli would say that I should have it looked at.

The thought of Skeli gave me a lift. I would see her soon. Another day at most.

Robertson. He would have taken the Kid back to the camp. The Kid was safe. Hungry, tired, scared, and thirsty—but safe. Hal? That fall had looked bad. Robertson would have had to send in a medevac team with stretchers. But shots had been fired. Would he have pulled his people instead? They were volunteers—heroes, not superheroes.

Where was the cliff? I'd lost it. The trees were taller, blocking out the horizon and much of the sky, but not sturdy enough to climb. Up ahead, I could see another hill. From that vantage, I would certainly get a sight of the rock.

Was I lost? Or just disoriented? Dazed by loss of blood or because I wasn't drinking enough?

I pushed through some thick sagebrush and found that my foot dangled over a forty-foot drop. The ravine. It felt like stepping into an empty elevator shaft. I threw myself onto my back and landed with one leg hanging over the edge. Safe. I did a quick inventory. All body parts were still attached. My hat and sunglasses were where they were supposed to be. The binoculars I had been holding in my left hand were gone. The sunscreen, too. The power bars were gone. I had only one water bottle. The other was forty feet down a crevasse in the earth that looked like the mouth of a Venus flytrap, waiting for a trusting fool to crawl down into it, only to be swallowed forever.

No food. Acceptable. One bottle of water. Marginal. I recalculated the odds of my survival. They had plummeted from their recent high. I was already feeling the effects of heat prostration and now I would have to conserve even more of my meager supply.

But my head was clearer. The sudden terror had given me another shot of lifesaving adrenaline. If I gave in to the fog surrounding my mind, I was a dead man.

I wriggled away from the drop. At least I knew where I was—not a small blessing. I was covering ground. I may have drifted too much to the right—south—but not by much. The detour around the ravine looked to be no more than half a football field away. I picked myself up and kept putting one foot in front of the other.

As I rounded the end of the deep cleft, I got a glimpse of the rock cliff. I pictured the map again. The arroyo was coming up. The underbrush was more sparse and shorter. I would be able to move more quickly. But I would lose my invisibility. I'd be an easy target for a rifleman shooting from a helicopter, or even from the top of one of the surrounding hills. Weighed against the certainty that I would soon run out of water and soon thereafter drop from the heat, the risk was a necessity. I angled more to my left to reach the open land of the arroyo sooner.

The sudden openness of the terrain gave a false sense of security. My universe was no longer defined by the distance to the next pinyon tree blocking the horizon. In another half mile I would find the collapsed eastern wall where we had crossed just a few hours earlier. From there, the trek to the camp was clear, the trail easier to follow and all downhill.

The helicopter was coming.

I heard the growing blare and began to run without looking back. It was idiotic, atavistic. I couldn't outrun a helicopter. I was no brighter, and just as terrified, as those javelinas. Only, they could run faster and hide easier. I was trapped in the open.

A shot sounded. I'd once heard an actor in a movie say that if you heard it, you hadn't been hit. How stupid was that? But I hadn't been hit. I kept running. I now knew the answer to whether those thugs would kill me if they couldn't catch me. The path was ahead and to my left. I would have to scramble up through the soft sand that bordered the dry riverbed, and in another few steps I would be safe in among the pinyon trees. I just had to keep moving.

The helicopter passed directly over my head, the pilot confident that, with no trees in the way, he could bring it in that low. It swung around and hovered twenty feet ahead. He wanted to herd me away from the sanctuary of the woods. I refused to let him. I kept running.

The rear window opened and a rifle poked out. I zigged and zagged wildly. They were too low, the wash from the rotors was stirring up a brown cloud.

A second shot. I didn't care; I kept running. The choice was to stand still and die or to take a chance and possibly live. The dust was in my eyes, my nose, my throat. The helicopter rose up and away to escape the blinding plume.

That was my break. I knew I wasn't going to get another. I zigged to my left—straight for the trail into the woods. I scrambled my way up the side of the arroyo on hands and knees, and when I reached the top, I rose up and kept on going.

Police, military, and Hollywood stuntmen practice extensively together as teams to make the kind of shot these amateurs were attempting. The shooter sent three more bullets whining off into the desert, none of which came anywhere near me, as far as I could tell. I didn't slow. In seconds, I was in the trees and out of their sight.

I chose one of the larger trees, and after checking for snakes, scorpions, and other unpleasant fauna, I scrunched down beneath it and waited. The helicopter roared overhead, like a predator robbed of its prey. Four times, the machine swept by, inches above the treetops. I stayed low, took a sip of water, and waited. They would, I was sure, see the futility of trying to find me from the air and finally retreat back to the abandoned farmhouse.

They surprised me. I had not expected such tenacity or risk taking. The helicopter flew back to the flat, relatively clear arroyo and, with a mad spray of dust in the air, settled down just feet above the brush. The rear door opened and the shooter jumped to the ground. He was going to hunt me on foot.

And I was leading him directly to the camp, where unarmed volunteers waited. Where, I hoped, my son was recovering, if they had not already sent him on to a hospital. For the first time, I regretted having thrown away Willie's handgun.

I had a lead of forty or fifty yards and the freedom to run as fast as I could. He would have to move slower. He only knew where I had entered the woods. He was no tracker. Every cross trail would slow him down, as he would have to decide which way to go. On the other hand, he didn't have to catch me to kill me. I took another swallow of my dwindling water ration and ran.

66

The camp was gone. The horses, tents, the tables, all the equipment had been packed up and hauled off. The searchers had followed Robertson's instructions to the letter. At the first sound of gunfire, they had cleared out.

I sensed it the moment I came over the rise, even before I had a good view of the clearing. There should have been a change in the air—the scent of hydrocarbons, the hum of a generator. Those were the conscious thoughts that only came later. The first awareness was from the subconscious and it led to despair.

I was done. I could not walk another hundred yards, much less run. Somehow, I had lost the Yankees cap. My head was no longer merely hot, sweaty, and achy—it was starting to cook. There was not a single bit of shade. I should have had gone back under the pinyon trees. I heard the helicopter again. It was too late. They were back. I could no longer move fast enough to hide. It was over. I sank to my knees and waited.

The helicopter hovered for a minute before landing. Dust swirled around me. I shut my eyes against it and held my breath. The noise subsided, leaving a high-pitched whine over the deeper hum of the engine. The dust settled a bit and I chanced a breath. I cracked open one eye. My vision was blurred from sand and dust, from dehydration, and from fear. But I forced myself to watch. I opened the other eye. It didn't improve the picture.

The rear door opened. Two men got out. They both carried long weapons. A moment later, two more men followed. They spread out and approached me slowly, heads turning, eyes alert. A tall man came directly over and stood facing me. I wanted to lift my face to him, so that he would know I had at least died bravely, but my neck wouldn't let me. I stared down at his feet. At his silver-tipped cowboy boots. Marshal Reyes.

67

I asked to share a hospital room with the Kid, but they stuck me with Hal instead. He had two busted arms, neither requiring surgery, fractured ribs, and a face that was disfigured with cuts and bruises but would eventually heal. I had a bandage on the back of my head and a bad attitude. I wasn't the ideal roommate.

"When can I see my son?"

"He's resting," the nurse said.

Do they take courses in how not to answer patients' questions? Or are uncooperative control freaks naturally drawn to the profession? Nature or nurture? What drew me to my profession? It had to be more than a simple desire to make a lot of money. I had been good at it and thought I was having fun, despite the fact that I rarely smiled. It was the intensity of the moment-to-moment existence of a trader, the constant jolts of adrenaline, the soaring elation of having rightly called a market move, positioned my book accordingly, and seen my bet paid off in millions that had all contributed to my addiction to the markets. I missed every bit of it. And when I had lost all of it, through stupidity or cupidity, but either way my own culpability, what had replaced that feeling of total involvement in my life?

"I want to see him." I may have spoken a bit louder than was strictly necessary.

"You should be resting. And please don't wake Mr. Morris."

Hal Morris was on a morphine drip. I could have set off fireworks and not disturbed the man.

"I can't rest because I'm worried about my son. If I could see him, then maybe I'd be able to relax."

"He's in the children's ward," she said in a tone that implied some-one of my ilk would never be allowed there.

"I'm dehydrated. I've got heatstroke. It's not contagious."

"You are not allowed out of bed. Don't make me have to strap you in."

"What's your name?"

"Why do you need my name?"

"So I can report you."

"It's Janice, and be sure and buzz me if you need anything at all."
She walked out.

Short of pulling the IV out of my arm and staggering bare-bottomed through the halls looking for the children's wing, I was stuck.

The four young killers who had holed up in the gas station had given up once their meager supply of ammunition gave out. That happened to coincide with the call from Robertson's people reporting shots fired up in the hills. The marshals had loaded back into their helicopter and flew to the rescue. I owed those clowns my life.

The door swung open again. Roy Robertson came in wearing a vintage Grateful Dead T-shirt—*Blues for Allah*—and a big smile.

"I just checked on your son. He's sleeping, but looking just fine. Give him a day's rest and he'll be good to go."

"That nurse won't let me see him."

"I'm sure she will in time. I get the feeling she's a bit overworked."

"I don't think I like nurses."

"I was married to one once."

"So you know what I mean."

"The woman was a saint. Next time you want to give that nurse a hard time, just think about your friend over there." He nodded toward Hal. "It's going to be at least a month before he can wipe his own ass."

"I'd still like to see my son."

"Let me see what I can do," he said, stepping out into the hall again.

He was back in minutes with a wheelchair and an attached IV pole. He moved my saline bag and helped me into the chair. I discovered that I was stronger than I had imagined. The mind had given up, but the body had not. That was a powerful lesson I would do well always to remember.

"How'd you manage this?"

"Janice lent it to me."

"What did you bribe her with?"

"I sweet-talked her. I find it works better for me than resorting to New York manners."

"Ouch."

He rolled me out and down the hall to the elevator.

"Have they caught those guys yet?" I asked, as he wheeled me inside.

"They arrested the pilot when he set down in Albuquerque, but he was alone. He could have set those two punks down anywhere. They're long gone, I imagine."

"Two? There was a third shooter. The one in the woods."

"He tried the Butch and Sundance strategy with those marshals. Bad decision."

The doors opened and he pushed me down another corridor and through a set of swinging doors.

"Who was he? Does anybody know?"

"A young man from back your way. That's all I heard."

"And Willie?"

"No sign of him. We'll have to go back in tomorrow and look for the remains. Any thoughts on where we should look?"

I thought back. The farmhouse. The hill. The distance from the cliff. The lines on the topographic map. "Bring me one of your maps and I'll pinpoint it," I said.

A nurse looked up as we passed her station. "Can I help you, gentlemen?"

"Thank you, ma'am," Robertson said. "We're looking for the little boy who was lost. This is his father."

"Room 108. Don't wake him."

"I just want to see him," I said.

She smiled. "I understand."

The Kid was asleep. Robertson was right. He was fine. He was sunburned, but, despite his pale skin, it wasn't bad. He must have made it into that cleft in the rocks early in the day. Another few days, though, and he would be peeling. That had the potential to turn into a three-act drama. But he was okay. They had already removed his IV and I saw that he had eaten. The remains of a grilled cheese sandwich and a juice box were on a tray by the side of the bed. What angel of mercy had known exactly what he would tolerate?

"Thanks, Roy."

"For what?"

"For bringing me here to see him."

I looked at that relaxed, pale pink face, at peace only when asleep and all of his demons were temporarily at bay, and I vowed that I would never allow him to be in harm's way again. No matter what the cost—in time, money, or blood—I would give it gladly.

Impossible. It wouldn't work and it wasn't fair. My son deserved more. It was a promise I couldn't deliver. The universe doesn't work that way. There's risk in being alive, in crossing the street, taking a cab, eating from a food truck. He wasn't a bubble boy who would perish at contact with the world. His world held more terrors than most, but that was no reason to give in to them.

I vowed to help make him strong. He was well along on that path already. That was a promise I could keep. One that would make me proud. It wasn't the easy path. There would be pain—both his and mine. But the Kid could do it. I could guide him. That was the best that I could do. That was the best that I could do for him.

I let Robertson reposition the IV bag while I slid back into my bed. I was surprised at how tired I felt after so little exertion.

"So, after shooting it out with that fellow from Ronkonkoma and rounding up the pilot, they still have no idea who sent those killers after you, do they?"

"That's all right. I do."

Virgil chartered a plane for us. The Kid had a history of being a "bad flyer," a history I never wished to revisit. Temple Grandin, the world-famous Aspy who redesigned cattle feedlots to reduce stress and subsequent damage to the animals, might want to take a look at airports and boarding procedures. It wasn't the flying that weirded out my son, it was the chaos that preceded it. The background noise would have been enough without the pointless lines, waits, jostling, contradictory orders and explanations, and the calculated passive-aggressive behavior of two-thirds of the employees, from check-in, to security, to flight attendants. To my mind, the Kid's tantrums were more than fully justified. I didn't know why more travelers didn't react as he did, screaming, weeping, sobbing, kicking, scratching, biting, and banging their heads on the bulkhead. Consumers first traded convenience and luxury for price, then they swapped freedom of movement and legroom for the sake of another few dollars' discount. Next, they gave up "perks" such as checked baggage and food. And still the marketing departments continued to focus on price, until finally travelers ceded basic human dignity. The Kid was incapable of making that adjustment, so he released his more primitive response.

But flying is always a trade-off. Even private jets have their drawbacks. The interior of the little Honda was a plastic-lined metal tube four and a half feet high, five feet wide, and twelve feet long. Too big for a coffin, too small for a submarine. At a tad over six feet, I was confined to my seat for the entire trip. The Kid, however, loved it. It was like a Lilliputian world created just for his enjoyment. He used his table to watch cartoons on his iPad and to line up his cars, but when he needed a change, he explored the minuscule bathroom—I didn't even try—and laid out on the rear bench seat that doubled as a narrow bed. The flight from Santa Fe to Westchester, an hour north of Manhattan, took a little under four and a half hours. When I got out, my first stop after landing—and working out the kinks in my back and knees—was a long visit to the lavatory. The Kid came off the plane skipping.

"Are you hungry?" I asked when we were settled in the back of a Town Car on our way to the Upper West Side.

"'Nilla."

I laughed. "Not ice cream. Lunch, maybe. A grilled cheese?"

"'Nilla," he said.

He was teasing. Joking. Interacting just for the fun of it. A rare and delightful occurrence.

"How about pasta? Spaghetti with butter?"

"Worms."

"Yes, but you like worms."

He stuck out his tongue in the universal sign for *Yuck*.

"Those kind of worms," I said.

"'Nilla."

"You got two chances of getting ice cream for lunch, sport. Thin and none."

He thought for a moment. "I'll take thin."

"Very good. Have you ever considered a career as a negotiator?"

He made the *Yuck* face again.

"All right. So, what do you want to be when you grow up?"

"A Dodge Viper."

"That's my boy," I cried. "Follow your dream."

He sat back and happily made car noises. I feasted on seeing the city again. The view of the Palisades across the river as we came down the Henry Hudson. Passed under the GW Bridge. The rise in anticipation as the car approached the turnoff at the 79th Street Boat Basin and I began to register that we were home. Back in our neighborhood. No wonder the Kid was happy. Four months of trying to fit our square pegs into southwestern round holes was over. Now the trick was to find a way to stay alive while fitting the rest of the pieces together.

But I had one more priority. I dialed Skeli's clinic.

"Is the doctor in?" I asked.

"Who's calling?"

"Hi, Kasey. This is Jason Stafford. Is she there?"

"OMG! She's not going to believe it. Where are you?"

"Seventy-sixth Street. Can I talk to her?"

"Oh my god, just a minute."

She put me on hold. It was so normal, so New-York-the-way-I-will-always-remember-it that not only did I not mind, I reveled in it. Tchaikovsky's Violin Concerto Op. 35 in D Major played in my ear. I knew that's what it was because Skeli and I had discussed the selection for August in one of our conversations weeks earlier. It was time to open discussions on September's hold music. We always started poles apart—contemporary country for Skeli, classic jazz for me—and ended up with classical. Soon we would no longer have a choice. Clients had already complimented Kasey on her taste in music.

"Jason?"

"*Ciao, bella*," I said.

"Oooh, I love it when you speak gelato. Where are you? You made the papers again yesterday. Not front page, though. I thought I might get a call. Are you all right?"

"Whoa. Wait."

"Well, tell me. I know you're okay because the *Post* said so. How's Jason?"

"The Kid is great. He's practicing to be a Viper when he grows up."

"*Euw.* A snake?"

"No, a Dodge Viper."

"Is that a car?"

"The greatest American car ever built."

"Can you be serious for just one moment?"

"Okay. The Ford GT may not have the same raw horsepower, but the Kid says it's a better car. How's that?"

"Why are you calling on this line? Is it safe?"

"It doesn't matter. I'll explain everything when I see you."

"What? Really? But how? I mean, when?"

"Well, the Kid and I are about to have a late lunch over at the Athena. Can you get away?"

She shrieked. "What are you talking about? Don't play games like that on a pregnant woman. Oh god, it's true, isn't it? It is. You're not mean like that. You're really here in New York."

"So you want me to order you a salad, or what?"

69

The next morning, Roger picked up the Kid and took him out to
Queens for the day to visit my father. Skeli left soon after. I worked
the phones for three hours, setting up a working lunch at Virgil's
apartment, and clearing the bureaucracy necessary to get my son en-
rolled in his school again—a feat that took infinite patience, per-
sistence, and a pledge of an amount equal to three months of consulting
fees. Carolina, our housekeeper, would need a few days to readjust her
schedule to accommodate me, but was happy to hear we were back in
town. I saved the most important for last, on the premise that failure
would be too disheartening to contemplate.

I needed to persuade Heather to return for one more year of shad-
owing the Kid. She was busy finishing her thesis and I knew that once
she was done, we would lose her. That was a given. But she had been
too important to the Kid's happiness to let her disappear from his life.
The key to getting her to return was not the money—she cared for the
Kid, and the money was already exorbitant—but safety. I guaranteed
her that I would take care of all outstanding issues in that regard within
one week.

"I don't know how you can make that promise, Mr. Stafford. I do
read the newspaper, you know."

"I understand how you feel. If I can prove to you that both you and
the Kid will be as safe as your average New York City resident can
expect, will you come back to work with him next week?"

"Average?"

"All right. Above average? How about top quintile?"

"And no bodyguards following us around with guns?"

"We won't need them," I said.

"Deal," she said.

Closing a two billion euro/sterling forward swap with the Bahrain Monetary Agency had given me less anxiety than that brief conversation. And my joy at hearing the magic word "deal" had never been greater.

f I'd had Virgil's money, I would have gone for Central Park West with views of the park and the Thanksgiving Day Parade. The Dakota or the San Remo. A building with character and history. The penthouse on Park Avenue was the kind of luxury sky-top aerie you might find in Hong Kong, Abu Dhabi, London, or Chicago. It was nice, if you liked living as far from the streets as possible. I preferred the streets. But I didn't have his money and could not even imagine what the place must have cost him.

The uniformed lobby attendant took me up to Virgil's floor, using his passkey to override the lock on the PH button. I stepped out into a marble foyer with a sparkling fountain and three sets of imposing mahogany doors. The center door was a double door that swung open a moment after we arrived.

Virgil, looking older and grayer, stepped out and grabbed my hand. "Jason, it is so good to see your face again. It has been a very long summer." We shook, and he peered into my eyes as he spoke. He must have seen something reassuring because he smiled with real pleasure.

"A summer I would just as soon forget," I said.

"Indeed. Come in. Larry is already here. We're just waiting for Agent Brady."

The dining room walls were covered with gilt-framed oil paintings of hunting and fishing scenes from the mid-1800s through to contemporary. There were too many and too diverse a collection for the whole to make any sense. But what should have been a jumble was surprisingly homey. Comfortable. The paintings were not there for show, they were there because they were loved.

Larry walked in from the living room and greeted me warmly. We all took places around the long table. I opened my laptop, plugged in my cell phone to access Wi-Fi—bypassing Virgil's system—and logged on to Manny's private chat room. He had stuck a piece of tape over the camera at his end, but he'd be able to see everyone in the room.

"We're ready. Just as soon as Marcus gets here," I said.

A long sideboard ran down one side of the room. On it were an assortment of beverages, including sodas, both sparkling water and still, a selection of beers in a bucket of ice, and a bottle of Veuve Clicquot Rosé. There was a platter of assorted sandwiches and wraps, three different salads, and a bowl of iced jumbo shrimp, cracked crab, and calamari. Virgil was brought up that way. It wasn't his fault he didn't know how to do anything but grand.

A soft gong sounded from the entryway.

"That will be him on the way up," Virgil said. "Excuse me."

Larry got up, took a small plate of salad greens and one piece of calamari, and poured himself a glass of Pellegrino. "Can I get anything for you?"

"No, thanks. I'll get it in a minute." I spoke to the laptop. "Manny? Are you going to be okay with this? An FBI agent in the room, I mean."

The voice of Amy Schumer assured me that he was fine with it.

"You're not going to use that voice in this meeting, are you?"

"Too much?"

"A bit," I said. "Do you have anything with a bit more gravitas?"

"Is this better?" It was Morgan Freeman.

"How about something in between? Do you have a Ben Affleck in there? George Clooney, maybe?"

"Just give me a minute."

Virgil came in with Brady, who came straight over and shook my hand. "I'm glad to see you, Stafford. Sorry I'm late."

"No one's late," Virgil said. "You're merely the most recent to arrive. We'll get started when everyone has a plate. I've given the staff the afternoon off and my wife is away with the girls on Nantucket. We will not be interrupted."

We all fixed plates of food and took our places around the table. Brady had a beer and a thick sandwich. I took some of the Tuscan salad and heaped cold seafood on top. I eyed the champagne but took a Pellegrino instead. Keeping the faith.

"Jason, I'm going to defer to you," Virgil said. "You asked for this meeting. It's your agenda."

"Thank you, Virgil. Let me start by saying that what I know and what I can prove may be two different things. I don't have anything that will stand up in court. Yet. That's why I've asked you here."

Everyone gave a brief nod of acceptance.

"Virgil has a very big problem coming up next week. His firm—the one that he personally saved from the ashes of his father's garbage heap and that, brick by brick, he rebuilt—may be taken away from him. If things go against him—and I think the deck is well stacked that way—the results of a shareholder vote will be announced, officially ousting Virgil and replacing him with a guy named Jim Nealis. Everyone with me?"

Larry and Brady gave another nod. The voice of Matt Damon came from the laptop. "I understand."

Larry smiled. He was accustomed to Manny's eccentricities. He may have been the only one in the room who knew Manny's real name.

"I have a rather large problem, too. People are trying to kill me. I've thought for some time that some Central American drug runners might still be after me, but I have recently found out that this is not the case. That leaves only the men who killed Aimee Devane and who came after me in New Mexico."

"The dead perp has been identified," Brady said. "No record. No connection to any other investigations, according to the DEA, NYPD, Nassau County Police, and us. The guy was a cipher. His father has an auto body shop in Brentwood. The son lived at home."

"He worked for that guy Gino," I said. "There's a connection. Your people are the best for finding what that is."

"We'll find it."

"But meanwhile, my butt is out there," I said. "We need to aim for the head. These guys are just muscle. They'll fade away as soon as we put the spotlight on the man in charge."

"I thought you said this guy we've got—this Gino—was the one giving all the orders," Brady said.

"Gino is the sergeant. He's dangerous, but you've got him and he's not going anywhere for a very long time. But the crew is taking orders from someone else. Someone higher up."

"Gino's not going to roll," Brady said.

"What about Scott?" I asked.

"We've got no way to squeeze him. He denies being there and he's alibied for the whole night. I believe you, but no AUSA is going to take a chance on your word against his."

Larry spoke up. "The stock fraud thing won't work, either. The FA and the other broker-dealer will go down, but at worst, Scott will get a small fine and an asterisk on BrokerCheck."

"Let me tell you all a story," I said. "For the moment, let's just call it that. A story."

"Is it a true story?" Virgil said.

"Maybe. Some of it is based on hard information, some is speculation—or at least extrapolation from the known facts. And some of it is based on nothing more than gut. But it may still all be true."

"Let's hear it," Brady said.

"Twenty years ago, Frank Scotto and a few semi-legit partners set up a financial services firm. They planned on running it on the up-and-up, but Scotto was too stuck in his ways—he couldn't help himself. He met a young investment banker named James Nealis and the two of them cooked up a plan. Scotto had a book of bad loans he'd made to blue-collar businessmen. You can imagine the kind of loans Scotto was making. Nealis cleaned up their balance sheets and brought these little companies to the market. 'Micro-cap stocks.' There's little or no oversight on these IPOs and the documentation is minimal. And there are always investors out there who will fall for the right spiel. It worked this way: The shares were sold to the public. The company owners got a big cash infusion—which they used to pay off the bad loans to Scotto. In return they got a cheap ninety-nine-year lease, with maintenance and storage, on a fleet of trucks, the main overhead expense for their businesses. Meanwhile, the banker, Nealis, earned a big fee—a chunk of which he kicked back to Scotto. End of the day— Scotto's happy, Nealis is happy, and Mack the electrician is happy. The investors, not so much. But that's life."

"Excuse me," Virgil said, "but Nealis has been a most reluctant, but quite efficient, proxy for me this summer. He has kept the firm running, and reported to me daily. I trust him."

"The guy's a snake, Virgil. Let me keep going."

"Can you prove any of this?" he asked.

"Not the juicy bits. Manny and I were able to reconstruct some of it. But the firm was shut down by the feds and there's not a lot of information available on something this old."

"Why didn't Nealis go to jail?" Larry asked.

"Because he had already moved on to the next big thing."

"Can you put Scotto and Nealis together?" Brady asked.

"I'll get to that. The relationship only becomes apparent when you look at the whole picture. Let me continue."

"Keep going," Virgil said. He wasn't at all convinced, but he was listening. He'd come around.

"About this time, the tech bubble was getting some legs. Scotto and partners bought another small bank and—surprise, surprise—a guy named Jim Nealis was soon running the new issue business for them. He specialized in zombies. The walking dead. Companies that were a bad idea in the first place. He buys up the outstanding shares for nothing, puts in his own new managers, and resurrects the stock with a new public offering. The regulators were buried back then with the avalanche of IPOs. They didn't have the manpower to police this kind of business. Remember, this was the era of financial deregulation. 'Caveat Emptor' on bumper stickers. Ever hear of TriLucta? Query?

Ultime? . . . No? Neither has anyone else. They all went bust within weeks of coming to market the second time around. These companies didn't have a product, or a business plan, or any chance of ever making a profit, but they didn't need any of that because they only had to stay upright long enough to issue more shares. Scotto and his partners—and Nealis—cleaned up on the banking fees. The managers moved on to the next sham outfit. And once again, the investors got nothing but a good story and a tax write-off."

"Didn't the feds catch on eventually?" Larry asked.

"I suppose they might have, but the market got there first. The bubble burst. This little bank was caught holding tens of millions of worthless shares. They closed the doors one night and never came back."

"And what happened to the stars of this little drama?" Larry asked.

"Scotto retired," Brady said. "It was around that time. Maybe a year or so later. He moved to Florida."

"I think he finally discovered that markets go down as well as up," I said. "Nealis stayed in banking."

"I'm amazed that he could even get hired after that," Larry said.

Virgil and I looked at each other and laughed. "When a crash like that happens, it wipes out a lot of people. So everyone is forgiven. Clean slate for all," Virgil said.

"And when you blow up large, everyone thinks you must have been a player, so you become even more valuable," I added.

Larry shook his head. "I don't think I understand your business."

Virgil gave another sweet-and-sour laugh. "Neither do I."

I got up and took another bottle of Pellegrino. "Jump ahead a decade or more to our current situation. Nealis is now a top banker, specializing in biotech, the next hot thing. Only, he's at a large, reputable firm. He can't play his old tricks. Competition is cutthroat, inside the firm as well as outside. He knows he's never going to get pegged for the top slot, and while he's making good money, it's not crazy money. And he wants crazy money."

"So he agrees to come work for Becker Financial?" Virgil said. He was definitely coming around.

"A firm he already knows a good bit about from his old friend's youngest son. His 'cousin' Joey."

"Who is running his own little scam," Brady said.

"Right," I said. "But I think Joey was a reluctant conspirator. Check the old employee records and you'll probably find that those guys in New Jersey were part of the original crew from twenty years ago. They traded in those same micro-caps because they knew where all the bodies were buried. They just needed someone to help park the securities who wouldn't ask a lot of questions."

"This is a good story," Brady said. "But that's it. A story."

"Admittedly. But I can point your people to the right records. And once on the trail, they'll find more."

"But you haven't tied Nealis to Scotto, to murder, or to any other current crime," he said.

"What was Scotto's first wife's name?"

"*What?* How do I know?"

"*I* do," I said. "Rosa."

"And?"

"Rose Holdings is the company that owns that bison ranch–slash–truck garage out in Manorville. The only document referencing that name is the deed on that piece of property. Rose Holdings, with a post-office box address in Lawrence, Kansas."

"Why Kansas?" Virgil said.

"Because Scotto and Nealis thought no one would ever look there."

Matt Damon's voice came from the laptop. "And Kansas has only recently digitized all of their old incorporation records. I found the file this week. Take a look."

The screen flashed and a document appeared. Larry and Brady leaned in to examine it. At the bottom was a list of the owners.

"These are all Scotto's old partners. Now they're all with him down in Boca. Sitting around the pool smoking cigars," Brady said. "Can we get a printout of this?"

"Virgil?" I said.

He nodded. "Send me the file."

"So what are these old guys up to now? And what's the connection to Nealis?" Brady asked.

"Rose Holdings is behind almost all of the purchases of large blocks of Becker stock in the last six months. They're about to take over the company."

"Wait," Virgil said. "Nealis has been fighting the board on this for months."

"Right. You told me two of the board members were making noises to give you the boot and install Nealis at the helm way back in June."

"Yes."

"And that Nealis held them off. He sided with the rest of the board, right?"

"Yes," Virgil said. "And he sided with the rest of the board when they demanded a shareholder vote on the question."

"Exactly. Meanwhile, his old buddy and his friends are busy scooping up shares. He might have lost a board vote, but he'll be stuffing the ballot box for the annual meeting."

Virgil folded his hands on the table and stared at them.

Matt Damon spoke. "When a sinister person means to be your enemy, they always start by trying to become your friend."

Brady spoke to the laptop. "You've got a paper trail? I mean, you can demonstrate that all of the trades lead back to this Rose Holding. That's what you're saying, am I right?"

I cleared my throat. "Before Manny answers that question, Marcus, I need to caution you. We've come to a point where you have to make a decision."

Brady looked up at me in surprise.

"Some of the information Manny has gathered has been the product of unorthodox means."

Brady squinted at me, trying to give me the federal agent hard-ass look. I knew him too well.

"And the solution to Virgil's problem—and mine—will require other unorthodox activities. I would not want you to compromise yourself in any way. We can break here and you can take my story and leave. You are free to make of it what you will. Tell it to Blackmore, research it on your own, or forget you ever heard it. As you wish. But if you stay and hear me out, be forewarned."

"You're not threatening an FBI agent, are you, Jason?"

"No, Marcus. Just the opposite."

He turned to Larry. "What about you?"

"Attorney-client privilege will only cover me so far," he said. "But I believe I can best serve my client—and my friend—by staying here and giving my best counsel."

Brady thought about it. "I want to help."

"And you *can* help. But I need you to trust me."

"If it backfires, I'll lose everything."

I turned to Virgil. He looked up and nodded. "I'm sorry, Jason. So much of this could have been avoided. It is my fault. I will do whatever it takes to make things right." He turned to Brady. "We can protect you. If Jason's plan blows up on us, I am comfortable testifying that you left the room at this point and did not return."

"No," he said. "I don't want anyone to lie for me. I'll stay. I'm all in. Bet the ranch. Or however you want to say it. Tell me what's next."

I took a deep breath. "Thank you."

"Yeah, yeah. Thank me when it's over. What's next?"

Everyone leaned in.

"Manny? Why don't you go first."

71

Rose Holdings doesn't own the shares in its own name, of course. But Rose owns a host of blinds, almost all of which are numbered accounts. I will provide you with the names, addresses, and banking information for each of these subsidiaries. Your people will have to be told where to look. Believe me, they're not going to stumble across it."

"They're pretty good," Brady said.

"Then let them try," Manny continued. "You'll be available to give out hints, though, if they need it."

"I can't use anything you got illegally. Any good defense lawyer will get it all thrown out."

"I would," Larry said.

"It will be entirely up to you as to how much information you share or whether you choose to reveal the source," I added.

"It won't be the first time an FBI agent has had to shave the facts when on the stand," Larry said.

Brady bristled. "We're not all as crooked as you like to think, counselor."

"No," Larry answered. "Only about a third or so."

Virgil half rose from his seat. "Boys! Boys! No fighting. We're here to work together."

"You're right," Larry said. "Forgive me, Agent Brady. You are being asked to take a wider view of the ethics of what is being discussed, and I respect your willingness to listen."

"Thank you," I said. I looked at Brady. "You okay?"

"I'm good."

"The weak link," I said, "is Scott the younger. Joey is out of his depth and afraid to admit it. But he is loyal. We won't get him to talk *unless* he thinks it's all over—that there is no longer any good reason to keep his mouth shut."

"Agreed," Brady said.

"But if we can get him to talk, we can roll up Nealis, the old guys in Florida, and maybe even the young muscleheads that keep coming after me."

"We need some kind of leverage," Virgil said.

"Leverage is the key," I said. "Look at it in reverse. If Brady's people arrest Nealis, the old man, and his cronies, then Joey will panic. Then Blackmore can bring him in, offer him a deal, and squeeze every drop out of him."

"This is the chicken and the egg story. We can't arrest them without hearing what Joey has to say," Brady said.

"Larry, what would happen if Nealis votes shares he doesn't own?" I asked.

"That's illegal. Major fraud."

"But he does own them," Larry said. "Or at least Rose Holding owns them and he will have the proxy."

"So we need to get Rose to sell. That's all."

"And how do you propose to convince them to sell before the meeting?" Virgil asked.

"You said it. Leverage. The old man and his partners don't have enough money to pay cash for all those shares. They bought them on margin. Borrowed money."

"That sounds right," Virgil said.

"We trigger a margin call. If the price drops enough, the banks will call in their loans. When Nealis's friends don't come up with more money, the banks will sell out their positions in Becker Financial. If Nealis tries to vote those shares, Brady arrests him."

Larry laughed. "That's quite a plan. And only a trader like yourself could come up with it. I love it."

Virgil looked confused. "You would need a substantial drop in price to pull this off. I mean, not just a point or two. How do you propose to do that?"

This was the part where I was afraid I might lose some support. Manny had assured me that it was doable, but the plan was like playing catch with a hand grenade. Or an atom bomb.

"We're going to crash the stock market," I said.

72

I think I'll have a beer," Brady said. "Anyone else?"

Larry got up and joined him at the buffet. "I think I'll try the wine."

I was exhausted and exhilarated. They had all approved the plan, but they had made me explain every step. I had tried, but it wasn't possible. The markets don't run on logic. It's fear and greed. And all I had to do was create enough fear to get the markets to drop by a hundred points on the S&P about a half hour before the close. A flash crash. Stocks would pop right back, but not all stocks would rally equally. It had been done before by a guy with a laptop. He'd done it for profit and gotten caught. I was going to do it to catch some bad guys. And I wouldn't get caught.

When a move that large and that sudden occurred, all the financial stocks would stay under pressure. Though the general market would rebound, there would be lingering fears that the bank stocks would be in trouble simply because of the volatility. I would need to keep the lid on only one of those stocks.

"It's important that we all keep our heads through this," Virgil said. "We cannot profit from this. No one makes a trade based on the plan. No tip-offs to your favorite aunt or sleazy brother-in-law. Nothing. The regulators will be looking at every trade connected with a market move like this. We can't have anything that could trace back to any one of us."

Virgil had been enervated when I arrived, but this cockeyed, highly illegal, and quite dangerous plan had rejuvenated him. He may have been issuing a stern warning, but he sounded more like a pirate captain than a responsible adult. I wanted to answer him with an "Arrgggh."

Larry and Brady clinked wineglass to beer bottle. "If this ever comes to light, you and I will be famous, Agent Brady. Every graduating law school class will know our names for decades to come."

"And every police academy graduate, too," Brady answered.

They drank.

A late-summer sunset was sending shafts of orange and pink light across the living room. It was late. Roger and the Kid would be back from visiting my father. I signed off with Manny and packed up the laptop. "I've got to get back home. The next time we meet will be next Friday before the annual meeting. If anyone comes up with a reason for us to rethink this scheme, give a call. Otherwise . . . Later."

Virgil walked me to the door. "I made a mistake. I see it now, the whole picture. Thank you and please accept my apology."

"Nealis looked too good to be true."

"And I was greedy and impatient."

I smiled at my boss and my friend. "I'll never tell."

"Good luck, Jason."

"Better to be lucky than smart," I said. I felt neither and I would need to be both.

73

Manny and I had a lot of work to do. The setup had to be seamless. We had to insinuate ourselves into the market without setting off a run too soon. We had agreed to meet in the chat room, just as soon as I got the Kid down for the night.

A full day with Roger, my father, and Pop's new wife, Estrella, had done the poor guy in. His stomach was bloated with vanilla ice cream. He nibbled at dinner with no enthusiasm. I imagined him sinking slowly into his pile of ketchup and fries.

"Are you too tired for a bath?" I asked.

He ignored me.

Often, I could tell what he meant by the *way* he ignored me. He had his tells and his tics. But that night he was too exhausted to even emit subliminal signals.

"All right. We'll do the bath in the morning. But I do want you to wash face and hands and brush teeth."

He sighed. A big, long operatic sigh. A Wagnerian sigh.

"I'll help you," I said.

"I do it," he said.

"Fine," I said, and then, when he didn't move, "Are you ready?"

"Why is Willie bad?" he said in a dreamy voice.

"Wow. That's a big question, sport. What makes someone do bad things? Is that what you're asking?"

He let his head flop to the right. That may have meant "Yes."

"I'm not that smart, son. Sometimes people make mistakes and then find themselves stuck and doing things they never imagined they'd be doing." That wasn't Willie. That was me. "I don't know. Maybe he didn't have good parents. Not everyone is lucky that way." The Kid had suffered from not having good parents. His one remaining parent was muddling through as best he could, but was still woefully inadequate.

He sighed again. A small sigh.

"Let's get you cleaned up."

He let me take his hand and lead him to the bathroom, where he surprised me by stripping off his clothes. I turned on the faucets in the tub.

The sunburn was on his cheeks and chin, his neck and the top of his chest where his shirt did not cover, and along both forearms. Otherwise he was a light honey hue. Though I'd done my best to shelter him from the Tucson sun all summer, it had left its mark, seeping through clothes and sunscreen.

"Does your sunburn hurt?" I asked.

He growled. It was annoying to talk about it.

He climbed in the water and sat down, waiting for me to wash him. Though he did not like to be touched, bathing was different. Like a Roman emperor, he was content to be treated like a lesser god. I soaped up my hands and gently rubbed him all over—he hated the feel of a washcloth.

He winced as my hand brushed over his arm.

"We'll put some cream on that when we're done," I said.

He looked at me askance.

"Okay. Not cream. Medicine. Gook. Good gook. It'll feel cool. You'll like it."

He let his head flop forward, resigned to a life stuck with such an idiot for a father. I lathered him up and rinsed him off quickly. While I worked, he entertained himself by making frog sounds.

"Okay, hop out, Mr. Froggy." I patted him dry with a smooth towel.

"Willie is afraid," he said when I was done.

I wrapped the towel around him. "You are very wise, little one. I think you're right. Willie was afraid, so he did some mean things. Were you afraid? I was afraid for you."

"*Rrrrribit,*" he said.

"Okay, brush your teeth and I'll get pj's."

I walked into his dark bedroom and before I could turn on the light I heard the weird, lonely howl of a coyote echoing through the apartment. Again. *"Yip. Yip. Aaarrrooooooo."* The Kid was a perfect mimic. My stomach muscles clenched. A chill ran up my back. Then I heard the sound of a small child brushing his teeth and I relaxed again.

Had he been afraid? I would never know. But I was, and always would be.

74

The sell orders had been building up all week. Manny concentrated on individual stocks in the financial sector, as well as the banks, brokers, insurance companies, and ETFs and other funds that specialized in those stocks. He was careful to keep the offers to sell just a bit above the market so that he never actually executed a trade. I picked the stocks and the prices. He entered the information into his computer, and the program he'd written placed the orders anonymously through many different brokers, making it look like the sell interest was broad-based. The market drifted sidewise all week, which worked in our favor.

We worked in my father's new apartment on 115th Street in College Point with a view of the airport and the city jail on Rikers Island. It was a constant reminder to not make any mistakes. Manny piggybacked on the Wi-Fi at St. Agnes High School—closed for the summer—so that if any watchdog entity tried to search back through the Internet to find where the selling pressure was coming from, they would run into a dead end.

Pop and Estrella stayed in my apartment and kept an eye on the Kid. Manny and I ate microwaved Lean Cuisine and never went out. We spelled each other during the night, keeping an eye on the overseas markets. By the weekend we were beginning to develop cabin fever, so we both agreed that a twelve-hour break was in order.

I flagged a livery driver on College Point Boulevard and paid him cash for a ride to West 110th Street in Manhattan. Skeli and I ordered Chinese, watched Bogie and Bacall in *To Have and Have Not* on TCM and went to bed early. Sunday, I rode the subway all morning, switching lines and cars until I was sure I wasn't being followed, and then took the Number 7 all the way to Flushing, Main Street, where I caught a bus that let me off eight blocks from Pop's place. Manny arrived an hour later, wearing a dark brown ankle-length djellaba. In the multicultural, polyethnic mixing bowl of Queens, he fit right in.

"The Pacific markets open in a few hours. I want to be ready," I said.

"We're ready," he said.

He was casual, relaxed. I was paranoid, anxious, and a nudge this side of explosive. It felt good.

We tracked the Sydney market, then switched to Singapore and Tokyo. The markets felt heavy, but at the same time somewhat skittish. It was perfect weather for a breakout session. By the time that London began trading, the world markets were all slightly lower on light volume. I was too hyped to sleep, so I made a pot of coffee and let Manny sleep for six hours. When he awoke, he scrambled eggs for us as we waited for New York to open. We ate while watching Bloomberg News on my father's giant flat-screen. Becker Financial got a mention for the meeting on Friday evening.

"I think that whatever the results of the shareholder vote, they want the markets to digest the news over the weekend," the guest talking head said. The banner at the bottom of the screen said that he was the chief portfolio manager at Boyle & Co.

"Do you have a stake in the vote, Tim?" the TV reporter asked.

"We're in the contrarian camp. We own BFG. I think Virgil Becker has done a good job and I hope he is reinstated once this vote is out of the way. He's been tainted by the investigation, but I believe he can weather it. And remember, the Beckers still own a large block of shares. I think the market will be very surprised if the vote goes against them."

"And markets hate surprises, don't they, Tim?"

They both got a good chuckle over that. The conversation switched to the restaurant industry and why those stocks' performance was tied to the price of oil. I hit the mute button.

"Shall we surprise them, Manny?" I asked.

He grinned. "Photon torpedoes ready, Captain."

Computerized trading has affected all markets, and the jury is still out on whether this is a good thing or a bad thing. My take is that it doesn't matter. You can't undo technological change. Celebrate the positive effects—greater liquidity, speed of execution, improved price discovery, transparency of information—and accept the fact that the guy with the biggest, fastest computer is always going to have an edge over the rest of us mere mortals. And also suck it up when, as will occasionally happen, the computers read the same signals and all lean the same way at the same time.

We started sending out those signals.

"It doesn't matter how far above the market you make your offer. Just do it large. The computer programs scan the order books of the floor traders, and size means more to them than price."

The program placed orders to sell Becker Financial two or three points higher than the market price. If any one of them had been executed, we would have been in deep trouble; Manny was offering tens of thousands of shares at a clip. I had him place similar orders to sell the S&P index on the Chicago futures exchange. Well above the current market, but again huge in size.

By midday, my adrenaline was starting to fade. I lay down and tried to nap for an hour, but I couldn't relax. Though exhausted, I was still flying on nervous energy. I made another pot of coffee.

The bulls tried pushing the market up late in the day on the weekly car sales report, and for a few minutes I felt a stab of panic as the market ticked up. They were getting dangerously close to our sell orders on the S&P index. If I told Manny to pull the orders, the market might read it as a bullish sign and really take off. Rather than watch the tape and fret, I went in the kitchen and made turkey sandwiches for the two of us. We hadn't eaten since breakfast.

"I hope you take mayo on your sandwich, because that's the way I made it," I said.

"Thanks," Manny said, though he had only been half listening.

"They had a little rally a while ago, but it didn't amount too much. The market is back down to the opening levels. What do you want to do?"

"What's the time?" I asked.

"Is this mayo? There's no mustard?"

"I'll get you mustard. What's the time?"

"Three thirty-one," he said.

Less than a half hour to the close of business on the New York Stock Exchange. Futures would stay open longer, and the aftermarkets would kick in right away, but the next day's margin calls for BFG would be based on the four o'clock price.

A graph in the upper right-hand corner of Manny's screen showed an ever-growing spike. Order flow toxicity, the measure of the relative imbalance in sell orders versus buy orders, was close to record levels. Hedge funds, market makers, and day traders would all be focused on that graph. And they'd be nervous. Soon, they'd be scared. Fear and greed, in the end that's what moves markets.

"It's time," I said. "Let 'er rip."

Manny hit keys on the laptop and all of our above-market offerings ticked lower. We still had not made one sale. We didn't need to. All we needed to do was to give the appearance of many different sellers all leaning in the same direction at the same time.

At 3:34, the computers kicked in.

I had timed it perfectly. The market was tired. Traders were bored, or off the desk, or complacent; very little had happened and the close was less than a half hour away. They never saw it coming.

A nanosecond later, the market got hit with thousands of sell orders. Prices on the terminal all switched to red, and minus signs appeared on the tape. The selling continued. S&P futures dropped by two percent. Then three, and four.

"Manny, put your ear up to the computer, and if you listen really carefully, you will hear the screams of traders in crisis."

"Cruelty has a human heart, Jason."

The market continued to plummet, overloaded with sell orders from computer-driven hedge funds. There were times when the market would move so quickly that a human trader had no time to panic and react. He or she could only sit frozen in awe. Sometimes, like this day, that was a good thing. Computers don't panic at all and they can react to market changes in an instant. So while humans watched, the computers behaved like lemmings and leapt off the cliff.

I checked the market for Becker Financial Group. After hitting a recent high of 52.1 a week earlier, BFG had been trading listlessly all morning between 50.06 and 50.12 with good size offered at 52.5. When the order came in to show twenty thousand shares at 51.5, all of the bids pulled out. The next sell order was from a computer to sell one thousand shares "at the market." Not a particularly large order, but there were no longer any resting customer bids and other sellers were jumping in. There were a few trades in the high forties, then nothing down to 42.4, 42.2, and 42.0 as a few human traders tried to stop the flow. The computers blew right through them. In another few seconds, BFG was down to 38, where stop-loss orders began flooding the market and trading was halted.

The other financial stocks were getting a beating also, but none as badly as Becker.

The only thing that stopped the market from trading lower was that there were no more buyers anywhere. The selling stopped and everyone got to take a deep breath. It was 3:43. Nine minutes had passed and the stock market had given up half a trillion dollars in value.

The pause continued. At 3:46, the S&P futures market ticked up. It was the first uptick trade since the selling began. That was all it took. Despite the instantaneous flash of information through the Internet, through cable and ether, and by methods more ancient, the human animal responds at its own speed. Once the information was digested that the market had suddenly, and without reason, become vastly cheaper, the buy orders came back in. The markets began trading back up again, and by the time the final bell rang on the New York Stock

Exchange at 4:00 p.m., most stocks were back where they started the day or slightly higher.

But not the financial sector. Those stocks lagged. And Becker lagged the most. When the closing price for BFG hit the tape, it read 39.8. Down twenty percent.

"Is that too much?" Manny said.

"It'll get a pop tomorrow. Maybe we overdid it just a tad."

"You never know what is enough, unless you know what is more than enough."

"You've pulled all of our orders out, haven't you?"

"Aye, aye."

"Then I'm going to bed. See you in the morning. Nice work, Manny."

everage is the great equalizer. It can make you or break you. Wall Street can't function without it, and yet it is behind every crash the market has ever seen.

The margin calls went out the next morning.

When you pay cash for a stock, the most you can lose is the amount you put up. But when you borrow money from your broker—on "margin"—and the stock goes down, you can find yourself in an ever-deepening hole. Of course, if the price goes up, your profit is magnified considerably, but so is the risk. If you lose, the broker will demand that you post more money to cover the drop in value of the stock. And if you don't come up with the cash in record time, the broker has the right to sell the position—usually right at the bottom.

Virgil met us in Manny's chat room. He was keeping his ear attuned to any and all rumors about the firm and the stock.

"I'm hearing that a couple of the bigger shops are already calling around, trying to round up buyers."

"If I had the money, I'd be one of them," Manny said.

"The market knows there are some big blocks that will have to be sold. We won't get an uptrade until that's out of the way."

"How's your mother taking it?" I asked. Almost all of her remaining wealth was tied up in Becker Financial Group stock.

"Mother is the proverbial immovable object. She called me last night to talk about Wyatt's birthday next month. She refused even to discuss the sell-off."

"The price will be back up by next week," I said.

"Or next month, or next year. Just as long as I'm at the helm," Virgil said.

"Is there any chance that Nealis will find some way to come up with the cash?"

"This is where his secretive system of blinds and false owners comes back to bite him on the butt. The margin calls are going out to lawyers and offshore bankers, who then have to scurry around individually to get hold of someone up the line. And they have no contact information. Nealis and his co-conspirators are stuck."

"I don't want to have to try and do this twice."

"No, I would imagine not. How are you holding up, Manny?"

"It's a shame. No one will ever know what we did. I can see myself years from now at a hackers' convention, listening to some blowhard tell the story of how he once crashed the market from his laptop. And I will have to keep my mouth shut."

"I'll know, and I do not forget favors," Virgil said.

Manny and I walked down to the shore and took turns smashing the laptop on the rocks, laughing happily at the devastation. When it had been reduced to a sufficient number of pieces, Manny threw them out into the East River—he had the better arm. There were many secrets resting on the bottom of the East River; ours would be comfortable resting there with them.

"I hope Larry comes up with some good news for you soon," I said.

"Yeah, well, I miss my girls."

"I understand. It's been great working with you."

"Keep me in mind if you ever want to make another attempt at destroying the capitalist system."

I laughed. "Is that what we were doing?"

"Think about it. It was you, me, and an HP. Imagine what could be done by someone who put some real effort into it. We're turning the world over to the machines, my man, and they're really not up to the task."

"That's a scary thought," I said.

"We weren't the first, and we won't be the last. But someday . . ." He didn't finish the sentence. Neither did I.

"See you," I said.

"Be in touch." He turned and walked back through the park and across Poppenhusen Avenue. I stayed there and watched the river flow. I had a lot to think about.

The Becker Financial Group Annual Shareholders Meeting was held in a secondary conference room down the hall from the main banquet hall at the New York Hilton on Fifty-third Street. There were not enough of those shareholders to warrant a bigger space. The hotel staff had set up one hundred straight-back chairs in neat rows with a central aisle that led to a solitary microphone stand. Facing the room, on a raised platform, was a dais for the board members, chief counsel, and Nealis. Two video cameras had been set up in the corners to capture the festivities.

BFG was not a widely held stock. Other than the family and the Rose Holding cutouts, the owners were all old creditors of the father's empire. They had been forced to accept stock in place of their missing cash. Other investors remained shy of supporting a name—Becker—with so much negative history attached to it.

I arrived a few minutes early and checked in with the two smiling interns who were outside the door, handing out badges on purple-and-gold-striped lanyards. My badge read SHAREHOLDER, which was accurate. I held one share, which I had purchased the week before, expressly for this purpose. Other badges read GUEST, PRESS, STAFF, BOARD, and EXECUTIVE, with the exec's title underneath.

"Might I take a look at your list?" I asked.

The two young women looked at each other and frowned. They were not prepared for the question.

"I won't steal it," I said. "I just want to take a quick look."

They still weren't sure.

"It's all public information, you know. I can find it all online. How about if I just look over your shoulder for a minute?"

That closed the deal. They really couldn't prevent someone from standing behind them and having a quick look, could they?

Rose Holding was not on the list, but all of the false fronts were there. Not one, as far as I knew, was a shareholder, their positions having been sold off by the banks, but the list had not been updated. At that moment, no laws had yet been broken. The list had not been updated in time for the meeting. There would be no securities fraud until those shares were voted. But the moment the results were announced, Nealis would be guilty of stuffing the ballot box. By itself, it was a serious charge, but not a fatal one. But it would be enough. His whole edifice of lies and manipulation would tumble.

I smiled at the two women. "Thank you again, ladies. You have made my day."

One of them handed me a printed agenda and smiled back. I showed my credentials to the hired security guard at the door and took a seat in the back of the room. I pulled my brand-new Yankees cap lower and slouched down in the chair.

There were a few people there ahead of me. Livy and Wyatt sat with Virgil in the front row. I recognized a grizzled, alcoholic reporter who had interviewed me for the *Wall Street Journal* back when we were both much younger. He had been grizzled even then.

At ten minutes to six, the room began to fill up with print- and digital-media reporters bearing notebooks, shareholders—most of whom were professional money managers who worked for the corporations or funds that were the true owners—and senior staff. Not one of the television channels had sent a team. I wasn't surprised. Blackmore would have alerted them all that the real news wasn't happening until after the meeting was over.

I read over the agenda. It was the usual bore. Speeches followed by speeches. The vote was the last item before New Business. It was the only piece of business of interest to anyone but the wonkiest of analysts. The big banks and major corporations made their annual meetings into industrial shows, some with Broadway stars, full orchestras, movies, laser-light shows, and performances by Bruce Springsteen or Elton John. BFG wasn't in that league, and I hoped it never would be. I thought shareholders should be scandalized by the waste, rather than bedazzled by the sequins. Maybe I was just becoming cranky.

An earnest young woman with a name tag that read PRESS: REBECCA FRANCIS—BLOOMBERG NEWS came in, looked around, and approached me. She was young, good-looking in a middle American farmgirl way, and very tall. I tried to repel her with body language and more cranky thoughts, but she put on a smile and kept coming. Good reporters are like guard dogs. They're relentless and they have an incredible sense of smell.

She introduced herself. "I'm sorry to bother you, but you do look familiar. Are you with the firm?"

"Shareholder," I said, folding my arms over the credentials hanging on my chest.

For the briefest moment, I was sure she was going to sit down next to me in my dim corner. She thought about it. I could not afford to be recognized by anyone. Not yet.

"What's your prediction on today's vote?" she said.

"They're paving over the wetlands," I said. "If they pave over all the wetlands, we won't have any crabs and we'll have to make our crab cakes with extruded fish paste. It's un-American."

There's one—or more—at every public meeting. The certifiable crank, who may or may not be mad but is certainly angry. Angry about something and who is willing to talk about it at great length, usually in front of a microphone, if they can get near one.

It worked. "Sorry to bother you," Rebecca said, moving away quickly.

Many of the shareholders made a pass by Virgil to shake his hand and make noises of support and encouragement before going off and finding a seat. And there were also some who avoided Virgil altogether. Tim Boyle, whom I had last seen on Bloomberg TV at the beginning of the week, was in the second row on the aisle. He had visited briefly with Virgil before sitting. The only shareholder that I knew personally was Ahmad Din. He managed a global equity fund. We had done business together in the past when he had asked for help hedging his foreign exchange risk. We had been friends. I had toasted him at his wedding.

I got up when I saw him come in and headed him off. I needed to be sure he wouldn't out me if he saw me hiding in the corner. "How are the markets treating you, Ahmad?"

He showed no reaction. He saw me. He heard me. But it was as if I had not spoken. As though I didn't exist. He walked by me and found a seat in the row behind Boyle. I was used to those snubs, and sympathized. My presence was a reminder of a broken trust. I went to jail and lost my career. He lost faith in a friend he had once valued—me. Maybe his pain was greater.

But I was no longer worried about him greeting me loudly across the room. I tried not to slink as I walked back to my seat.

At one minute to six, the few invited staff members came in and took seats in the farther reaches of the room. They were only there to make the crowd seem larger—and to applaud at the right moments. Senior executives filed in next and filled in the reserved seats in the front row on the opposite side of the room from Virgil and his family. Some of them gave him a wave or a smile as they went by, but none went over to chat or to shake his hand. Finally, the board members arrived and marched straight to the front of the room. Nealis was last. He was so wired, he practically glowed. There was a sudden tension in the room that had not been there a moment earlier. His pose as the reluctant replacement did not dispel the feeling that, in this small world, something momentous was about to happen.

Everyone took their seats and the sounds of murmured conversations and papers being rustled resolved into a taut silence.

Nealis opened the meeting with a joke. Something about golf and markets. It wasn't a very good joke and he made a dog's breakfast of it with his delivery. He had read the room all wrong. They weren't there to laugh.

"I know this meeting is spartan by Wall Street standards. But we're not here for ostentatious celebration. This is a solemn occasion. There are weighty matters before us. Champagne and rock stars would be inappropriate. All I can say, though, is stick with BFG. We're going to get there."

He had recovered. He introduced everyone on the stage before launching into the numbers. It was a formality only. Earnings, past and projected, had already been shared with the public. No one listened. They were all there for the results of the vote, the only information that had not yet been made public.

The shareholders were losing patience. People shifted in their seats, whispered to companions, or texted on their phones. Nealis pushed on, but it was all uphill slogging. It was not fun to watch. He gave himself a break.

"I'd like to introduce George Demarest, who can explain how we fared in fixed income this quarter. George?"

A tall, thin man unfolded himself from his seat in the front row, but voices from behind stopped him.

"Come on, Jim. Cut to the money shot."

"Yeah, I've got three hours on the L.I.E. to look forward to after this."

That brought out a chuckle from the rest of the crowd, as most of them also had summerhouses to get to. There may have been differences of opinion as to which way the vote should go, but there was unanimous agreement that it was time to just get to it and get it over with.

The fixed-income guy looked back at the shareholders and waited. Nealis could have helped him out but didn't. He was nervous. It struck me. He knew about the margin calls. He knew he was in trouble. He wanted this over as badly as everyone else in the room, but he had to play out his role or risk exposure. So he did nothing and let Demarest spin in the wind.

Rather than mounting the stage and speaking from the podium,

Demarest went to the microphone stand on the floor. "Nice to see you, boss," he said to Virgil. "I'll be brief." He *was* brief, but the shareholders were impatient. He mentioned low yields on bonds, narrow margins, and that the Federal Reserve was soon going to be forced to raise rates again. No one cared. When he asked if there were any questions, there was only one.

"You want to tell us about the vote?"

"Sorry," he said. "That's well above my pay grade." He retreated to his chair and folded his long frame back into it. I think he would have sat on the floor if he could have made himself less conspicuous.

Nealis was in a bad spot. If he gave in to the crowd and announced the results of the vote, without the full preamble, he risked looking weak at the very moment when he had to look most leader-like. A man with more self-confidence might have been able to get through the ordeal with a bit of self-deprecating humor. Virgil would have handled the situation. Nealis got pissy.

"Gentlemen, may I remind you that we are all speaking publicly. We have the press with us today." Besides Livy and the reporter, there were two other women shareholders in the room. None of them looked happy about being ignored.

The young woman from Bloomberg held up a hand at chest height and waved to the traders. It was the perfect gesture. It told the shareholders that, though she was merely an observer, she had already chosen her side. She was there to hear the results of the vote, too.

Tim Boyle stood up. "This is your show, Jim. Play it your way. But the only thing that anyone in this room cares about is the result of that vote. You're doing yourself no favors by stalling."

"I'm not stalling. I'm trying to keep to the agenda."

"You're the boss. Change the agenda." Boyle sat down.

There was Nealis's opening. He had the brains to see it. The only way to keep control of the meeting was to give the audience what it wanted. If he had agreed at the first signs of resistance, he might have been able to carry it off with dignity. But he'd held out, and acquiescence now wasn't the high road—it was the lifeline.

"All right! All right!" He was the one with the microphone and standing on the stage, but he still felt the need to shout down the opposition. "At least allow me to go over the events that got us to this point."

The crowd got quieter. They'd won and could afford to be magnanimous. To a point.

"Earlier this year the firm discovered that we had a compliance problem. Virgil Becker, the man who brought the firm back from the brink, was arrested and had to take a leave of absence. I took over and have tried to run things as he would have wished."

He looked out at the group and waited for the polite applause the line warranted. He didn't get it—not even from his supporters.

"Sometime later I was approached by two of the board members, who expressed their desire that Virgil be allowed to retire and that I take over on a permanent basis. They wanted my okay before taking the matter to the full board."

This was ancient history. He was losing them again. But this time they were angry. People were glaring daggers at the stage. The cell phones had all been put away. Nealis had their attention, but it wasn't the way he wanted it.

"I demurred," he said.

Nice word, I thought, *for treason.*

"They insisted, and we finally agreed that the matter was too important not to have the full backing of the shareholders. The results were tabulated earlier this week for all shareholders of record as of this date. I will now turn it over to our chief counsel."

He stepped away from the microphone. He couldn't help himself. He smiled.

The lawyer felt the crowd's impatience. He didn't waste any time. He strode up to the mic and announced, "The matter put before the shareholders is that the board will immediately accept the resignation of the chairman and CEO, Virgil Becker, and replace him with James Nealis." He looked down at Virgil sadly. "The resolution is passed by a margin of thirty-two votes with ninety-six percent of shareholders voting either aye or nay, and no abstentions."

I jumped up. "Question for you, counselor."

The reaction was muted. I thought that most of the crowd was surprised, but not shocked. A loss for Virgil had always been a possibility.

Nealis saw me for the first time. His eyes bulged.

"Yes? The man in the back with the Yankees cap. Please state your name and give me your question."

"Jason Stafford. Are you in possession of a list of all beneficial shareholders?"

"Please step to the microphone and repeat your question," the lawyer said.

"No!" Nealis yelled. "This man was not invited to this meeting. Security! Where's security?"

I strode quickly to the microphone and repeated the question. "Do you have the list of all true shareholders who voted in this election?"

Nealis may have suspected where I was going, but he was a step behind. "You don't have to answer his questions," he said to the lawyer.

"Let him answer!" someone yelled from behind me.

"Just answer me this," I said. "Is it the same list that was used for entry to the meeting this evening?"

The lawyer was facing an angry, vocal crowd and thought he had just been lobbed a floating-softball question. "Yes, that is the same list. I have a copy that Mr. Nealis provided me earlier today."

"Thank you." I turned away and texted Brady.

All yours.

The doors in back of us opened and the room filled with policemen. Uniformed NYPD, U.S. Marshals in light windbreakers, and FBI in suits and ties. A uniformed sergeant with a bullhorn was telling everyone to remain calm and to stay in their seats.

The crowd was in shock. No one spoke or moved.

There was a pause, and in walked Wallace Ashton Blackmore, U.S. Attorney for the Southern District of New York, and the man who most wanted to be the next mayor of the city. He was flanked by four AUSAs and followed by a stream of television camera crews. Big lights on dollies followed them. The room was crowded and lit up like Yankee Stadium. And Blackmore stood on the pitcher's mound.

"James Nealis?" he called out.

Nealis was stunned. "I'm James Nealis," he said.

"You are under arrest, Mr. Nealis. Please cooperate with these policemen. They will read you your rights."

"This is ridiculous. What am I being charged with?"

"We'll start with securities fraud and defrauding the investors in Becker Financial with regard to this vote. Take him away."

Blackmore turned to the cameras and began answering reporters' questions.

78

Virgil and I spent most of Saturday in the office going through Nea-lis's email. We needed to identify any senior staff who, because of their misguided support of Nealis and his campaign, might be happier working somewhere else. It was an ugly job, but necessary.

We found three certifiable rats. Virgil called them individually and asked for their resignations, effective immediately. A senior banker was playing golf with friends out at Shinnecock Hills in Southampton. Virgil caught him as they were setting out for the back nine. The second, also a banker, expected the call—he was one of the golfing foursome and had just watched his buddy get the axe. The head of IT was on his boat, fishing for stripers near Gardiners Island. None of the men squawked.

"I have some spots to fill. Any thoughts?"

"It's a tough time of year to get anyone worthwhile to jump ship," I said.

Virgil waved his hand as though erasing the thought. "That depends on price, doesn't it? I'll spend what's needed. I'll also have two board seats open in the near future. Would you be interested?"

"No, thank you. I'm not a politician. Has Aimee's position been filled?"

"Her number two is 'acting chief.' I don't really know him."

"I have a suggestion. Let him stay acting for now and bring in a guy I know to back him up. A year from now, you'll know which one you want running compliance for you."

"Who is this?"

"His name is Hal Morris. You can trust him. I do. He risked his life for me and the Kid, so I owe him. He knows nothing about securities or compliance, but he's smart. He'll learn."

"Fine. You handle it."

I would have someone in compliance I knew I could trust. Someone who would have my back if I ever needed it. And Hal would be intimidating enough to be very good at the job.

"I'm leaving," Virgil said. "See you tonight?"

"I wouldn't miss it."

79

Rather than subject Skeli, seven and a half months pregnant and insistent upon wearing spike heels to Virgil's victory party, to the vagaries of a New York City cab ride, I paid for a limo for the evening. The car picked us up at the Ansonia and the driver was patient and polite as I detailed exactly how I wanted him to drive—both route and velocity—to Park Avenue. Skeli found my concern on her behalf both annoying and entertaining.

"You are very sweet," she cooed, "but I'm pregnant, not disabled."

"I'm treating my anxiety, which does not recognize that you are in far better shape than I am."

"I'm thirty weeks and counting. I'll be careful."

The party was a small one by Becker standards. There couldn't have been more than a hundred guests in the living room, on the deck, or circulating on the roof garden. We made a polite circuit before Virgil's wife swept Skeli from me and steered her to a comfortable chair in the living room.

The carpet was white, the leather-covered furniture was white, the walls were white. The only color in the room came from two Roy Lichtensteins on the far wall—both pictures of the same blond woman, one weeping, the other smiling.

Skeli slipped off the shoes and hid her bare feet under the ottoman. Virgil's wife saw her and smiled.

"You go talk to your cronies," she said to me. "Wanda and I are going to have a chat about babies, and you men always get so antsy when the subject comes up."

"Before I go, what can I get you?" I asked Skeli. "A plate of canapés? Caviar? Real food? They're grilling steaks outside."

"Just some water," Skeli said.

"Still or sparkling?"

"Still. If I burp, I'm liable to pop out a baby."

Trays passed by with little morsels of exquisitely designed food, flutes of champagne, and wineglasses filled with red, white, rose, and sparkling water. I took one of the latter and headed for the kitchen to get Skeli a tumbler of tap water, when I noticed across the room that a handsome, tuxedoed young waiter was already presenting her with one. Sparkling water in hand, I went back outside and made another pass through the rooftop garden, looking for someone who might talk to me. There were more of them than I expected. The story of my part in rescuing Virgil and the firm at the meeting had spread.

Livy was holding court out on the deck, seated in a wicker throne. She lifted a large glass of clear liquid when she saw me. "Mr. Stafford, the hero of the hour!"

"No heroes here, Livy." Heroes didn't crash the market—a story that I hoped would always remain secret.

"Nonsense. Tell us of your ordeal in the desert."

I looked around at the expectant faces surrounding us. Some of those people had snubbed me or whispered behind my back or laughed at bad jokes at my expense. Now I was their hero.

"Maybe another time," I said.

"You must come and visit with us in Newport again. Wyatt so enjoys your visits."

I agreed that I would and excused myself.

I found Larry and Brady sitting across from each other on white metal filigreed lawn chairs. Each had a glass of something amber. A bowl of crushed ice and a decanter sat on a small table between them.

"Greetings. You two look like you're becoming good buddies. What's in the carafe?"

"It's a handcrafted, limited-edition Kentucky bourbon that Virgil insisted we try," Larry said.

"How is it?"

"Ask me again in an hour or so." He poured himself another shot and dropped a single small ice chip into the glass. "It seems to improve with quantity."

"We are deliberating," Brady said. "Care to join us?"

I pulled up another chair. "I'll sit with you, but I'm not drinking 'til the baby's born."

"It's a night to celebrate," Brady said.

I raised my glass of expensive seltzer. "I agree. How was your day?"

Brady spread his arms and grinned broadly. "Spectacular. We picked up young Mr. Scott late last night and gave him a few hours to appreciate the intensity of life experience at the MCC."

The Metropolitan Correctional Center served as the intake jail for the federal justice system in New York. As an introduction to life in the BOP, it was violent and terrifying. Virgil's father had killed himself there. He wasn't the only inmate to arrive at that desperate decision. Larry called it The Zoo.

"He knew we had the old man and his friends in custody down in Florida and, of course, he knew about Nealis."

Blackmore's stern and noble visage had been on every news station—national and local, business and all-news—nonstop for the past twenty-four hours.

"He lawyered up, but one of the AUSAs gave him a crash course in federal racketeering law and the bargaining began. He sang. Arias. We now have Nealis for ordering the hits on Aimee Devane, Mark Barstow, and you."

"What about that other punk? The one who washed up in the Great South Bay."

"It seems Gino did that guy on his own initiative."

"And the rest of the gang? Gino's crew." The men who had tried to kill me twice, and who had hunted me in the desert.

"Scott gave us their names and they are all in jail. There were only four of them left, you know. And their loyalty was to Gino, not Nealis.

Once we started asking questions, they opened up, pointing fingers, and all trying to be first to cut a deal."

For the first time, I really did feel like celebrating. I had not known how much pressure and fear I had been carrying until the moment when it lifted. My son was safe. I was safe. My family was safe. I wanted to share the news with Skeli.

"That's great news. Thank you, Marcus."

They both raised glasses in salute.

"One more request?" I said.

"What's that?" Brady replied.

"Manny Balestrero."

Larry and Brady shared a look. They both knew his real name. Neither could admit it to me or to each other.

"We're working on it," Brady said.

"There would be no case at all without him," I said.

Larry nodded. "And we're making progress. For the moment, he's safe."

Which might be all any of us could expect. I walked back toward the living room, but before I got there, I saw Skeli on the deck looking for me.

"Hello, Dr. Tyler. Your boyfriend just got some terrific news."

"Good." She was unsmiling and brusque. "It's time to go."

I was sure that Brady's report would bring a smile to her face.

"Fine, but just give me one minute. I'm dying to share this with you."

She looked me in the eye. "No. It's time to go."

And it hit me. It wasn't just time to leave the party. It was time to go. We were about to have a baby.

AUTHOR'S NOTE

On May 6, 2010, the Dow Jones Industrial Average dropped six hundred points in a matter of minutes, wiping out approximately one trillion dollars of wealth. Dedicated computers, all with similar if not identical algorithms, read certain signals and all generated sell orders at the same time. Five years later, regulators determined that high-frequency, computer-generated trading was not to blame, but only a contributing factor. Who *was* to blame? Authorities arrested a man in the United Kingdom who had been trading via a laptop while sitting in his parents' home in a London suburb. He was accused of using various sophisticated, and illegal, trading strategies. On the day in question, he was said to have profited by as much as nine million dollars.

ACKNOWLEDGMENTS

So many friends, fellow authors, and relatives—and all the myriad combinations thereof—are deserving of mention that I fear giving offense to those I might omit. But if I included everyone who has helped me, the list would be as long as the book.

One man deserves special recognition, both for his generosity to me in giving of his time and expertise, but also for who he is and what he does. Bob Rogers heads the New Mexico State Police Search and Rescue Division. He coordinates the search teams when a pair of hunters fails to return home, or a team of spelunkers gets trapped in a cavern, or a child wanders off in the high country. May you never need his help, but if you do, be assured you are in good hands.

Thanks once more to the usual suspects: the Muses—you know who you are; Larry Ruggiero and Richard Fiske; Tim and Melissa O'Rourke; Dr. Cornelia; the Pawley's crew; Judith Weber and Nat Sobel; and Neil Nyren and all of the great people at Putnam.

ML   1/2016